The Hand of the Arch-Sinner

The Hand of the Arch-Sinner

TWO ANGRIAN CHRONICLES OF
BRANWELL BRONTË

A Reader's Edition

Reconstructed and edited with an
Introduction, Notes, and Commentary

by

ROBERT G. COLLINS

Initial Transcription by John Barnard,
May Collins, Judith Bates, and Robert G. Collins

CLARENDON PRESS · OXFORD

1993

Oxford University Press, Walton Street, Oxford OX2 6DP
Oxford New York Toronto
Delhi Bombay Calcutta Madras Karachi
Kuala Lumpur Singapore Hong Kong Tokyo
Nairobi Dar es Salaam Cape Town
Melbourne Auckland Madrid
and associated companies in
Berlin Ibadan

Oxford is a trade mark of Oxford University Press

Published in the United States
by Oxford University Press Inc., New York

© Robert G. Collins 1993

All rights reserved. No part of this publication may be reproduced,
stored in a retrieval system, or transmitted, in any form or by any means,
without the prior permission in writing of Oxford University Press.
Within the UK, exceptions are allowed in respect of any fair dealing for the
purpose of research or private study, or criticism or review, as permitted
under the Copyright, Designs and Patents Act, 1988, or in the case of
reprographic reproduction in accordance with the terms of the licences
issued by the Copyright Licensing Agency. Enquiries concerning
reproduction outside these terms and in other countries should be
sent to the Rights Department, Oxford University Press,
at the address above

This book is sold subject to the condition that it shall not, by way
of trade or otherwise, be lent, re-sold, hired out or otherwise circulated
without the publisher's prior consent in any form of binding or cover
other than that in which it is published and without a similar condition
including this condition being imposed on the subsequent purchaser

British Library Cataloguing in Publication Data
Data available

Library of Congress Cataloging in Publication Data
Data available
Includes index
ISBN 0 19 812258 6

Typeset by Best-set Typesetter Ltd., Hong Kong
Printed in Great Britain
on acid-free paper by
Biddles Ltd.,
Guildford and King's Lynn

ACKNOWLEDGEMENTS

Acknowledgement is herewith made to the Board of Governors, Brotherton Library, Leeds University, owner of the two manuscripts the title pages of which are reproduced here, as well as to the Brontë Society (Haworth), owner of Branwell's sketches identified here as 'Northangerland as a Youth' and 'Northangerland in Middle Age', which preface the two chronicles.

The preparation of this edition involved several years of work, during which the kind assistance of a number of people made the task much lighter. My thanks are extended particularly to Mr Christopher Sheppard. As custodian of the Brotherton Collection of Rare Books and Manuscripts at the Brotherton Library, Leeds, he not only arranged for the availability of the materials, including magnified copies, but over an eight-year period, on my repeated visits to verify an obscured reading yet again from the original manuscript sheets, invariably provided every assistance and that with the utmost courtesy. My thanks, also, to Mr Dennis Cox, former University Librarian of Leeds, who initiated the project; to Mrs Sally Stonehouse, former Librarian of the Brontë Parsonage Archives (Haworth); and to her successors, Dr Juliet Barker and Ms Kathryn White, all of whom were of immeasurable help in making various Brontë papers available to me. Ms Nancy Coffin and the late Robert Taylor of the Robert Taylor Collection at Princeton University were most helpful as I researched associated materials, as were archivists and other librarians in the Readers' Room, British Museum; the Humanities Research Center, University of Texas (Austin); the Berg Collection, New York Public Library; and the Huntington Library (Pasadena), among others.

Particular thanks, also, is due to Dr Ralph Berry of Stratford-upon-Avon, whose brain was picked in the identification of Shakespeare references in the two chronicles; his quick recognition was of great help. As is true of all present-day writers on the Juvenilia, I owe a considerable debt to Christine Alexander's superb ordering of the narrative lines in *The Early Writings of Charlotte Brontë*

(1983), surely the most important work on the Angrian writings since that of Fannie Ratchford a half-century ago.

Above all, my deepest gratitude is owed to my fellow-labourers in this task: to May Collins, whose uncanny eye puzzled out so many obscured lines on which I was about to give up, and who took almost total responsibility for the final typescript; to John Barnard, whose patience and exactness resulted in giving initial order to the transcript; and to Judith Bates, who noted so many ambiguities that had to be resolved. They have helped to make finally visible to the world these two manuscripts, the first words of which Branwell put to paper almost 160 years ago. Having gasped out an apparently wasted life on his deathbed to his old friend, the sexton John Brown ('In all my life I have done nothing—either great or good!'), Branwell would surely have been happy to see the appearance in print of a major part of that continuing story to which he devoted much of his short life.

Robert G. Collins

CONTENTS

List of Illustrations	viii
Introduction	ix
Editing the Manuscript	xliv
Select Bibliography	lii
A Chronology of Patrick Branwell Brontë	liv
The Life of Field Marshal the Right Honourable Alexander Percy, Earl of Northangerland, Lord Viscount Elrington, Lord Lieutenant of Northangerland, Premier of Angria, Major General of the Verdopolitan Service	1
Real Life in Verdopolis: A Tale	121
Explanatory Notes	213

LIST OF ILLUSTRATIONS

Facsimile of manuscript title-page I   lviii
Facsimile of manuscript title-page II   120
Both facsimiles reproduced by permission of the Brotherton Collection, Leeds University.

The drawings reproduced between pages 92–93 are all by Patrick Branwell Brontë, most of them originally appearing in letters by Branwell to Joseph Leyland. All are reproduced by permission of the Leyland Collection, part of the Brotherton Collection, Leeds University.

1. 'Bendigo taking a "Sight"'.
2a. Self-portrait, 1848.
2b. 'The Rescue of the Punch bowl, a scene in the Talbot'.
3. 'Myself'. Self-portrait as Prometheus in chains.
4. top: 'Cooper's Anatomy'.
   middle: Self-portrait, on a catafalque.
   bottom: *Hic Jacet*. 'Martini Liugi Implora Eterna Quieta!'

INTRODUCTION

> I only feel that every power—
> And Thou hadst given much to me—
> Was spent upon the present hour,
> Was never turned, my God, to Thee;
>
> That what I did to make me blest
> Sooner or later changed to pain;
> That still I laughed at peace and rest,
> So neither must behold again.
>   8 August 1841.[1]

To reduce a man's life to a chronology is, paradoxically, to leave everything—or nothing—to the imagination. For a century and a half, Patrick Branwell Brontë has been defined as absolutely as anyone associated with literature could conceivably be. However, his image to even the cultivated mind is certainly that of a literary character, a Dickensian grotesque, rather than of a complex personality who produced a body of creative work which might conceivably be interesting in itself. Branwell's influence on literature is, simply, that of a horrible example impressed to great effect on three gifted sisters. As phrased in a dubious tribute in the 1940s, a century after Branwell's death:

In due time, each in her own fashion and according to the light in which his personality and his actions were regarded was to set down her reactions in writings that stand today among their finest work. As a figure in literature Branwell was thus destined to play no mean part; not, indeed, the part he had been encouraged to hope for and believe in; yet a form of immortality not less secure for the exchange of role to that of pitiable, sordid, but undoubted inspiration.[2]

---

[1] *The Poems of Patrick Branwell Brontë*, ed. Tom Winnifrith (Oxford, Shakespeare Head Press, 1983), 121. Subsequent references to the poetry refer to this edition.

[2] Lawrence and Elizabeth Hanson, *The Four Brontës: The Lives and Works of Charlotte, Branwell, Emily and Anne Brontë* (Oxford, OUP, 1949; New York, Archon, 1967), 189. Branwell-bashing goes on apace, sometimes quite vigorously considering the length of time since his death. In a letter to the *New York Times* (travel section, 30 June 1984) a member of the US branch of the Brontë Society, identified as 'Book Reviewer for the *Brontë Newsletter*', warns literary tourists to eschew the lure of the

INTRODUCTION

At about the same time that this was written, the most serious attention that had yet been accorded to the Brontës' early writings resulted in three books by the scholar Fanny Ratchford which appeared between 1933 and 1964. In *The Brontës' Web of Childhood*, Ratchford made great claims for the so-called Juvenilia as 'the conclusive answer to most of the long-studied, much-discussed Brontë problems'. However, she then went on to declare: 'They explode the myth of Branwell's mental endowments, showing that his earlier precocity held not a spark of genius and that his development ceased after his fifteenth or sixteenth year.'[3]

How complete a view Ratchford actually had of Branwell remains a question, but her conclusion was less original than she suggests. Long before, in his *Charlotte Brontë and her Circle* (1896), Clement Shorter had delivered a near-contemptuous dismissal of the Brontë son. Characteristically, the chapter of Shorter's work devoted to Branwell, rather than being a sampling of Branwell's own work, consists almost completely of excerpts from the later letters of Charlotte in which she bitterly complains of her brother. However, Shorter himself had, as an approved judgement on Branwell, Mrs Gaskell's authorized biography of Charlotte written some thirty-nine years before (in fact, Shorter edited a new edition of that biography in 1900). Thus, the standing view leads back in a straight line to Charlotte herself, who in those final three years of Branwell's life saw her brother succumb fully to despair and that despicable weakness of which she grew completely intolerant.

It was, of course, Charlotte who largely defined the family to her friend and subsequent biographer, Mrs Gaskell; Charlotte who at

---

Black Bull in Haworth. 'May we suggest that a walk on the nearby moors might prove more enjoyable and helpful to an understanding of the Brontë genius? Bemoaning the wastrel brother's downfall and making a shrine of the chair in which he sprawled drunkenly would be to waste precious time, as he did.'

[3] While Fanny Ratchford was undoubtedly the most active scholar dealing with the Juvenilia prior to Christine Alexander's magisterial study (see n. 7 below), she seems to have felt no great obligation to read the original manuscripts, with the possible exception of those written by Charlotte. In her notes, she makes frequent reference to transcriptions that she has received from C. W. Hatfield. The indefatigable Hatfield worked for years on the unpublished manuscripts, producing extensive transcriptions that survive in longhand and typescript, most of them in files in the Brontë Parsonage Archives, Haworth. A chaotic but fascinating collection that includes copies of many odd sheets of Branwell's work, the originals of which are scattered, the Hatfield transcriptions are probably the chief means by which most visiting scholars of the last half-century have had access to the Brontë Juvenilia. Hatfield, of course, did not transcribe the two chronicles presented in this volume.

this time wrote the many letters to Ellen Nussey in which Branwell's disintegration is recorded; Charlotte who reported to Mr Williams, of Smith, Elder, her London publisher, the final days and hours of Branwell's life and the death that she defined as a welcome, if sad, blessing upon the weary family. But there had been twenty-eight years of life for Branwell before his dismissal from the Robinson family in 1845, in that clouded incident that propelled him finally and irretrievably into the darkness of opium and alcohol. And for at least half of those years, he wrote.

But the image of the lost soul quickly became fixed, and Branwell Brontë has had few defenders since that autumn of 1848 when, after three years of crushing personal agony, he became the first of the three young adult Brontës to die within an eight-month period. Often vilified, at best he has been damned with condescending pity as the weak-willed, drunkard brother of those tragically romantic heroines—Emily, Anne, and Charlotte—who burned with brief, brilliant accomplishment before being snuffed out by the iron hand of an impersonal fate. (There is, obviously, as much romance inserted in the Brontës' life as exists in their fiction.)

Such a dramatic view of destined end is, to be sure, a natural stimulus to myth, and fatality is the guiding element of what has become the Brontë legend: the myth of the lonely house in the remote northern reaches where three sisters of divine genius uttered their inspired thoughts together, while all around the darkness closed in. They have become priestesses through whose voices timeless spirits spoke briefly, all too briefly, as though a Shelleyesque veil had momentarily been lifted and Eternity had made itself manifest. In this legend, such intense power cracks its human vessel; with their mission fulfilled, the chosen spirits are drawn back to a truer, happier existence, while those of us who remain behind as readers in their timeless texts are witnesses, testifiers to the truth that has been ritually revealed.

But such a legend requires another presence in the house, Caliban to their collective Miranda, an earth-bound demon whose nature is that of the debasing flesh. Branwell is the faulty fourth vessel, flawed in the emotional fire of life just as they were refined and made beautiful by it. He is the element of pathos at the edge of the drama, by the contrast with which their greatness is known more immediately, the shining prince to whom great ability was attributed and on whom great deference was lavished—and wasted—for, with poetic justice, it is the shy sisters, the trio of Cinderellas, who are resplendent under their burlap. It is they who prove, through dramatic reversal, to be the true heiresses of a grand destiny. If life was not kind, the verdict of romanticized history is.

As for Branwell, what use does history have for him after that? He is, without question, the faltering weakling, the boy who never grew up, the golden lad turned into the contemptible 31 year-old failure who virtually took his own life, distraught over an unhappy love affair. In some literary Madame Tussaud's of the collective mind, he is forever staggering up the Parsonage lane, gin-soaked; he is the drug-crazed Branwell, hallucinating all night while his aged father lies, a haggard sleepless guardian, beside him. He has become rigidified as the human rubbish that Charlotte—that single-minded soul suddenly on the brink of the greatest personal success to be achieved by any one of the family—could scarcely bring herself to speak to for the last two years of his life, the lost brother whom Mrs Gaskell called 'the bane of his sisters' lives, and who, when she saw a piece of his writing, perplexed and astonished her by his mastery:

> In a fragment of one of his manuscripts which I have read there is a justness and felicity of expression which is very striking. It is ... drawn with much of the grace of characteristic portrait-painting in perfectly pure and simple language, which distinguishes so many of Addison's papers in the *Spectator* ... But altogether the elegance and composure of style is such as one would not have expected from this vehement and ill-fated young man.[4]

She had, of course, never met Branwell, and her knowledge of him was derived chiefly from Charlotte's letters and directly from Charlotte during the visits they exchanged before the younger woman's death. In any event, Mrs Gaskell seems to say, as a wastrel Branwell should not have been such a good writer.

Obviously legends are made out of more than the figures in them—and less, also, for the figures must always be trimmed and shaped to fit the form which validates the legend. What need has the Brontë legend for such factual elements as that the author of *Wuthering Heights*, the romantically reclusive Emily, was apparently the most tolerant, forthright, and best-natured for the four Brontë children who lived to adulthood; that from mid-childhood until

---

[4] Mrs Elizabeth Gaskell, *The Life of Charlotte Brontë*, ed. with an Introduction and Notes by Clement K. Shorter [The Haworth Edition] (New York and London, Harper and Brothers Publishers, 1900; AMS edn., 1973), 190.

well into her adult life Charlotte wrote romances of adultery and emotional drama which match modern soap operas; that the father, Patrick Brontë, was a published poet and novelist of competence, if not genius, well before the children were born; that the entire family was extraordinarily interested and well-read in current politics and public affairs; that Branwell, in the surviving accounts of friends who knew him well, is everywhere described in warm and admiring terms; or that for a period of at least a dozen years, from early boyhood on, Branwell was an incredibly prolific writer, turning out hundreds of thousands of words of prose narrative, as well as poetry which has been misattributed to Emily because of its merit?

But legends and sympathetic reaction aside, the question remains as to whether Branwell is important *only* in relation to his gifted sisters, as a model for them of the pampered youth living at feverpitch, the dissolute young man caught in the addiction of opium, alcohol, and self-pity. That Branwell, the abject failure, certainly did exist; at least there is considerable evidence supporting such a view of him. The testimony of Charlotte in the Gaskell biography and in her correspondence—indeed, Branwell's own letters—as well as the accounts of drinking-friends and observant neighbours verify that Branwell's addictions were deep-rooted and destructive, that he was every bit as much of a burden on the family as has been said. And fairness aside, there seems a rough poetic justice in the fact that the favoured son proves himself unworthy; without the romance in their personal lives that one might wish for them, the three sisters of genius seem to deserve a foil, if nothing else. And there is a sense of balance for a modern generation devoted to redressing the inequities of the past: as he failed, they rose; brother and sisters alike were touched with fatality, but theirs was triumph where his was failure.

None the less, the evidence establishes that Branwell was for many years the reverse of an idler. He wrote a great deal of both prose and poetry, by some counts more than all the published writings of his three sisters. As Winifred Gérin, the most reliable of a small number of generally unreliable biographers of Branwell, observed:

Of his vices and misfortunes, all too much has been written by his sisters' biographers. Everybody knows he drank, took opium, and wrote equally fluently with both hands—at times with both hands at once, and in moments of bravado in Greek with his right and in Latin with his left. Of the multiple and contradictory facets that made up his complex personality, however, very little has so far been made known.

And, as she also noted: 'The greater part of Branwell's writings has remained unknown and even unsuspected by the general public.'[5] Thirty years later the situation remains essentially the same.

It is probably best to begin with an admission. If what survives today is a clear indication, Branwell's writing, when forced into a comparison with that of his sisters, is inferior by almost all the traditional criteria with which we judge serious fiction. With regard to structure, drama, and psychological sensitivity, for instance, his work is easily criticized. Structure to him was relatively the same from the age of 12 or 13 until his death; it consisted of an apparently endless series of incidents detailing military and political battles, punctuated by riotous carousing. Drama took the form of restless action; flaring anger, morbid brooding, and brutal arrogance constantly recur in place of inner sensitivity. In short, Branwell chose to record the ego, which he not infrequently seemed to believe was the soul—although instinctively he treated it as the soul's curse; embodying it in the character who quickly assumed the central position in his writings.

And yet there are any number of striking scenes and memorable characters in his narratives. Rarely sentimental, although often melodramatic, frequently stirring in his tales of brutal conflict, often lyrical in his observation of landscape and nature generally, Branwell shares qualities with his sisters although he is a writer very different from them. Unlike Charlotte, Branwell did not write tales. His writings of passion, vaunting ambition, and war are the histories of an elaborate social myth, a fictional grid that turns Angria into England, Africa into the contesting powers of Europe, his 'great men' into the brutal barons of a feudal anarchy. Splendour, luxury, emotional hyperbole, and dissipation are everywhere present; the heroes—Northangerland and Zamorna—each are married at least three times and have additional mistresses. With Charlotte, he makes a world; unlike her, he did not write formal novels. He is, simply enough, the author of fictional chronicles. As such, his structure is under-

---

[5] Winifred Gérin, *Branwell Brontë* (London: Thomas Nelson and Sons, 1961), pp. vi, v. Gérin, in a companion biography, *Anne Brontë* (London, Thomas Nelson and Sons, 1959), further observed: 'Branwell, who has found such scant sympathy among the biographers of his sisters was yet, it is too often overlooked, adored by them all. Even at his most degraded he was cast off only by Charlotte, who having loved him best from early childhood, was the most disillusioned by his failure' (p. 180).

standably episodic and digressive rather than a formal shaping of an integral idea arising from the subject. If he is to any degree a novelist, it would have to be the picaresque form with which he is to be identified.

His most important work was a long, continuing biography of the fictional Alexander Percy, an amoral adventurer whose characteristics, appetites, and activities both explore and open out the range of the exotic romantic hero/anti-hero of the earlier nineteenth century. Known familiarly at an early point in the writings as Rougue (Rogue, in Charlotte's more orthodox spelling when she wrote about the same character), as his career unfolds Percy becomes established formally as Lord Viscount Elrington (Ellrington, to Charlotte), the Earl of Northangerland, and Prime Minister of Angria. In the later years, Northangerland is the name commonly used.

The most dramatic figure in the kingdom of Angria or, for that matter, in any of the so-called 'Angrian writings', he is also one of the most realistic of the Luciferian villain-heroes of the period. Created in full character by Branwell, Percy became, in the view of later biographers such as Daphne du Maurier and Winifred Gérin, a succubus who fed upon his master, a model of asserted will for which Branwell's own actual life could provide no parallel. He lived with that figure from his tenth year to the last desperate days of his life.

Moreover, it is evident from his very approach that Branwell became closely identified with his anti-hero long before he began to sign his own letters with the name of Northangerland. Because of this fascination with his fictional character, Branwell presents him as a gigantic figure caught in the toils of his own perversity. Since he thus tends to dominate Branwell's narratives, traditional structure is made irrelevant, for Northangerland lives for each passing day, frequently cursing the past and contemptuous of the future. In some ways, then, Branwell is a modernist who created an amoral protagonist making his existential way through life, literally creating in himself each new day, which would not otherwise exist. *I am—therefore the world is.*

On such grounds, then, one may approach Branwell's chronicles and find still alive in them the intense pressure of the youthful writer's own personality. All writers, but perhaps children in particular, necessarily present images towards which they are by their nature drawn, which their mind has first invented and regarded. Just as, in the early pages of the novel, plain Jane Eyre emerged as a rebellious child from the Red Room, imbued indelibly with Charlotte Brontë's independence and integrity, so Alexander Percy, however grown in height over his youthful amanuensis, utters his words of disdain and shakes his fist to the dark heavens which Branwell himself thus defies. As a projection of Branwell, Alexander Percy is of some immediate intrinsic interest to us, of course, since he rages against the limitations of this world and finally stands, like all creatures of ruin, as a metaphor for the limitations of the stalwart individual confronted by indifference, hostility, or persecution. *Jane Eyre* is a success in part because Charlotte Brontë, in her writing, grew out of herself into the finer, most purposeful, more ideal human personality realized in Jane. Alexander Percy, on the other hand, while taller and more powerful physically than Branwell, is less than him, only a part of him, and that not necessarily the better part; a literary character, unlike Charlotte's Jane he is not made more fundamentally human, but is rather a warped part of a man, an exemplar of the destructive impulse, the defiance, even hatred, of the involuted ego towards anything that would restrain it in any way.

None the less, some of the fascination that such a figure had for Branwell is transferred to us, for the man who will not serve and is indomitable, whatever force is applied against him, is more than a curiosity. He has deep roots in us, however ashamedly we disavow them; while we probably dislike Alexander Percy, we do not have the contempt for him that, through the literary relationship, we suspect he feels for us. He is the outlaw, the anarchist, the despoiler, the unnatural father, the taker of women, the man of unrestrained appetite, who respects and concedes little and fears nothing. Like Lucifer, he is the arch-revolutionary; he will not serve.

But Branwell himself gets caught in Pandemonium; he has no god greater than himself to bring him out of the pit. Having created an Antichrist in his own image, he becomes locked inside the figure. Consider those late letters to Joseph Leyland or John Brown, the former begging an hour's company and signed Northangerland, the latter pleading pathetically for gin on credit even as his life shortens to weeks. He has created himself as a Hindley Earnshaw—one might have said a Heathcliff, except for the fact that Emily's protagonist, raging egoist that he is, still yields to one power greater than his solitary self, that of the passion of profound love. (In contrast, Percy's great love for his second wife Mary becomes nothing more than intensified bitterness when she dies. This loss may, as Branwell suggests, help to explain his contempt for all other creatures, but unlike Heathcliff, Alexander Percy sees his dead beloved as Lear regards the just-murdered Cordelia—dead, dead, dead.)

Branwell's fiction lacks traditional structure, then, because the familiar interplay of negative and positive values is not present in it; there can be no resolution, only a succession of encounters. As such, his narratives are at odds with the highly structured and largely domestically pointed English novels of the mid-nineteenth century, and find little place among them. However, as chronicles of a particular sort they resemble certain aspects of twentieth-century fiction, those works of encounter and strung-together incident out of which is created the life-progress of an individual as a series of events which encapsulate chance and fatality, and so deny order.

Certainly it is too much to say that Branwell Brontë consciously sought such a definition. His work, however, is composed along precisely such lines; his life-view was involuted in a similar way, and it may be that a modern reader can follow his narratives with a greater appreciation of character regarded for its own sake than traditional literary critics might believe. In fact, Emily Brontë's masterpiece shares some of the same characteristics; despite the double frame mechanism as a device for getting the story told, the story itself is the chronicle of a thirty-year-long fatal relationship containing much of the same feverish exchange of self-centred passion which characterized Branwell's fiction. But without that equal intensity of personality which dramatically links Catherine Earnshaw and Heathcliff, Branwell's work seems to lack an end, a destination.

This is not to say that there is no contest present, for underlying all the Juvenilia is the complex love–hate relationship of Percy and Arthur Wellesley, Northangerland and Zamorna. But despite the tens of thousands of words lavished on it by Branwell and Charlotte within the early work, the Northangerland–Zamorna relationship is never made clear; nor is it resolved—to the end it remains the continuing struggle of two gigantic personalities caught on the same ground. Charlotte retained the essentials of it, of course, and refined it in the successive contests of will which Jane Eyre, William Crimshaw, Lucy Snowe, and the two heroines of *Shirley* each successfully undergo. (Interestingly, while Charlotte and Branwell each wrote about both Northangerland and Zamorna, Charlotte's picture of her ideal hero tends to darken in the later accounts; she makes Zamorna closer to Northangerland in ruthlessness and egoism. Yet Branwell, in 'The Life of...Northangerland', actually makes Percy evolve into a lost soul for us, while Charlotte simply changes her attitude towards Zamorna from the earlier to the later figure, as can be seen in the more sentimental 'Marian Hume' writings when compared with the later 'Elizabeth Hastings', episodes where Zamorna is treated as a cliché womanizer.) But Branwell was to make no greater use of the emotional exercises of the Juvenilia, and it is on this material that we must judge him.

Although the 'Angrian' writings of the Brontës were, in fact, a body of material that was added to well into their twenties (in Branwell's case, perhaps, up to within the last year of his life), casual readers of *Jane Eyre* and *Wuthering Heights* are apt to think of these writings as a charming, rainy-day activity shared by four talented children. The miniature books on display in the Brontë Parsonage Museum, looking like dummy volumes in the library of a doll's house, reinforce that view. Their contents, since they are largely illegible to the unaided eye, do not intrude on their charm; they strike one as the artefacts of play, much like Branwell's famous toy soldiers. However, such a sentimental impression is a far cry from the larger part of the actual narrative content of the so-called Juvenilia, which has come to be known synonymously, if somewhat inaccurately, as the Angrian writings. The word 'Angria' is traceable to a pirate kingdom on the Malabar coast of the Indian Ocean, long forgotten today but famous for its successes at the end of the seventeenth and during the first half of the eighteenth century; it took its name from its founder, Kanhoji Angria, an Indian admiral who organized a powerful pirate fleet which for many years not even the European powers could defeat, a corsair who reared a city state which became legendary in its wealth.

Actually, the kingdom of Angria itself was a late development for the Brontës as writers. Branwell created it in 1834, when Charlotte was almost 18 and he was nearing 17. Emily, 16 that year, and Anne, a year younger, at the same time created a kingdom of their own, Gondal. Since that name, coincidentally, is taken from a plateau in the central part of India, they may well have chosen it in part through Branwell's influence; in any event, the coincidence of characters' names in the Angrian and Gondalian writings is quite striking. Anne and Emily's early pieces of prose fiction have not survived. Over the five years preceding this split of fictional territories, however, the four young Brontës had written a great many tales centring on 'the Great Glasstown Confederacy', an associated group of kingdoms, each with its own capital and ruler but with a common capital city and parliament in Verdopolis. The fictional founders were English soldiers and explorers; the setting, that of coastal western Africa, the topography of which the Brontës were acquainted with, partly from travel books and geographies, partly from their current reading in *Blackwood's* and other magazines.

In time, in their own tales they transformed the landscape and climate to that of England. As early-nineteenth-century English children, they had been reared to see Africa not as an integral foreign culture so much as an extended England, a base for a transplanted English society. A study of the periodicals read by the Brontës at this time reveals that articles on the colonial experience, the founding of capital cities and government buildings in such places as Sierra Leone, and the opportunities for fortunes to be made and personal distinction recognized and given free rein were all extremely popular. Imperialism, in one sense, meant the transfer and expansion of English institutions; in short, making the world English. Consequently, there is not too much of the exotic fairy-tale in these so-called 'juvenile' writings. In fact, after the first few years what little fantasy element there is will more often be found in Charlotte's work rather than that of Branwell.

Simply stated, the stories tell of an English society, colonial but independent, building a parliamentary monarchy and beset by certain wars and revolutions, into which elements of current European history are laced. Most of the interaction is between the aristocracy and their respective followers of the adjacent states which make up the Confederacy. Many of the confrontations take place in parliament; much of the intrigue occurs in gaming-rooms or in city streets; the wars which erupt are composed of battles that take place on realistic sites—as in the the famous 'Massacre at Dongola'—transposed from such recent events as the Ashanti Wars or the Peninsular Campaign.

The rulers in the earlier of these writings were objects of youthful hero-worship. In several cases they were drawn from actual contemporary public figures, such as Arthur Wellesley, better known historically as the Duke of Wellington, and his two sons, Arthur and Charles Wellesley, as well as from the celebrated explorers, William Edward Parry and Sir John Ross (all of whom, ironically, outlived

Branwell, Emily, and Anne Brontë). Some of the Angrian characters were composite figures, whose names were drawn from literature, as in the case of Percy, or were phonetic echoes of actual persons (for example, the name Elrington), while some were simple descriptive names which clearly survived from childhood into the adult writings (such as Sneaky, or Sneachi, as it is variously spelled). In fact, the associated kingdoms of the Verdopolitan Confederacy are an empire; to spend much time in the great mass of surviving manuscript, particularly that of Branwell, is to realize quickly that it represents a fictional reproduction of the imagined political life of the United Kingdom itself, fraught with the scheming and intrigue of Shakespeare's history plays, with an added heavy emphasis on the more modern contest between republican and conservative views, as well as the logic behind the extension of empire.

Further, except for certain of the wars (and even these have a distinctly modern-European character), the natives are not very much dealt with, since the imagination of the Brontës was not stimulated by the exotic reality of Asia and black Africa for its own sake to any great extent.[6] Rather, it was a form of realism, a freshly invented European or (even more specifically) British culture that they chose to work with; a world familiar but new, in which they created a society notable for its political manipulation, avaricious greed, ruthless and reckless contest between powerful personalities, and—related to the latter—invariably unhappy romantic love relationships. Within this society the basic philosophical conflict is between anarchy and order, republicans and royalists, individual ego and social responsibility, liberal and conservative, with the authors apparently coming down on the latter side in each case. None the less, both Charlotte and Branwell were fascinated by (and demonstrated at length) the attractiveness of the rebel figure. As noted, for Branwell, less conservative than his sister, the larger-than-life arch-sinner becomes a lonely world unto himself. This is the subject that lies at the core of their narratives, the ruined Lucifer, the title figure of one of

---

[6] An exception is the native prince Quashia Quamina, who opposes the English and wars against them, after being adopted and raised by their leader, the Duke of Wellington. In Branwell's accounts, he later becomes a cohort of Alexander Percy, and is said to have engaged in various criminal activities, including the slave trade. In successive writings he becomes progressively lighter-skinned, golden, even. Eventually, with his contemptuous manner, exotic origin, and adoptive background, as well as his striking appearance, the later Quashia might be said to anticipate the image of an early Heathcliff (described as a 'Lascar'), who may even have been inspired in part by him.

Branwell's better-known poems (1836), hurtled down to the dark wasteland, unconquered from without but victim of his own nature. It is an image which had become a living concept for Branwell by his adolescence.

Traditionally, the Brontë legend has as its first chapter the magical story of Branwell's toy soldiers, the incident which is said to have released the great flow of creativity in the four young Brontës. The story is told by Branwell himself in one of his early Glasstown manuscripts, as well as by Charlotte in a separate account. In 1826, when Branwell was 9, his father went to Leeds on a trip and returned late at night. He brought back a present for the boy, a box of twelve toy soldiers. Far from being a first set, they represented a supplement to an older one, which by then was battered and incomplete. It was not Christmas but, as Branwell carefully dates it, 5 June. Next morning he called his sisters from their beds to see his new figures. Each of the girls was allowed to select one, which became her soldier and for which she chose a name, although they were to remain his possessions. (Soon after, he gave each sister full ownership of her chosen figure.) Charlotte named hers 'Wellington'; Branwell, significantly, named his favourite 'Buonaparte'. These effigies became the Twelve Adventurers—later, the 'Twelves'—the focus of a series of childhood games of a dramatic and then a literary nature, an imaginative extension of the recent Napoleonic wars, which had been the greatest public concern of the earlier part of the century and, in the years following, a particularly strong and continuing interest for all of the Brontë household, in which the icons of Wellington and Nelson gave way only to that of God himself. In a family headed by a father whose who greatest secular interests were literature and military matters—Patrick Brontë had wavered between a career in the Church or the army, and all his life retained an interest in military ordnance—the Brontë children began writing at length, creating adventures involving the heroic figures from whom the soldiers had been named.

First they began with games—called 'plays'—such as the 'Play of the Islanders' which Charlotte subsequently dated to 1827. Initially their heroes were known as the 'Young Men'; Branwell's 1830 account of the 'History of the Young Men', while not the first reference, lays out in detail much of the foundation of the Glasstown saga. Composed of elements drawn from contemporary explorations, such as those of Mungo Park in Africa, and the *Blackwood's Magazine* accounts of the arctic explorers Parry and Ross, there were intermingled references drawn from the *Arabian Nights* and *Aesop's Fables*. The four Brontë children, for example, created themselves as Genii, the immense creatures who built Verdopolis at a stroke. The toys themselves were soon ignored; a few years later, Branwell wrote that the actual effigies had already disappeared. However, they had served their purpose; they had been the catalyst that unlocked a world of inspired imagination, a taste for heroic activity and profound emotion. The story of the toy soldiers is a beguiling one, and therein lies its danger, for such guile leads us down the garden path. These soldiers were not operetta sentimentalists.

Since almost all of the succeeding manuscripts, including many of the later years, were written in an extremely minute hand, which does not always yield readily even to modern magnification, only scholars in modern times have read at length in them. When first written by Branwell and his sisters, the narratives apparently were read aloud, probably selectively, by the individual authors to one or more of the others. However, they were certainly kept as a secret between the four younger Brontës; in many hundreds of letters to Ellen Nussey, sometimes on what was practically a daily basis, Charlotte never divulged the fact of their existence. If their father ever read them it would logically have been only after Charlotte's death, when he was in his eighties, and since he had serious problems with his eyesight for much of his later life this seems unlikely, although not impossible. Charlotte's brief marriage meant that the Reverend Arthur Bell Nichols, her husband, became custodian of all the family papers after her death, and had forty years in which to read them before selling most of them to T. J. Wise in the last years of the nineteenth century. Most certainly he would have glanced at the manuscripts; he may well have read in them at length. However, such solitary acquaintance would be largely inconsequential except for the possibility that, if he did read Branwell's manuscript material carefully, he would very probably have destroyed any amount of it out of kindness to the memory of the unfortunate youth. It is clear that Branwell's writings would have seemed both immoral and anti-religious to Charlotte's husband and Patrick Brontë, when one considers that many of the passages in the pages still left to us have been described in such terms by critics of our own time. Even Charlotte, youthful freethinker that she was in her Angrian writings, in her mature years had become more religiously conservative, as is evident in both *The*

Professor and *Villette*, as well as in the Gaskell biography. As recorded in her letters, she regarded with condemnation what she not unreasonably viewed as her brother's atheism, and was relieved, if not forgiving, when he apparently prayed on his deathbed.

Their writings for the first few years are adolescent, if not childish. However, by about 1833 the manuscripts of Branwell and Charlotte fall into a very different pattern than might be expected. Now young adults, their interests are those of serious political conflict and personal emotions, tied to the archetypal heroic figures who have attracted them for most of their lives. They are writing fictional history now, but it is not that of a remote period. On the contrary, it is history foreshortened, crammed into a forty- or fifty-year period, with the costume element eliminated and with all of the characters of this history still very immediate in their interest. The Anglo-African nations of the Confederacy evolve even as the model-soldier figurines of their childhood fade into august personages, who retire to the rear of the drama as two younger generations successively occupy centre-stage.

Increasingly, too, while the characters and the overall story-line are common to both Branwell and Charlotte, the protagonists of his manuscripts are more often Alexander Percy and his sons, while the central male figure in Charlotte's tales is most often Arthur Augustus Adrian Wellesley, the Duke of Zamorna and Emperor of Angria, son-in-law of Percy. Wellesley is, of course, a more conventional hero; in the Angrian chronicles he assumes the role of the historical Duke of Wellington, becoming his own father as the saviour of Europe in defeating the anti-monarchical menace of Napoleon. He returns to the kingdom of Wellington's Land, in the Anglo-African empire, where he summarily demands of parliament in recognition of his services to them the vast undeveloped lands to the east which will then be known as Angria. The Duke of Zamorna receives his kingdom much as, say, Marlborough had received Blenheim and large estates from a grateful nation, or as large tracts of land in the American wilderness had been granted to aristocrats in the seventeenth and eighteenth centuries. However, Zamorna overcomes the opposition on this occasion largely through the support of the powerful Northangerland, now his father-in-law and subsequently prime minister of Angria.

Writing continuously after 1834, it would seem, Branwell and Charlotte rapidly developed Angria as a mighty nation in its own right, with large and elegant cities and a Byzantine political situation. Zamorna's life, detailed by Charlotte, is a mixture of firm and wise government, accented by a series of sensual encounters, legitimate and otherwise, with various beauties from the Verdopolitan aristocracy, and climaxing in the civil wars raised against him by Northangerland. In Charlotte's hands the romances, the emotional consequences, the tragic realization of love and death are recounted over and over, much of it through the eyes of the several women who are romantically related to Zamorna and, to a lesser extent, Northangerland.

Branwell's chronicles are made of more brutal stuff, as is his chief character, Alexander Percy. In the six volumes of 'Letters of an Englishman', written between 1830 and 1832 (the manuscripts of which are in the Leeds University Brotherton Collection), Branwell details Percy's role as a destroyer of civil peace, the revolutionary architect of a civil war that rocks the Verdopolitan Confederacy. Executed at the end of that early work, Percy is revived and goes on to a career as an outlaw and general rogue. By 1834, with the establishment of the new nation of Angria, Percy, now generally known as Northangerland in his middle-age and grown publicly respectable in the role of chief minister to the emperor, is none the less the same man as the early atheist intellectual, the pirate, the compulsive gambler, the rapacious cattle-dealer, the adulterer, the seducer and betrayer of countless women, the master of and rallying-point for all the thieves, swindlers, and republicans of the nation. He is cursed as always with a compulsion towards power and the inability to defer to anyone, even the monarch he helped to create and towards whom he always has a sinister advisory role. Inevitably he reverts to the role of the Dark Archangel, crying havoc as leader of the anarchic Republican faction. In what must be regarded as the dramatic high point of Angrian history, he raises a mighty rebellion and at first succeeds, to the point of making Zamorna a fugitive. In a significant episode, however, Percy secretly arranges for Zamorna to escape just as his followers are about to execute the defeated monarch; always there exists between the older and the younger man a bond of fused love and hatred.

As 'The Life of... Northangerland' and 'Real Life in Verdopolis' clearly show, Alexander Percy, throughout his long career, from early years through jaded middle-age, is a classic demagogue. In this, too, the echo of the Council in Hell in *Paradise Lost* reverberates. Branwell, in his time, was not alone in seeing demagoguery as a manipulative device commonly employed by the rebels and destroyers of history, and in being thrilled by it. Democracy, as a growing force, always seemed to be the fine face of demagoguery; in this view, the leader of the mob is perforce a powerful personality who uses lesser men by natural right. At that, Branwell's Percy is not the least effective of his species. His role as head of a group of scoundrels, most of whom are lifelong associates, is one he has inherited from his even more dissolute, but less effective, father, the first Edward Percy. (Subsequently Alexander Percy's own oldest son, disowned by him, is also an Edward Percy.) As a law unto themselves, the Percy men have been violent and rebellious back to their first appearance in the north of England, before Shakespeare spoke of them.

Reminiscent of an eighteenth-century Hellfire Club in many ways, the present Northangerland group is as unprincipled a collection of individualists and quarrelsome scoundrels as might be imagined (Branwell knew his *Peregrine Pickle* and other Smollett novels very well). The gang follows Northangerland because he exceeds any one of them in ferocity, drinking capacity, womanizing, and contempt for authority. Sharing both his good fortune and his bad, they display not so much loyalty as a bond of interwoven crime, a common conviction that scoundrels must hang together or they will assuredly hang separately. Over the years, the members of Percy's party are always out for vile pleasures and the main chance; they amass considerable wealth through cattle speculation, piracy, highway robberies and hijacking of goods, and manipulation of public funds and political interests; but they throw away as much again in endless gaming, drinking, sexual debauchery, conspicuous waste, and over-reaching. These are the 'rare lads' who appear repeatedly in the Angrian chronicles.

Paradoxically, however, most members of Alexander Percy's personal guard are themselves professional men and, in fact, make up the wealthier elements of Angrian society. With their great mansions and frequently ruinous gambling activities, they exist just one step below the great titled aristocracy, most of whom are entrenched royalists, loyal first to Wellington and then to Zamorna, and thus natural opponents of the opportunistic adventurers led by Northangerland. An exception to this, the Earl of Caversham, one of the few old titles in Percy's company, is a particularly unsavoury figure, who for brief financial gain conspires without hesitation in the murder of his oldest friend, Alexander Percy's father.[7] Caversham and Jeremiah Simpson, the usurer (and, known in other writings as Macterrorglen, a revolutionary commander), were early cronies of the first Edward Percy, who as an adventurer on the run had established the Percy family line in Anglo-Africa. Several others—Hector Montmorency, Arthur O'Connor, George Gordon—are the sons of early companions of the elder Percy. Thus the *posse comitatus* that Alexander Percy heads throughout most of Branwell's chronicles is, in large part, shown to be an inheritance from his father. Actually, the word 'inheritance' is inadequate, for a received *curse* would more accurately describe what operates in Alexander Percy's life.

In two major elements of earlier nineteenth-century Romanticism, Branwell is not only a man of his age but a particularly intense voice of it. He shares with greater poets such as Byron the concept of the extraordinary man and the 'received curse', the latter deriving from the solitary role, the alienation, which the former, the ego, inevitably imposes; these two psychological elements constantly recur in his narrative. They are, in fact, represented in a curiously intertwined way at the dramatic level.

From an early age Branwell was an extensive reader, steeped in Elizabethan and Jacobean revenge drama, as well as in classical literature with its sense of a curse as an expression of fatality. This notion accorded well with his own dramatic sense of life, since it confirmed the special identity of the self. The contempt of Byron's Manfred for all other beings except the object of his fatal love, or—from the same poet—the Gaiour's single-minded revenge for the loss of his beloved and his subsequent withdrawal from the world, is not dissimilar to Alexander Percy's brooding upon the loss of his second wife and regarding the rest of the world with hatred thereafter—except, of course, for the art that went into each work. But the Brontë *Milton* was also an extremely well-thumbed volume (the hand-annotated copy still exists). Like Blake and many others, Branwell took the romantic view of the dark angel. The figure of Lucifer as a first principle of rebellion against law touches upon basic

---

[7] Caversham is, incidentally, also the villain of Charlotte's 'Something About Arthur', in which he betrays the youthful Arthur Wellesley. See Christine Alexander, *The Early Writings of Charlotte Brontë* (Oxford, Basil Blackwell, 1983), for information on this and other 'juvenilia' of Charlotte Brontë.

religious myth and explains man in contest with his God, as well as—and again this is seen in Byron—the three successive 'falls',[8] in the third of which Cain through envy introduces violence and murder to the world. The three stages are necessary, one to the other. As a principle of pride and rebellion, Lucifer is the incarnation of a curse engendered by man's fateful indomitability, human courage carried to the heavens, which itself is linked to his unhappy destiny by its false promise of a self-determined destiny. Lucifer has many minions— those who live by him are gathered unto him, in an involuted form of the good man's relationship to his God—and it is these emissaries of Lucifer who represent the tempters and deceivers, the figures of Mephistopheles pretending to serve the dissatisfied Fausts of the world.

But for Branwell, interestingly, the curse is first dramatically manifested in its ugliness. The demon is scarcely disguised. Throughout Branwell's chronicles the avatar of sin and death is Percy's mentor and familiar spirit, the repulsive old Yorkshireman Robert Patrick King, better known as 'Sdeath.[9] Effectively, the figure of 'Sdeath is the embodiment of the curse on Alexander Percy and, though less interestingly, his father before him. One is reminded of the figure of Gil-Martin, a much more sophisticated demonic familiar in the *The Private Memoirs and Confessions of a Justified Sinner* (1824) by James Hogg, a *Blackwood's* writer for whom Branwell had the highest regard (and whom, in a well-known letter to *Blackwood's*, written when he was 18 on the occasion of Hogg's death, he praised fulsomely as the author who had had the greatest shaping influence on his life). Where Hogg has the antinomian protagonist of his novel create the demon in his own image through his damning of mankind generally—Gil-Martin, whose features reflect the successive victims of hatred, begins as pleasing and handsome but eventually becomes a repulsive mirror-image of Robert Wringhim—Branwell has 'Sdeath as both the shaping tutor to, and the mocking tool of, his master. The role of the grand sinner, however, is reserved for Alexander Percy himself; it is he who corrupts others, having been first corrupted

---

[8] The first fall brings discord into heaven. Envy, born of pride, is the archetypal sin of Lucifer. He in turn feeds the pride and envy within Eve (cf. Milton) resulting in the second fall, which alienates man from Paradise. The third fall is that of Cain induced by Lucifer (cf. Byron's *Cain*) which alienates man from man.

[9] The name is an imprecation common in the eighteenth and nineteenth centuries, standing for 'God's Death', in analogy to the old oaths ''sblood' or ''swounds'.

himself; it is he who begins, like Milton's Lucifer, to show the marks of his degradation, a ruined archangel who has debased himself.

In contrast, 'Sdeath is a *principle* of evil. While withered and repulsive, he stands outside time, at least on a human scale. When beaten, as appropriate to a foul thing, he cannot be killed. Already described as an old man when he originally becomes the attendant of the first Edward Percy in that man's dissolute youth, he emigrates to Africa with him, pandering to his master's vicious whims always. A constant source of Biblical quotation in mocking fashion, the devil quoting scripture, the old man will later be echoed, radically reduced in importance, in the figure of the vicious old retainer, Joseph, in *Wuthering Heights*. In Branwell's 'Life of ... Northangerland', 'Sdeath names himself as tutor to the small boy Alexander Percy, encouraging the child's wilfullness and rudely displacing Sergeant Bud, here shown as a cultivated, intelligent, and responsible figure who henceforth has no influence whatsoever over Alexander's moral life. Subsequently 'Sdeath is the murderer of his old master, Edward Percy, whose murderous tool he has long been (the sword that Percy has lived by), as well as of Alexander Percy's first wife, Augusta, who is first admired extravagantly by 'Sdeath for her resoluteness in crime. He remains the vicious tool and counsellor in villainy all through Alexander Percy's youth and middle age. At that time, 'Sdeath, a centenarian at least by any reckoning, is still practising his trade of assassin and evil messenger, still exhorting Alexander Percy—and spouting Biblical injunctions, since no one is a more obvious believer than the devil himself.

The heart of any Faustian legend is, of course, the infernal demon as willing tool; as such, he makes it possible for the protagonist to sin mightily. In a symbolic lending of his demonic powers, he makes the victim extraordinary but thereby also enmeshes him inextricably. In short, such a devil serves only in order to conquer in the end; the devotion of 'Sdeath to his 'master' is that of the demon who cherishes the victim he corrupts, for the very sake of the growing corruption. Correspondingly, the ostensible master of such a tool abhors him as demon increasingly, even as he is more and more completely dependent on him. It is this aspect of the relationship to which James Hogg devoted the later part of the *Private Memoirs and Confessions*.

However, it is in the early life of Alexander Percy that 'Sdeath as demonic principle is defined explicitly for us by Branwell. The incarnation of evil, seen in its most unvarnished and repulsive form,

'Sdeath none the less cannot be dismissed. As the Devil himself, he is the true father of a possessed Northangerland. The following exchange from 'The Life of... Northangerland' is far too purposeful to be taken as banter:

> 'It's a braw cheild that doesn't know its own feyther. Thawrt greeting [weeping] to part wi' thy Daddie [Edward Percy], Aw guess, and doesn't know that here he is beside thee, and, lad, that thaw can nivver part wi' him, eh?'
> 'I think you are the Devil', shouted Alexander....
> 'And Aw am', he shouted in return. 'And thaw's made war' guesses nor that, and Aw made falser answers, too.'
> [Later, on departing, he says] 'Goid neight t'ye, my Son.'
> 'And eternal night to you, Old Satan', exclaimed Alexander.

If God is the merciful Father of the redeemed, Satan conversely is the merciless progenitor of the sinner. Embodying intrigue, corruption, betrayal, and murder, he is both necessary to Alexander Percy and an object of his hatred. Evil having its own immortality, on the several occasions when he is shot or otherwise violently attacked by Percy, he reappears shortly after, more hideous for his ugly wounds but grinning mockingly as he takes his accustomed place, which is never then denied to him. In short, parallel to, but the reverse of that between Percy and Zamorna, there is a special kind of love–hate relationship between Percy and 'Sdeath; even as the former is himself seen as a towering Lucifer, he abhors the contemptible figure of his most devoted underling.

What Branwell seems to suggest through the 'Sdeath figure is a projection of evil which is also a reflection of self. 'Sdeath is, so to speak, the evil deed, while Percy is Lucifer, tormented by his own self-love. Milton's Satan is primarily treated as 'the adversary'; he remains Lucifer in Branwell's hands, is himself a victim, damned through a monstrous ego that cannot accept restraint and which in time makes opposition his own reason for existence, yet writhes in a horrible suffering, too. Interestingly, in Branwell's earlier story 'The Pirate' (1833) Alexander Percy tries to kill 'Sdeath:

Rougue [Percy] crying, 'I have done with thee, thou wretch', took the ugly heap of mortality and hurled it into the sea. When it touched the water a bright flash of fire darted from it, changed it into a vast genius of immeasurable and indefinable height and size, and seizing hold of a huge cloud with his hand, he vaulted into it, crying: 'And I've done with thee, thou fool' and disappeared among the passing vapours.

Ere he departed, three vast flashes of fire came bursting and round them were the Chief Genii Talli, Emmi, Anni; he that ere this [was] the little hideous old man was the Chief Genius and Branni.[10]

The dramatization of Branwell and his sisters as 'Geniuses'—in the Arabian Nights' sense of the *jinni*, a nature spirit or tutelar deity—went back to the enactment of fanciful scenarios leading out from the inspiration given them by the episode of the twelve toy soldiers. What is astonishing here, given his lifelong use of old 'Sdeath as the embodiment of evil, is Branwell as author deliberately identifying himself with the repulsive figure, with the principle of the demonic. In an obviously Manichean twist, he unites the evil 'Sdeath with the 'Chief Genius' or ruling power. Thus, he himself is both Percy and 'Sdeath alternately. Also, there is particular interest in the fact that Branwell linked his sisters, as writers, to the evil figure, even as he made himself synonymous with him in a psychological fusion of seducer and victim, of the pure and the impure, of the damned and the innocent. Unquestionably the writer is pouring his complex characterization out of himself, but Branwell would begin his seventeenth year shortly, and was no longer playing with supernaturalism for its own sake. Certainly Charlotte, and probably all three of the girls, heard this tale from Branwell and would seem to have accepted it casually. Whatever the limitations of 'The Pirate' as straightforward adventure narrative, it was an integral part of the Percy saga, of which Charlotte was writing tandem versions along with Branwell at this time.

For Branwell, as for Byron before him, the Pirate figure is very important. It becomes an avatar of the Luciferian figure in the actual world of physical strife and contest, a world where men are not saved by sentiment. While much has been said concerning the influence of the Byronic hero on the Brontës generally, it is probably equally true to say that the Pirate figure was a parallel influence on first Byron and then Branwell, for 'the Pirate' was a real identity in the eighteenth and early nineteenth century. He was not simply lawless, but a law unto himself, the ruler of his own personality, in a world where all

---

[10] 'The Pirate', *The Miscellaneous and Unpublished Writings of Charlotte and Patrick Branwell Brontë* [The Shakespeare Head Brontë], ed. T. J. Wise and J. A. Symington, 2 vols. (Oxford, Shakespeare Head, 1936–8), i. 174 ff.

other men were lesser creatures and his authority was absolute. The island of Madagascar in the eighteenth century was divided into pirate principalities, for example. The original Angria, the Malabar pirate Kanhoji Angria, whose principality was named after himself, is more striking yet. But his kingdom fell, too, in time. The curse on such figures is the ancient one of rivalling the Godhead, and damnation is the price paid. It is, surely, a situation fascinating to the mind of a dreaming youth.

Daphne du Maurier has written an interesting modern account of Branwell Brontë's life on the guiding theory that he was early enslaved by the 'infernal world'. In fact, the very designation was a descriptive phrase used by Charlotte and Branwell, even when they were adults, to refer to their imaginary empire; they referred to it also as 'the nether world' and saw it as a place of enchantment, with themselves as the enchanted. Hogg (whose *Private Memoirs and Confessions of a Justified Sinner* was published only six years before Branwell wrote his 'History of the Young Men' and 'Tales of an Englishman') had suggested that Satan could usurp one's body and thus carry out any excess, any evil, of which the soul of the self could be supposedly innocent. If God could descend into one's body and inform it with the sweetness of grace, then the opposite could hold true, as the Manichean view assumed. It is a thrilling notion but, too long played with, perhaps a dangerous one.

Admittedly, a fascination with the demonic, which is the flamboyant element of the spiritual, is natural to imaginative children, and the Brontë sisters were also gripped by it. But Branwell moved farther afield than his sisters for, as noted earlier, from some time in his boyhood he became a purposeful atheist. Living recurrently in his father's parsonage throughout his life, from the age of 15 he apparently ceased to be a regular church-goer. At the time of Aunt Branwell's death, when all of the girls were away from Haworth and he was there as the sole mourner with his aged father, it was remarked among the parishioners that he had not been in the church for several years preceding.

But if one is an atheist, all activity reduces to relative values and impulses. Simply put, at one end there is the social benefit of the many, which requires a subordination of self in the name of common love, symbolized by Christ, who represents the *victim* as hero. At the opposite end, though, is the assertion and enhancement of the individual, the egoist who *will not serve*, represented in myth as

Lucifer and in human history as the hero of self-determining action, or the extraordinary man. Christ as selfless love, Lucifer as rampant ego; these symbolic values probably transcend orthodox religion sufficiently for us today. That they did so a hundred and fifty years ago for a youthful atheist surrounded by traditional religion is doubtful.

Branwell's lifelong fascination with the figure of Lucifer is well known. His first acquaintance with his close friend Joseph Leyland followed hard on an exhibition sponsored by the Northern Society for the Encouragement of Fine Arts at Leeds in the summer of 1834, in which one of the outstanding pieces was Leyland's gigantic bust of Satan. (There is a significant coincidence in the fact that among Leyland's few surviving pieces is a life-size relief medallion of Branwell in profile.) As mentioned earlier, the Brontë family copy of Milton's *Paradise Lost* was a basic text for the children, and like many of their books was freely annotated by them with observations and questions. The poetry of Branwell, recently collected, is filled with Lucifer poems, linked with Northangerland and himself. The romance of Lucifer, for Blake or Byron or Branwell Brontë, is easy to chart, for it accorded very well with the times and the expectations of late Romantic and early Victorian world-views, a world of early industrialism, colonialism, and exploding energy. For the young pre-Victorians, the dynamic myth told them that the world was there before them for the taking if only they were indomitable enough, if only they dared to be as great as they could be, if only they chose to be the extraordinary man.

The importance of this figure for an understanding of Branwell's writing cannot be over-emphasized, for in his chronicles and particularly in the extraordinary man, Alexander Percy, one clearly sees both the attraction of the rampant individualist for Branwell and his own eventual tragedy as it developed from that attraction, and is recorded in a poem such as his 'Azrael, or Destruction's Eve':

> We say that *He*, the Almighty God
> That framed Creation with a nod,
> His wondrous work so well fulfilled
> That—in an hour—it All rebelled!—
> That though He loves our race so well
> He hurls our spirits into Hell—
> . . . .
> That though He says the world shall stand

> Eternal—perfect—from His hand,
> He is just about to whelm it o'er
> With utter ruin—evermore!—
>
> (85–98)
>
> 'Away with all such phantasies!—
> Just trust your reason and your eyes!—
> Believe that God exists when I
> Who, here—this hour—His name deny,
> Shall bear a harder punishment
> Than those whose knees to Him have bent.
> Believe that He can rule above
>   When you shall see Him rule below;
> Believe that He's the God of love
>   When He shall end His children's woe...
>
> (103–12)
>
> A Thought for Earth far more beseems
>   Than childish gazing at the skies.
>   'Tis Earth—not Heaven—shall shortly rise;
>   'Tis Man—not God—shall soon avenge;
>   And if there be a paradise
> We'll bring it in the coming change!—
>
> (125–30)

But, not surprisingly, out of this serviceable rationalist verse comes a final view that is destructive, even cataclysmic. Azrael, we remember, is the destroyer, the Angel of Death, and as he drinks with his own familiar, Moloch—'just a simple glass of wine | Will drive the demon power of evil | To his and our good lord, the Devil! | Come, drink this draft and—feel divine!'—he plots the overthrow of Heaven. 'So—when Lord Azrael saw the wide | Commencing waste assume its form, | Grim Gladness buoyed his heart—.'[11]

In this and other works of Branwell there stirs the Luciferian urge towards power, power over men and power over things which, some decades later, would be manifest in the development of the dynamo for Henry Adams or in the philosophy of Nietzsche. But there was no such singleness of thought for Branwell or Northangerland, no system of belief, only the emotional impulses of an undirected and over-stored mind.

Time has edited the great Romantic thinkers, of course, to accommodate the subsequent growth of egalitarianism, which in any event

---

[11] Winnifrith, *Poems*, 141–54.

had its roots in the late eighteenth and early nineteenth centuries. But a fiery poetic attack on prevailing institutions and monarchical privilege, as uttered by Shelley or Byron, is far from being a belief in undifferentiated equality. The great dream of the Romantic artist was not based on democratic anonymity but on the heroic individual who would assault injustice; it envisioned the shattering of traditional barriers to allow the uninhibited fulfilment of the naturally extraordinary person. This view celebrates freedom as the *release* of personality to accomplish its greatest *individual* destiny. Emerging democracy for the general, as manifested, say, in the new American proletarian, was a mental and, literally, a social disease which was little approved as a practical reality by most serious thinkers. This was the age of Carlyle's *Heroes and Hero Worship*, of Emerson's *Representative Men*, of history composed of larger-than-life figures leaving footprints in the sands of time. From 1750 to 1850, certainly, the greatest writers of the time call for a meritocracy but not for the unrestrained democracy we are apt to think of today. It is worth remembering that most educated Europeans thought of the French Revolution as a bloodbath, and the reactionary Napoleon was the most popular figure in Europe as emperor. Republicanism went wrong when it was taken over by the great unwashed; they properly remained the raw mass they had always been, but the use of them as a means towards enlightened power by the worthy individual was as right as was their obligatory acceptance of him as leader.

Such an individual was to be recognized through his indomitable 'Will' or asserted strength of personality, of course. Yet this temperament led him to a contradiction of roles, eventually. The demagogue was justified in that, as *antagonist* to the entrenched authority or system of values, he is seen as the *protagonist* of the masses who consider themselves excluded from the benefits which they covet. In an underlying logic, he frequently embodies for his followers their private ambitions, frank avarice, or secret desires. Perversely, then, the use of personal popularity to organize the masses becomes acceptable to those manipulated. The egoist as leader often establishes his independent role by being the most haughty, the most contemptuous of figures; but as an outsider to the Establishment, who asserts himself as the role model for the anonymous rebel in the mob, he will be applauded in his personal arrogance so long as the objects of his attack are believed to be established privilege and long-entrenched positions. Where legal authority is viewed as a barricade, the protection of the *status quo*, the archetypal rebel tears down such barriers to the cheers of the multitude and has a thousand hands raised to do the actual demolition.

So Branwell creates Alexander Percy in the levelling of the jail in 'Real Life in Verdopolis'. Quick to recognize the invariable resentment of the numerical majority in any social body, the demagogue asserts himself as their champion, and is granted licence by them. Ironically, having been so placed above them, he sees himself as entitled to (and generally receives) the actual fruits of the rebellion.

Branwell, born two years after Waterloo, perversely adopted Napoleon as his early hero, the first great modern leader in this tradition of the dictator lifted up and idolized by the populace. That he chose Napoleon as the name of his preferred figure in the toy soldier incident is initially significant in that the French emperor was a resurgent foil to Wellington, Charlotte's ideal figure as 'the Saviour of Europe'. At the same time, he was a figure of majesty, of absolute right. As Branwell recognized, the extraordinary man always rises by a combination of aristocratic opposition and popular worship. The image goes back to the early tyrants of Greece whom Branwell read about in his father's study. It is, of course, a precarious role: once the demagogue ceases to be the active antagonist of the *status quo* he loses his popular identity, unless still another outside force threatens the community and so restores his role as champion. So it is that Northangerland must ceaselessly agitate and manipulate, for he cannot be a builder. A primitive ordering of society recurs each time a new popular champion is crowned, just as—seen from another point in the social process—each new revolutionary success begins a process of consolidation that eventually leads to another revolution.

In any event, the man of destiny must first know himself as an extraordinary man. As we see in Alexander Percy (and as we can extrapolate of Branwell), to be only one of the mass, even to be initially satisfied to be such, is *ipso facto* an impossibility for him. Thus, the loneliness, the separateness, the emotional strain, the trial imposed by his incipient destiny for Percy, as conceived by Branwell. If he is really an extraordinary man, he is, paradoxically, *compelled* to be free, he must, like Lucifer, Napoleon, Byron's Manfred or the Giaour (or somewhat later, but more clearly still, Dostoevsky's Raskolnikov) prove his distinction by his freedom from the restraints, the moral law, imposed on and accepted by others. Hence, the insistence on being a law unto himself.

Admiration, then, is the force that propels such an extraordinary man to power; not only Napoleon but his nemesis, the Duke of Wellington, was a popular hero, as are equally Northangerland and Zamorna. The many admirers of Napoleon saw him as fighting against the inertness of an outworn world, and so they believed that any who opposed him acted out of resentment of his natural merit. His astonishing initial success then created a new leviathan, the self-crowned emperor, against whom would appear Charlotte's youthful champion of Britain, Arthur Wellesley, the fictional Duke of Wellington. The standing argument between Robert Moore (on behalf of Napoleon) and the Reverend Helstone (championing Wellington) in Charlotte's second published novel *Shirley* is an exact parallel in fiction to the debate that engaged western Europe in the earlier years of the century. Essentially, the separate Angrian writings of Charlotte and Branwell can also be recognized as a contest. That is, the drama of Wellington and Napoleon, fictionally carried forward through Zamorna and Northangerland, is one in which Charlotte eventually reasserts the primacy of society and domesticity.[12] Branwell, obdurate to the last as Northangerland, drinks the bitter dregs of the unregenerate rebel, the unbroken egoist.

To begin with, the two young Brontës were philosophically alike in their conception of their respective heroes, although in practice each of their protagonists expressed himself primarily according to the temperament of the respective author; that is, through protection of the state and impassioned love-relationships for Charlotte's Zamorna, and through rebellious action for Branwell's Northangerland. The historical Wellington was, of course, prime minister of England from

---

[12] By 1848, the year of Branwell's death, Charlotte's rejection of her own earlier, and his lifelong, celebration of the rebel figure was absolute. In a letter to Miss Wooler, dated 31 March, she says with a certain self-consciousness about her impending thirty-second birthday: 'I have now outlived youth; and ... certain things are not what they were ten years ago; and, amongst the rest, "the pomp and circumstance of war" have quite lost in my eye their fictitious glitter ... little doubt have I that convulsive revolutions put back the world in all that is good, check civilisation, bring the dregs of society to its surface; in short, it appears to me that insurrections and battles are the acute diseases of nations, and that their tendency is to exhaust, by their violence, the vital energies of the countries where they occur. That England may be spared the spasms, cramps, and frenzy fits now contorting the Continent, and threatening Ireland, I earnestly pray. With the French and Irish I have no sympathy. With the Germans and Italians I think the case is different; as different as the love of freedom is from the lust for license' (Gaskell, *Charlotte Brontë*, 366). Angria, in either the life of her Zamorna or Branwell's Northangerland, reveals little distinction between the love of freedom and the lust for licence, ego being the hallmark of both heroes.

1828 to 1830, just when Verdopolis was built. Charlotte's tribute to him in his middle age consisted in restoring him as a youthful romantic hero, giving him all that he might want in his political life, and more. As noted, she did this by turning him into his own son, reconceived as the saviour of Europe against Napoleon but now emperor himself of a new and shining nation which he is building through force of personality. At the same time, in her own youthful tolerance, she granted him the personal freedom of countless mistresses and an imperious manner with subordinates. She even allowed him, as an extraordinary man, the ruthlessness needed to set aside his own wife out of resentment against his father-in-law, Northangerland.

Such admiration espouses no popular political system; it celebrates Zamorna as a remarkable individual whose personal qualities are the justification for whatever he does, however unacceptable such actions might be from another person. He is, by his own view, beyond question; when he demands and receives a kingdom from a nerveless parliament, its very response confirms his greatness in the text. With *both* Charlotte and Branwell, then, at this time, the aim was not towards a benign average, of which they were themselves contemptuous, but a heroic reach towards the tangible forms of power.

Branwell's childhood hero, Napoleon, goes through an even more significant evolution. This figure was quite early transformed into Sneaky, or Sneachi, who becomes one of 'the Twelves', the founders of the Confederacy, and is in turn retired to the background as a royal eminence. While Alexander Sneaky has children, they do not, as in Charlotte's case, take over the foreground. Branwell, without regressing, simply switches characters, bringing in Alexander Percy to be more active, ruthless, and daring than any other of the Angrian characters. Literature is a great seducer, particularly one's own writings, and it seems that for Branwell, at 14 or so, Rougue was the figure towards whom everything so far had been leading, as though at the beginning of manhood he required this surrogate to live through.

During the early childhood of the Brontë children their father, according to his own account, kept a mask in his study. In a family game, he would give it to each of the children to wear in turn, while they were asked questions, which the wearing of the mask allowed them to answer freely. Analogously, Alexander Percy was developed as the figure through whom Branwell spoke to the world, however hidden from the world in his nearly invisible handwriting the tales of

Angria remained. Eventually a vital shift occurred, and it was as Northangerland that Branwell himself regarded the world. Briefly stated, through Percy, Branwell became the outlaw, the antagonist to Zamorna, who, as authority or law, eventually reasserted the traditional values through the pen of Charlotte. Through Percy made real on his sheet of paper, Branwell became the pirate, the thief, the contemptuous lover, and the tragic consciousness whose emotional demands the world was inadequate to fulfill. The mask of the elder Patrick Brontë was turned into the tiny booklets of 'Letters of an Englishman' and the sheets of 'Real Life in Verdopolis', which came to life far too successfully; the young writer who, except for his sisters on occasion, was also his own exclusive audience eventually could not remove the mask.

Branwell's obsession and his fate, then, seem traceable at least in their general outlines to certain aspects of his time. It is worth repeating in this connection that the Brontë household in the 1830s was probably as well-read and intellectually informed as any in England. Charlotte and Branwell's generation is that of the agonized sceptics—Tennyson, Browning, Arnold. In a sceptical world the romantic demagogue as popular hero is himself a displacement of supernatural force, which in some way he tries to take into himself, either physically or intellectually. Accordingly, while aristocracy as a concept continues, it is no longer an established order but a natural order made up of those with the will and intelligence to create themselves as such. Nature's noblemen, many self-proclaimed, replace those of hereditary title. By 1848, the year of Branwell's death, the thrones of Europe in the familiar image are teetering; everywhere, it seems, the 'common man' is exhorted, invited to take hold of his own destiny, generally under the guidance of a revolutionary leader. What Branwell's contemporary, Dostoevsky, the revolutionary turned conservative, called in the Epilogue to *Crime and Punishment* a brain infection, a disease sweeping into Russia from Europe, in which men were driven mad with the belief that they were God—this epidemic was already in full course.[13]

---

[13] Improbable as it may seem, Dostoevsky and Branwell were born within four years of each other, with Dostoevsky's first novel appearing two years before Branwell's death. While they obviously did not know each other, they shared the same dramatic post-Napoleonic world.

In some ways, then, Branwell's chronicles are those of the imagination of his time. His problem may, in fact, have been that he imbued Northangerland with characteristics which it was too easy for him to believe in himself; he was his own best reader of these private chronicles. As noted, Branwell in his adult years commonly used the name of Northangerland in correspondence with his friends, who apparently came to accept it readily, sometimes addressing him by that name in their responses.

Obviously he was both hypnotized by the figure he had created and aware of the inevitable self-destructiveness of such a character, for in time this self-destructive element is what Branwell himself purposefully reveals about Percy. Ironically, Northangerland in the chronicles provides a pattern of despair which Branwell will eventually follow.

Without the redeeming ordinary emotions of a Raskolnikov, Branwell's hero has nowhere to go. Like Emily's Heathcliff—or even Anne's Gilbert Markham—to whom in many ways he bears a remarkable resemblance of personality, he can unhesitatingly smash another man in the face in a moment of spontaneous anger; but unlike the two of them he lives only for himself even when he broods on and on over the death of his beloved wife. Since Mary Percy in Branwell's tales (in contrast to Emily's Catherine Earnshaw) is irretrievably dead, she remains a death agony within the bitter Percy. Suffer from her death though he does, he cannot believe in anything outside himself, not even her spirit, as Heathcliff believes in an enduring Catherine. Both are prisoners in the flesh, but while Heathcliff eventually finds his heaven, Percy has nowhere to go outside himself. Conversely, while Zamorna probably represented Charlotte's ideal at an early stage of her life, she grew beyond him. Northangerland achieved a more immanent, a more compelling existence in Branwell's life; and rather than growing out of him, he was taken over; life creating fiction was in turn taken over by it.

In this, Branwell was an invisible member of a diverse community of European writers of his time, all of whom individually saw the heart of that moment with extreme clarity. Better men, perhaps, saw it as the loss of a necessary principle; Branwell's curse was that he was swallowed by the world which he envisioned. Stendhal created a Julian Sorel in *Le Rouge et le Noir* who, faced with a world in which cynicism had apparently displaced human love, chose to reassert love even though it meant dying out of this life. Like Raskolnikov or Heathcliff, it gave him a place to go to, to earn, to win redemption by the selfless love of creature for creature even if it be in some trackless Siberia of the human spirit. Emily Brontë, Dostoevsky, Stendhal—all were far greater than Branwell in what they achieved.

But perhaps none suffered through the crucial question of the self without the mitigating grace of love more painfully than did Branwell. And perhaps none needed it more than did he, as evidenced by the Lydia Robinson episode that sits as a terminal illness over the horrifying last few years of his life. Again, that nineteenth-century clinical term—'marasmus', a 'wasting away', the death certificate with which his life was sealed. Almost a hundred years before the literary discovery and exploration of that trackless desert of the Waste Land, Branwell had become one of the skeletons bleaching in the pitiless sun.

Since little of Branwell's work has been available for the common reader to judge, its merit has remained largely undefined. One thing that is clear to anyone who has studied the existing manuscripts is that they are the surviving portions of a much larger body of work. This is rather to be expected than otherwise. The Brontë family rapidly dissolved after Branwell's death; two of his sisters died within the next nine months; his surviving sister, within another seven years; his father, already of advanced age, shortly after that. The home was taken over by strangers and extensively remodelled; the personal effects of the Brontës were scattered or destroyed. Some (no one knows how many) of the surviving manuscripts were eventually taken to Ireland by Charlotte's husband, Arthur Bell Nichols, where, a half-century after Branwell's death, most of whatever remained in Nichols' possession was sold to T. J. Wise. Wise added to the confusion by separating portions of manuscripts and selling off single sheets. What was lost in each of these long periods of neglect will never be known, but certainly Branwell, as the least known, least published, and most readily dismissed member of the family, would not have had much chance of being preserved in manuscript through special consideration. On the contrary, when we consider that even the manuscript of *Wuthering Heights* has not survived, it is remarkable that we have as much of Branwell's work as we do.

His writings, in any event, have so far had little effect on his reputation. Since so much of his work was done between his thirteenth and twenty-fifth years, in a great sustained outpouring, with little of the prose recopied and very little of it edited, and since almost all of it was in that scarcely legible minute hand, practical problems of accessibility have denied Branwell's work a reading. Prior to Tom Winnifrith's *The Poems of Patrick Branwell Brontë* (1983), the only trade-book publication of Branwell's work[14] was that included in the grab-bag two volumes of the *Miscellaneous and Uncollected Writings of Charlotte and Patrick Branwell Brontë* in *The Shakespeare Head Brontë* (nineteen volumes), of some sixty years ago, of which one thousand copies were printed, guaranteeing that circulation would be restricted for the most part to libraries (and not a great many of those). Further, much of what is included there of Branwell's work is in the form of facsimiles of undeciphered manuscripts, thus remaining virtually illegible to casual readers.

Even Branwell's friends from his Bradford and Halifax periods, Joseph Leyland, William Deardon, and Francis Grundy, would have heard only some of the poetry and at best a page or two of the more dramatic prose—as suggested in the famous episode where, a few years before the publication of *Wuthering Heights*, Branwell allegedly read a scene from that work to his cronies in a local pub, speaking of it as his own, and raising a storm of controversy that continued into the following century. To be sure, few scholars today pay much heed to the notion that Emily's masterpiece was written by Branwell. Yet there are more substantial reasons for knowing Branwell's writings.

The Brontës were a very close-knit group, and all through their childhood and youth shared an interest in writing, both in subject-matter and world outlook. For much of that time the evidence indicates that Branwell established the direction of their writing, and as the only boy tended to dominate his sisters with their generally willing compliance and even admiration. There is a significant echo in the characterization of all the youthful writings of the Brontës, with the basic figures probably those of Branwell. (Certainly the AGA of Emily's poetry, particularly as reconstructed by Fannie Ratchford, seems closely related to Alexander Percy's ruthless first wife, Augusta di Segovia, in Branwell's chronicle.) A very limited number of names

---

[14] At the time of the present writing, the release of a new edition of *The Poetry of Patrick Branwell Brontë*, ed. Victor Neufeldt (New York, Garland Press) has been announced.

recur in all of their writings, as do kinds of characters—for example, Ellen, governess of young Alexander Percy, and Nelly Dean of *Wuthering Heights*, whose proper name is Ellen; as well as the repeated names of Arthur, Alexander, Gerald/Geraldine, Mary/Maria, and others. Heathcliff, and even Rochester, can be seen in more than embryonic form in the personality of Alexander Percy, while Arthur Huntington of Anne's *The Tenant of Wildfell Hall* could be Percy in any one of several of Branwell's manuscripts, were we to read Anne's account from the side of the male figure. A good number of Branwell's better poems closely resemble those of Emily, in part because they bespeak a similar emotional and dramatic context, while there is absolutely no indication and little likelihood that he knew her work before he wrote, or even that her poems were written before his. (For example, she was clearly active in the five-year period before the publication of the Bell poems, during most of which time he was with the Robinsons when he either wrote no poems or, more likely, passed them on to Lydia Robinson, who would certainly have destroyed them in the family crisis that ensued.) There is, in short, a rich opportunity for a comparison of his work with that of his sisters, which may well add considerable colour and depth to our understanding of all their writings.

Before this can be done very seriously, we need to see Branwell's work in a parallel form to theirs, corrected and edited, transposed from the frequently confusing flood of inspiration in the manuscript, the almost completely unpunctuated, indifferently spelled, ink-blotted, sometimes repetitious cataract of words.

The two works edited here, 'The Life of... Northangerland' and 'Real Life in Verdopolis', form an excellent introduction to Branwell's art, and give an accurate view both of his strengths and limitations as a writer. For this reason, the aim of the editor has, throughout, been that of providing a reader's edition, that is, a work readily available in form and meaning to any intelligent reader.

Since Alexander Percy was far and away his most important literary character, 'The Life of... Northangerland' is of obvious importance. Written in 1835 when Branwell was 18 and had already been writing about his hero/anti-hero for several years, it is necessarily retrospective. That is, having shown the imperious and egoistic demagogue as a mature man, having made him in his own chronicles (if not in Charlotte's) what was called the leading light of that shadow world of Verdopolis, he had, in fact, turned his own fictional world into a backdrop for Alexander Percy.[15] Thus, when he writes of the family background of his hero, of his childhood experiences, youthful passions, and eventual share in the murder of his father, he is obviously explaining how Alexander Percy got that way, accounting for the man who stands as the Lucifer figure in the chronicles generally, and in doing so revealing his own state of mind. Appropriately, then, the chronicle entitled 'Real Life in Verdopolis', although written two years earlier by the 16 year old Branwell, shows Alexander Percy as the mature demagogue, Rougue/Elrington, in his later marriage to Zenobia, in his rabble-rousing, particularly, and in his hidden role as leader of the thieves and outlaws of the nation, as well as in his compulsive opposition to the Aristocrats in parliament. Taken together, while both display the open-ended characteristics of Branwell Brontë's chronicles, they provide us with an effective portrait of his obsessive vision.

---

[15] Although Charlotte's characterization of Alexander Percy is milder than Branwell's and conveys little of the passion attributed to the figure by her brother, she surely was familiar with his Alexander Percy. It is surprising, then, that in a letter transcribed by Hatfield and printed in the *Brontë Society Transactions* (1950, p. 16), she refers to herself as a 'Richardsonian author' who might write a six-volume work in which the Angrian characters would appear, with 'Percy my Mr B.' The latter is, of course, the lusting hero of *Pamela*, and the playful reference suggests that she scarcely considered Percy to be a contemptible figure. Mrs Gaskell prints part of that letter, omitting the reference to Percy. (Gaskell, *Charlotte Brontë*, 194) Charlotte, then 24 years old, obviously still had Percy as a spontaneous reference. It is worth noting, too, that Charlotte in her 'Devoir' 'Sur La Morte De Napoleon', written in Brussels and dated '31 *mai*, 1843', spells out appreciatively the very traits of the Extraordinary Man celebrated by Branwell, although she contrasts them subsequently with those of the man of integrity—the noble Wellington. This exercise, written when she was 27, could easily be an Angrian manuscript.

EDITING THE MANUSCRIPT

While it may drown a reader, a flood of words carries an enthusiastic writer along so swiftly that he has little time to observe landmarks, and Branwell Brontë's output as a youthful writer was certainly prodigious. As Winifred Gérin has pointed out, he 'would appear, as a child, to have worked at fever heat, speed and intensity being the condition of his writing'. And

between the ages of ten and seventeen he became the author of some thirty named and distinct volumes of tales, poems, dramas, journals, histories, literary commentary, etc. and of almost as many fragments. It has, also, to be taken into consideration that a quantity of others may have been lost.[1]

Branwell's biographer is certainly right about lost manuscripts; we have many odd pages surviving that testify to a much larger bulk. Furthermore, there is nothing significant about his seventeenth year as a writer of Angrian manuscripts; he continued afterwards, and for periods of time at the same speed and intensity, as is revealed in 'The Life ... of Northangerland' printed here. Above all, because so little of his writing has been published, what has been publicly said about it has generally been from writers on Charlotte, Emily, and Anne, most of whom seem to have sampled a manuscript page or two out of passing interest and pronounced it indigestible. Small wonder, to be sure, for it is a daunting physical task to read through as much as one minutely inscribed page—which in normal handwriting might cover up to ten pages. Then again, consecutive pages of manuscripts still remain widely separated in libraries far apart from each other.

'Real Life in Verdopolis' (1833) and 'The Life of Field Marshal the Right Honourable Alexander Percy, Earl of Northangerland' (1835) have had an unusual modern history which yet reflects the characteristic confusion of critical attention to Branwell's work. For one thing, both manuscripts 'disappeared' for several years. 'Real Life' is listed in volume two of Clement Shorter's *The Brontës: Life and Letters* (1908) under Appendix V (p. 434), as noted by Christine

---

[1] Gérin, *Branwell Brontë*, 41.

Alexander in her comprehensive study of the Juvenilia. Alexander, however, writing in the early 1980s and noting its absence, cites it as a lost manuscript by Branwell. In another note she speculates (logically, but in this instance inaccurately, as it happens), that an 'unnamed and undated fragment' given in facsimile in the Shakespeare Head *Miscellaneous And Unpublished Writings of Charlotte and Branwell Brontë* (i. 296) was possibly part of the 'missing' 'Real Life in Verdopolis'.[2] Both Daphne du Maurier (1960) and Winifred Gérin (1961) in their respective biographies of Branwell make no reference to 'Real Life', although both refer at length to Branwell's manuscripts in establishing the association between the author and his literary creation, Rougue/Northangerland, who stands as the central dramatic figure in 'Real Life'. Equally, in the omnibus *Everyman's Companion to the Brontës* (1982), Barbara and Gareth Lloyd Evans do not mention the work.

The same is true of 'The Life of... Northangerland', which Christine Alexander refers to as now untraceable (although, with her unparalleled grasp of the known manuscripts, she acutely observes from a single facsimile sheet of the title-page in the Harvard College Library that the manuscript was an account of major events referred to in other fragmentary writings). Considering that Charlotte often wrote separate versions of situations; that she and Branwell moved back and forth filling in events, a process which sometimes involved a reworking of the circumstances, including name changes and the re-ordering of relationships; that a large number of Branwell's manuscripts are scattered and any amount of the material may have long since been destroyed; and that his tales are episodic—in view of all this, a coherent account of Branwell's full narrative writings has seemed almost impossible. It is, therefore, of particular value that these two manuscripts, among the longest of his surviving ones, should have resurfaced and entered the purview of scholarly attention.

In fact, it is not surprising that studies published early in the 1980s did not encounter these two works, for they only came back into view at that time. In 1980 a benefit auction of literary rarities was held in New York by the Grolier Society. Among the offerings were the original manuscripts of 'Real Life in Verdopolis' and 'The Life of Feild (*sic*) Marshal the Right Honourable Alexaner (*sic*) Percy Earl

---

[2] Alexander, *Early Writings of Charlotte Brontë*, 273.

of Northangerland'; both were donated by an anonymous owner.[3] Purchased by the Brotherton Collection of Rare Books and Manuscripts at Leeds University, the two manuscripts proved to be in excellent general condition, all things considered.

None the less, they displayed all of the problems of transcription and editing characteristic of Branwell's work. The specimen manuscript sheets reproduced here before each of the two chronicles illustrate essentially the sort of thing that was there to be deciphered. Also the Notes include a number of examples of the original form of the text in some passages crossed out by Branwell. Although no longer in the minute lettering of the manuscript, they will give some idea of such problems as that of deciphering his syntax.

Written on pulp paper, considerably darkened with age, and in ink now turned brown by time, the manuscripts are inscribed in the extremely minute hand that has guaranteed the inaccessibility of Branwell's writing to the casual reader for almost a century and a half. Although not the doll-size booklets of the imitation *Blackwood's* of Branwell's earliest years, the sheets, measuring approximately 11.5 cm. × 19.3 cm., are written to the edges, top, bottom, and sides, with as many as 137 lines to the page, and an average of about seventeen words to the line. Written on both sides of the sheet, the total pages number, respectively, thirty-five for 'Real Life' and thirty-two for 'The Life of . . . Northangerland'. When one considers that a page without chapter breaks—that is, most of them—can carry as many as 2,300 words, it will be seen that the two narratives are substantial works.

In addition to the obvious problem of deciphering such extremely small writing, there was Branwell's own hand as a difficulty; in comparison, the letters in Charlotte's microscopic writing are very much clearer. One suspects that in time Branwell wrote these tiny letters without the need even to read the words as his practised hand shaped them. It is, further, a jerky hand, that makes it extremely difficult to distinguish, for example, a 't' from an 'l' or at times even

---

[3] A third Branwell manuscript from the Grolier auction was purchased by the bibliophile Robert Taylor for the collection bearing his name in the Princeton University Library. According to Mr Taylor, he knew only that it was a Branwell manuscript at the time. Examining it a few years later I found it to be a major chunk of Branwell's so-called final novel, 'And the Weary are at Rest', which had been published in a private edition of fifty copies with an Introduction by C. W. Hatfield in 1924. This finding suggests that other, unknown segments of that strange work may have been separated or lost.

an 's', or a 'v' from an 'r'. Then, too, he commonly used either no punctuation or false punctuation; that is, his pen nib touched down constantly and at random between words, frequently giving the effect of end stops after each word. Paragraphing, too, is capricious and often forgotten for long periods; at times, words are inadvertently repeated and at other times omitted. In short, Branwell was writing at a gallop, and it must have been an extremely rare occasion when a page was revised at all once it was filled.

There were other problems with the physical text. For example, over the years some of the manuscript pages have become worn and abraded at the edges, obscuring or destroying parts of words or sentences, a problem exacerbated by Branwell's habit of filling his sheet completely. In an effort to halt the deterioration, an earlier owner encased the edges in a surrounding matting, the overlap of which compounded the problem of transcription since parts of lines beginning and ending a page are sometimes indecipherable or missing, as are odd letters or short words at the beginning or end of a line. Repeated readings have, in most such cases, made it possible to eventually determine what is missing with a fair measure of accuracy, but the necessity for reconstruction involved hundreds of minor but time-consuming decisions. All of this was complicated by random blots, smudges, or unassociated words or markings where Branwell had made use of a sheet already partly written on, or where a later writer had scrawled a now-meaningless reference.

In short, it is easy to see why much of Branwell's writing has remained unpublished or why a publisher would simply print an odd sample sheet of manuscript without transcribing it. Yet there seems little value in reproducing as a text the original distortions of meaning embodied in the manuscript; anyone who has searched for material on Branwell surely has been frustrated by the largely useless facsimiles in the Shakespeare Head edition of *The Miscellaneous and Unpublished Writings of Charlotte and Patrick Branwell Brontë*. What has clearly been needed is a sensitive and careful transfer of meaningful text from the faded, jumbled, and mutilated first draft that survives in manuscript to a printed narrative in which the intensity of Branwell Brontë's imagination is fully visible.

Having purchased the Branwell manuscripts, Dennis Cox, the Librarian of the Brotherton at Leeds University, recognized the potential significance of the two long manuscripts and approached Professor John Barnard about preparing them for publication. With the assistance of Judith Bates, Professor Barnard began the transcription. However, soon after, when the complexity of the task became evident, and with approval of the Librarian, he invited the present editor to join him in the task. After the rough transcription was done, John Barnard, under the press of other scholarly projects, found it necessary to withdraw, leaving myself, assisted by May Collins, to carry forward the editing and reconstruction of the transcript, along with the Notes and the Introduction. Thus, the present reader's edition, with whatever questions remain, must be seen as the responsibility of the surviving editor. (On the other hand, since the greatest single difficulty was in the initial deciphering of the manuscript sheets, there is no question that the intelligence, patience, and fine perception of John Barnard, May Collins, and Judith Bates contributed largely to a basic text within which the resolution of individual questions became possible.)

Characteristically, the first steps were dictated by the manuscripts themselves. The basic transcription consisted of four separate readings by Judith Bates, May Collins, John Barnard, and myself. Each reader used a set of high-definition, several-times magnified, photographic copies of the manuscript and, in frequent instances, illuminated magnifying lenses, although the reproductions were useless for portions of the text hidden under the matting on the original sheets. The readings were then correlated, resulting in a very rough master transcript. The unrevised condition of the manuscript became evident with the very title, where Branwell's indifference to spelling results in the omission of the letter 'D' from Alexander Percy's first name. Although Percy's name is set off by Branwell in block capitals, he probably never noticed the error and never returned to correct it. He certainly did not intend the name as an oddity, since he spells it accurately everywhere else. It quickly became apparent, also, that each reader might see a given word differently. For example, still in the title, the phrase 'Premier of——' was completed in the various initial transcriptions as 'Premier of Duguid', 'Premier of Dongola', and the obviously correct 'Premier of Angria' (a quick glance at the manuscript facsimiles included in this edition will reveal why anyone first experiencing the Angrian manuscripts could make such a mistake). Hundreds of questionable readings became evident, all of which had to be resolved on an individual basis, including the many incomplete words and lines referred to earlier. Unlike his sisters, Branwell had, of course, never prepared any of his prose manuscripts for a publisher or had them edited by a publishing house, for in his chaotic world writing them *was* publishing them, just as the little books of his childhood had made him the publisher known as 'Seargent Bud'.[4]

The original rough transcription, where every line was studded with question marks, was only the beginning, and the editor found that he could never get very far away from the manuscript sheets. A reader's edition, the logical objective, imposed somewhat different demands, too, from those normally faced by scholars working with manuscripts. Often, where textual correction is the aim, a scholar makes his way back through successive editions of a literary work to an original manuscript, seeking to find in the authority of the author's unadulterated text a more accurate reading. On the other hand, since the intent in the present case was to rescue Branwell's work from the limbo in which it has existed by virtue of its peculiar and partly accidental condition, one had to thread one's way not only into the labyrinth but back out again, in the process paving a road for a future common reader. In order to do so, the editorial procedures had to be extended beyond the routine ones involved in working with a normal manuscript for purposes primarily of verification. One necessarily became (though to a judicious and limited degree) the copy-editor/proof-reader whom Branwell never had. Essentially, these demands led to the following editorial procedures, given in something like the order of complexity.

1. Correction and standardization of spelling. For example, like many youthful writers Branwell repeatedly transposed letters, as in the ie/ei combinations. Where an error exists, correction has been made. On the other hand, certain forms characteristic of archaisms, such as the use of 'past' instead of 'passed' as the past tense of 'to pass' are retained, where the meaning is clear to the reader.

2. The introduction of standard punctuation and regularized paragraphing. Little of either exists in the manuscript, and a conservative form has been introduced throughout. Not infrequently,

---

[4] In contrast, according to Mrs Gaskell, Charlotte Brontë was a painstaking writer who 'never wrote down a sentence until she clearly understood what she wanted to say, had deliberately chosen the words, and arranged them in their right order' (*Charlotte Brontë*, 323). Even Charlotte, however, appreciated a copy-editor; in two letters to Smith and Elder concerning the proofs of *Jane Eyre*, she thanks the publisher for correcting the punctuation: 'I found the task very puzzling, and, besides, I consider your mode of punctuation a great deal more correct and rational than my own'. (ibid. 338).

even so apparently small a thing as indifference to punctuation by the enthusiastic young writer has created run-on sentences or questionable fragments which, once punctuated properly, suddenly become perfectly intelligible. Again, dialogue in the manuscript on occasion was hashed together in a single crowded paragraph, sometimes leading to a confusion of voices; these were fairly readily identified by appropriate paragraphing, resulting, too, in an increase in sharpness and significance.

3. Deletion of meaninglessly repeated words (dittography—the same word sometimes repeated where no emphasis is achieved, resulting in a stutter) and the addition of words, such as articles, clearly omitted in haste by the writer.

4. Infrequently, the correction of syntax when a given sentence is completely obscure as given, and where the change in position of a given phrase clarifies without altering.

5. Making a choice between probable alternatives when, as is not infrequently true in the manuscript, a given word is not absolutely decipherable. In the second sentence of 'The Life of... Northangerland', as a simple example, the early transcriptions yielded 'from the *fights* of a Marlborough...' However, the basic metaphor in this paragraph is that of *stars* ('luminaries', 'flashing', and so on), so while it is not absolutely beyond question, a second reading leads to 'from the *lights* of a Marlborough', which suits the context much more. In almost every case, resolving a questionable word or line was a matter of turning over possibilities until, like a missing piece of jigsaw, the right one suddenly became evident.

6. Reconstruction at many points where the manuscript was worn off on the edges, covered by firmly glued-down matting which could not be removed without damage, or where the upper half of a top sentence or the lower half of a bottom one had been trimmed off by an early owner interested only in the novelty of the manuscript as a physical object. One distinct example is that of manuscript folio 2, verso, of 'The Life...', where the top line is largely missing and the reconstruction is based on the surviving visible letters and the context. 'Upon [my being shown to a waiting room, within a few minutes a] magnificently dressed lady of about thirty years of age entered...' (p. 16). Another, similar in nature, is found on page 42, where the words between 'soon' and 'on him' are largely illegible. However, reconstruction resulted in: 'A certain aristocratical circle was soon [assembled, their interest centred] on him.' In this case,

too, certain legible letters, as well as the narrative context, accord with the bridge portion finally determined. In some cases parts of words or even of a single word are present as a bridge; sometimes a letter-count is useful, and so forth. In no instance has material been introduced which has no substantial basis in the manuscript. Throughout, the editing procedure has been faithful wherever possible to Branwell's phrasing and structure. (Some of the more difficult decisions are recorded in the Notes.)

Usage and stylisms have been preserved generally. Branwell frequently uses a split form for compound words such as 'in to' or 'over head'; not infrequently, too, he uses as a present tense what we would regard as a past tense of words such as 'rung' and 'drunk'. Where the meaning is perfectly clear, such usages have been preserved as characteristic of his style. He also had a habit of putting in quotation marks phrases which we would regard as ordinary figures of speech, for example, when Northangerland is described as 'to be of "salt of the land"'.

In all of the above, the attempt has been to follow Branwell's thought and to remain as faithful as possible to his style as it is revealed in his many other unpublished manuscripts. Basically, I have tried to identify and correct inadvertent errors, and bring Branwell's text back to life in the present day. Undoubtedly, there are individual points on which another editor might draw different conclusions. However, the edition presented here will, I am confident, give the common reader a long-overdue experience of the mind and imagination of the fourth Brontë, and of the prose on which he spent much of his early life.

SELECT BIBLIOGRAPHY

The following list does not include articles, most of which are on Branwell's poetry in any event. While some of the titles given are primarily concerned with Charlotte Brontë, such works as those by Christine Alexander are valuable contributions to Branwell studies also. The Hatfield transcriptions and the Leyland manuscripts provide easy access to original Branwell writings for scholars visiting Brontë country.

Primary

Brontë, Charlotte, *An Edition of the Early Writings of Charlotte Brontë*, ed. Christine Alexander, *Vol. I, 1826–32*; *Vol. 2, 1833–4*; *Vol. 3, 1834–5* (Oxford, Shakespeare Head Press, 1987, 1991, 1991).

—— *Legends of Angria*, ed. Fannie E. Ratchford (New Haven, Conn., Yale University Press, 1933).

—— and Brontë, Patrick Branwell, *The Miscellaneous and Unpublished Writings of Charlotte and Patrick Branwell Brontë*, ed. J. A. Symington and T. J. Wise, 2 Vols. [The Shakespeare Head Edition] (Oxford, Basil Blackwell, 1936, 1938).

—— *The Poems of Charlotte Brontë and Patrick Branwell Brontë*, ed. J. A. Symington and T. J. Wise [The Shakespeare Head Edition] (Oxford, Basil Blackwell, 1934).

Brontë, Patrick Branwell, *And the Weary are at Rest*, ed. C. W. Hatfield (privately printed in an edition of fifty copies, 1924).

—— *Brother in the Shadow: Stories and Sketches by Branwell Brontë*, ed. Mary Butterfield and R. J. Duckett (Bradford: Bradford Libraries and Information Service, 1988).

—— 'The Leyland Manuscripts', letters and sketches by Patrick Branwell Brontë formerly in the possession of Francis Leyland. The Brotherton Collection, Brotherton Library, Leeds University, Leeds, England.

—— 'Miscellaneous Transcriptions of the prose fiction of Branwell Brontë', made by C. W. Hatfield. Unpublished manuscripts and typescripts. Archives, Brontë Parsonage Library, Haworth.

—— *The Poems of Patrick Branwell Brontë*, ed. Tom Winnifrith (Oxford, Shakespeare Head Press, 1983).

—— *The Poems of Patrick Branwell Brontë: A New Text and Commentary*, ed. Victor Neufeldt (New York, Garland Press, 1990).

Secondary

Alexander, Christine, *The Early Writings of Charlotte Brontë* (Oxford, Basil Blackwell, 1983).

du Maurier, Daphne, *The Infernal World of Branwell Brontë* (London, Victor Gollancz Ltd., 1960).

Evans, Barbara and Evans, Gareth Lloyd, *Everyman's Companion to the Brontës* (London, Dent, 1982).

Gaskell, Elizabeth, *The Life of Charlotte Brontë*, ed. with an Introduction and Notes by Clement K. Shorter [The Haworth Edition] (New York and London, Harper, 1900; AMS, 1973).

Gérin, Winifred, *Branwell Brontë: A Biography* (London, Thomas Nelson & Sons, 1961).

Grundy, Francis H., *Pictures of the Past: Memories of Men I Have Met and Places I Have Seen* (London, Griffin and Farrar, 1879).

Law, Alice, *Patrick Branwell Brontë* (London, A. M. Philpot, 1925).

Leyland, Francis A., *The Brontë Family, with Special Reference to Patrick Branwell Brontë* (London, Hurst and Blackett, 1886).

Lock, J. and Dixon, W. T., *A Man of Sorrow: The Life, Letters and Times of the Reverend Patrick Brontë* (London, Thomas Nelson & Sons, 1965).

Ratchford, Fanny Elizabeth, *The Brontës' Web of Childhood* (New York, Columbia University Press, 1941).

Shorter, Clement J., *Charlotte Brontë and her Circle* (New York, Dodd Mead and Co., 1896).

A CHRONOLOGY OF PATRICK BRANWELL BRONTË

1817 (June 26) Patrick Branwell Brontë (known in family as Branwell) born at Thornton (Bradford), Yorkshire, fourth of six children born in a seven-year period to the Revd Patrick Brontë and Maria Branwell Brontë.

1820 The Revd Patrick Brontë accepts position as Perpetual Curate, St Michael's Church, Haworth (Keighley), Yorkshire.

1821 Mrs Maria Brontë dies of cancer; her sister Elizabeth Branwell (Aunt Branwell) joins the household as surrogate mother.

1825 The two oldest Brontë children, Maria and Elizabeth, die of consumption. Branwell may have been a pupil for a short period about this time in Haworth Grammar School; otherwise educated by his father, a good classical scholar, at home.

1826 (June 5) Branwell receives a set of toy soldiers on his father's return from a visit to Leeds. While not his first set, they are 'the Twelves' that stimulated his and his sisters' incredible output of writing from that point onward.
(December) 'The Play of the Islanders', first kernel of the Glasstown Confederacy.

1829–30 'Branwell's Blackwood's Magazine' (then 'Blackwood's Young Men's Magazine') begun by Branwell, taken over by Charlotte. Late 1830, Branwell begins 'The History of the Young Men', an extended development of Glasstown. Branwell now writing under the pseudonyms of 'John Bud' and 'Young Soult, the Rhymer'.

1831 Charlotte goes to school at Roe Head; Branwell continues Glasstown chronicles by himself.

1830–2 'Letters of an Englishman' (6 volumes), describes the civil war which 'Rougue' (Alexander Percy, Earl of Northangerland) launches. Percy will become Branwell's chief character and alterego. From this time on, through 1842, Branwell writes constantly, producing many prose narratives, of which the titles referred to below are only a few.

1833 (January) 'The Pirate', Branwell's account of Percy's criminal career, and ascendency to the aristocracy.
(May–September) 'Real Life in Verdopolis'.

CHRONOLOGY

1834   (June) 'The Wool is Rising'. This long piece on the founding of Angria is one of a half-dozen written that year in which the focus shifts from Verdopolis to Angria. It is about this time that Emily and Anne establish their fictional kingdom of Gondal.
Branwell begins art lessons with portraitist William Robinson; he paints the famous group portrait of his sisters at this time.

1835   (April[?]–November) 'The Life of Field Marshal The Right Honourable Alexander Percy, Earl of Northangerland', a major segment of 'The History of Angria', which he wrote for the next two-and-a-half years.
(Autumn) Unsuccessful trip to London as a potential candidate for The Royal Academy.
(December) Attempts unsuccessfully to establish connection with *Blackwood's Magazine*. During this period, close contact with Emily, the only one of his sisters then at home.

1836   Joins Masonic Lodge; continues to write 'History of Angria'. Long walks on the moors with Emily.

1837   (January) Sends samples of his work to Wordsworth without response; again attempts to establish connection with *Blackwood's*.

1838–9   Branwell sets up as portrait painter in Bradford. Continues to write Angrian chronicles. Close friendship with sculptor Joseph Leyland.

1839   After some success as portraitist, runs out of customers at Bradford and closes studio.
Home in Haworth, reading classics again and beginning translation of Horace's *Odes*. Again, of his sisters, only Emily is at home.

1840   (January–June) Branwell employed as tutor by Mr Postlethwaite, Broughton-in-Furness. Initially successful, he is discharged for neglecting his duties.
(May) Visits Hartley Coleridge at nearby Ambleside and is encouraged by him in his writing.
(August) Branwell appointed as 'Asst. Clerk in Charge' with the Manchester–Leeds Railway.

1842   (April) After almost two years, discharged by the Railway Company for 'carelessness'.
(Summer) Several of his poems published in the *Halifax Guardian* and *Leeds Intelligencer*.
(October) Death of Aunt Branwell, a great shock for Branwell who of all the children was probably closest to her. Period of close contact with Anne.

1843   (January) As tutor, Branwell joins Anne, who is governess, in the Robinson family at Thorp Green, beginning (according to his

	account) a long intimacy with Mrs Lydia Robinson. Apparently a very happy period. Very little of his writing from this two-and-a-half year period survives, perhaps because he was not living at home and perhaps because he was writing primarily poetry, of which the bulk may have been given into the hands of Mrs Robinson and subsequently destroyed.
1845	(July) Branwell summarily dismissed by Mr Robinson, allegedly because of his affair with his employer's wife. Shock drives Branwell to intensified alcoholism and drug use. From this point, Branwell makes ineffectual attempts to write a major novel, 'And the Weary are at Rest', of which only a small part is extant.
1847	(October) *Jane Eyre* published. (December) *Wuthering Heights* and *Agnes Grey* published.
1848	(24 September) Branwell's death at 31 of 'chronic bronchitis and marasmus' (a 'wasting-away').

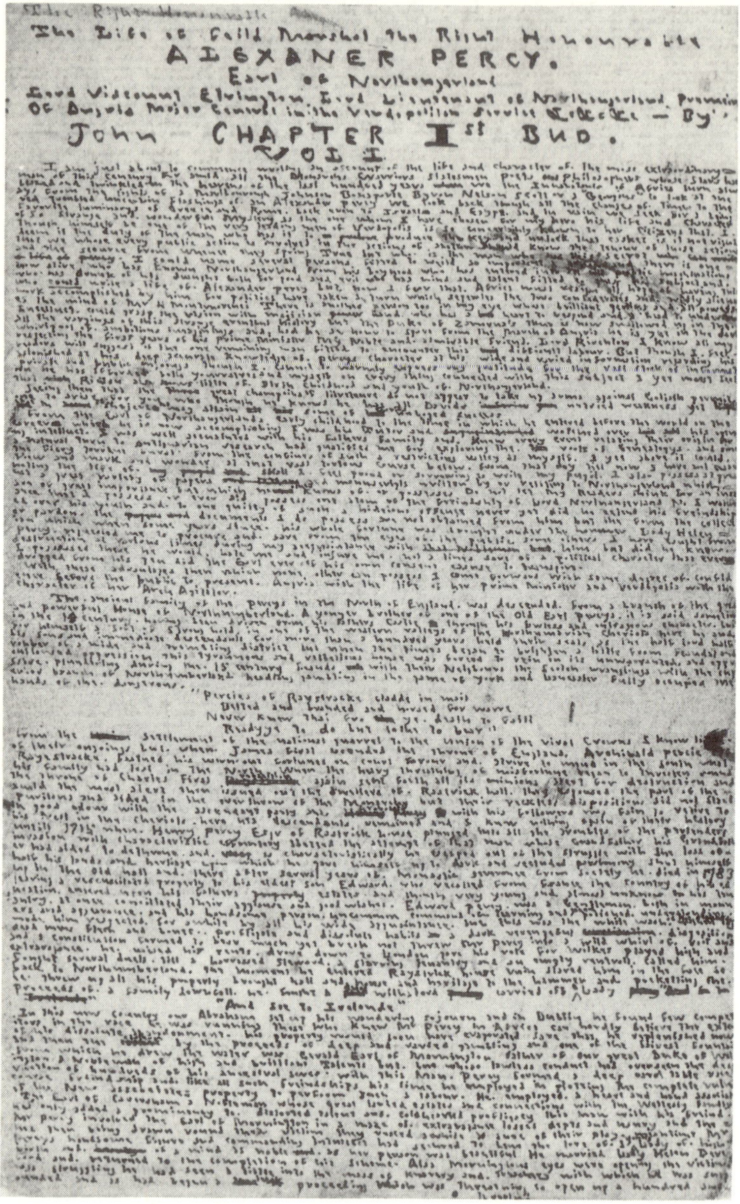
The Life of feild Marshal the Right Honourable
ALEXANER PERCY.
Earl of Northangerland
Lord Viscount Elrington Lord Lieutenant of Northangerland Premier
Of Angria Prime Councill in the Verdopolitan Senate &c &c &c — By
John CHAPTER Ist BUD.
VOL I

The Life of Field Marshal the Right Honourable

ALEXANDER PERCY

Earl of Northangerland
Lord Viscount Elrington, Lord Lieutenant of Northangerland,
Premier of Angria, Major General of the Verdopolitan Service
&c &c &c—By

John Bud

VOL I

CHAPTER Ist

[Chapter I]

I am just about to commence writing an account of the life and character of the most extraordinary man of this century. Amid all the monarchs, warriors, statesmen, poets, and philosophers whose stars have blazed and twinkled in the heavens of the last hundred years, we, the inhabitants of Africa, turn always from the lights of a Marlborough, Johnson, Bonaparte, Byron, Nelson, Scott, or a 'Georgius' to look at the red, troubled, uncertain flashings of an Alexander Percy. We look back through all of the changes of time to the favourite luminaries of Greece and Rome, back even to Israel and Egypt; and in vain we seek for a being of so strange and wonderful mystery as the one I have chosen for my hero. His life and character, though he is one of the leading men of Verdopolis, is so uncertainly known to her citizens that I deem it the duty of the man who has it to produce the key and unlock the casket.*

Is it not vital that we, whose every public action is influenced by the actions of another, should know the tenor of those actions and the source from where they spring? True. But who is the man who has this sacred key?

I could name several persons fit to yield so important a secret. There is one now alive who has known Northangerland from his boyhood, who has entered into all his machinations of public life, who has drunk of his draught for both good and evil, who has mind and talent fitted to grasp his subject, and who *could* write a life of Alexander Percy. But now, I fear, Africa must resign all hope of having this work accomplished by him, for politics has taken a turn which now separates the two confederates, and widely aliened is the mind of Mr H. Montmorency.

To my eye, there is another person, too, whose brilliant genius and all-powerful intellect could grasp the vision with magician's wand, a man who has a heart to respond and a head to understand all the various parts of this strange and eventful history; but the Duke of Zamorna's time is now swallowed up in the whirlpool of his own ambitious imagination. And had he an hour to spare from the March of Angria, he is yet in the dark respecting the first years of his prime minister. I know all my readers will suggest my noble and admirable friend, Lord Richton, as the one remaining man fit to encounter this difficult labour. But, though I am astonished at his deep and accurate knowledge of Percy's character, at his wide and varied information regarding Alexander Percy's private and public ongoings, though I cannot too warmly express my gratitude for the vast stock of information he has afforded both to yourselves and me on everything connected with this subject, I yet feel that Richton, alas, knows too little of the birth, childhood, and youth of Northangerland.

Seeing, then, that these three great champions of literature do not appear to take up arms against the Goliath task permits one to arise for you, who, though he knows he has all of David's untried weakness, yet trusts that within the subject he may attain some of David's untried success. From the Earl of Northangerland's early childhood to the time he entered on the career which he is now accomplishing before the world, I was his tutor and watched over his opening intellect. I was well acquainted, too, with his father's family and knew every event relating to their origin, for a natural turn to antiquarian research had qualified me for exploring the roots of genealogy. And since that fiery torrent, Percy, burst from the confines of such a restricting valley as myself, I, though yet above it, could view and mark and wonder at that vast, tortuous course below.

From that day till now I have continuously noted the life of—shall I feel proud or sorrowful to write—my pupil. I also possess at hand a great variety of papers and manuscripts written by or related to Northangerland, which are of great importance and which no other person even knows of. But do not let my reader think for an instant that I possess one atom of the friendship of Lord Northangerland.

No, I watched over his youth; and to one guilty of such a hideous offence, never yet did he extend his friendship or pardon. The documents I possess were not obtained from him. They form the collection which, when some years since his whole fortune was brought under the hammer, Lady Helen Percy requested that I procure and so save from the eyes of the public. Others I have caught from destruction at various times during my acquaintance with him; but did he know I possessed them, he would both hate and do injury to me. Not a line, save of a political character, that ever dropped from his pen did the Earl ever of his own consent cause to transpire.* With these advantages, then, which none other possess, I come before the public with some degree of confidence to present Angria with the life of her prime minister, and Verdopolis with the character of her arch agitator.

The ancient family of the Percys in the north of England was descended from a branch of the great and powerful House of Northumberland. Sometime in the fourteenth century, a younger brother of one of the early Earls Percy, having been driven from his father's castle through his lawless and outrageous character, built for himself a sort of stronghold in one of the western valleys of the Northumbrian Cheviots. Here, he and his sons and immediate descendants for more than a hundred years held their seats as the half-lord, half-robber* of a wide and trembling district. But when the times began to brighten a little from feudal and outlaw oppression, this tyrannous and rebellious house was forced to rein in its unwarranted and aggressive plundering. During the fifteenth century, feuds with their neighbours, the Scotch, wrangling with the superior branch of Northumberland, headlong gambling in the game of York and Lancaster fully occupied the hand of the dangerous

> 'Percies of Raystracke, cladde in mail
> Belted and branded and horsed for warre,
> Never knew thai fro ye death to faill,
> Readdye to do but lothe to bear!'

From the settlement of the national quarrel to the union of the rival crowns,* I know little of their ongoings. But when James First ascended the throne of England, Archibald Percie of Raystracke fastened his worn-out fortunes on court favour and strove to mend in the south what his family had lost in the north. When heavy misfortune began to threaten round the throne of Charles First, opportunism again sent forth all its minions, alert for destruction, and amid the most alert there issued out the dwellers of Raystrick Hall.* They espoused the part of the Puritans and so sided in the overthrow of the monarchy. But their reckless disposition did not stand in good odour with the party now in ascendancy, and Archibald with his followers was fain to retire to his hall in the Cheviots.

Here his descendants remained; and I know nothing again of their history until 1715, when Henry Percy, Esquire, of Raystrick House plunged into all the troubles of the Pretender's invasion.* With characteristic effrontery, he aided the attempt of that man whose grandfather his grandfather had aided to dethrone; and, as characteristically, he escaped out of the struggle with the loss of half his lands and his heritage. Upon which, he gave himself up to dark and secluded parsimony, shut himself up in the Old Hall, and there, after several years of monastic severance from society, he died in 1783, leaving a resuscitated property. His eldest son, Edward, recalled from France, the country of his education, entered upon his father's estates, and though very young and almost unknown to his tenantry, at once conciliated their applause and good favour.

Edward Percy was a gentleman both in manner and appearance, and his handsome person, uncommon command of bearing, and polished understanding made him respected for a while by all his wide acquaintance. But this was the whitewash of plaster washed off dead men's flesh and bones. Profligate and dissolute habit, a dark revengeful disposition, and a constitution formed to bear much, yet break not, soon threw Mr Percy into a wild whirl of riot and extravagance. He raised his rents, drove down to London, gave his vote for Wilkes, played high and fought several duels, until a harassed steward, a starving tenantry, and an empty rent-roll called him back to Northumberland.* The moment he entered Raystrick House, ruin stared him in the face. So, he threw up all his property, brought hall and house and heritage to the hammer and, pocketing the proceeds of a family downfall, he fought a duel with a Lord, withstood, and carried off a Lady—

'And soe to Irelande.'

In this new country, our Abraham set up his sojourn, and in Dublin he found few competitors in the race he was running. Those who knew Mr Percy in Africa will hardly believe the extent of his dissolute abandonment. His property would soon have evaporated, save that he replenished the cistern now and then by the proceeds of deep and varied gambling. One of the fairest fountains from which he drew water was Gerald, Earl of Mornington,* father of our great Duke of Wellington, a nobleman of high and brilliant talents but whose lawless conduct had overseen the destruction of hundreds of his ancestral acres.

With this man, Percy formed a deep card-table, race-course friendship; and, as with all such friendships, he employed his time in plotting the complete ruin of the new acquaintance's property. To perform such a labour, he employed a heart-and-hand associate, the

Earl of Caversham, a nobleman whose great landed estates and connections with Mr Wellesley's family had only added a prominence to distorted talent and cold-hearted profligacy. This man, with his friend Mr Percy, involved the Earl of Mornington in a maze of extravagance, losses, debts, and usury; and the net then being drawn around their victim, they rested awhile, sure of their prey. Meantime, Mr Percy's handsome figure and commanding intellect had secured to him the love of a young lady of high birth and a mind as noble as her person was beautiful. He married Lady Helen Beresford and returned to the completion of his scheme.

Alas, Mornington's eyes were opening; the victim was struggling. He had seen a little into the maze of knavery and treachery with which he was surrounded, and so had begun a proceeding which was threatening to open up a hundred similar actions. The two confederates, convinced that there remained only one way by which to quash proceedings so detrimental to their projects, called into their councils Robert Patrick King,* the valet of Mr Percy, a native it was supposed of Yorkshire, who had been in the service of the Percy family for thirty years.

The age of this servant was perhaps then, as near as they could guess, fifty or fifty-five; and of his life, though Percy had so long known him, he was very little acquainted. An air of strange and impenetrable mystery hung over the fellow's course, and stories were not wanting respecting him which might make the hair of one's head stand up with horror. As far as they all knew of his character, there was no thought, however foul, no deed, however monstrous, no word, however perjured, which he would not say or do or think for money and the love of seeing a man's death struggle. A hundred men in the metropolis, of all ranks and titles, had employed this man as the instrument of their crimes. While in London with Edward Percy, he had attained the proud eminence of general tutor of vice among the young; and now, in Dublin, he was actively employed as its instrument among the old. To such a spirit of evil, Percy and Caversham had recourse in the time of their difficulty.

He taught them at once a ready method of removing the 'inconvaniense'; and after his insinuating himself into the confidence of the Earl of Mornington, that nobleman was one day found dead in his dressing room, his features blackened and distorted as by some sudden struggle. He was buried with all the usual honours, and for a while all suspicion seemed laid at rest. But his lady, the Countess, believed rather in death by visitation of man than by any other visitation whatever. She again instituted an inquiry into the causes of this event; and, erelong, matters had come to the inauspicious pass that the Earl of Caversham, Mr Edward Percy, and Mr John O'Connor began to look oftener towards the Atlantic Ocean than to the hills of Ireland.

At this time, 1790, the fame of our rising empire in Africa had spread itself abroad through the whole of Europe. All men heard with astonishment of vast conquests, of the rapid rise of a few hardy Adventurers whose leaders had twenty years before sailed from England without exciting one word or other sign of notice from the population. And though very lately one of these heroes* had delivered Europe from slavery, and had departed for Africa with 50,000 followers, yet no one could have hoped that in so short a time the Twelves would have beheld the whole course of the Niger, the Gambia, and the Senegal as their own kingdom, and the people as their own. But all now in Europe as they saw the light of Fortune waning in their hemisphere looked on Africa alone as the new seat of her capacious reign.* Everyone who had heart and enterprise, whose hands and purse were empty and his shoulders both broad and bare, now embarked with joy for this Canaan and Promised Land. That enthusiasm with which three hundred years ago Europe had looked on America was now rekindled with triple ardour when she gazed toward Africa.

Towards this shore, so hopeful for the future, the three blood-stained confederates directly turned their eyes. Gathering together in haste all his lawless gains, Mr Edward Percy fled to London to escape immediate apprehension; and next, early in 1790, set sail from England with his newly wedded bride, Lady Helen Percy, more than £100,000 in his purse, and his tutor in crime, R. P. King, following faithfully at his back. But so close, I understand, were the officers of justice after the criminal that the worthy valet only escaped being whirled back to Ireland by levanting, in the night of departure, from Portsmouth jail. The Earl of Caversham and Mr O'Connor, both being Irishmen, had just before set sail directly for that part of Africa lying westward toward the Atlantic and known to be under the sovereignty of the Duke of Wellington.

Here, too, Mr Percy directed his wanderings, though in so doing he knew he should place himself in the power of the son of the man he had murdered. But his desperate character hardly brooked caution

THE LIFE OF . . . NORTHANGERLAND 9

and, muttering 'It's best to sit near the fire when the chimney smokes', he anchored after a tolerable voyage at the mouth of the noble Gambia.

My readers must know that forty years ago £100,000 was no mean matter in Africa; and let them not wonder if, however bad his character, Mr Percy when he landed established himself on a high footing in his newly adopted country. His wealth, his own able and energetic character, as well as the high station, beauty, and accomplishments of his lady, opened to him a fair reception at Court. He entered as Member of the General Parliament for Wellington's Town, bought an old house built by the English of 1500 AD* amid the woodlands east of the capital; and, adding new fronts and paths to it, he christened it Percy Hall and made it his family's country seat.

In 1790, Africa presented a very different appearance from what it does now. The white inhabitants were comparatively few in number. Almost all soldiers, ever bearing arms and possessing a rough, iron, and ambitious character, they ruled with haughty despotism over a lately vanquished and half-unexplored region of burning Africa. Verdopolis itself, almost the only great city of consequence, towered on the Niger, the very queen of our dominion; and her population, a vast whirlpool of mingled YOUNG MEN, French, Spaniards, Americans, Italians, Moors, Turks, Persians, Burmese, and Egyptians, all inured to bloodshed, alien from each other, and each ambitious for supreme, sword-gained dominion. General awe only of the English Adventurers, the Twelves, prevented the other nationals from throwing confusion into absolute chaos. While the YOUNG MEN kept up a desperate warfare against the French, all the remaining bands persecuted and worried each other; while, over all things, the GENII, small and great, wandered the continent, oppressing and exacting with demon malignity.

In those days the man who beheld Verdopolis at midnight would fancy he saw the streets of a stormed city, so ferocious and outrageous were the feuds, fights, and murders amid its varied inhabitants. Just at this time arose the Great Rebellion against the GENII* which shook Africa to its centre for nearly a year. I know that it was only the undaunted energy of the Adventurers which kept them from the conviction that everything about them was verging to everlasting ruin.

The picture I have drawn of Africa at the end of the eighteenth century is a strange one but as true as strange. I was then in my twentieth year, a soldier in the armies of the YOUNG MEN, and day and night I was occupied in a series of such battles as would have given surfeit to many a gallant spirit. But my mind, naturally inquisitive and attentive to learning and acquirement, was always observing things around me; and I, one among these thousands, only saw in the anarchy the noble struggle of a rising empire. In 1793 I received a temporary discharge from my military duties and hastened to Wellington's Town to visit my parents, who resided near its suburbs.

I remember, when I turned up the road which led towards the scenes of my childhood, with what wonder I looked over the wide expanse of newly planted wood and great sweeps of just-clipped verdure, all circled by the park walls and poplars erected and planted just that year. I could not but wonder at the creation, for it spread, leviathan-like, over many a spot and many a cherished nook of boyhood recollection. I hardly liked to see the old house on the knoll of woodland now transformed into a great gentleman's hall, half hidden among its many columns.

One of the first questions I asked when I reached home was to whom belonged that fine domicile which had sprung up since I left home, over Alderwood Shaws and woodlands. The answer which I received was that the park and house belonged to Edward Percy, Esquire, a gentleman who had landed two or three years ago, who was said to be worth a great deal of money, and whose wife was a distant connection of the King.* That this Mr Percy was a great man, that he lived very high but was extremely proud and haughty. He strained his tenantry as hard as they could bear; and if the rents were not brought in exactly on the day appointed, the unfortunate defaulter was at once cast into jail. He never gave one farthing in charity; and if he knew of a poacher trespassing upon his manor, it was hard indeed for the unfortunate culprit. He would hang the man if he dared, though he had stolen only an egg. In short, the character of this gentleman was drawn as that of a man whose life of dissipation and extravagance having begun to turn tide, his mind had hardened into an extreme of selfish and grinding tyranny.

In such esteem was held Edward Percy, Esquire, MP, of Percy Hall in Wellington's Land. He little cared, himself, what another man thought of him, so long as he could find room for his revenge over the thinker. But I have lingered too long over times and persons who might have been dispatched in a much shorter space. I must hasten to be ready for an advent of importance, for about such appearance, all I have yet spoken of (and, I fear, Africa) must mark with a black cross the year 1793. Then, on the first of December, on a bleak, stormy morning was born at Percy Hall his country's pride and scourge—Alexander Percy.

[Chapter II]

I have said that the birth of Northangerland* was marked by a rough and stormy day. Certainly there appeared no prodigy either in heaven or earth, but clouds and wind and rain beat round the ancient Hall when its young lord first opened his eyes upon that life which, for him, has seldom been one of happiness. His father and mother were proud, indeed, of their infant son, and the domestics and retainers talked greatly of his beauty and 'wonderful wit'. Yet, despite the strange anecdotes told by nurse or servant, little Alexander was at first like any other child. And as no feast or other entertainment would Mr Percy give in celebration of his infant son, as he did not release a single debtor or give back one penny of the rents, as the christening was void of all show or ostentation, the tenantry and other people around began to forget that their young master was alive in the world.

So, amid the old oaks and elms, his early infancy passed on in silence and seclusion, watched over by the fond and anxious affection of his noble mother. Cherished as the pride and glory of his nurse and attendants, gazed on now and then with complacency but often without notice by his dark and haughty father, Alexander's first year or two exhibited all the little hopes and fears, joys and sorrows of early infancy. And then when he could walk and speak, he was often carried out around the park and to the houses of his attendants' acquaintances, that they might see the young heir in all his rising glory.

I remember his favourite nurse used very frequently to bring him down to my father's house, where I myself (Oh, how different since!) was his special delight and attraction. I had just returned from war, was young and active, could tell him stories of battles, and play and rattle on with him to his heart's content. I fancy now I can see Ellen Hope coming in at the garden gate with her charge in her arms, a wild, rosy-cheeked, bright-eyed little fellow of three years old, his large straw hat covering his light golden hair; and, as he was borne, his voice raised in a cheerful scream by some high-waving lily or other pretty flower hanging almost within his reach over the hedge or paling. He always sat down on the grass by me to hear about some bloody battle with the Frenchies; and, though he ever began to listen with all the fire and enthusiasm of a military hero, I cannot recollect that on any of these occasions he ever came forth with any astonishing display of brilliant genius or far-sighted sagacity.

No, the cat or dog, or his young nurse, or a horrible shriek at the sight of my sword and gun, generally diverted the future rebel from the dark details of battle and murder and sudden death. However, upon the conclusion of my narratives, 'Mr Bud, do take me to see the Duke of Wellington', or 'I will be a General, whether Papa says so or not' formed the fervent aspiration of my ambitious listener.

And yet, even in these times of childish gaiety, there was one tone in Alexander's mind which presaged something of his future strain of feeling. One fair, bright afternoon, as I sat with him at the honeysuckled door of my father's dwelling, delineating all the horrors and bloodshed of the storming of Doverham, an Italian minstrel came up to the garden gate—one of the various bands which existed at that time amid the Babel confusion of Africa. This man had in his hand only a single flute on which he played the airs of his native Apennines. However, ere he had concluded the first piece, Alexander, who had lifted his head in deep attention to the music, dropped it again and, covering his face with his hands, burst into a long fit of weeping. He sat in tears till after the music was done and the man had left the gate. Then, raising his eyes, he looked hastily round him and, rising, ran with all speed out the gate and down the gravel walk. His nurse who, hearing his crying, had hastened to reach him, now ran after him and found little Alexander fighting vigorously with the minstrel for possession of the attractive instrument.

Home he was carried, weeping and chattering by turns or biting his nurse and struggling to recommence his attempted robbery. From this moment, music formed the chief passion of his soul. All then thought that the child would never heed anything else, and his father cursed him for a silly idiot. Perched upon the music stool of a large harpsichord of Lady Helen's, he sat spreading his small fingers over the keys and imitating with instructor's precision every snatch of a song or bar of a tune which he had chanced to hear. Daily and hourly he plagued his mama to teach him the mystery of his adored music; and almost the first question which he asked of every lady who visited the Hall was 'Can you play?' or 'Will you teach me to play?' The ladies themselves, attracted by his beauty and cheerfulness, were always glad for amusement's sake to accord with his wish and show their powers on the instrument, and many a time has the Countess of Caversham or the Countess di Segovia or Lady Tracy or many another fair visitor taken him into her chariot for a drive to some concert at Wellington's City.

Music was his sole delight; and of all airs, the slow, solemn, funeral ones best pleased him and made his fingers tremble with excitement. When listening to the organ at his father's church, I have often seen him clasp his hands together and look more like a little seraph than any mortal child.

At this time, when he had attained his fourth year, the war with the Frenchies and Americans again broke out most furiously. I was recalled to the army and bid adieu for a time to my native scenes and acquaintances. On the morning of my departure, as I stood with my bundle in my hand, my Elzevir *Vergil* in one pocket, and my half-collected 'Songs of the YOUNG MEN' tied up in tape in the other, little Alexander Percy came running before Ellen Hope toward me, crying that he would 'go to fight' with me under the Duke of Wellington, that he didn't 'care for Papa any more than if he were a Frenchie', and he was sure that Mamma could never like him the worse for coming back dressed in scarlet and gold—and if Ellen would only leave off holding him, he would marry her when he got back and make her a general's wife.

My business here is not to write a life of myself but one of the great Northangerland. Therefore, I must pass over without a word all my toils and travels and warfare in the Third War with the Frenchies, from 1796 to 1800.* Hostilities being concluded, I again returned to Woodchurch, raised to the rank of captain, and resolved to rest for a while from the fatigues of service. During this interval of four years, however often thoughts of home had recurred to my mind, the confusions and changes of constant fighting all conspired to drive far from me any ideas unconnected to my nearest and dearest imaginings; and among these repressed feelings, Alexander Percy, of course, faded in my remembrance. My acquaintance with that little child, however pleasant, was of far too light and casual a character to bide the brunt* of battles and sieges. When I reached home, raised in consequence and circumstances, I don't recall that I ever asked about the heir of Percy Hall.

One evening in August, 1800, as I sat in my study at home,

engaged in the delightful task of correcting the sheets of the fourth edition of my lately published maiden work, *Leaf's History, with Commentaries*,* a production which had spread my name through much of Africa, Betty stepped in, announcing a fine gentleman as desirous of speaking with me. Much to my astonishment, ere she had half finished her message, the said fine gentleman himself without further stay walked into the apartment. Not over-pleased with his excess of familiarity, I gazed at him with considerable resentment, demanding the reason of his insolence. But that gaze soon convinced me that what I had taken for familiarity was, in right, directly contrary.

The stranger seemed a Lucifer of pride. Coldness, revenge, and despotic tyranny was shadowed strongly on every lineament of his handsome and haughty features, and the averted twist of the eye and sunken corner of the mouth told me I might add to these pleasant qualities present or past dissipations of the wildest character. This man, whose tall form and dark attire carried forth his aspect as a gentlemen, turned a chair to the fire and, seating himself, began. 'I understand you are my tenant. Bud is your name, I suppose?'

'May I ask', I answered, 'by whom I have the honour of being addressed?'

'And you are the same person as the man who wrote the *History* lately published?' continued the stranger, without noticing my question.

However, I had guessed who this should be and spoke: 'Mr Percy, for I believe, Sir, you as my landlord claim that name, I should certainly demand on account of my profession a different style of language from the one you, Sir, have chosen to adopt.'

'If you are my tenant, I shall require you either to accept the station of tutor to my son or I will turn you from my property without delay. Your work shows much sense, learning, and information, and its writer perhaps may prove a man fitted for the office I mention. Remember, Sir, I am not to be trifled with; and if I think you, as I do, qualified to teach the heir to my estates, I require you either to obey me, or I'll make you repent it.'

Now the pleasure felt by a young author flattered by a person so much above him was just sufficient to repress my inclination to rise and turn this intruder from the door; and when I reflected that this gentleman could do much of what he threatened, the share of prudence which I always have possessed determined me to refrain from a harsh answer to his tyranny. I told him that, as he was my landlord, as I always had felt a regard for his son, as it was not inconvenient to me to accept the station, I would consent to enter upon the engagement he wished me to, stipulating that in case of one word or action used to me which becomes not one gentleman to another, I would leave his house directly, as I had an independence of my own which secured me from despotism.

'Fudge,' he said, 'you have nothing to do with regard for my son. Train him to have a regard for me, or at any rate to act as if he had. And as to your treatment, Sir, don't dictate to me.' He then mentioned a very handsome sum as salary, told me that the Hall must be my home, appointed a day for my arrival there, and, without giving me time to answer, left the room. I heard his horse trot off, directly after.

Now, reader, in this strange interview do not suppose that Mr Percy's conduct was the bluntness of honesty, or the unceremoniousness of ample wealth. It was the real, sour, insolent tyranny of his own mind; and, as such, it did not surprise me who, by report, had long been acquainted with my landlord's character. Viewing it in this light, I thought it folly to resent it. And as the situation was really excellent and highly respectable, as I knew I should be treated as I deserved like a gentleman by all save the Master of the Hall, as I should thus enter society where I fancied my abilities would find their way, and as I really, now, recollected my future pupil as a cheerful, handsome, and intelligent child, I obeyed the assignment.* On the first of the next month, I set forth from my dwelling for the great house, over the park before me.

As I passed over the long stretches of short green verdure and by the great masses of dark, thick foliage and saw the great extent of the grounds and the high order they were kept in, and when I looked up at the broad, irregular, but stately and imposing edifice before me, and above all when I entered its magnificent apartments adorned with everything which could make life a paradise, I began to hold a high opinion of the opulence of the owner of the mansion.

Upon my being shown to a waiting room, within a few minutes a* magnificently dressed lady of about thirty years of age entered the apartment, his wife Lady Helen, her countenance—now still majestic but then eminently beautiful—expressing not dark, brooding pride but stately and queen-like condescension. To say that Lady Helen did not look haughty would be to talk like a fool. She looked very haughty, but with this look there shone intellect and grace and condescension in every feature. She knew in what office I appeared, she knew my profession and the humble abilities I had shown, and she directly made me feel myself at ease and at home.

After preliminary conversation where, however, aristocratic manner was never absent,* she smilingly said, 'I believe, Captain, that you will naturally ask from me a little insight into the character of your future pupil. You will certainly wish to know your ground before you advance on it. But I fear I can hardly satisfy you as I ought to do. His mind has puzzled even myself, who I believe must know him as well as anyone. I can hardly tell you, Sir, whether he will prove affectionate to those who like him, or if he will regard authority however exerted. He wanders strangely, is bent upon certain things at times, and badly neglects everything unconnected with his capricious pursuits. He is passionate, too; and as yet only two persons have been found to quiet his passion. And as I fear both myself and his immediate attendants, deluded by his most frequent disposition,* have sadly indulged him, those noxious weeds have acquired a root which render them very difficult to extract.

'But remember, Sir, that you are appointed the gardener of this garden. I must trust to you its management, and you know that it will not become you to neglect it. For the eradication of his bad qualities, I look to you, Sir, but I also know what human nature is, and I do not expect more from you than you will be able to perform. I hope you have been told, Captain, to make this house your home. And now, Ellen, where is Alexander?'

'In his own room, my Lady; he would not come out with me.'

'Then tell a servant to show Mr Bud there.'

So saying, Lady Helen bowed graciously and left the room.

I entered a handsome little apartment, filled with a confused heap of all the playthings and gewgaws which children usually admire and, in its first appearance, presenting little difference from the studio of any indulged child of aristocracy. But to one who looked further than first appearances, there could something be seen which, in these places, we do not usually see. I walked to the upper end of the room; and, as Master Percy could not be found here, the servant went to fetch him. Meanwhile, my notice had been attracted to a beautiful organ, of fairy dimensions, which stood before me. A book of music upon the front was opened at a 'Stabat Mater Dolorosa', 'Veni Creator', and 'Dies Irae', and upon the keys a sheet of paper scored over in a childish and informal hand with a succession of *breves*, *semibreves*, and *minims* in an *andante* movement which the writer was adopting to the words

> We leave our bodies in the tomb
>   Like dust, to moulder and decay,
> Then while they waste in coffined gloom,
>   Our parted spirits, where are they,
>   In endless night or endless day?

underlined between the staffs till met by the lines

> Buried as our bodies are
> Beyond all earthly hope and fear,
> Like them no more to reappear,

written in an elegant and feminine handwriting. A little Bible lay open on a music stool at Ecclesiastes 5: 1 ('Remember thy Creator in the days of thy youth'); marked in pencil, 'I shall arrange this'.* And around on the carpet were scattered five or six engravings of battles, a whole collection of hymn books, many odd volumes from a vast variety of books, odd little drawings in pencil, a little fife, *Joe Miller's Jest Book*, and a much fingered copy of *Jewel's Sermons*. Amid this ludicrous heap of morsels, I, naturally remembering the errand for which I came, looked for grammars, accidences, and usual steppingstones to learning. Alas, I sought but could not find. It's true, there was a leaf of a spelling book but it floated, like a boat, in a vase of water, where a little well-filled ship was resting with its tiny silken sails.

At the fireside, I saw a very little but very luxurious satin sopha piled with soft cushions, a pair of gloves, a brass cannon showing the seal,* and a warm Indian shawl thrown over the back. If I mistake not, thought I, my pupil's intellect has received many impressions since I last beheld him; but to what I can permanently direct his mind, save music and luxury, I at present cannot tell. Of Alexander himself, I saw nothing that afternoon. He could not be found by his attendants, and I was left to amuse myself and survey my own apartments till evening, when I was called to tea.

I recollect, as I entered the room, being struck first not by the rich and splendid furniture or the princely service of silver on the table, but by the owner of these rarities who presided at their head. I could hardly leave noticing Mr Percy as he sat, gloomy and lowering, his dark eyes fixed upon any one who happened to be moving or speaking with such a look of bitter habitual malice that, though very likely quite unintentional, it gave the idea of his really hating everyone about him.

Next to him, I saw the Earl of Caversham, whose high shining forehead, bald before its time, and stately, aristocratic person gave at first sight a very different impression from that which you owned after attentively noting the athwart glances and craftiness of his countenance and the unrestrained, unprincipled sentiments of his conversation. The half-worn out profligate Sullivan O'Connor,* and the handsome, stately Lady Caversham, who sat next to the still more stately (but as condescending and proud) Lady Helen Percy, completed this small party of a few of those aristocratic and wealthy families in this part of the country who acknowledged the sour, ambitious, and dishonest Edward Percy as their political guide and companion.

Of course, amid such high company my business was rather to hear than speak, and although (and let me be indulged the vanity of an author) the fame of the work I had just published attracted to me more notice than I expected, that evening I employed myself chiefly in noting the character of the turbulent spirits who sat before me. And I know that as soon as what I saw began to settle in my mind, I felt that dreary, ominous feeling steal over me which we experience in our recollections of these old haunted mansions and the predestined fate of dark, evil-guided children, the miseries and glamour of the old romances and tales that claimed our youthful admiration. All the sentiments and paths of activity of my master and his associates seemed from the conversation so twisted, so blackened and dangerous, that Ruin and Downfall stepped in as their inseparable companions. Nay, ere the company parted, my imagination had pictured the room hung round with sable, the stately mistress robed in mourning, her look fixed and despairing, Mr Percy dead and coffined, the Earl of Caversham chained and prisoned: all fallen to ruin and, as predestined, to decay.

Withall, and in many respects, how just have been those forebodings, how truly they have lighted these fortunes. Yet, in one case, I did not prophesy right, I did not point out the author of this woe.

No, my suspicions were far from alighting on the head of the handsome boy who burst into the room as the company were concluding their repast, his face looking so wild and excited, his hair fallen back from his forehead, and his eyes wandering around the room with such an earnest glance of comprehension. He ran to Lady Helen and, grasping the hand she held out to him, leant against her knee, gazing at everyone as if unconscious of their presence.

'My dear Alexander,' said his mother, alarmed. 'What is the matter with you?'

Her son only started, as if appalled at her voice. But a servant, who had entered after him, answered. 'My Lady, young master had just returned from we don't know where. He came running into the Hall, and without noticing any one made directly for this apartment.'

'Sirrah! Sit! What is this? Answer your mother!' cried Mr Percy angrily and with violence.

Alexander, roused by this, spoke.

'I have seen the Angels,' he said, and his face assumed a ghastlier paleness than before.

'Trash!' was his father's harsh answer. 'Have done with this nonsense, sir! What have you been talking to him about such stuff for, Helen? He's fit for nothing.'

'Why, Percy, your son is strongly excited,' remarked Caversham, earnestly.

'He'll be mad before twenty,' said O'Connor.

Then, all three left the room for Wellington's Town, leaving Lady Helen, Lady Caversham, and myself with the alarmed, excited child. The moment his father and the other two departed, Alexander leant his head on his mother's lap and burst into tears. It was long ere he could be prevailed on to raise his head, speak, or attend to anyone, but he hid his face in the folds of her gown, grasped his hands convulsively, and seemed to shudder if he was touched. At last he again looked up and gasped abruptly.

'Mamma—I have seen the Angels. I was playing on the organ at the church. It was quite dark. I had only a candle by me and 'Sdeath was blowing behind the instrument.* I was trying something of my own. It was the thing Augusta had set words to. But I had got a much grander music in my head—while I was playing from my own thoughts, I shuddered and felt a coldness on my cheeks. I could hardly see the paper and had to gasp for breath; I was quite shivery and looked back hastily—' here he stooped, as if reason had left him.

'I—I saw them in the dark, standing just at my back, quite white and very high—they reached to the roof and looked down at me, smiling like spirits—there were a great many of them, and one had its hand on the seat behind me. It pointed its finger to the paper on the keyboard, and the others waved their wings impatiently. I—I couldn't speak. So—I began to play and played far, far better than ever I did before, but I don't know what I did. They all sighed and stooped down their heads from high. I couldn't bear it, so I screamed out, got up—I don't know what happened further—they were all so white and solemn! Oh, Mamma! Mamma!'

He clung to Lady Helen and shut his eyes in apparent agony. His mother carried him from the room.

'This child', said Lady Caversham to me when they were gone, 'is a very singular one. He is exceedingly engaging, but I fear he won't live long. I have often noticed him and wondered sometimes at his vivacity and cheerfulness, and next at his silent abstraction. If I take him with me in my carriage for a while, I cannot satisfy him with caresses and attention, erelong he sits wrapt in his own dreams and starts if I speak to him. He is constantly excited; and I suppose this night he worked himself into delirium by his enthusiasm for the music he had hit upon. Indeed, the art fixes all his delight. He plays, and sweetly, too, for hours together and is quite uncertain in anything else he learns or toys at. I cannot tell his disposition. At times it seems cruel, careless, and vindictive. He would kick a little dog or strike a child if they stood before him, and is so proud that he affronts the attendants who take notice of him. And his father increases his wanderings* by his angry manner of noticing and checking his peculiarities. You, Mr Bud, must be cautious in your plan of dealing with him. I cannot think the boy will last long.'

This strange vision, the result of excited imagination, produced such a violent illness on Alexander Percy that for many days it was totally impossible for me to make him show the least sign of acquaintance with me. And, of course, I could not commence with my duties as tutor to him. After some time, however, he recovered the usual tone of his mind and became himself again.

Alexander was now eight years old, but his mind had been left entirely to itself. What he knew, he knew unassistedly, for though his mother was a woman of the clearest and strongest understanding, yet her great affection for her only son seemed to be taken advantage of by himself, to secure him that unlimited indulgence which affection is too often prone to give. And now I found his temper much more self-willed than it had been four years before. At this age, he was often passionate, revengeful, and headstrong, and when I, as in duty bound, attempted to inculcate on his mind those studies in which youth are in general first initiated, the drudgery and labour of the first lessons were not all forgotten in those that followed. Wayward to the last degree, my pupil so obstinately persisted in refusing to learn that at length I almost began to consider him incapacitated to understand.

One afternoon, I had been remonstrating with him on his idleness at some length.

'Mr Alexander,' said I, 'at this age you ought certainly to be able if not to understand wisdom at least to know that she ought to be understood. You are heir to a large property and will, one day or other, enter upon a station in which he who is poor in mind, however wealthy in estates, must be poor, indeed. Your advancing age also calls upon you to work hard while the daylight is before you, for remember, child, that the youth who sets to learning Latin or Greek when he ought to be employing learning already acquired looks laughable and lamentable, likewise.'

'I know it all. You've said so twenty times before,' answered young Percy pettishly.

'Yes, and if you no more hearken to it, I must say so twenty times again. Sir, will you commence your lessons now, or loiter there longer? Get up from the sopha and throw down that hymn book directly, Sir!'

I was rather irritated, for Alexander had been lolling on a pile of cushions for two or three hours, doing little but singing and sleeping and asking a hundred strange questions on a hundred different subjects (on his part returning for my answers such astonishing pieces of information as 'I have asked for wine after dinner, Bud, and am going to have it' or 'I'm going to sleep now', and 'I have asked Mamma to tell Papa to be off to the City that I may have plenty of time to range over the park and countryside, but she won't do it'). At last I rose and said, stepping towards him, 'I'll tell your father if you don't set to work this minute. He, at least, will not suffer you to neglect that for which he pays so much that you should attain.'

'He's going to strike me! Bud, if you offer to touch me, I'll tear your tongue out, you dirty half-pay! I don't care for either you or Papa. I'll do nothing!'

This announcement was followed by a summary protest of a cushion delivered in my face in earnest. I walked to the door, but he arose and, running before me, crying out 'I'll tell Mamma he has struck me', flew as quick as a greyhound out of the room and half through the house. I returned, destining for him a stern message from his father, when young Alexander again entered the room, his cheeks pale and his eyes flashing, holding by the hand a low, mean-looking blackguard of seventy, habited in an ancient brown coat, and whose shuffling gait, insolent address, and malignant countenance I at once recognized as the distinguished attributes of Mr R. P. King, Mr Percy's valet, rent-screwer, and man of all work, an hoary-headed villain who was detested by all the tenantry round him.

'Naa!' ejaculated this precious ancient with a squirt of tobacco and look of insolence. 'Naa! What wor' yew saying to young Measter? It fits yaw sure enough to be hodding up yer head and hectoring and doctoring about th' place at this time o' day! Yaw wor'nt brought into th' Hoyle to rule ower him nor ower me, nother.'

Here followed another drencher of spittle and a dash across the mouth with his coat sleeve.

'Aw'd hev ye to knaw that Aw'm the maister o' this room and noabody else. Aw'm this lad's preceptor, and Aw think it's myseln that should point him his larning and noane o' your ilk. Aat of the haase, un' smartly, or you'll like to repent ont! Aat, mun!'

'Mr 'Sdeath, I believe I—.'

'Silence, Aw say! What have yaw to do with th' lad, indeed! Come hither, marry, Aw know how to diddle the likes of yaw.'*

And here the mean-looking old rascal clenched his fist, grinned with his exaggerated features, and cast on me such a look of demoniacal malignity that I don't know whether I could for a minute have restrained myself from felling him to the ground. As it was, I had not the trial. Mr Percy's stern voice was heard below.

"Sdeath—King! Here, this instant!' The speaker followed his message directly, dark-angered and scowling.

'What in heaven's name have you let the fool slip for? Why, I could have made £10,000 out of soul, body, and estate. How dared you, villain, to neglect the law case. To the jail with him directly and to——!'

Here, Mr Percy cast an enquiring glance of ill humour on me, and rage upon his minion, who boldly faced him with a loud expectoration.

'Now, Maister, Aw'm moan the man thaw taks me for. Do yaw think Aw'll be bothered with cases and judgements when Aw've getten sich a case o' me awn to look after? Aw say to ye, mun, do you see what yaw'n sarved me with here? Here while Aw hev labboured, heart un hand at yon hight (pointing his skinny fingers towards the City) and warked me poor old conscience till it creaks like a cart wheel, yaw've dispossessed me of my darling office at hoam and capped me i' the matter of yawr young hopeful here wi' an old prigmadainty book-larned chap like yon.'

Another vehement ejection of tobacco juice.

'Aw willn't have it; nor will yaw, nother', and here he stroked the curls of his young pupil, who shook his head back and laughed at me with real contempt.

'Naw,' continued the Senior, 'thaw sees the drift, Master Percy, hey, thaw sees what I want. Thaw knows what thaw's done, and—and mind, Sir, if I don't remember you for such conduct as this!'

With a fiendish sneer, first at Mr Percy and next at Alexander, Mr R. P. King—or 'Sdeath—dashed his old hat over his brow and strode* out of the room. Percy himself cursed me with an oath, knocked his son down with his riding whip, and followed his man directly. Alexander got up, in tears, certainly, but bitterly hating myself and declaring he would obey only 'Sdeath, whatever he told him to do. I had rather my feeling imagined than described.

Still, under such auspices, Time swept unstayingly on. Alexander Percy saw birthday after birthday pass over him, and every year beheld him taller and handsomer than ever. But while his expressive and beautifully chiselled features ripened in a lifting animation, his mind and disposition seemed to grow constantly more strange and dark and impetuous. Music at all times formed his chief amusement, but it had ceased to be his chief employment. Truly, his learning was only taken up by starts and goaded, as it were, towards its goal, but there were other thoughts and employments which exerted all his opening faculties and kept his fine forehead at all times corrugated with thought.

The first strong pulse of Ambition beat through his veins and roused every fibre to enthusiasm. To be a great man, to equal or eclipse all those great characters he was constantly reading of in his delightful *History*, to be the mover and controller of vast events, to send his name down time renowned either for good or evil seemed, day and night, to be his great wish and endeavour. He was constantly thinking of his future life and picturing to himself its changes and greatness, questioning me upon all manner of subjects which he wished to lay hold on for this journey, and listening with delight and excitement to the tales and speeches of his constant companion, old 'Sdeath. But amid all his wild and wandering desires and ever-extending yearnings of ambition, Religion—that subject, that name—was first and foremost to claim his rapt attention. How often have I seen him seated on his favourite sopha, his hand supporting his forehead and his elbow buried in the cushion, his own Bible spread upon it, and his calm blue eyes wandering over its pages for hours together. Sermons and strange old works of divinity he read through and questioned me on almost daily, and often where no mortal could answer him. 'Mr Bud, where shall we go when we die?' 'What are our Spirits like, Sir!' 'I wonder where (naming someone lately dead) is, now?' 'Do those who are dead know anything of the people of this world?'* 'Can anyone tell what Christ was like when he came into this world?' 'Why isn't it swallowed up today or tomorrow?' 'Why doesn't the Judgement Day come now, when men are so wicked?' And 'I should like to live till the Judgement Day to see the world destroyed and the end of time.'

'How can people tell that the Bible was written or not written, and how were those who wrote it inspired?' 'It isn't written, is it, Sir; it is just the setting down of the strange things that happened long ago.' 'Oh, how I should like to have lived in the days of the Bible and seen Christ or David or Abraham and the patriarchs and the Angels—Bud—Mamma! Are Angels about us? If they are, they know how I want to see them! Why, why don't they appear?'

And then he would remain thinking and picturing to his mind the sublime events he had spoken* of, or reading and rereading the holy volume he grasped in his hand, or singing or playing for an hour or two together his favourite hymns*—'Twas in that dark, that doleful night', 'Why did my God and Saviour bleed?' 'When I read my title clear', 'There is a land of pure delight',—or any such song or composition of sacred and solemn tone.

But what deeply grieved me to notice was the gradual manner in which, as he grew older, he left off speaking of religion by degrees. From questioning every one at any time upon this subject, in a few years he had so changed as never to give the slightest hint or speak a single word to any person upon anything connected with it, to maintain the sternest and most inflexible silence upon his own opinions, and indeed to shrink absolutely if anyone made an allusion to them. Now, I do not think that at this time young Percy was either

Deist or Atheist or that he thought less of death or eternity. No, far from that. His thoughts had become deeper, more intense, more absolutely delightful to himself, though to think them always made him both gloomy and sad, as well as vindictive.

He had grasped the subject altogether in his opening mind, but, alas, that mind was always darkened* to error and sorrowing. Religion never for a moment having acted as a guide to his steps, as a hope for an hereafter, or as a reason for the world before him, he at last, unable to prove it true so as to satisfy his own yearning and over-strained mind, dashed from his guarded ways and trampled it underfoot in despair. Here, here indeed the overmuch, unassisted thinking of an impassioned, melancholy, and unbridled mind produced the crisis from which that mind revolted with horror and affright, fixed and hopeless and rayless Atheism.

But I am straying far forward in my subject. In his early years, this cloud had not yet darkened over Percy's expanding intellect, and only his own wild, solemn, and unsettled imagination wandered unstayed over the sublime expanse of heaven and eternity. For myself, I was grieved to know that however Alexander delighted in such a subject, it never for an instant operated beneficially on his capricious affections, vindictive pride, or unbridled passionateness of disposition. No.

Men, on noticing in a cursory manner the youthful heir of Percy Hall, beheld a slender but active boy, tall for his years and possessing a countenance whose constant play of varying expression showed in every light its eminently handsome features. They, in general, thought him conscious of his aristocratic beauty and, though a lad, rather disagreeably vain of it, yet on observing his expressions were struck with an effeminacy and girlishness. The expansive forehead, the anxious eye and the sensual lip, the hasty abruptness of his general manner, and the harsh, daring tone of his conversation, all tended to shew them a proud, handsome, ill-tempered, and indulged boy, one who, it seemed, could dash through life and oppose all who opposed him. The seraphic sweetness of Alexander's childhood had left him in his youth, and by the time he had reached his fifteenth year, his vindictive haughtiness had shaken from his friendships every one save those Ladies with whom he was acquainted. To these fair and lofty visitors of his father's noble hall, an instantly assumed ease of manner, a very pleasing and polished aspect, and that warm, ardent tone of thinking which here glowed in openly expressed admiration of themselves, passionate fondness for music, and all loftier feelings of humanity shone round and adorned him with such a delightful grace and poetry that few there were of the Ladies of the metropolis who left his company unprepossessed in his favour.

My readers may think that I am describing nothing but contradictions, but I tell them that Alexander Percy was contradiction itself. To me he seemed a living paradox; and I could trace none of his various feelings and actions to any common source, save—generally and widely taken—to ardent and tumultuous passions, with an exquisitely sensitive nervous conformation acting upon a mind from its earliest dayspring totally destitute of religious restraint or moral principle.

I know that often, and deeply, I sorrowed to see my pupil wandering about by himself through the park of his father's hall, miserably sunk in a chaos of his own imaginations, perhaps having rushed out of his father's presence in violent anger at Mr Percy's stern, harsh-tempered check of his error or angry threat of future punishment, and then running over in his own mind that held too-frequent like scenes, cherishing that poison so often instilled into his soul by his own chosen Mr 'Sdeath. Thinking of myself either with impatience or dislike, chafing and spurning at* the unavoidable obstacles which lay between him and his hundred still far-off, but desired attainments, often thinking: When should he know what he wished to know, when could he do what he wished to do? Next, striving to look into his future life, to chalk out future paths to power and glory amid the crimes and darkness which he conjured up before him; from this, he would ask himself: What was he, and where was he? Then, think on Religion and the State of Nature and of the Future World, of the Creator, and his own favourite and cherished subject—death and eternity.

He would form in his heart stanzas and passages leading to this train of thought, would run over in his mind, and to self-created strains, imaginary bursts of music and snatches of harmony, till the colour had left his face and tears had dimmed his sight. And then, evening perhaps drawing on, himself far from home, he would return toward where he had started and enter abruptly into the confusion of a splendid entertainment, harsh and resentful and gloomy, to meet the black, threatening frown of his enraged and vindictive father.

[Chapter III]

Percy Hall and the splendid domains around it, stretching wide over the woodlands of Wellington's Town, formed to the eye of the stranger the principal and noblest features in that direction, east of the metropolis, where on every side of its spacious parks, along the banks of the Gambia north to the wild hills of the frontier and south to Alderwood and Rio Grande, numerous seats and possessions of a proud and wealthy aristocracy presented attractions hardly second to itself in the scenery of the environs of the Capital.* But noble as were the features of that scenery, they, like many things beside,* were only pleasant to the eye. Their merits could not stand the test of reason, for here, in this portion of the kingdom, was lodged a nest of ambition, crime, and treachery from which that high culture, democracy, has since flown, as the scourge and curse of all Africa. Aye, here under the eye of the Duke of Wellington himself, Edward Percy, Esquire, MP reigned, the prince and ruler of a band of men whose chief wish and aim was revolution, anarchy, and blood.

Fitzgerald, Earl of Caversham, held his abode in the noble mansion of Ravensworth House, a few miles south of Percy Hall. Sir William Streighton, on the other side of the river, claimed the lands of Riverton Hall. The Earl of Jordan, in the north, resided at the foot of the mountains, and Sullivan O'Connor nearer town, while Mr Henry Montmorency, Richard MacArthur, Philip St John, and Carey and Gordon spread their stately houses over the well-peopled countryside. All these men I have mentioned lived in first-rate style, kept up splendid establishments, plunged headlong into play and dissipation; and, in consequence, grasped every penny they could lay their hands on and without mercy wrung out all the savings of their harassed tenantry. In everything they did, however, Edward Percy was pre-eminent. His expenditure, his avarice, the dishonest and extorting means he used to gain money, his tyranny over his tenants, his dabblings in the darkness of politics: all formed the most perfect and highly finished portrait of an ambitious, unprincipled, and tyrannical oppressor.

Well, these wicked and unprincipled men have since met with the punishments of their wickedness; and of all the persons whose names I have enumerated, there is not one now alive. No, the short space of twenty years has swept them all from the earth; they have long heard their eternal sentence and entered on their eternal doom. Their own deeds destroyed them, and their own children hastened their end.

At this time, twenty-five years ago, almost all these aristocrats had sons and successors, and young Caversham, young Montmorency, young O'Connor, young Carey, and many other lads and men then ranging from fifteen to thirty years old seemed likely enough to perpetuate and strengthen their ancestral qualities. If Mr Percy ruled among the fathers, certainly his son did among the children, and young Alexander from his fifteenth year upwards led from mischief to crime those whom since he has led from crime to death.

And I have forgot to mention as the great mentor, the infallible oracle in all thoughts and actions, R. P. 'Sdeath as he was now called, that Robert King who accompanied Mr Percy from England and Ireland. If Earth holds a fiend more infernal than this hoary villain, Earth has darker tenants than ever I could think on. But such writing as this takes me from my immediate subject, and I must now strive to regain my narrative. Though at the loss of some years of Northangerland's existence, I will again catch a glimpse of this brilliant meteor and reintroduce to my readers Alexander Percy, now in his seventeenth year.

Alas, when I saw him at that age, it was with clouds gathering thicker over his sky, all the best of his strange character deepening and darkening, and his future dreary wilderness of life beginning to close its horrors fast around him.

Alexander, at this age, had shot up from a pretty little child into the grace and energy of springtime youth. His height equalled that of many men, and his fine figure, polished manners, and ever-impassioned expression, with that voice whose melancholy sweetness —melancholy without intention or meaning, I can even at this distance of time distinctly remember—gave everywhere to his first appearance an air of refined and noble aristocracy. I shouldn't have said everywhere, for often, very often, all these graces were hidden in him by morose, silent gloom and harsh, passionate impetuosity; and the youth 'whose bright blue eyes' seemed now suffused with the light of love and thought and poetry would next moment oppose to an angry father scowls of threatening sullenness, kick an unoffending spaniel from him till it ran off howling, and beat a restless horse with all the unfeeling brutality of a savage. But if anyone attempted to aid or instruct him in his conduct, sneers of contempt or a pointed insult might well chance to be the payment of the ill-timed kindness.

Alexander's information from excursive reading was at this age prodigious beyond description. An exquisite memory and a power of getting a sense of an author in a glance, united to an ardent and eager thirst for books of any description, stored his mind with a mass of knowledge and information which has aided him since, in all he has attempted. In languages, the same qualities of mind had done the same service, and Greek and Latin with all their noble authors were as familiar to him as his native tongue. Modern languages he attained proficiency in immediately. But as for mathematics, his warm imagination could not fix itself on that stern study of reason until years of unhappiness, a contempt of all human enjoyment, and a strange yearning after some thing of certain truth, after some thing on which he could rest his harassed mind, as immovable by the paltry will and not resting on the shallow arguments of man, urged him against whom abstract Religion seemed forever closed to seek in her sister, philosophy, a final shadow of omnipotent truth. Alexander Percy at seventeen cared nothing for mathematics, though Alexander Rougue* at thirty was the finest mathematician in Africa. But let me now proceed in the relation of this strange, eventful history. Although I cannot attempt to detail every event and incident of Northangerland's boyhood (for my space will be too limited even for a mention of the deeds of his manhood), yet ere I bring Percy into active and public life I must describe to my readers that scene and incident which struck the keynote of his life and whose chord has never since ceased to vibrate.

On a wild autumnal evening in AD 1810, when Alexander was in his eighteenth year, the wind howled in mournful gusts round the walls of Percy Hall, as if chafed and angry at its vain attempts to spoil the splendid rooms within. The private parlour was lit up; and the great red velvet curtains flowing down before the windows, the gilt and mirrored walls, the rich Turkey carpet all received a redder and richer glow from the bright, warm blaze which roared up the ample fireplace.

Why cannot man ever be happy? The owner of this splendour sat in the full radiance of it, on a soft, luxurious sopha, his feet resting on the warm hearthrug, and himself apparently with nothing to do but listen to the voice of his chimney, and think of his wealth. But yet, as Mr Percy sat, his face turned to the fire and his hands rested on his knees, I never recollected to have seen a countenance more expressive of the troubled and tormented feeling of a harassed and exasperated mind than that over whose high, dark forehead the flame flung its strange, flickering light. A heart ill at ease and a soul soured by the distractions of Ambition shewed all their clouds and misery in that haughty, handsome face.

But why should I proceed thus, like a notary writing down the furniture or persons of an apartment? I cannot hope to give my reader a living image by such a dead manner of painting; and if I could hit on a brighter colouring, I would fain spread it on my canvas. As it is, let me work out by laboured touches that scene which exists in my memory in such broad, indelible masterstrokes.

That evening and in that parlour there sat opposite Mr Percy, and beside his Lady, a form which, once looked on, you would hold in mind whether absent or present. A woman it was—and such a one! Oh, I feel I *cannot* describe to my readers Lady Augusta Romana di Segovia!* Only daughter of the late Earl of Jordan, she was then in her twenty-fourth year; and her father and mother being both dead, she was left sole guardian and director of her young brother and, until his majority, of his great and princely fortune. Descended from a high Florentine family and born in Italy, every thought and feeling of her mind breathed of the sweet and sunny South. High birth, high wealth, high intellect, and high passions centred in the form of the highest, the loftiest beauty. Surrounded from childhood to youth by wealth and admirers, being early bereaved of all natural or parental protection, given to life with a soul determined to take life and enjoy it, all this had made her what she was. Noble, lovely, dazzling in mind and person, warm as Italy itself in all her thoughts and actions—but, beyond this, all was wild waste and desolation.

Religion would have shackled her feelings and bound her to duties and humility, therefore she was a determined and unthinking atheist. Yet atheism showed her fears no refuge and held out no real cure for the conscience, and so she flew at times into superstitious Popery. Society and customs imposed on her certain rules of conduct and decorum, so she trampled on and despised the world; but without society, she could no more shine than a taper in vacuity. Beyond it, her mind felt no ease in contemplation; therefore, she grasped with passion on to the world, its glare, its vanity, and its dissipations, and her burning and passionate feelings kindled a fire in her heart which at once illumed and consumed her.

I knew nothing of the extent of that passion nor the power of her pride nor the wild waste of her profligacy. But I do know that when I beheld her in her usual magnificent drapery seated on that sopha which took from those grand folds of velvet the aspect of a regal throne, regarded her stately, arching neck and the light of deep emotion which quivered in her large, dark eyes and black, arching eyebrows, when I heard her rich voice of melody and the warm enthusiasm of her language, it cost me no struggle to keep in the background that dreary conviction that the meanest peasant girl in Africa might have more hope of peace here, and happiness in the hereafter, than Lady Augusta Romana di Segovia.

I have said that amid a luxurious apartment and the rich glow of fire and tapers there sat this night a gloomy distraction on the features of Mr Edward Percy, the aspect of deep concern on the noble countenance of his Lady, and a glow of excitement on the soft cheek of their lofty visitor. In truth, young Alexander Percy had been absent from the house for two or three weeks. No one knew where, but all supposed that he had run to sea.

The autumn was unusually wild and stormy. Of late, especially, the wind and rains had risen to an hurricane, and now they were blowing and beating most mournfully round the old and sheltered Hall. I had stood at the window with curtain drawn back, looking over the tempest till Lady Helen desired me to close it round again, for it only added to her depression to view the wild waste of clouds drifting over the moon and piling in the dark, dreary sky. Her Ladyship had naturally an almost spartan command over her feelings. But often this evening I beheld her eyes lighten with a look of agony when her husband informed her that if Alexander were at sea, then he must be under it and not above, for it was hardly possible that any vessel could live out the storm, amid such a whirlwind as the day had passed in. However, Lady Percy gave no way to expressions of grief; but servants had been despatched to all the ports adjacent, and a very short time would clear doubt whether the youthful adventurer was alive or dead.

A short time did clear it. Just as I returned to assume my seat, I was stopped by hearing a well-known voice in the hall, and raised, too, in a tone of exasperation. The door opened, and in dashed Alexander Percy, drowned in the rain, his handsome face shining, and his hair all dripping over his forehead. As he gazed hurriedly over the room, he crimsoned through the paleness of exhaustion up to the eyes as they fell on the form of the luxurious Augusta. But ere anyone could speak, Mr Percy, who had risen with a tremendous scowl of threat, demanded angrily:

'Sirrah. How dare you leave the Hall unpermitted? You are come back, but I wish to heaven you had dashed your brains out against the sea bottom! Begone, fool—!'

'Edward,' exclaimed Lady Percy, 'pray be silent. Anger cannot prove useful now. Alexander, you might have guessed that I could not feel easy in your absence amid such dreadful weather. Why did you depart so suddenly, Love?'

'Why, Mamma, I care so much for the sea in fine weather as I do for blustering nonsense in foul, and now that I could grasp a rough-raging Atlantic, I would take advantage of it. I would not cause you a single tear uncared-for, but never drop one over me. I cannot die yet. I will dare twice as wild an ocean tomorrow without heeding it. Stuff! What care I for blustering?'

'Silence, Sir!' broke in Mr Percy impetuously. 'Silence your nonsense. I tell you that if you leave the Hall again without my express permission, be it for one day or a month, I will decide at once whether you can die or not die.'

Lady Augusta had sat no unmoved spectator of this scene. Her dark eyes flashed with animation, and as her beautiful lip curled in a sneer, she said, emphatically:

'Mr Percy, your son Alexander loves a storm. Do not act like a fool and so caress him when he disobeys you. Punish him with a calm, Sir.'

'Do you say so, Lady Segovia?' asked young Percy, turning to her with eager excitement.

'Yes, and I think much more, Alexander', was the answer, and its tone of music thrilled through the heart of him it was addressed to. He turned round with a lightening glance of triumph.

'Then I don't care *what* you say, Sir!'

Mr Percy's broad, black eyebrows centered in a scowl of hatred. He fixed his countenance with the ghastliness of a dying man and muttered determinedly, 'Dare you speak so, Sir?'

Alexander faced his father with a fierce, vindictive flashing of his eye and a curl of defiance on his whitened lips. 'Aye, and think more, too!'

With a dreadful execration, his father dashed his closed fist to his face, but Alexander warded the blow with his hand and, turning with a strange look to Mr Percy, sprang from the room. He did not stop till he reached the hall, and there he sat down, wearied with the day's wild weather. Exhaustion and excitement combining spread a deathlike paleness over his face, and he could have dropt from the seat when, roused by a coarse, sneering cough behind him, he turned around and saw the hideous figure of old 'Sdeath, his little eyes flaming and his fiendish features writhing with sarcastic laughter.

'Naw what ailes thee, mun?' asked the old villain.

''Sdeath, I have been treated as by Heaven I'll never be treated again.'

'Aw knaw, Aw knaw. But what'l ta do, lad?'

'I'll never speak to him again.'

'That'l be nought, and wor nor nought.'

'What shall I do, 'Sdeath?'

'Kill him, mun.'

'Kill you!' cried his pupil, with a loud oath at the suggestion.

But the tutor, dashing his greasy cuff across his misshapen nose, came up to young Percy with a chuckle of delight.

'Aw'll tell thee what, young man, thaw's a gooid lad and a clever. Thaw weddnt deny it, and thaw's shewn as much sperit this evening as would fill a score o' hogsheads. And Aw'll tell thee what: they's no way for thee but one. Thaw mun look to the Lord, man, and abide by his will. There's a providence ower were heads which alluss provides for the best, and what says the Scripture? *Come unto me all ye that are heavy laden, and I will give you rest,* and agean, *though your sins be as scarlet, yet they shall be as white as wool.* Naw them texts were never intended for ought but the help of the needy, and Aw hav often and often thought on 'em as Aw read that blessed book. There's as much store of comfort atween the two boards of the Bible as have lasted me fro the rocker o' the cradle to the brink o' the grave. And Aw say that, though Aw have been young and now em old, yet Aw have nower seen the righteous wanting, or his seed begging their bread. And Aw wad hev ye look to this betimes and think out ere the hour cometh when no man can think. Aw hev brough yaw up from infancy, and Aw've thought many a time to myseln that Aw wad nevver let ye go. And naw, Alexander, naw that times are lighting hard and vexations affright ye, naw is the hour of trial, and naw look to storms unless—. Aw spake. Look, for thy deliverance cometh!'

As the ancient fiend spoke thus, with a godly sanctity diffused over his puckered features, the door opened and a young man stepped into the hall, who with an air of familiarity threw his hat and cloak aside and strode toward the fire. He was a tall, muscular young man about six-and-twenty, with a brawny frame, red whiskers, and handsome, wicked-looking features. This newcomer stretched his arm towards Alexander, shook the clenched hand unoffered to him, and asked—somewhere between sneering and speaking in earnest—'Heyday, Percy, what now say you?'

Alexander, with all the energy of hatred, told him of the language and blows his father had bestowed on him, and concluded, 'Hector, I'll never stay another night under the roof while he is alive.'

'No more should you. Come, clear up. What, Sir, there's a way to use such an affair as yours. 'Sdeath, have the walls ears just now?'

'No one at present, Aw think.'

'Hum, well. Sit down a moment and listen to a fairer friend than Elihu was. I fancy the little knowledge I have of law affairs will just aid me so far as to know the treatment of a business like yours. Tut, man. Of course you'll never touch this doorstone yet a while. Why, you're seventeen, and it's time to set up yourself.'

Young Percy caught the idea with lightning quickness. He started up and said, 'You mean that I should borrow money, don't you? And I will! Where shall I do it?'

'Hem. Very satisfactory, but not so loud. And, on second thoughts, it were best to tell you under another roof than this old house, so we'll just take a ride to Wellington's Town. It's a middling night,* and I can show you a cask that'll tap as freely as any.'

''Sdeath will have our horses in a twinkling.'

As he spoke, Alexander himself ran out to the stable, brought out two, vaulted on to one while his advisor mounted another, and both then galloped quickly down the avenue in the wild, howling night.

The gentleman I have introduced to my readers was no other than Hector Matthias Mirabeau Montmorency,* son of William Daniel Henry Montmorency, Esquire, MP, of Derrinane Abbey, and the very man who may be found at the moment diving in the wildest ocean of our country's politics. Twenty-three years ago, however, he was only known as a young lawyer of astonishing learning and ability, burning with ambition and fast for the top of the tree. But his reckless habits, squandering extravagance, and total want of principle kept him down from the height on which was fixed his most anxious wishes. He was a deep confidant of Alexander Percy, and observed with wonder his young friend's fast-opening intellect, overwhelming impetuosity, and eager alertness in crushing all marks of goodness or principle.

Well, Alexander Percy, accompanied by his firm friend Hector and followed by their common father 'Sdeath, hastened to Verdopolis and entered under the portals of the Right Honourable the Earl of Caversham. This noble they found sitting alone as calmly and quietly as a Christian anchorite; but 'there was within that did not shew', for a very little conversation and a short explanation of the scene above described drew forth first from his unspotted soul a gentle and soothing condolence and a moderate endeavour to heal all disagreeable difference. But when he saw the distaste with which his words were received, when he saw his young visitor break into a passionate fit of cursing the instant that reconciliation was mentioned, he quietly put by all secret artifice and at once sounded Percy on the subject he appeared to come for.

Money for the purpose of dashing on by himself, money to squander in all the wildest riotings and gambling and extravagance was what Alexander just now wanted, and this the Earl of Caversham determined he should have. He knew that Mr Percy's huge estates were entailed upon his son, and that if he lent him now a good round sum, he could be sure hereafter to get it back again. He was known through all Africa as a rich* and pitiless usurer, for Caversham, however dissolute and abandoned he might be, had always an eager greediness, avarice, and a cold, calculating craftiness which made him lay by all the pride of aristocracy and proceed with exquisite skill in his detestable profession. The wealth he gained by this conduct was immense, but it was all lying in the hands of poor wretches to whom he had lent at enormous interest and whom he snatched from the verge of bankruptcy only to plunge into deeper and more hopeless ruin. But the essay of this night might be classed among the most successful bits of business he had ever a hand in. Here is the monument of his villainy:

'I hereby promise to advance to Alexander Percy, Esquire, the sum of £25,000 upon security of the entailed estates of his father, Edward Percy, Esquire, and at an interest of 20 per cent per annum, to be paid either yearly or along with the principal when he arrives to his paternal property, but in such case burdened with an additional interest of 20 per cent upon the accumulated interest of the principal to fill up the loss sustained by the lender from not having that superior interest in his hand to traffic on.*

       signed Caversham
       Witness R. P. 'Sdeath
            H. M. M. Montmorency'

 Alexander, the moment this paper was signed and all things settled in due legal formality, drafted a bill on the Earl's banker, and as soon as he was satisfied took his hat and left the town. Though the night was dark and bleak and stormy, and though he himself was dreadfully fatigued by the journey from the sea shore and the constant restlessness of his ongoings when round home, yet the conflicting passions of his mind so harassed him as entirely to drive underneath observation all the faintness and weariness of body. He mounted his horse and urged it madly through the streets till the spurned and frightened beast brought him straight before the banks of the Gambia; and then he recovered recollection of where he was sufficiently to guide it upward along the road which winds north towards the boundaries of Wellington's Country. He cared nothing about where he was going, or what hour of night it was, or whether calm or stormy or wind or rain, but all his thoughts were fixed on that situation and aspect of life into which his own wild passions had so suddenly and irretrievably plunged him.

 Nay, the very word 'Life' alone was enough to make him start, for that morning he had been only a wild, spoiled, passionate, and headstrong boy, residing at his father's house, all his prospects watched over by parents, and his footsteps guarded as those of an inexperienced child. Practically, what did he know of the world? What had he to do with the ongoings of men? He certainly possessed a wide circle of companions and acted as the very prince of a host of humanity. But these acquaintances were youths and schoolboys; or, if men, yet acting as his mentors and teachers in frolic, rioting, and boyish extravagances. And truly, too, that morning he had been still only just returning from an expedition alone, through the country to the sea, and among strange scenes unaided and unwatched over. But all this was having no more than an outburst of unfledged daring and wild imagination. It had been in reckless play with the tempests of nature and much-relished buffeting with the waves and weather.

 Truly, too, he had thought much before this night, but his

thoughts, entirely exempted from the influence of the world's events, were the mere creations and paintings of his opening and unbridled mind. He himself knew that it was nowise what the world calls thought; and though much of his musing was on the future, it was all just so little foresight. He knew that he did think intensely of his early childhood, of his present scenes, of what was in store for him hereafter. He weighed his own powers, his own splendid mind, and fast-widening stores of information.

That he was determined to be known in the world and that he cared for no one who should ever arise to thwart him, he was well aware; that he did possess within himself such a soul, such powers, such immensity of talent and genius that he must, if he lived, gain at some period the eminence he looked for. He knew, too (and few know that), what he was, where deeply rooted were his faults, and what those qualities were that were likely to ruin him. He knew his extreme violence of passions, his headstrong and unreasonable pettishness (for that name could he call it), his total want of governing principle, and his scorn and contempt for all the various aspects of goodness. He saw all that black melancholy which has since so miserably embittered his cup and which even then with its strange, poisoned draught, with its first bewildering fumes, deranged his soul. But though he saw all this, he could not tell how to amend it, and when amendment was suggested to his mind, he fiercely and contemptuously repulsed it.* He knew all that was wrong with him, but he gloried in that wrong; he cherished it and laughed and scorned at the idea of setting his heart aright.

Here, then, we have the key to that bitter mood with which this night he regarded all thoughts of his father. No thought of revenge presented itself openly to his mind, but he determined never more to attend to, or live with, or in any wise obey him as a father. He thought, too, of his mother; but her he loved, and he knew that she loved him. And if one tear was dropped by him that night, it was over the feelings of long-rooted affection, the memory of his early childhood, the image of her who had watched over him with the unchanged endurance of a guardian angel, who had attended to all his capricious wishes, had nursed him in sickness and smiled on him in health, whose voice he always heard, and whose countenance, still present, looked at him in all his often repeated visions of that which to him was never again to return. These feelings Percy has always felt with the most utter intensity; and now, in this present lonely, stormy night, they filled his heart with an agony which no pen or tongue can describe. And when he looked at the return which he was now going to give for eighteen years* of unchanged, unwearied affection—that he was going to separate himself at once from his mother to pass into a life where she could neither smile on him nor advise him, and which must certainly embitter all her thoughts for him and cause to her many a weary thought and many an unavailing tear—when he thought of all this and felt that his spirits would not let him change or soften the keenness of separation, he stopped his horse, and with clenched teeth he shook his fist up to the sky and cried with a horrid curse that he would that he 'might this moment be struck dead for ever!'

As he wildly looked round for the bolt which should strike him to annihilation, an object passed his sight which in a manner forced him from the illusion of his agony. A decrepit old man on a grey horse trotted up, and though the night was so black and stormy, touched his shoulder with a coarse greeting of familiar recognition.

'Who the Devil are you?' asked young Percy vehemently.

'Naaw,' returned his fellow journeyer with a disgusting, nasal laugh of derision. 'It's a braw chield that doesn't know its own feyther.* Thawrt greeting to part wi thy Daddie, Aw guess, and doesn't know that here he is beside thee and, lad, that thaw can *nivver* part wi him, eh? And sure enough, thaw's the guid will o'heaven above thee, for A'm noane clear tha sich a blessed height have Aw ever been aat, in above what tha'rt, fair clothed with sunbeams withaat and glowing wi happiness within! Sich a lookaat for thee, Aw've gotten, lad. Hold up thy head, for I'll be hanged if I do not see a crown over it, a crown of white, my lad, silver, I should guess, and plaited into as many rays as there is hairs o' thy head and thaa's robes of white, too, but they muffle thy feet and hand sadly, and thy face looks too resigned and pure, lad. And thaa's carriage just ahint thee, nabbut its rather o' the smallest and as black as the midnight, and thaw mun lie in't instead o' sitting ont, and thy palace isn't as large as some is. But what o'that, six feet is as much as thaa'l need an Aw'll warrant thee...

'Naa, Naa! What naao!' cried the old blackguard as his exasperated listener pulled out a pistol and fired it with an oath in his face. The old fiend drew back, let his young master proceed forward, and followed him jeering at the unsteady aim he had taken.

'What, thaa's all of a fluster. Has thy father stricken thy wits, aaso, or aar'ta, thin, kin o' thy mother? Lad, nivver heed her, say Aw, nivver heed her. But, happen, thaw thinks old Caversham's taken thee hold by the thrapple ower this £30,000.* Thaw's gotten it, and Aw say never heed that, too. Aw say thaw hev getten it, and that's enough to heed one awhile. But, lad, Aw'll tell thee what it is. Aw have trotted me old bones so far for it to make of a neight. Aw've news to tell thee, and what'l tha give for em news as gooid as gold? Ane better than some gold that Aw hev known, for they're true news and noane coined ones—Aw say, lad, what does that think o'—Lady Augusta!'

'I think you are the Devil,' shouted Alexander, turning round on his tempter with a fierceness that might have started anyone but this marred old sinner.

'And Aw am!' he shouted in return. 'And thaw's made worse guesses nor that, and Aw made falser answers, too. But what says Scripture, that a man shall leave feyther and mother and cleave unto—.'

'By Heaven, 'Sdeath—!'

'Noa, noa, Heaven's nought to do with 't matter, nor earth, nauther. But Leddy Segovia!'

'Ho, you blasted villain, will you drive me mad—? Ha, I'm mad already—but, old scoundrel, silence with your hateful ... your ...'

'Yawr what, na? Yaw wad saw sommut sweet, waddn't yaw? But Aw do say that she's as wild as yaw are, and a bonny handsome couple yaw'll make, and a good and a decent, and am sure yaw'll both live *will--I, nill-I,* as the saying is; and for the matter, yaw'll both die and be buried and—why, after that, rest your souls, for I'm sure they'll both need rest. Wither they'll get it is another question. Ha, ha, ha! But mind, lad, yaw be at the fayte at the Duke of Wellington's tomorn at neight. There's a card for ye lying at yere feyter's, and look weel about ye there, and—goid neight t'ye, my son.'

'And eternal night to you, Old Satan!' exclaimed Alexander as R. P. 'Sdeath turned his old horse round and trotted off towards the city amid the wild rain and wind and darkness. But the appearance and the conversation of the hoary rascal had changed somewhat the current of Percy's feelings, or at least had made an outlet to their intensity. Determined now to cast off all melancholy, to crush all thoughts of old associations, and as usual to laugh at every idea of religion and rectitude, he too turned his horse's head toward the city and rode forward, thinking of the readiest mode of opposing his father, showing him that he could live without him and cut out his own scheme of life so that every event should prove to be what Mr Percy might hate and wish to be otherwise.

'Curse the frenzied tyrant,' said Alexander to himself. 'As truly ought to be, his own dear friends will play the double part and, underhandedly, will cherish what he himself will urge them to crush. He may rave and storm at his will, now, but he shall feel I have the upper hand of him. Thirty thousand pounds in my purse, and from the pocket of his best associate, too, is a glorious beginning, even though I myself shall smart for the fingering of it. But hang it, shall I regret the interest I have to pay for this foundation of my future fortune? I think it's the very picture of human life. No blessing without ten times its weight of cursing; not a step to climb, but I've a dozen yards to fall for it.

'Oh, curse that, too. It's as bad as my father, and I wish him and all such work was even now at the bottom of the Gambia. However, I must so act as to seem all careless of the future. I will hire today a nest in the Western Hotel; and daily and nightly I'll issue forth from my stronghold and blaze away at fêtes and balls and entertainments and the opera and the theatre, and—mind, lad—at the gaming house, too! How in the world am I to pay up the interest of the cash I have laid hold on, except I stake chance after chance as fast as I can lift my hands up? One risk over, another comes on, till either I blow my brains out or the mercy of providence holds out hope of resuscitation!

'What a fool I am! Always overlooking the bright side—or, till I find my purse, progressing in the best arithmetical manner that old Bud ever pointed out or spoke or dreamed of. Old Bud! Old fool! Old before his time. The scoundrel shall leave his lobster hold on me; what I learn, I learn without his aid, and I'll let that pedantic coxcomb feel the punishment of his disgusting hyprocrisy. Does he suppose that he knows more than me, that his brain is better furnished than mine? Ah, Captain, your conceit could never carry you so far—. But what need is there to trouble myself about him! Have at the world now, and leave moral-buckled schoolmasters to their hornbook and accidence. Hang me, am I turned fool myself to be riding on here trying to decceive myself into lightness and heedlessness? Stupidity's at high-water mark, I think, and I am careering full sail in the deepest of it! No. No, I am entered at last on what men call the Ocean of Life; and if ever anyone had a sailer, a rudder, or a chart or a compass, I have none—nor shore or harbour, either.'

So he went on trying, as he owned to himself, to blind his own eyes to consequences and keep from his sight the stern reality of his prospects, till morning rose through the storm, and he entered again the crowded metropolis of Wellington's Land.

That night Alexander Percy appeared at a splendid fête given by His Grace, the Duke of Wellington, at the Palace, and many of those present remembered afterwards when his ongoings first rose before public attention. What a singularly reckless and distracted air, a look between fierceness and misery, was cast over his features through that gay and gorgeous night! His fine person and stature so much above his years, with a face of such varied expression and such refined and fascinating manners, gained him always in public far more notice than his youth and his father's enmity to the government could otherwise have given him. But he hardly ever seemed to care for this notice, and that evening least of all. He wandered apart from the splendid throng and sat down on a sopha in the most silent and empty saloon and passed an hour of inward thought, unconscious almost of everything around him.

At length, the familiar aspect of a grand piano, which stood open opposite, roused him to rise and step toward it. His fingers once placed on the keys, he could not think for a while of taking them off, and so he sat running over the sheets of music and playing by starts, each bit longer than the preceding one till he fairly had launched out into the tide of a passage of ancient and sacred harmony.

Soon, those within hearing who had ears could not fail to catch the tones of this exquisitely skilful playing. And as it was affirmed 'Young Percy was playing', that name (so well known was his extraordinary musical genius) directed the foot of many a lord and lady toward the room from where these sweet sounds proceeded. A certain aristocratical circle was soon assembled, their interest centred* on him with such looks of admiration as his performance deserved.

Then one forefinger pointed to an opened leaf and a voice itself of music desired him to play some piece, whose title I have long forgot. He turned to the speaker, and as he looked on the Lady Augusta di Segovia, all saw his changed expression and the bewildered stare when he resumed his playing. In a minute, after a half-connected prelude, he struck his fingers impatiently from the keys and said confusedly 'I cannot play', left the instrument, and the room altogether. Lady Augusta herself smiled derisively at those who turned to her for an explanation of this conduct. Her dark eyes seemed almost to say 'The deer is struck, and well you regard in envy of the huntress'. To those fair faces who returned looks of reproach and astonishment, she answered only with a triumphant and insulting glance, which soon subsided to her own characteristic look of Italian fervour.

Now, far indeed was Lady Augusta from a coquette. Her character had none of this surface of lightness and vanity. Her almost solemnly musical voice, her serious, earnest smile, the expression of her dark and lustrous eyes, all most vividly showed forth a character far indeed removed from the everyday silliness of frivolity and giddiness; and she knew that Alexander Percy had a spirit far too like her own to be enslaved by nonsensical airs of goddess-like caprice and disdain. She knew that one hour of such a display would rouse him only to contempt, and her own arts and wiles and snares were of an order. For her commenting upon those which excited all her scorn when she saw them employed round her had always earned her more malice, animosity, and inveterate hostility than fell to the lot of any other woman than this star of western royalty.

When morning dawned, the guests departed, and Alexander Percy entered upon the wild, irregular life which he had chosen out for himself. Since he had hardly yet numbered his eighteenth year, fixed and melancholy misery could not forever dwell on his mind, and the task of driving it off was easier then for him than it would have proved in later life.

His mornings he generally spent at the professors of boxing, fencing, and such athletic exercises, in whose rooms he learnt all the art of defence, acquired ideal skill and strength, and repaired or warded off the inroads which the life he led was making on his naturally strong and springy constitution. Then, during the day, the presence, company, and ongoings of young Caversham, Montmorency, O'Connor, or Gordon, and old Caversham and old 'Sdeath and an hundred of the like profligate villains of the city afforded him vast instruction and amusement, and completed the day's course of study in the art of holy living and dying.

Every night the countless feasting and gaieties and splendour of a wealthy, royal, and aristocratical city swallowed him irretrievably in its whirl of dissipation, except now and then when the hours of midnight were spent in sullen, gloomy thinking or fitful, intermittent study. Such a round of existence as this, he well knew, accumulated vast materials for bitterness; but he felt it chased away the present burning of his heart, and so he eagerly flung himself into its vortex and left future time to future thinking.

Among all the many splendid edifices which thronged the capital and illuminated its streets with the blaze of their nightly assemblies, none stood more eminent than the noble Segovia Palace, for within a couple of hours after sunset its pillared front was sure to be surrounded with equipages, and its long rows of windows to fling forth their blaze of glaring light. Certainly the nominal owner of this aristocratic mansion fully bore out the truth of Zamorna's maxim that no man is so little master as at his own hearthside. For in the unhappy-looking youth, all clothed in silks and velvet and possessing a countenance coloured so like the keys of 'My Grandfather's Harpsichord', who might be seen lounging about on the sophas of some secluded saloon, no one could have thought to find the Right Honourable John, Earl of Jordan. It was his stately sister, Lady Augusta, who held all the sovereignty of his lands. Castle, palace, and revenues, she controlled everything as she wished, and through her own profuse expenditure would soon have drained all her brother's immense wealth; yet she possessed sources from which to acquire new.

Well, at the Segovia Palace and its far-renowned entertainment, Alexander Percy was seldom absent. Augusta had never dreamed of better success than over this wild and wandering creature of his own passions; and, for himself, he loved her enthusiastically. So did she also in like manner love him, and neither of the two were among those pale-faced beings whose life and wishes are ever wafted off in the breath of a sigh, who as such know themselves and dare not take a step in life without being hurried on by the power of fate and circumstance.* No, Augusta herself laughed at both fate and circumstance; she cared little to what end her course was tending, and Alexander—why, he cared certainly, for his aim was to force his life straight against both fate and circumstance.

When I think of these two beings, of mind so noble and of forms and feeling so calculated to adorn and exalt the world and the life they moved in, when I look back to twenty years ago and picture them as they were placed in such lofty station and so much the admiration of a great and royal capital, and think of their reckless, determined, headlong course of ruin, the race which each seemed most desirous to run to death, and their troubled and bewildered life and (of one, at least) the sudden and melancholy end, I turn from their strange, eventful history with a mind more strongly impressed than by any of the wild, unreal, romantic fiction that ever my ear listened to. Hardly any one can look on the present estate of Northangerland with such extraordinary interest as I can, for few so well as myself know what that nobleman has caused to be done and has himself passed through.

But I am running out of the main course of my subject. The countless crowd of visitors at the nightly fêtes of Segovia Palace as they entered into its splendid and glowing saloons were always, after a while, sure to be received not only by the well-known, admired, and detested Lady Augusta but by young Percy, the remarkably tall, handsome young man attired in such scrupulous and fashionable elegance (for this was before the Northangerland clothed in solemn black), with such an extremely proud and haughty air, yet ever again bursting—through his exclusiveness—into fits of passionate impetuosity. Politicians weighed in their minds his demoniacal father and his noble expectations and remarked one to another that the 'tyger of opposition' was in his spirit, and those who lived would very likely soon view his ravages. People of keen observation thought him a young man of uncommon personal and mental endowments, but— and they shook their heads at this aspect of his character and rumours of his conduct. As for the ladies of Wellington's Land, he held almost the place then, as regards them, which the 'Sun of Angria'* holds now. His natural elegance was the perfection of grace; his extreme passionateness of temper, his fiery animation. His utter melancholy was indeed the quality which placed the capstone of his character, the halo which shone round him and deified him. But when the sharp observers noticed his frequent appearances and graceful lordliness at the Segovia Palace, and how his manner altered and his blue eyes lightened in the presence of its splendid mistress, they one and all deplored and compassionated his destiny, and vilified and execrated the spells of the much-hated enchantress.

There were not wanting in Wellington's Town many fair heroines who, I believe, both would have attempted and could have succeeded in saving him from her toils. Who could fail to notice how, when the urgent and earnest solicitation of some lovely and aristocratic circle had prevailed on him to show his admirable powers and genius on organ or piano, as he sat at the splendid instrument creating its varied and noble harmony, he would look upon the stately plumes, and raven or yellow curls and heavenly faces which hung over him with a look of rapture and excitement not all, I know, derived from the music he was playing. And it was then that he seemed capable of feeling pleasure undashed by some bitter weight of care.

But when he entered those saloons where more sombre attire, more anxious countenances, deeper and sterner voices showed the presence of beings of another description, feelings, too, of another description seized on his soul, and brought down again over his spirit black, depressing thoughts and dreary outlooks for the future. In his position with the ladies' circle that I have mentioned, he triumphed and gloried though he cared precious little for their good will, but here he wished, longed, burned for distinction among them, to lead them or oppose them in all the walks of fame and empire. To command in the field and senate, rousing and employing all his energies with them or against them, to carry out his schemes of ambition and establish his name as the highest and most celebrated man of his time. But the bitter consciousness had come over him that the life he was now leading, though it might ensure him favour among the women, could never give him sovereignty among the men of Africa.

But I must make a vigorous effort to proceed with my narrative, or the life of Percy may linger in thoughts and reflections. Lady Augusta saw that there might some time be some danger of her enchantments losing their power, while Alexander was left at his own wild will, as now. So, in the month of May, 1811, there was announced through the city the marriage of Alexander Percy, Esquire, with Lady Augusta Romana di Segovia. The fashionable circles immediately resounded with hints, innuendoes, and violent invective, uttered perhaps with a sweet voice but certainly with most bitter feeling. However, there was one in Africa whose voice was not very sweet, though his feelings were bitter indeed on the occasion.

My readers may have wondered why, since Alexander was yet a minor, being only in his nineteenth year, his father did not enter and put a stop by the strong hand of the law to his rebellious and unauthorized conduct against him. To do this was most certainly Mr Percy's fixed resolution, but unfortunately only a day or two before Alexander had left Percy Hall, one of Mr Edward Percy's numerous debtors, a gentleman who had been one of his associates and to whom he had lent large sums of money on usury which he had proved quite unable to pay, after a long and miserable imprisonment was freed by insolvency. Now desperate at the greediness of the man who had thus ruined and persecuted him and seeing all his prospects through life destroyed by Mr Percy's cruel avarice, he publicly abused and insulted him under very aggravated circumstances with the intent to bring on a duel with him. Mr Percy's cold-blooded, hardened feelings would have despised and laughed at the challenge, but his black and revengeful passion urged him to punishment of the offender.

Nature contended against nature on the question, until the skilfully manipulative old valet 'Sdeath represented to him that he had seen Mr Sullivan, the unhappy insolvent, and that 'his hands trembled uncommon; there wad to be ninety to one agean his hitting'. This hint succeeded. Mr Percy accepted the challenge, and the two had a meeting where he shot Sullivan right through the heart. A duel in Africa neither was nor is considered anything very heinous. But in this case the friends of the slain man took it up and pursued Mr Percy in an action for murder on the grounds of unfair play which were very apparent in the transaction, for old Mr Gordon, a true fellow of 'the Justice' (Mr Percy), acted as Sullivan's second, and suspicions were afloat that gold had drawn that unfortunate wretch's bullet from his pistol while 'the Justice' was known to have used two in his own.

Men believed all this as very likely to have happened, so as matters looked desperate at present, the Magistrate of Percy Hall fled from it in hot haste and took refuge over the seas in Slumpsland till the storm should blow over. However, it thickened and blackened till on a sudden, as if by a blast of wind, it just disappeared, and men heard no more of the prosecution for murder. In real truth, Mr Percy used his old agent, Money, at a liberal rate to quash the zeal of the friends of the deceased, and, it seems, he succeeded perfectly. So, after three months absence from Wellington's Town, he arrived again at his seat in the beginning of June. But during his temporary exile it was that all these events happened with regard to his son Alexander, and the news of the marriage with Lady Augusta saluted his ears as he passed through the metropolis on his way to Percy Hall. When he arrived there, I for one saw directly that the fiend of passion held full possession of his heart.

He called his lady apart. When, in an hour or two, she left the room, I was commanded to appear. The moment I entered, I was saluted with 'Fool! Traitor! Toad!' and a host of the like decorous epithets. He was in a towering passion, accused me of conniving at the conduct of his son, said he would hang me for it if I did not take care, and then threatened Alexander himself with the most dreadful effects of his parental affection.

As soon as I parted, Old 'Sdeath was ushered in; and the two—master and man—remained closeted together all the evening, at first, it was said, abusing and storming at and cursing each other in the most unmeasured violence but all the rest of the time in deep, secret, and anxious consultation. Now this wretch 'Sdeath, during the whole period of Mr Percy's absence, had been at Verdopolis aiding Alexander and hurrying him on to all manner of vice and dissipation; but when the father returned, 'Sdeath repaid this companionship by informing against the son and suggesting all means for stopping his courses. At night, Councillor Daniel Montmorency,* Mr Percy's lawyer, was called for; and early in the morning, our master, accompanied by 'Sdeath and five or six trusty servants, left the Hall on horseback for Wellington's Town.

Alexander was swiftly riding toward town on his return from a shooting excursion among the hills when old 'Sdeath met him and persuaded him to take a short cut toward the city. Unthinking of treachery, Percy followed his advice, and they cantered forward through a large plantation belonging to his father. At a sudden turn of the road, 'Sdeath blew his nose with portentous loudness; and, as Percy turned his steed to give him a blow for the din, six mounted men burst suddenly through the thicket, seized hold of his horse by saddle and bridle, and laid hands on him to pull him to the earth. Alexander, with a succession of oaths, fired his pistols into the faces of two, and exerting all his uncommon muscular agility had nearly succeeded in freeing himself from the grasp of all of them. But with a horrible curse from a well-known voice, another man burst upon him and threw him on to the ground. Alexander directly knew his father, who had grasped him with desperate violence; now the other servants, except two disabled by the son's tremendous resistance, secured him and hurried him into a covered carriage which stood horsed and waiting not far off. His father himself bound his hands with most painful tightness, thrust him into the chaise, and entering with old 'Sdeath and an athletic attendant ordered the coachman to drive forward.

While these four remained in the carriage, a profound silence was observed. Alexander sat, as pale as marble with hatred and exhaustion. It was not until after many hours' furious driving, when the vehicle drew up at an inn in the harbour of Wellington's Town, that Mr Percy informed his son:

'I have stopped your opposition to my will; at length, marry whom you like! What the devil has dared you act as you have done, fool! What will you be good for, think you, man? I here have you, and off you must go directly, for the Philosophers Isle. While I was away, I had settled all things for your reception there. But by——! I little thought to find you married on my return. However, to college you shall go or die for it, and you'll embark this very evening aboard this vessel just now weighing anchor. Your berth is secured, and bid adieu to your Lady, if you can. 'Sdeath is to accompany you there; and after you're fixed, he returns again. Away with him! Servants, away with him, and begone!'

'You devil!'

Alexander only uttered the words and was hurried out, on to the vessel and into a cabin ready prepared. The ship weighed, set sail, and left Africa with the future Earl of Northangerland, thus rudely snatched from the life he had chosen and his goddess-like Augusta, to drudge in a far-off college along the usual rough road to learning, advancement, and distinction in the world.

[Chapter IV]

My readers, in perusing the account of Alexander Percy's youth which I have just concluded, will perhaps be inclined to wonder at the few apparent traces which it exhibits of all those vast powers of genius, ability, and natural and acquired knowledge by which he has risen through life to the rank and station which he now holds in the affairs of Africa. But I must tell them that, if this is their judgement, it is a weak and short-sighted one. I know that, in all the pages just finished, I have detailed no vast exertion of bodily or mental capabilities, no huge strides made toward power and importance, no sudden plunge and rapid rise in the warlike or political events of the time. The warrior, the statesman, the rebel, and the legislator have not yet appeared in any act or aspiration of the soul of the future Earl of Northangerland. I have described only the caprices and wanderings of an indulged and passionate child, the vice and errors of an unbridled and impetuous youth, plunging now into a chaos of dissipation and folly, then led by others to ruin and crime.

This melancholy train of events has formed the staple, the main plot of my narrative; but what is it that constituted the by-play, the under-plot, that portion which is usually by far the most interesting and important part of a novel or tale? Why, it has been the gradual ripening and opening of an imperious temper, ungovernable passions, excitable feelings, undaunted recklessness of purpose! Yes, but what truly great genius ever appeared in this world without a character like this, and does not this character contain the seeds of a powerful imagination, mental energy, fixed resolution, and that spring and life blood of all noble actions—unquenchable, untiring Ambition!* And must not a mighty genius possess all these? Yes, also, but if the greatest genius have all these, and yet have not a determined line of conduct to pursue, and an immediate, and constant system of acting on that course he has taken, he will spend all his powers in vain, may perhaps astonish the world for a moment but then must vanish:

> *Like a bright exhalation in the evening*
> *And no man see him more.**

All this I know, and I know that while Alexander Percy possessed all these powers of intellect, he also had fixed on some tangible mode in which to strengthen and bring them into action. He was yet only in his nineteenth year. Till this time he had done nothing, thought of nothing to any tangible purpose or with any determination to proceed. But now—now, when he was landed on the shores of the Philosophers Isle, forced by his father and deprived of all hope of escaping, he saw distinctly that only two ways were left for him to act: either to remain at college and relinquish for the present all the pleasures he had left in Wellington's Land, or by flying to that country again relinquish forever all hope of power and glory in life to come.

If he fled, a short, troubled life of dissipation awaited him, to be followed by an early end. If he stayed, labour, exertion, and absence from what he loved but—and here was the reward that so firmly chained his feelings—but to be followed by vast information and knowledge acquired, probable elevation and distinction at the noble University in which he studied, and when he returned to Africa all the means and appliance at least for rising to the topmost height of any station, any aim he might fix his heart on. All this, Alexander Percy saw most vividly. He knew what he wished to be; and he felt that now was the hour for fitting himself to accomplish that wish, for how through the wild life he was sure to plunge in on his return could he attain any degree of eminence in any of the knowledge that men set value on? He saw that it was now or never, and so he instantly put his hand to the plow, his shoulder to the wheel.

What were Alexander's feelings upon his arrival at the Philosophers Isle may best be gathered from his own writing; and that my readers may have at least some insight into their wild and wayward character, I feel it to be my duty to present them with the following letter addressed by him, shortly after he landed, to his wife, Lady Augusta Percy. It has been in my possession ever since the wreck of his fortune in 18—,* and I have always considered it a most striking example of his thought and feelings before these terrible storms of misfortune came upon him to cover all his spirit with their own oppressing gloom.

Don't think, Augusta, when you receive this letter that I wrote it from a feeling of the necessity of making my wife acquainted with my sudden and unexpected departure from herself and my house and country, or that I felt anxious to quiet all your well-grounded fears for my safety and your uncertainty of where I may be, or even that my anxiety arose from a very proper desire to know how you yourself were and to bewail with you our sudden separation. No, Augusta, none of these thoughts influence me, for you must be, by this time, well aware of the causes of our separation.

I, for my part, will not bewail what for eleven months to come I am determined to endure, and as to my safety, I, at least, know how little I care for that and how very little I care whether yourself be assured of it. I write to you, Augusta, as I would speak to you, because wherever I am or whatever I may be thinking on, you are always present to my mind, and you seem to be present to my eye. Have no fear, Augusta, that I shall soon forget you, for perhaps if I so constantly recurred to your recollection as you do to mine, you would think in good truth the words were literally fulfilled that we two are made one.

Augusta, how strangely rapid is the flight of time, and what changes it is forever bringing over our destinies. It seems to me not one day since, with thee, I laughed at home and parents and prospects and the future, and determined to make sure only of pleasure in this life, jilting* pain till the life to come when, if there be nothing of that sort in waiting for us, pain must go about its own business. If there be, why we shall have plenty of it. When I was with thee, I did not feel it; and when now absent from thee, two or three lesser, insignificant sensations such as hatred, revenge, and so forth prevented it from entering my mind—and since we two are one, was not this the case with you? I can answer that you have felt the delights of hatred and revenge as often, perhaps as strongly, as I have. Well, Augusta, take up those pleasures again, and I entreat you—feel them now.

I foresee that through this letter I shall be acting as I have been doing all my life, wandering and digressing (read transgressing) continually. Come, then, let me shake off all ceremony. If I judge your heart aright (and it is not so easy to guess where its right lies), you will not seek for anything more than my thoughts and feelings expressed to you as they occurred to me. And if when I give you them they appear erroneous and unintelligible, let the fault lie on those thoughts and not on my head for writing them. Augusta, I HATE *my father. I hate him. He is a demon. He has through all my life and through that nineteen years of his own made it his constant aim and endeavour to thwart and oppress and crush me. I have beheld nothing of him but his black, bilious passion, brutal temper, and base, crafty dishonesty. It cannot shock you to hear me speak thus of him for you have heard me speak so before, you know I speak the truth; and you yourself have received from him the dislike that I have, and you yourself feel toward him* as I have felt. Then listen to me, Augusta, think of him, remember him—I know you love revenge—and exercise that revenge on him in any plan you may have for injuring and shackling him. I shall always be ready to assist you to the utmost of my power—what did I say, to assist? To lead you, to direct you, not to bind the victim to the altar but to stick the knife into its heart's place. Write to me if you observe any change in his health. Of all things, I most wish him to die. He is worth £30,000 a year; and out of that, £15,000 is entailed to me. Augusta, you know that a property of £30,000 certain, in spite of all his endeavours to devolve it from me, is what neither yourself nor myself will affect to turn from; and before I am twenty-one, I see that I must either possess it or run myself into desperate embarrassment. (Ha! I have done that already.) And as to your own property, Augusta, I know you regulate it all, but it must in a few years devolve on that pitiful creature, your brother, the fatted calf, curse him. If I return, I'll give that to him which it will be long ere he is cured of.*

It seems to me as if nothing but trouble is waiting to hail me on my majority. Yet, among all the clouds waiting, there is one thought to give me delight. Thou, too, art in waiting. I am not going to fill my paper with idle protestations of 'constancy', 'affection', and all that sort of trash. But, Augusta, I love thee, and thou knowest that I love thee. You are the heaven on which all my hopes in the hereafter turn, the paradise in which every pleasure I can trust is centred. I know well that you are as bad as I am, that you are almost (as men say) as bad as you can be, but this does not matter a straw. You are Augusta di Segovia, my brightest light of the past. You are Augusta Percy, my only hope of the future. A minute ago I said that you know I love you, and now I say I know that you love me; and it is a love as warm and unthinking and inconsiderate on your part as on mine. I could not trust you one moment, I could not look forward to one bright day before me, but that I am certain you cannot leave me. You want, Augusta, to make me prisoner without committing yourself forever, but you fell into the gulph you wished for me, and when you wanted only to clasp my hand, you found I had as firmly clasped your own. Oh, when shall I clasp it in reality, when shall I see you again?

The woods and hills of Africa, her noble rivers and her crowded metropolis, the stately towers of Jordan Castle and the noble saloons of the Segovia Palace, they have no pleasure of recollection in my heart but what they derive from thy Italian eye and raven curls and Satanic soul. Yet, there is one other whom I grieve to part with, one other whom I do wish to behold again, and that one, Augusta, is my mother. She, I know, loves me, and whatever of goodness my soul possesses, I owe it all to her. I cannot forget my *childhood; and in every thought connected with those times and their feelings, my mother's form, my mother's voice mingle in the dream and give it half its charm and all its comfort. Childhood to me seems to have been a period of unmingled happiness as I view it now; contrasted with the storms of my later youth, all looks like the sabbath. All seems like those evenings in summer when the sun was setting in golden light over the glades and dark green trees of the park, its yellow lustre flung over the wide-spread towns and shining with such soft and glowing light on the front of the Hall and the golden, glittering windows and the sides of the white cows spotted over the grass.*

And my mother then would walk with me alone, sometimes trying to call my wandering mind to a little sense of what I had heard at church that day, checking my wandering feet from the countless objects of interest which distracted my attention and made me run every moment from her hand, till satisfied curiosity brought me back again. I might seem then heedless, wild, spoiled, and uncontrollable but, in truth, if I cared for no one else, I did for her; and she seldom had to reprove me twice in one day for the same fault, though all her caution was forgotten on the morrow. While I remembered it, I heeded it, or at least often did . . . But it was not in attending to what she said that I showed my affection for her, but rather in unconscious delight in walking with her, in sitting beside her, in chattering to her, and crying when separated from her. When away from her, I was passionate, wilful, cross, and troublesome; when with her, delighted and far milder and calmer than children often are. But when my father joined us, as he sometimes did, I caught a faster hold of her hand, shrunk closer to her side; and several times she caught me making apish grimaces at him. It was only then that I would willingly leave her and run to my nurse, when Ellen* found in me at once a considerable pleasure and a very considerable plague.

But curse all this! What am I doing? Ah, I forgot—writing down my thoughts as they occur, and you must e'en take them as they occur. I know you don't like my mother. I know that you won't like to hear of any pleasant days of mine if unconnected with you. You wish only to hear of my thoughts of yourself and remembrances of the noble girl, the wicked Italian, the glorious enchantress who made my later days one stream of fevered excitement. Ah, Augusta, these feelings are different, indeed, from my dreams of childhood. These fill my eyes with fire, and those with tears. And now, when I think on, these thoughts bring suddenly upon my mind a host of different beings yet, who have had almost as much to do with my later life as thou.

Ha, I begin to feel the demon within me. I begin to feel those burning sensations which called from his Grace, the Duke, his short prophecy that I *should throw Africa into as great a fever as I seemed in myself. Come, let me give way to the inspirations of that Deity within. Let me ask: how are my noble friends, my hands, my weapons? My noble Caversham and Montmorency and 'Sdeath and Simpson and St John, and all the rest of the everlasting tribunal of immortality. How are they, and how do they get on? They have my life in their hands; and I, theirs in mine. We are linked together, but I am yet above them, and I will yet be far above them. But I look to them as the swords wherewith I shall slay the foe, as the weapons of my arm.**

Yes, Augusta, here I sit in my secluded study in one of the solemn cloisters of St Patrick's College in the Philosophers Isle. What am I? A young gentleman of considerable expectations, snatched by his father from an imprudent marriage and sent here to complete his education for the life of an independent squire* and perhaps future Member of Parliament. Ha, is this so? Nay. A young—a young—why, let me say for courtesy a young man, retired of his own private accord, whether hurried by force or not, into these accustomed* precincts of learning with a determination to sit down and study night and day, to plunge into the most recondite mysteries of the classics, languages, mathematics, practical science, political economy, the Art Naval and Military, all the wide range of history, and all the treasures of ancient and modern literature. To study them indefatigably and unceasingly until a high degree, victory over all his fellow students, the honour of Senior Wrangler send him from the Isle the wonder and respect of all the university, his mind strengthened and furnished with all the stores and acquirements of learning, armed at all points, his weapons sharpened and his spirit fortified, to do that which he is determined to do—to fulfil his destiny! To obey his own soul, to spread his name, fame, words, and actions wherever there is a world to spread them in and one single human being who can feel or hear!

Augusta, do you know nothing of AMBITION? *If so, you know nothing of my heart. Ambition, that single word will rouse me when no other thought or feeling can.* It drives away joy and sorrow, love and hatred, crime or religion, drives them away or makes them bend instantly to serve its own ends and work what it imagines. If ever human being had this feeling, I have it, and all its fullest force is resistlessly centred in me. I cannot describe to you what I feel or how it affects me, Augusta. The influence is really irresistible. My ambition is not that pure and heavenly feeling which prompts a man to do what will prove to the glory of God and the benefit of his fellow man. It is not that effervescence of youth which makes a man admire great actions and strive to imitate them. It is not the generous ardour* *which prompts him to distinguish himself among heroes and sages, which catches fire from poetry or accident and which can rest content with a Sicilian and a miner.* It is not that sordid passion which directs the energies to the accumulation of power and the acquirement of wealth and luxury. No, by Heaven, Augusta, it is none of these!*

Oh, that I had the powers that my spirit longs for, that I could tell you in living letters what it is. I say it is none of these, but it may be all these; and I think it is, and twenty times as much, besides. My bodily conformation is excitable, my nerves acutely sensible, and they work on my brain till my feelings can be roused like gunpowder. I have a mind, from these causes, naturally sensible of the strongest and most constantly recurring and most unquenchably raging emotions of love, hatred, sorrow, and anguish. But its exaggerated tone, though it can be driven almost to madness by these feelings, cannot be moved at all by friendship, respect, kindheartedness, platonism, the ties of religion, or the customs of the world. The fiend within me drives me over all such feeble barriers and tramples upon these, the passions of cool reason and reflection.

You see, all my actions in this light proceed from the animal, from the natural conformation; and so they do, nothing can be plainer. I have all these nervous feelings and all the—the—let the first word stand; all these nervous feelings which other human beings have, but excited to a ten-fold degree of intenseness. As a vast deal of the mind really lies in the nerves, as the brain could only be called the seat of the soul inasmuch as it is the rallying point of the nerves, so, since my nerves are naturally, dreadfully excitable, my imagination is to the highest degree vivid and burning. I see everything in a far stronger and more distinct light than others around me see them. Whether they be natural objects, the emotions which arise from the sight of scenery, of the sky or the earth or the sea or from their glorious and god-like associations, the thoughts which must rise when I gaze on the star-spangled heaven of midnight or the stirring whirl of the city at midday, and from hence religion with its mysteries and associations has such effect on me that I am in daily agony that my searches shall find it to be untrue. Oh, that day (and come it will), that day shall I lament to see. Nay, that is not strong enough, but—away with this and hence.

Music has always had so irresistable a charm for me; and hence, the vehemence of my feelings has always shewn me forth like one mad with pride, passion, and waywardness. And hence, I am what I am—insane—a madman. But in order that I may prove a curse to the world, that I may exercise my powers! Where, if I was left to my personal feelings and my own organization, I should spend a short life in a whirlwind and die at twenty of pure old age, shaking like an aspen leaf! Burnt to white ashes!

God, if there be a god, Chance, if there is none, has gifted me with an intellect, strong, vigorous powers of reason and thinking. Ha, and it is from thence, from this mind uniting with this body that I am what I am. Not a mere madman, not a mere profligate, not a mere enthusiast or poet or painter or musician or soldier, not one whose spirit is bent upon one subject and guided by one feeling, or one whose reason is upset by his nerves and who is driven by all manner of feelings, or one who is hurried into a waste of profligacy and has no thought for anything else. But, Augusta, I am—Alexander Percy. Aye, for by no other name can you call me, unless I be—following the doctrine of Pythagoras, and it may be so, for his metamorphoses forget their former life—a bodily incarnation of Lucifer himself! Augusta, if there be a Satan, I am he!*

Oh, why today, when I was wandering by the seashore, why did I stop so before the full front of the Atlantic and gaze on the clouds rising far beyond it, and the sunlight on their sides, and their deep black shadows and changing, fleeting masses driven over all the soft azure sky; and why did I listen to the wind coming over the sea and whirling through my hair, and to the roar of the ocean dashing on the beach and surging so ceaselessly all around the shore? What was it for that my feelings were so roused, and my mind was so filled with thickly on-coming fancies? Why did I feel at once so unutterably miserable and roused to such a pitch of energetic Ambition? Yes, then I felt even as I do now, and what—what has my Ambition to do with the clouds and skies and seas of the shores of the Philosophers Isle? Why did I not speculate on what I saw, on the mighty works of creation and the greatness of the Creator, or on the nature and qualities of the sea, on the causes of its tides, on the mystery of its formation, the unknown depth of its waters, and the shores round which they may flow? I have imagination, why did I not think on things like these?

But no, I dreamed first of thee, Augusta. First, all my feelings dwelt on thee, and then they dwelt on all the west of Africa, and on all my prospects and all scenes of my past life, on Percy Hall and on Wellington's Town, and all old times past marshalled before me. Till, on a sudden, like a strong wind, the thoughts of still older times swept through my mind and without my being able to guess well how—the times of the Flood and after, Egypt, Nineveh, Babylon, the mighty nations of old, their empires, conquests, and the strange, dream-like nature of their might and glory. But I knew they had long passed away as finally as the waves which rolled over the sands *before me, and how, by two powers, the force of death and the power of man. Sosostris and Israel and Cyrus and Persia and the Greeks and Alexander must e'en appear to my sight, and I could not but ask: and what were these, and for what did they live, and what did they do?*

Carthage, Rome, Hannibal, Sulla, Caesar appeared with them, and then still mightier and still more powerful, Napoleon and the War. I could almost hear the thunder of Aveola, Marengo, the pyramids, Austerlitz, Jena, Wagram, Borodino, the mighty struggle of '14 and the resurrection of '15 close after this,* while sights and sounds created by my own soul were yet hovering before my eyes and lingering in my ears. Our own nation, its rise, the foundation and ongoings of the African kingdoms, the people, the days, the events among which I was born and which had not yet lapsed into mere pictures of remembrance but existed now, and were now capable of being acted on by the human hand and mind. These thoughts rush upon my mind and shut out directly every other thought unless they can connect it with themselves.

What am I, I ask myself, and I am not long in finding an answer. And what shall I do in this world, and what is this world? What are its one thousand million of inhabitants, what have they been doing from the creation till now, and what are they going to do? What will the next twenty years bring forward, and what shall I be at the end of that time?*

Our nation cannot stand still; it is now rising and hurrying forward, either upward or downward. Mighty events are every day unfolding themselves, and I know that Africa is the cradle of a new era in history. And is it for me to sit down and see the world directed by the coarse minds of twelve northern Adventurers, or by the routine intellect of twelve hundred southern noblemen, or by mere fate or events over which no one man has any control? And shall I return to Africa and settle at Percy Hall—Ah, I forgot. My father is alive—well, at Wellington's Town, enter Parliament under the auspices of His Grace, the Duke, give a silent vote, live splendidly, perhaps enter the Army and die Colonel Percy or Viscount Alnwick, a member of the Western Aristocracy? Or shall I be reconciled to my dear father, fight under his banner in the House of Commons for a seat in the ministry and, as he would do, having become Home Secretary, die a—why, like the other picture—a member of the Western Aristocracy?* Do you think, can you believe, that such will be my lot?

No! By Heaven, no! Oh, 'Sdeath; oh, Caversham, old and young; oh, Streighton, Montmorency, Gordon, Simpson! Well may you hope for my life and preservation. It is you, my father's phalanx, which I trust to make the stepping stone, the weapon of my advancement. But, oh, Wellington's Land,

Parry's Land, Ross's Land, Sneachiesland, Verdopolis, ye deserts of the east, and mountains of the north, and woods of the west, and plains of the south, thou City of Verdopolis, thou land of the French, ye islands of the sea. I know what you are now, but what is your future course, and will you be ever doomed to be cursed with the name of Percy? And if you, why not look at all—Africa, Asia, America, Europe, all the world! For all the world is open to me. May not all the world be mine? When I look at the world, at its state of blinded stupidity, its mighty shackles of religion,* the vast trammels of customs, laws, kings, kingdoms, aristocracies, factions, manners, morals—faugh! Hence, away with them all! Earth to earth,* dust to dust, ashes to ashes. All Creation groaneth and travaileth in pain, until now it is one damned ulcer which—how can I hope to cure?

But I will cure it; by my heart, I will!

Oh, Augusta, Augusta, would that you knew what at this moment I feel. I am a heap of wretched contradictions, thinking of impossibilities, dreaming and waking to a consciousness that all of which I've felt and thought and seen and read, of all the past, and present, and the future is a Slough of Despond. Misery and disappointment, and hope without fulfilment, and labour without recompense, and religion without righteousness, and—sorrowing without end.

Well, what is the future to me, Augusta, or the past? What do I care for aught but thee? When shall I see thee again? Thou knowest how thou hast enchanted me, and willingly I bear thy enchantment.

> Augusta, though I am far away*
> Across the dark blue sea,
> Still, eve and morn and night and day
> Will I remember thee
>
> And though I cannot see thee nigh
> Or hear thee speak to me,
> Thy look, thy voice, thy memory
> Shall not forgotten be.
>
> I stand upon this Island shore
> One single hour alone,
> And view the Atlantic swell before
> With sullen surging tone,
>
> And high in heaven the full moon glides
> Above the breezy deep,
> Unmoved by waves or winds or tides
> That far beneath her sweep.

She marches through the midnight air
   So silent and divine,
With not one wreath of vapour there
   To dim her silver shine,

For every cloud through ether driven
   Has settled far below,
And round the mighty skirts of heaven
   Their whitened fleeces glow;

They join and part and pass away
   Beneath the heaving sea,
So mutable and restless they
   So still and changeless she.

Those clouds have melted into air,
   Those waves have sunk to sleep
But clouds renewed are rising there
   And now waves rouse the deep.

How like the Chaos of my Soul
   Where visions ever rise,
And thoughts and passions ceaseless roll
   And tumult never dies.

Each fancy but the former's grave
   And germ of that to come,
While all are fleeting as the wave
   That chafes itself to foam.

I said yon full moon glides on high
   How'er the world repines,
And in its own untroubled sky
   Forever smiles and shines,

So dark'ning o'er my anxious brow,
   Though thicken cares and pain,
Yet in my heart, Augusta—thou
   Shalt still forever reign;

And thou are not yon wintry moon
   With its melancholy ray,
But where thou shinest is summer noon
   And bright and perfect day.

The Moon sinks down as sinks the night,
   Thou ever beamest on;
She only shines with borrowed light,
   But thine is all thine own!

And now, Augusta, fare thee well till thou meetest again, and rousest to strength and energy, thy

Alexander Percy.

I have given the whole of this long letter because I think it elucidates Northangerland's character and feeling at this time better far than anything I myself could say of them. We see displayed in it all that enthusiastic spring of mind, that ardent ambition which melancholy and grief had not yet withered within him, and all those ideas of the world and its condition and ideas of what he should accomplish in it and how he should attempt it which have since so direfully operated and which he is now endeavouring to carry further into effect. There runs also through this letter the strain of contradictory thinking of himself, the overpowering glimpses of this world's vanity and vexations which laid the foundation for his later miserable depression. But I have lingered long enough over this interesting mirror of his strange character. Let me now proceed with the details of its practical development.

The instant that Alexander found himself fairly transplanted into this new academic soil of the Philosophers Isle, he laid such effectual restraint upon his wayward wildness as to enter his class and pursue his studies with a vehemence and vigour that speedily brought down his fine healthy complexion to the true tint of student pallor. All the day, half the night, for the whole of the first month he was incessantly plunged into Greek, Latin, mathematics, and every branch of learning and science that his capacious intellect could lay grasp on.

His tutor, Dr Chillcott, an intimate friend of myself and, since that time, the respected prelate of Wellington's Town, thus writes to me in March:

'You told me, my dear Bud, that my new pupil would prove almost impossible to control. I believe 'impossible' was your very expression. And when he walked into my study one morning and abruptly announced himself as 'a Devil of the brood of Percy, come to receive lessons in the arts of destruction', I must say I looked at him with some feelings of unquietness on reflecting that I was to have charge of such a desperate young fellow as he seemed to be. Without waiting till I told him, he took his seat beside the fire and asked, with another oath, what the ——— was he to do to be saved?

I said, 'Leave off swearing, Sir, and your chance will be improved.' With a third exclamation he cried, 'I did not come here to bandy words with you or, by God, to be taught religion, either. I say, Doctor Bolus, I want a prescription, a tincture of humane letters. My brain is as empty this morning as your brandy bottle was at the end of last night.' Seeing that it was useless to grapple directly with his humour now, I determined to follow it; and, without answering him, I wrote down in the form and language of a prescription the studies he was to enter upon and the amount in which each dose of learning was to be taken each day.

He perused the paper with a moody look, which cleared up once or twice into a sneering laugh, and in conclusion said: 'Are you fit to teach me these trifles, for I hear some good fellows of your parts have their bellies lined a damned deal better than their skulls—have you eaten your brains, Master? Eh? I'll not be humbugged.'

'Sir,' I said, 'I am fitter to teach you than you are to learn.'

'How do you know that?' was his answer, and so I told him distinctly that his manner and language must be presently* altered to me, or he would not do long here. I pointed out to him the consequences which would follow obdurate conduct: disgrace and expulsion from college, a character broken, self-respect in himself and the respect of others towards him all fallen away, life begun without a single prospect of honour or happiness. And then I asked him what would follow.

'I'm the Devil,' he said, 'and I know what you say is true. Doctor, I'll call again this night', and so he rose and departed from the room.

At evening he returned again and sat with me for three or four hours engaged in conversation respecting the course he was to pursue, the branches of learning he was to follow, and what he already knew in them. I was truly astonished to see his powers of conversation, the wide extent of his information, and the depth of his knowledge in language and history. I told him that with the foundation he already had gained nothing but energetic attention was requisite to enable him to soar to the highest branches of human acquirements. But attention, I perceived (this, I told him), was what above all things must be exacted from him, for I feared his character was neither so calm nor so steady as I could wish it.

'Why do you think so?' he asked rather sharply.

'Your father, Sir, has informed me so and given me proof of it.'

'What proof?'

'Your marriage.' I didn't think that this string was one that could vibrate so. The word 'marriage' was hardly out of my lips when he started up and cursed and swore at me for a 'damned old fool who would be minding everybody's business but my own', told me to be damned with my advice, and left the room in a fury of rage. However, as you had informed me of his character, I determined to stomach this; and I have since had reason to believe that all his inflammable restlessness of reproof arises from the sting left in his mind by his father's harsh manner of sending him to this island, for from this first week of his arrival to the present time, a period of three months,* he has not for one moment relaxed from the most intense and ardent study. Night and day he is plunged in the very deepest fount of learning, and his astonishing application has reduced him almost to the paleness and tenuity of a senior wrangler. He is struggling for a seat in the July examination, and truly I think he will obtain a high one. I have entreated him to rest for a moment, but no; he only curses me if I speak of it. He says 'I will be first or die for it', and indeed, no pleasure, no dissipation seems to possess power over his unshaken perseverance. I think, Bud, you erred in describing him as you did in your last letter. At least, such is not the opinion which three months' experience has enabled me to form of him. I think him to be a young man of a stern, inflexible mind, ardent and resolute in his determination to gain distinction and having an astonishing command over a fiery and impetuous temper. His religious principles, judging from his behaviour at devotions, seem far more serious than those of the generality of our students, for a look of more real and unaffected seriousness I seldom see or an aspect of deeper attention. He associates with nobody and is as temperate and frugal as a *Spartan*. But he will be a great man and, I hope, a good one.

Such were the fruits of my excellent friend's experience to that date. Well, many a man has been almost as much deceived as this. At the conclusion of another three months, when the summer examination came on, Alexander Percy—in spite of some awkward rumours which had spread among the Colleges—still maintained among the heads of the University that character which has just been given of him; and on the awful day of trial, he bore the questioning and cross-questioning firmly, showed such rapid progress and astonishing acquirements in Greek, Latin, Hebrew, mathematics, history, and the sciences of war, demeaned himself* with such ready alertness, calm scholar-like possession, and with so triumphant a success in all the examinations that he was unanimously called the 'first freshman' on the list. And though several students were then from priority of time and such considerably in advance of him, yet everybody saw that efforts for another term like those for the one past would carry him up to the top of the tree.

Such success was not in the nature of events likely to pass off without detractors. Instead of the rumours which were afloat being quashed by this victory, they only thickened and wandered in on one's ears like motes which, the stronger the light, the faster thicken over the eye. They were disregarded for a time as the mere suggestions of envy and malice; and so in truth they were, but they were not the less well-founded. Dr Chillcott's letters to me soon began to show some signs of doubt as regards the character of his pupil.

In the month of August, a synod of the Grand University Council was suddenly called by the President, Manfred; and after a long deliberation during which sundry officers entered the hall with several persons from the Philosophers Town in custody—among others, an old man who had lately settled there and who was supposed to have more to do with the students than was at all warrantable—these custodees not reappearing but being placed under lock and key, the meeting broke up. And lo—an Order was issued for the immediate apprehension and imprisonment of 'Alexander Percy, of St Patrick's College', with

Arthur O'Connor	M. Barmsworth
St-J. G. Streighton	P. St John
G. J. Gordon	L. Caversham
J. Gordon	N. Gordon

and one hundred students from various colleges.*

No sooner was this order promulgated than the officers proceeded to act upon it; and amid dismay and suspense on the part of all the University, the delinquents were apprehended and secured. But, when the roll of numbers came to be told, it was found that all the persons mentioned in the list above given were wanting, absconded clean, evaporated. A reward of £500 was offered for the body of any one of them, and £5,000 for that of Alexander Percy.

Such an event as this was unprecedented, and accordingly the excitement it occasioned was unprecedented. Among those apprehended were many of the heirs and representatives of the highest and most noble families in the Twelves' countries, and others the most talented and brilliant of all its rising genius. The blight had particularly fallen on the youth of Wellington's Land. As it would not do to keep long everything in this suspense, His Highness, Manfred, promulgated the following manifesto.

In consequence of various reports and rumours from many quarters and all them tending to affix suspicion upon many of the most distinguished young men in the University, I, on the first of August, 1812, deemed it my duty to call a secret Grand Synod of the council of the Philosophers Isle, where were examined several of those men to whom the rise of the reports could chiefly be traced, and among them a highly suspicious and ill-disposed person who within the last six months had settled on the island. This man, upon being promised a reward and immunity, said he would declare the truth of all which he knew respecting the subject we were met to consider. Having given in his name as Robert Patrick King of Wellington's Town, he upon oath deliberately and advisedly taken swore that:

There exists at present in the Philosophers Isle a society composed of a number of the students and scholars of the entire University, whose object and intent will best be given in the oath which he declared that each member took upon his entrance into this society and which runs as follows.

'*I swear in the name of all Nature that from this day henceforth, without drawback or subterfuge, I devote my whole soul and body with all my mind and energy to*

Firstly, *the utter extermination of all religious creeds and modes of belief;*

Secondly, *the overthrow of the whole religion and theocracy of the Verdopolitan Union;*

Thirdly, *the utter extermination of all kingly governments;*

Fourthly, *the overthrow of the present Constitution and Twelveship of Africa;*

that in order to accomplish these ends, I enter as a member of the Society for the Creation of the World, the members of which society have all sworn the oath which I do here swear, and are determined as I am to

(a) keep this association a profound secret to all the world,

(b) to consider each member when he leaves this island still a member wherever he may settle or whatever he may do,

(c) to pay yearly into the funds of this Society £50 of current money,

(d) to keep up a constant communication with the president and council of the year running,

(e) to leave all the regulations of the Society to that president and council so long as they continue in office, and I swear to perform all that I have promised—so help me, my mind.'*

Furthermore, the deponent, R. P. King, declared that this Society elected officers who were to hold office annually, that all the members were to strive to enter Parliament as soon as they could legally do it, and that their

President must be in Parliament at the age of twenty-one, and that there he should control their movements, subject to the decisions of the Council and whatever it should determine.

Furthermore, the deponent swore that the intent of the Society was to form a nucleus among the rising men of the Empire for the spread of revolutionary and republican opinions; that they were determined to proceed in their open courses legally, and as if acting independently as thinking and reflecting men, while underhand they should form a compact, well-ordered, and energetic association.

Upon being pressed to declare the names of the officers and originators and members of this Society, the deponent demurred till, as he expressed himself, 'Good terms were settled' with him. Upon this being confirmed, he declared further upon oath that the originator of the association was Alexander Percy, of St Patrick's, that it was performed in May of the present year, that the Society Council was composed of [here the manifesto enumerated the names of those heirs of Wellington's Land whom I have above given] and of the members he gave a written list of which the following is a copy [this copy, comprising all the membership, of course, I cannot give here], that they met once every month in the vaults under St Michael's Church,* and the Council once a week at Mr Percy's rooms.

The deponent demurred to give the names of the Society's treasurers, as they were not members of the University; and therefore, we had no power over them. His demurrer was accepted.

Upon examining, cross-examining, and searching into all the minutiae of this business, I found that the whole of what this witness stated was substantially and perfectly correct. He was thereupon ordered instantly to quit the island, now and forever banished; and Orders were promulgated by me for the detention and imprisonment of every man mentioned in his examination.

Judgement will be given on the case on 17 August, 1812.

MANFRED.

This affair was truly awful, as it showed the tremendous character of the future premier of Angria and the effects which his wild ambition had wrought in secret. Yes, reader, here were the effects of the noble and enthusiastic spirits that earlier were developed, as in the letter I quoted a few pages back. All the University, I may add all Africa, was struck with horror at the wild and extravagant madness displayed by this hundred of her youthful and rising suns.

I cannot tell what my feelings were when the news reached Africa.

All the thoughts which filled my mind on the future course of my strange pupil now flashed on me with resistless vehemence. I remember that I dropped the paper and cried out 'What will he do next?' However, as he and the officers of the Society could not be found, judgement was delayed till they could be secured by the civil power of any kingdom they might be lodged in; and on 17 August, judgement was given to the following effect. 'That all the members of the society be fined £5,000 each and be imprisoned six months in the University dungeons; or, in default of payment, they suffer expulsion from the University and the erasure of all their degrees, titles, or honours therein. That the members of the Council be fined £10,000, with six months' imprisonment, or instant expulsion from their college with the erasure of their degrees, honours, and titles. That the President be either imprisoned one year with, after, expulsion and incapacity to attain any public office, Parliament, or orders in the Church, Army, or Navy of Africa, or that he pay a fine of £50,000 and be degraded from all the last term's honours and stations.'

The announcement of this terrible sentence was followed by instant action. Twenty of the members paid their fines. Eighty were expelled from the University. As to the Council and the President, all waited in suspense to see how they would act. Their punishment was tremendous. In the latter part of August, a letter was received from the Government, stating that no one knew where they were, or what they could do in the matter, and their assigned punishment* was so high as to involve severe consequences in either sentence. But I must now relate how that group acted.

On the fifth day of August, 1812, there assembled a party in one of the saloons of Lady Augusta Percy at her mansion in Wellington's Town which if not numerous was certainly as striking in its character and aspect as could well be imagined. This saloon, then, a splendid and mirrored room, was carefully closed in, the great curtain hanging before the windows and the lustre from the ceiling shedding its rich yellow light all over the hangings and furniture of the noble apartment.

On an elevated sopha reclined the stately Augusta Percy, the wife of the revolutionary student; her splendidly attired form and sparkling Italian eye giving back her own aspect of Juno-like grace and dignity. Near her sat the Earl of Caversham with his bald forehead and suspicious courtliness of manner, looking with a hard, cold, and unaristocratic keenness at the assembly. Mr Thomas Steaton, the steward of Mr Percy, stood smiling sardonically, Mr William Montmorency and the Counsellor looking ditto at him as if the two execrable traitors were laughing at their own Judas-like conduct of their dear friend or master's interests. Counsellor Hector Montmorency, with Sir Thomas Streighton at the table over a pile of written papers and ledger-like, red-backed volumes, was standing looking both eager and aghast at a little shrivelled old man in top coat and top boots of the shabbiest order who remained near the door, talking in a coarse, hasty, and impudent manner, garnishing his discourse by a comfortable flourish of the fingers and nose and a more than due mixture of oaths and execrations. As he went on in his declamation, the company waxed more and more aghast till, he said:

'And Aw aloon em escaped to tell ye!'

All looked at each other with an appearance of blank dismay.

'Come,' said Lady Augusta, rising, while her dark eyes seemed to flash literal fire as she spoke. 'Come now, rouse yourselves. You see what has transpired. You see the detestable treachery of this infernal old villain. But what is done, you know, cannot be undone. What is to be done is what we must here decide upon. Alexander is ruined forever. You, Caversham, lose £30,000; Simpson loses £20,000. You, gentlemen, lose your sons. I lose—but we know our losses, so let us know our gains, too. Oh, that you felt as I do, and that execrable master of yours, Steaton, would not live another day! 'Sdeath, will you—?'

'Eea, eea, eea, eea, say aat, say aat, Aw will, Aw will; a commission, a commission!'

Hullaballoo...

'No, no, no!' cried the company at once. Lady Augusta seemed about to transfer her anger on to the company present, when the Earl of Caversham spoke. 'Now I am Treasurer of the Society. Its funds are in mine and Simpson's hands. If we pay the fines, they will amount to a loss on our part of £100,000. If we do not pay, we lose £60,000, our sons, Alexander—our hope and glory—and all the prospect of unlimited joys in the world to come. You all know well about young Percy: £50,000 payable with smashing interest on the death of his father.* Now, if we don't pay his fine on this damned occasion, he will be barred from title to his father's estates; the usury comes to the ground, and all is blown up between him and us forever. You see how the case stands. But if we do pay the fines, we shall lay it to his account. We'll lay £100,000 more, lent on interest, mind; and payable on the death of his father. The estate can afford the loss of a cool £200,000; mark you all this, eh?'

All present did mark it, and Augusta said, 'And his father shall die soon, that I declare to you.'

A paper was drawn up stating that Lord Caversham had lent Mr Alexander Percy £100,000 on interest of 20 per cent per annum, payable by instalments or on the estates of his father as soon as he should inherit them. Mr 'Sdeath was despatched with the bills to Stumps Isle where Alexander lay hid with the members of the Council. On the first of October, Alexander delivered himself and themselves up to justice, paid the fine of £50,000 himself, and £50,000 for them, to the perfectly electrified astonishment of all present.

Upon laying down these terrific bills, he said, 'And now damn you all, heads and feet together! I'll enter as a student again, and see if next January I don't bear away the palm. Oh, Manfred, indeed you have ruined me privately, but publicly you have made me great in deed.'

Truly did this strange young man speak, for he saw the dreadful embarrassment the payment of his debt must occasion at his father's death. And he felt in his own heart an intensity of hatred to the lenders, Caversham and Simpson, when he saw the crafty manner in which they had made a good business of this dreadful discovery.

Alexander was now known, emphatically, in the university. He was watched with the utmost vigilance, but he shut himself up and literally, day and night, studied to recover the ground he had lost and to gain so much more to satisfy his revengeful feelings, as he thought how they would be forced to give the palm to him whom, of all, they would most willingly refuse it.

The Society was quite blown up by now, but matters were hushed after the exaction of the tremendous fines, amounting in all to £200,000. No one knew how these fines were paid so readily. No one knew the strange ramifications of this conspiracy against Africa, and no one knew what years of blood and tumult it would ultimately occasion. No. And no one else knows this, now.

On the first of January, 1813, Alexander Percy came up to the examination, almost fainting, deathly pale, emaciated to a skeleton, and his eyes fired as with near insanity. It was at this expense that he that day astounded all the most learned men in Africa, outdistanced the most able competitors, and in that hall of perfect impartiality—

though feared and hated and usually frowned upon—he for his splendid success in languages, mathematics, history, and all other acquirements of learning received the splendid honour of SENIOR WRANGLER for the year 1812 in the University of the Philosophers Isle. He did not hear this word pronounced, for he had fallen, fainted, from the fatigue of the successive examinations of three days, superadded to his almost superhuman exertions since the fatal month of August.

The Life of Field Marshal the Right Honourable
ALEXANDER PERCY

Earl of Northangerland,
Lord Viscount Elrington, Lord Lieutenant of Northangerland,
Late Prime Minister of Angria, Major General in The Verdopolitan
Service &c, &c, &c, &c

By Sir John Walter Bud, Bart.,

Major General* In the Verdopolitan Service

VOL II

June 3, 1835*

[Chapter I]

I now, reader, commence the second volume of my 'Life of Northangerland'; and I commence it at a time when your interest in it will be stronger than the work itself will warrant. I know that no person looks with greater interest upon the present situation of Northangerland, no one knows more of it than I do now; and when I see this terrible ending to so long a career of misery, this last fatal wreck of all power and hope and happiness, it makes me look upon him at this time with a shuddering sensation at his agony, and upon his life with wonder at its stormy darkness.

And now, then, feeling as I do the desolateness of his present existence torn at once from all power and distinction, deserted by every one of the millions who lately looked up to him as their saviour, proclaimed to the world as a convicted and degraded traitor, forbid on a penalty which makes an attempt impossible to touch or even look on any of his few sources of ambition and exertion, the scornful execrations of all men ringing in his ears, the triumphs of his slaves or enemies flashing on his eyes and the bitter upbraidings of an evil conscience rending his heart, and all the despair of his stricken spirit poisoning every feeling of his mind—I say that when I so strongly feel all of what he is, I recur with a double sorrow and astonishment to the recital of what he has been. Whether the cup of agony shall pass away from Northangerland or be filled again, I know not. But truly, he has already drunk of it often and deep and long.

Now miserable as at present all the world sees Northangerland to be, yet when I look back over all the events in his life which I am now about to detail, I myself know, and I must let my readers know, that Alexander Percy has before this been as miserable and more despairing still. Indeed, when I run over in my mind the heads of the chapters in his life, I wonder how he has at all survived its events, how he is still able now to face pain or sorrow.

With the commencement of this volume, readers, I am about to recount an incident which it will be most disagreeable to me to write or to think about. Through all the last volume, you saw that I was chiefly engaged in describing the expanding mind and feelings of Alexander Percy, latterly only in his marriage with Lady Segovia and his unsuccessful association of republicans; just entering upon a glimpse of the train of events to which that mind and those feelings were bearing. I showed just dimly among what a set of friends and helpers he had got entangled. But now I shall show something more, and oh, what tongue can tell, what pen can write the latter dreadful wickedness of the higher classes around Wellington's Town? Yet, all their crimes shall shortly fade before the blackness of Percy's own.

I lately, in conversation, heard a foppish* person of this city declare that to seek true poetry it is necessary to shut oneself out from humanity, from the stir and bustle of the world, from the commonplace wearisomeness of its joys, sorrows, and greatnesses, to look in solitude into one's own soul and conjure up there some visionary form alien from this world's fears or sympathies. I have heard another person of the weaker sex say that it is the music of humanity which constitutes the essence of poetry; but it is a music in which trumpet and organ must have no sound, where everything real in this world's ongoings must give place to some pretty tale of true or false love or the orisons of some simple maiden, or the gambols of fairies in a flowery vale. I have heard, too, of another person, and of the shorter sex, too, who though I could not clearly understand her notions, yet seemed from her likes and dislikes in poetry to believe that everything is to be placed below that rambling story of versification, which doles out by the thousand lines descriptions of nature, clouds, rocks, and ruins—wild forms and mighty visions of half-forgotten times and people, dim old traditions—but nothing, not a glimpse of real life or real feelings; not a wind, not a breeze of that glorious humanity which carries with it some soul-rousing or heart-depressing vision of what a mortal may feel or see, some flash of that stir and glory which every age has presented to us, something of the actual shadow or sunshine which I know to be the greatest foundation of what I call poetry.

Well, let these three classes of people think a little more, and they will surely see the littleness of their doctrines. I for one will always fly from the sickly tales of mental concoctions or monstrosities, sentimental decoctations or airy fairyism, and shadowy fancies of what has never been, a Barmecide feast* which can never satisfy my hunger—to what has been, is and will be, to what I am now writing, to his very life, take it in public or private, to this very man, to the greatest, the mightiest poetry:* Alexander Percy and the history of Africa during the last eventful twenty years.

Reader, excuse this digression. But it was forced upon my mind when I thought that here, through all the ensuing pages, there will be no visionary legend, no wild tradition for the imagination to rise on, nothing of light lyric fancy, nothing of mere mental bubble-blowing. I shall detail nothing but the stern misfortunes and coldness and blight of ordinary life, the struggles of a great mind bowed down and often prostrated beneath the world, with a side glance at the mighty ongoings of empires and politics and war. My reason for speaking at all about poetry now is my knowledge of the fact that poetry is something in language which rouses or sways the mind to itself. Northangerland's life does so, therefore Northangerland's *Life* is poetry. To begin, then....

My first volume concluded with a chapter which described the consequences of Alexander Percy's education in the Philosophers Isle, and showed the discovery of that wild scheme of the Revolutionary association, which I am convinced was first set on foot by the Earl of Caversham, old Montmorency, Gordon, Simpson, and all the circle of the fallen spirits in the West.* They authorized Mr 'Sdeath to give young Percy a sketch of the institution, and that mind so fertile in the cultivation of evil produced the secret Society for the Creation of the World. I need not again detail the consequences of this conduct. How old 'Sdeath discovered the whole to the President of the University, what vigorous measures the Grand Synod took to root out the evil, and how the sentence past wrung £200,000 from young Percy's future property and expelled from their colleges eighty of the principal young men in Africa. I have brought into notice the diabolical manner in which Caversham, Steaton, and Simpson wound the coils round their victim by relieving him from the terrible embarrassment of fines which he could never otherwise pay, disbursing all themselves and agreeing with him to repay themselves with an usurious interest when he should come into possession of his father's estates. Percy saw that that wished-for day would now prove a day of double gloom, for then, at a blow, half his property must fall into the hands of usurers, and leave the claims of rank, station, extravagance, and waste to eat up soon the rest.

This volume I must commence with another and yet darker subject, where my prayers cannot be heard for the blood which cries for vengeance. It is with extreme reluctance that I approach this year of Percy's life and take my pen, to indite nothing but crime and misfortune. Oh, how soon, how shortly after its rising, was that Sun of Brightness hidden in clouds and storms!

After the disclosure and punishment of the secret Society in the Autumn of 1812, little further was heard in Africa of Alexander Percy, save that he had re-entered into his studies with even greater earnestness than before. He rarely wrote to anyone except his mother and his Lady. Communications to the latter, of course, I did not see, but Lady Helen, knowing the interest I felt in him and the time I had bestowed on him, often showed me extracts from those that were addressed to her. I have forgot to mention that about a week after Alexander had left for the Philosophers Isle, and while I was preparing for my departure from the Hall, Mr Percy called me to his study. As I entered, the old scoundrel 'Sdeath was concluding a tissue of bitter falsehoods respecting me. Without telling me to sit down, Mr Percy rose and furiously swore that 'You are a damned rascal, eating of my bread and drinking of my wine without the shadow of a service rendered to me! You have afforded facilities for my damned son's damned marriage, and you wish to live on me now, when your pupil has been taken away from you. Do you mean to teach *me* next, Sirrah?'

'No, sir, my rival tutor here seems to have taught you too well.'

'Begone, sir! I say, begone.'

And as the Master concluded, the Man broke out: 'And Aw say begone, yaw insolent upstart; it's yaw that's done mischief and misguided—.'

'Silence, King,' interrupted his Master, 'the fool misguided himself.'

'No, sir,' I replied. 'It was you two who misguided him.' And so saying, I left the room and the house together. From that moment my connection with the family of the Percys was dissolved, but my interest in their fate was undiminished and my gaze kept upon them as before.

I have mentioned that during the winter of 1812 the fears and hazards consequent upon the discovery and punishment of the Society for the Creation of the World had apparently subsided, though deeply indeed had they sown the seeds of sorrows and dangers to come. Alexander pursued his studies with impetuous fervour at the University, and his friends and connections dived downward* in their schemes of wickedness at home.

In the last page of the former volume of this Life, I showed my reader a glimpse of the interior of that splendid pile, The Segovia Palace, Wellington's Town; and the transactions there in progress regarding the freeing (?!) of Alexander Percy from the vengeance of law must add a new proof to the truth of that proverb which says that a fair outside often conceals loathsomeness within. Now, in the same pillared and lighted mansion, I must open Scene the First of the forthcoming tragedy.

It was wild and wintery in a dark January night, but neither storm nor darkness could enter the magnificent saloon where Lady Augusta Percy reclined on a sopha by a glowing fire and beneath the radiance of a noble chandelier. The still, solemn folds of the great curtains and hangings of velvet from cornice to carpet shut out all the storm, whose dreary gusts were howling through the western metropolis. Her Ladyship sat in solitary luxuriousness with one of her youthful husband's letters in her hand. She had just perused it, and now her soul seemed absorbed in reflecting on it; yet, whether her thoughts were pleasant or mournful could hardly be understood from those dark, lustrous eyes, whose glance either in joy or sorrow beamed with the same fervent glow. But if I speak of Lady Augusta, I can hardly restrain myself from entering into prolix minuteness and speaking with too much enthusiasm of one whose virtues I fear have long since been found wanting in the balance.

But my reader must bear with me when he reflects upon what I am, and how these thoughts must affect me. I have attained an age in which man is fonder of looking back than forward. I am an old retainer of the Percy family; and before I had attained the station I now move in, for fifteen years I daily strove to maintain there,* with pride, my honesty and independence. And few know how difficult it was to do so while yet looking up to these people I write of as my superiors and as among the loftiest in the Western Aristocracy. But more at heart and to the point, whoever has not felt it can hardly know the feelings with which an old retainer looks back to the buoyant morning of his life and the days he spent in the service of a great family.

Their antiquity, their traditions, their person, their marriages and intermarriages and secret history and strange whispers and gloomy glimpses: all are wrapt up in his soul with his own nearest thoughts and imaginations. I could readily feel these impressions always, and was not the Percy family calculated to inspire them? Was not its fate calculated to keep these impressions alive until my dying day? While I lived at the Hall and the town residences of Mr Percy, much, indeed, I suffered calculated to leave bitter feelings in my mind. But the rememberances of these feelings *now* leaves sensations which I cannot very readily describe—does not my reader enter into what I feel?*

And in spite of those scenes, though rather perhaps aided by them, the noble heart, the unvarying condescension of Lady Helen Percy, the wondrous spirit of her unhappy son, the mysterious family, the impassioned fervour of his Italian wife, these things bound me to those chequered days. The total breaking up of the Percy family when Alexander Percy left Africa, with my leaving the west at the same time to reside in Verdopolis, have separated all this first portion of my life from this second; and this, too, has added—how strongly!—to throw this solemn feeling over old, bygone days. How long could I run on, in what I am digressing about! How I could describe, in the tales I have to tell, these high and ancient houses, as a servant who remembers the personages he held communion with as higher than any he sees around him now. The great Duke's family, the House of Wellesley, with the dark Pakenham, that double marriage which then was so much spoken of, the youthful brides and especially our gracious Queen. The Humes, whom another pen than mine,* engaged on later but not lower subjects, has since thrown to other minds the same troubled poetry that they have in mine.

But I must end this digression, which I began by apologizing for my language respecting Lady Augusta Percy. My apology is before my readers. Such a being, so lofty, so lovely, despite her many and reckless crimes; is she not one of the very chief of these visions which are passing before me? Her life, her death—but let me hasten to detail them and that dreary tragedy whose scenes I trembled to behold.

'Does he say that he cannot return as yet, that he is involved beyond extrication? He shall return, if what he speaks of alone hinders him. I know its difficulty. But, oh, my dear Alexander! What would I *do* to see thee once more. And who knows thee, who is worthy to love thee but me? I know how many in this city and in Verdopolis hate me for taking what they would industriously vie for. But I have seized this prize from them, like others, and I laugh in my soul at their envious disappointment. It is the old cry again. "She, indeed! How insolent!" and "What a fool he is." What fools *they* are! And how many of those haters have made their calls on me this morning—and would fill this house tonight if I said the word!'

So Augusta spoke to herself, her full, rich voice giving bitter earnestness to her words, her lips curling in a smile of derision till again she gazed on the letter and her dark eyes filled with impatient tears.

As she sat, leaning her forehead on her arm and tracing the hurried lines which lay opened on the sopha, a young lady suddenly entered the room, wrapt in a large shawl that sparkled with rain.

'Oh, Augusta,' she said, 'it is a wild night! But I am come to tell you news which, when I heard, I directly put on my hat and shawl and hastened here through the streets with only a footman to guide me. I could not think of waiting for the carriage, and my father with the others will be here directly. What a spectacle I must be!'

So, standing before a large mirror, she took off her hat, shook the raindrops from her hair and, arranging it again, proceeded with what she had to say. But it is fit first that I should speak something of one whom well I knew and to whom, while sitting on my knee, I had often told stories.

Miss Harriet O'Connor* was the eldest daughter of Sullivan O'Connor, Esquire, and only sister of the unfortunate Arthur O'Connor whose life has just so miserably ended.* Mr O'Connor's other children were by a later wife; these two, by his first, Miss Woodfall, old Mr Percy's first cousin. Harriet was now about eighteen years, a handsome girl with red hair and commanding features. She had always been her father's favourite, was hated by her stepmother, and grew up amid constant scenes of quarrelling with her and crossings from her half-sisters. Her brother Arthur, with all his culpable wildness and evil principles, had a sort of good nature which he never used abroad but rattled through with at home; and as he stood by 'Mr Harry' in all the tempests at Woodfall House, 'Mr Harry'* in return stood by him till his father sent him to the College School at Verdopolis. Then 'Mr', or I ought to say 'Miss Harriet', was left alone.

Poor girl. She had not what she much needed, a director and a real friend. When I think of her and her life, I can hardly keep down a sigh. Her father indulged her, and her mother treated her harshly; for the first she felt grateful, the last she laughed at and forgot. I used often to call at Woodfall House or their residence in town; and my attention from the time she was eight years old was always attracted to the little girl with the curled red hair who, if she came in crying, was sure to go laughing out. But when, several years after, she returned permanently from school (for her stepmother successfully resisted her having a governess at home), when she returned with the finished form and rising grace of seventeen, I began to think more deeply of her prospects and her mind, and from that time my forebodings were never bright concerning Harriet O'Connor.

At first sight the impression she produced on strangers was not entirely agreeable. She was totally without the restraint of pride, and animated and cheerful but sometimes blunt and sudden in her address. And though of most pleasant conversation, still her egotism, even when ridiculing herself, and many erroneous and unusual notions which she constantly repeated, sometimes offended those who did not know her. She grieved those who did. But the friendly look of her eye and the odd way in which she shook her acquaintance so heartily by the hand, with her evident pleasure in seeing again those whom she had seen before, forced many to feel toward her otherwise than harshly. And though she was possessed somewhat of vanity and thought well of herself, her plain dark frock and pearl necklace most seldom intruded it on others.

But this is only the surface of her character; there was something lying underneath. This seeming impossibility of feeling anger, this complete freedom from pride, this unguarded abruptness was not the strangest feature of her mind. She was not altogether what she seemed, for underneath lay a heart filled with strong impressions, a mind overgrown with eradicable errors, habits of constant thinking which always end in thinking wrongly. But also—and mark the folly of judging, entirely from outward appearances, feeling always stretched and far too often troubled and restless and melancholy—I am convinced that her mind was of the highest order but rendered useless through want of training to the right. I mean not as regarded education, for her information was remarkably extensive.

One night as I was proceeding toward the House, I met her on the lawn, looking steadfastly up to the stars. After her 'Ah, Mr Bud, how do you do?' she said, 'In what direction should Christians turn to pray?'

I answered, 'Miss Harriet, I hope you are not scoffing?'

'Scoffing! Do you think I do not believe?'

'You have often spoken wrongly on the subject.'

'Indeed, what should I do if I did not believe in religion? I should have nowhere to look to, often, and I can't afford to part with my only refuge. But, Sir, I dare not call it a refuge, because if the Bible is true it is no refuge for me; and again, not for all the Bibles or religions in the world would I give up the opinions I hold. I have prayed to be guided right and have afterwards found that nothing could guide me but where I wished.'

At another time, she confessed, 'I am very melancholy, Sir, for I feel as if I was not made to be what I am. Everything that I do from my heart changes from what I wish it to be; and I can see that nobody thinks of me as they should do, nobody knows me. I do not care for my mother's scolding or the ill will of anybody else, and yet there is nothing I so much want, nothing I feel so glad for as any person's good will. If I can feel sure that anyone, no matter how low, thinks well of me, it is to my mind a delightful pleasure. But it is one I seldom feel. I am not quite sure whether all who know me do not hate me. I say that I was not meant to be what I am! And because no one does know me, is it well, do you think,

"To be alone on earth as I am now?"

But, Sir, at any rate, as the author of that line says,

"Before the chastener humbly let me bow
Our *hearts divided* and our *hopes* destroyed!"'

And so she turned away, while ere another hour I saw her among her mother and sisters, harshly abused by them and answering in a most bitter passion, but shortly declaring she would give in to them and consider herself worse than they did.

A page back, I mentioned her twice under the name of 'Mr Harry' rather than Miss Harriet, and for this reason: it came upon my ears as the well-remembered name bestowed on her in the very time I was writing of those who used it.* When she was seen associating with such friends and meddling with such matters as she did, who was her guide and director? Augusta di Segovia! This lofty and wicked woman saw what Harriet was; and Harriet, knowing her talents and admiring her splendour, and—as was her usual custom—captivated with her mode of setting the world aside in scorn at its customs and reproaches, spoke her mind to her with double freedom. She defended her in company with reddened cheek and sparkling eye not by extenuating her faults but by praising them till the smiles of one half the room and the frowns of the other threw her (and more than once did I see it) completely off her guard in a passion of embarrassment.

She could not long be in Lady Augusta's society without being in society which truly she ought to have kept out of. But this she could not do; and accordingly Lord Caversham, Mr Montmorency Senior and Junior, Mr MacArthur, Lord Edward Vernon, these she spoke of and to as friends and acquaintances. And if a caution was breathed to her respecting them, the usual showing up and exaggerating of vices as virtues stopped the mouth of the friend in complete dismay. Nor was this all the danger that covered the path of one who was formed in a higher mould than hundreds happier than her. There was another thing which I saw, soon; and when others perceived it, they counted her as little else than lost.

Always, where the Lady and the gentlemen I have above mentioned were, there had been one other among them, the one whose life I am now writing. A young man most noble in form, breathing in all that restless whirl of feelings whose settling has left the dreary waste we now see. I recall vividly to my mind how, when I was seated in the drawing room at Mr O'Connor's town residence conversing with Miss O'Connor, her attention seemed constantly directed to the group where young Mr Percy, with manner different from the person who will recur to my Verdopolitan readers, was talking earnestly and rapidly to Augusta Segovia and Lord Edward Vernon. In a little while, he advanced towards us. Then Harriet's face turned pale, and he said, 'Now, Hal, why so shy this morning?'

She exclaimed emphatically, 'Why d'ye call me Hal, Percy?* I might as well call you Alexandrina. You have no right to do it. I get called down enough for you—bored and scolded—while I act far wiser than my advisers. D'ye really think my name's Henry? If it were, I should know what to do.'

'Eh—call him out, perhaps?' interjected Lord Edward, lounging against the mantelpiece.

'Stuff. But I must call myself in!' answered Harriet, and Percy, who had stood in thought, muttered *sotto voce* 'Damnation' and strode to the piano.

A short silence ensued, when Harriet cried, 'Forgive me, Sir. I have spoken harshly. I *did not* mean it.'

'It is I who ought to ask forgiveness,' he replied seriously. But the entrance of other company put a stop to the subject, and I left the room, not admiring the succession of visitors.*

Certainly you will think that Miss Harriet O'Connor ought to have been silent to those to whom Captain Bud did not think it proper to speak. But, no, and with fervour I say it; Mr Jeremiah Simpson, Mr Charles Steaton,* and Mr Robert 'Sdeath had business with Alexander which Miss O'Connor very fully understood and very warmly entered into.

On looking over what I have written, I find that I have digressed so much and to such little purpose that it is incumbent upon me to resume the course of my narrative.

'Now,' said Harriet, turning from the glass. 'Now then, I am handsome again, as I can be, at any rate, although—but what is that, Augusta? A letter, eh? From whom? Alexander? Do give it me, do let me look at it!'

'My dear Harriet, what made you visit me in a night so wild as this? You forget yourself. What is 'Sdeath coming for, and who beside?'

'Why, I have the most delightful news to tell you could imagine, that old scoundrel—but do let me see the letter. How is he?'

'What is the letter to thee? He is ill, and I know not how to cure him.'

'Ill! What? Both at once?'

'Art thou ill, or am I? Which does thou join as both?'

'The old rascal has broken his head!'

'What! Who? The old devil—do you mean?'

'Yes. He was fox hunting this morning; and the ground being so splashy from the sleet, as he was checking his horse to threaten a farmer guilty of slaying a fox t'other night in his poultry yard, his horse missed his footing in the sludge and down he came with his rider beneath him. They took him up completely senseless, and he was conveyed through the city in a chaise this evening to Percy Hall. He never spoke, and they say he's dead; but the devil is hard to kill at any time. Would to heaven he may be!'

'Sancta Maria! I would die to have it so! Hast thou deceived me, child? Oh, Jesus! When do they come?'

Lady Percy rose and paced through the room with clasped hands while Harriet, bending over the table, was eagerly perusing the letter. As she laid it down, saying 'What would he have done? This comes just in the nick of time', the door opened to admit a servant announcing visitors. These followed close on the announcement: a great dark man with a squint, and Lord Vernon, Lord Caversham, Mr O'Connor, and young Montmorency.

'By God!' swore the harsh leader of the group. 'It's done at last, and my old friend has nabbed him, however!'

'What, Mr Simpson, then you've been dead yourself, if Death is an old friend of yours.'

'Be silent, Harriet,' interrupted Lady Percy. 'Simpson! Caversham! Is it true? Oh, Vernon, is he dead, indeed?'

'Dead as a door nail,' answered the Earl of Caversham. 'I saw him lifted into the carriage, white as a sheet—who, when he was he, was black as a thundercloud.'

'If he is not, we shall soon see,' said Mr Simpson, 'for we have despatched our dearly beloved 'Sdeath up to the Hall after the carriage, and he promised to bring us down a faithful report of how the balance stood, besides, if doubtful, a shrewd guess as to which way should kick the beam. But by the powers of villainy, we are likely to get our money sooner than I expected. But what's Miss Harriet walking about so troubled for? Felt a little twinge of affection for the deceased—heart-broken, eh?'

'No, Sir, no, Mr Simpson. But—but I thought after reading that letter—is Alexander to remain in ignorance of this event so long, so many days? How miserable, and him so surrounded with fears! I was thinking that he sha'nt, and Sir, for God's sake, let us give him intelligence directly. Let us think about nothing else. Something may happen if we delay. I—I'll go myself! And that directly, I'll go tomorrow!'

'Well, that's considerate, now! Ha, ha, ha! The young devil! Let him find it out himself! But "*A Dios*"! Doesn't thou know there's such an art as that of letter writing?'

'Oh, it won't tell all, or half!'

'Which I want to tell him,' thrust in Lord Vernon.

'Stuff, my Lord. Who'll go? Cannot I go, Augusta?—nay? Well, Caversham!'

'What? Harriet!'

'How will you send him word?'

'Segovia, Mr Henry wants to set sail tomorrow for the Philosophers Isle to acquaint your innocent infant with the demise of his father and give him a little fraternal admonition as to the manner he should bear it.'

'What is that, girl! Whither do you want to go? Have your senses fled up with the sins of that scoundrel? Know, child, that if anyone in particular shall go to the Philosophers Isle, it shall be myself and not thee. Your ignorance, or insolence, is too great...'

'I will not be silent, now. I will write to him this instant. He shall not suffer from your cold-blooded selfishness!'

'Thou young fool, do you know that I am in the room? But', she drawled, 'my dear Caversham, when does King arrive? I cannot feel easy till he be here. Oh, if the wretch be dead, that, that is all I want. I pray for nothing more!'

'You forget yourself, Madam,' said Simpson. 'I trust you don't pray for even that. By Satan! A bishop himself would swear that such a prayer would lack an answer, and so will I, on my heart! But—here he comes.'

A tantalizing hawing and scraping was heard at the door. The gentlemen stood still, the two ladies were ready to fly and throw the door open. The ugly old fiend they wished for entered. Wiping his nose with his coat cuff, he began with a satanic leer.

'Soa, yaw're met to consult, are ye? But yaw'd better gat away hoam. He's nother dead nor like to be dead. He opened his maath and spaak, just after Aw'd getten into 'th roam. But, oh, he wor beside himsell! He did talk wide! He swure! Eh, how he did swear! Yaw, me leddy and yar bonny husband. He damned ye as oft as he oppened his maath. There's no body i this roam but he tilted off to 't fur spot* in the emptying of a pint pot. Dr Duncan bled abaat temples; and when Aw left, he wor mending fearful weel. Yaw better be agoing, for there'll nought be done this last. Yaw're fit for so little that there's no use trying on ye. Yaw mun sleep ower't as well's ye can, my Leddy, for Aw sudn't wonder but he'll be stirring by this week end!'

'By this weekend!' Augusta said unconsciously, and with eyes to which tears would have given relief.

'By me soul, he will, and I'll stick by it and dee by it' (*sotto voce*: '*Hang 'em, they ern't worth a rotten filbert!*')

Simpson, whose shaggy eyebrows had bent blacker while 'Sdeath spoke, burst out in a loud, contemptuous fit of laughter.

'Simpson,' said Harriet, weeping, 'dare you rejoice at it! You know how embarrassed Alexander is, and you ought to know how this turn must disappoint us.'

'And I do, Miss. But I laughed at the old gentleman here. I'm guessing at his meaning! Eh, old boy? We are acquainted, aren't we?'

'Aw knaaw nought abbaat it. Do not trouble me. Yawr all fools thegither. Od! Awm plaused at o' me life ower ye.'*

'Good God!' said Augusta passionately. 'And was the event so near completion only to pass off and leave me more miserably defeated than before? Was I to feel such hope and see such a glimpse of happiness, only to be hurried again into disappointment and suspense? It cannot be! I will not bear such a succession of evils! I will overcome so unnatural a tyrant; let them not speak to me of religion and laws, I care for neither. I have trampled on both ere now, and yet never for such a cause as this. Shall I hesitate when all I care for is concerned; do I feel cowardice when I am to save Alexander from ruin? Myself from utter ruin? Oh, if *thou* wert here, if *thou* could'st know what I am thinking of, I should find aid equal to the enterprise. Yet, without thee I will do what could but be done even with thee, and it shall be done to aid thee!

'Old man, you look as if you comprehended me. I can trust your heart of steel, I feel that I can rely on you. If I know you, Simpson—(but I rashly venture myself among those who really hate me). Oh, that others could possess my mind, that old customs, old superstitions would weight so light that fear would be absent, that feelings and impulses of the heart—which is the only mind—would burn as strong and as brightly with them as with me. But we should have Hell in the world, should we not? Jesus! And can there be a deeper pit than men have dug in the world already! Oh, if I were alone and could do my own bidding with a wish, where should my path be taken, and by what means should it be made! Am I to receive him then with the account of happiness having knocked at the door but passing by ere it was opened, a great good thing let to slip through the hand? And is he silently and within his own heart to blame me for losing the opportunity of vengeance, for perpetuating all the countless evils to come? Oh, if there were an evil spirit here, I would entreat of him some counsel. But there *IS* an Evil Spirit...! Old man, can I trust thee?'

'To *DEATH*, Madam!'

'You speak well. And I *will* trust you, to *DEATH*!* Yes, Robert, you know your young master's difficulties. You—you know what would end them, what alone would end them. Ha, do not mention the word. I wish it to be uttered by myself. Yes, I will repay him, with Lord Caversham's interest, for the misery he lent, or attempted to give to me. But I am not formed for misery, and I will shake it from me. I care not for the risk or hazard. But then, why do you hesitate, you say? It's known to me. Sir! *WE MUST KILL MR PERCY!*'

Amid another company, horror would have compelled silence when Augusta ceased. Here, the minds of all present were too well used to sin to start at the suggestions of the tempter.

'My soul,' said 'Sdeath with emotion. 'But you have spoken well this day! Aye, when I brought 'em together, I know what they were and what they would do! Oh, thou art something like a woman!'

'Eh, Bob, is she?—Between ourselves—but no matter! A good move, by God! But what says our friend, the Lord Harry? More like a woman still, perhaps? Eh?'

'Lord Vernon, by my soul, this is no time for nonsense. Harriet sees the affair more seriously than you. But your Ladyship has thrust home, and your words shall not fall to the ground.'

'Stop, Caversham,' said 'Sdeath. 'Stop. Let's see about this spot of work and get it settled to our minds. Oh, but thou'rt the Queen of Heaven, and I shall never forget thee for this! Sit there for the best seat in the room is thine, and my old friend Jerry Simpson, sit thou on her right hand. 'Sblood but thou'rt true steel, and I've known thee as many a day. Caversham, sit thou on her left. Stand ye round now; and for myself, why, 'Sdeath, I'm but a servant and e'en must kneel before her.'*

The old wretch fell upon his knees; and while the fire glanced from his withering eyes, he grasped a long knife he had drawn from his coat and extending it towards them continued in a tone different from his usual mode of speaking.

'I needn't tell ye now the virtues of this old blade, but if ye want anything doing sure and short, here's the thing that'll do it for ye. And I needn't tell ye what this iron has accomplished, for this is not just the hour for cracking over old tales of sports that have been had; but it's the time to scheme a play that is to come on, and which God grant may be the merriest we've played since we opened our eyes in the world. My soul, but thou'st done well, woman! But trust me for doing better yet—'

'But the knife,' said Augusta, 'the knife. It leaves marks. Such a death—it will not appear to have been received in hunting. His cursed wife will discover it.'

'Trust me for that. I merely hold out my old blade as the symbol of my office. My soul, must it not be these very old hands which dandled him when a baby that shall handle him when a man? Did not these old bones hold him before he could walk, and shall not they HOLD him now when he can't walk? By God, but I will give him an embrace at parting; one grasp of the hand ere he sets sail on the voyage from whence no man returneth. He's oft black in the face with passion, and such a fall as he has gotten may well bring on apoplexy. By God!'

'Now, let it be done soon!' cried Harriet. 'Do not delay, for the sooner it is finished, the less suspicious will it seem.'

'You're right, Miss,' said Simpson. 'My old friend ought to have him in limbo before this week-end, roasted black as a bilberry. I'll furnish you gratis with the suit to rig him out for his journey. He sent his son on a voyage, let him go now on one himself. God! A thought strikes me; Caversham, shan't we go and see our old chum? By Jove, a good move. Let's up and condole with him over his misfortune, and talk to his Lady of a change for the better.'

'And let Harriet go,' said Lord Vernon. 'It will perfect her in the only sin she is not accomplished in—hypocrisy! Ha, ha!'

'Never, my Lord! Oh, God, have I not sinned enough already!' and as she spoke with hands clasped, she shed tears of bitterness. But Augusta's Italian eye smote her soul, and she dried them to drown conscience in the passions of that bloody hour. She gazed on Lady Percy with awe when she viewed her in the fire of untamed nature, with her black eyebrows corrugated by hatred and her majestic form erect in the triumph of revenge.

Augusta extended her white, statue-like arm as if grasping the magic dagger, while she said to the malignant 'Sdeath: 'What thou doest, do quickly.'*

And the wretched old man, donning his tattered hat, answered by a sneering laugh of satisfaction. To Harriet's excited mind, the stately, lighted saloon seemed to contain only fiends from the eternal pit. The wife of Percy with her voluptuous form and dilating eye; Caversham, with that high, noble forehead and scanty silver hair shining above his mean, greedy eyes and a coldly treacherous smile; Vernon, whose very smoothness of aspect shewed the deep villainy that lay beneath; Montmorency—young Montmorency (not now young, nor then young in crime). Him she looked at often for he stood backward, spoke little though laughing at every peculiarity in the conversation, but with those features massy even in youth fixed in deep thought, his brown hair falling over his knotty brow, and his grey eye sometimes bent on her with such a searching, strangely gleeful glitter. And old 'Sdeath, who paced to and fro with his hat struck over his brows, his hands plunged in his pockets and croaking with satisfaction over the misery that seemed ready to come, while the rest were talking together in a low voice over their projected deed of blood.

Harriet again took up Alexander Percy's letter and gazed at it as if its pages hid some profound meaning. As her eyes dwelt on the very form of the hastily written words, their impassioned meaning stole insensibly on her soul—

'I know not at all whether I am miserable or happy; nay, nor whether I have the materials for being either. I fancy that I cannot receive one good without I lay down another. Can I love any one but thee? And yet, my Augusta, forms and feelings crowd round me which are not of thee, whether I am with thee or from thee!'

As she read these words, she looked up and half started at the look with which Montmorency was regarding her, as he leant with folded arms on his yellow cane. Lady Augusta, who had been speaking to Simpson, extended her arm to him with a motion for silence. Old 'Sdeath was slouched down with his ear toward the door; and he sprung up with an emphatic oath as it flew open, and Alexander Percy strode wildly into the apartment.

He stopped when he saw those who were in the saloon. But in a moment, Augusta was in his arms. Affrightedly, she gazed on his face, where she saw a ghastly and emaciated look. But convulsively repressing all sign of joy and motioning her to keep silence, he said, looking hurriedly round him—

'My God! What are you hatching here? Why gathered and with such an expression? By Heaven, tell me what you are doing!'

The son of him they were about to murder had appeared among them with the suddenness of a thunderbolt. Lady Percy did not answer because in gazing on that unexpected form she had forgot everything and every sound. However, poor Harriet was in tears, for when Percy entered she sprang unconsciously to meet him, and the sneer with which Montmorency beheld her harshly called her back to reality. The others present dared not speak the awful answer, save two, Simpson and 'Sdeath, whom nothing could appall. And these both replied in a breath.

'We are murdering your father!'

'Murdering my what, Sirs?'

'Your father.'

'By Heaven, I will not be jested with!'

'And by Hell, we will not jest! But, good Sir', said Simpson, 'you give us no time to pay our respects on your sudden and unlooked-for return.'

'To death with respects! I see you are on some infernal business—Mr Satan! Explain!'

'Ha, ha, ha! A good move! But you're mistaken. Satan has only entered this moment, and knows as much of the matter as you do. But we are only met on our usual business—finding a new way to pay old debts. Your father on hunting this morning fell from his horse and has injured himself so severely as to cause hopes of his death for two or three hours on end. We hurried to your Lady to have a bit of chat over the news, and old Bob, my friend, was packed up to see how his master got on. As we were all speculating upon the expected catastrophe above there, Bob pops in and tells us it's no go, and all's blown over like a sea sickness. Such news struck us in a heap, but your good Lady, who lives in a sort of "Inferno" and is not so soon frozen fast, arose and gave us a hint which we are not slow to improve on.'

'Says her Ladyship, "We must kill Mr Percy!" Says Bob, "We must throttle him." Says I, "We must get in our monies", and say you, "They shall be paid every stiver."'

'Alexander,' said Lord Caversham, 'here were an opportunity which must be improved upon. If not, why you pay up your interests and lose your principals, we remain without our capital, and your father lives on, refusing your allowance or shuffling off the entail.'

'Do not persuade him,' interrupted 'Sdeath. 'Let the lad take his own mind. He'll come abaat, ya'll see.' And the old villain stood regarding his pupil with a gleam of fiendish satisfaction. Percy stood still in utter silence. He looked on the ominous faces about him, and almost recoiled from their expressions.

Gazing steadfastly on Harriet, he said with emphasis, 'And do *you* approve it, too?' She could not reply but answered by her kindled eyes.

''Sdeath,' said Percy, turning to the old man. 'Attend in my dressing room tomorrow morning. Gentlemen, meet me then at breakfast here. Go now, and to Hell with ye all!'

'Good night, my Lord and Lady Macbeth,' said Montmorency. 'We'll produce our *habeas corpus*. But Miss Harriet, how do you go home?'

'I—I don't know,' she said, starting.

'Ha, Harriet! But I will see you tomorrow. I shall call on O'Connor. Good night to you, at least.'*

'And I again', said Hector, 'will have the honour of escorting you home.'

At this moment, a servant called from the Hall, desiring 'Sdeath to go up directly, as his master could not do without him. The villain laughed heartily at his confiding ignorance and preceded the rest from the room.

Augusta and Alexander were now left alone. He stood, and with clenched hand raised upward, cried, 'Oh, my God! Upon what a course of destruction dost thou drive me!' Lady Percy, whom his sudden ghastly and exhausted appearance had shocked into silence, burst into tears and throwing her arms around his neck she said, 'Oh, my Love! You affright me by your voice and aspect. You are, indeed, dreadfully ill. In Heaven's name, has any irremediable evil happened, that you should arrive so unlooked-for and so despairing?'

He laughed with a hollow mirth and, seating himself with her on a sopha, answered.

'Evil, Augusta! Certainly not. Ha! Why, I am first man of my year. I have been made Senior Wrangler, my Love. *Vi et armis,** as the saying is. I have forced them to grant their highest honours to the man whom most they hated. Is not that a sweet comfort? Thou at least can appreciate its value. I left the Island the week after my examination, shaken to pieces with nervous exhaustion, my soul full of horror and sleepless anxiety, threatened by my creditors, detested by my superiors, cursed with the brand of treachery, almost outlawry, atheism, and destruction. I sailed over, ruminating on some plan to free myself from my chains before circumstance rivetted them upon me. The Devil tempted me day and night, and—now! I have arrived, on land, full into the midst of a vast conclave of demons. I have not cast off the Evil Spirit, but I have received seven new ones. My God! They tell me to murder my father! Ere I saw them, I was brooding madly on the deed, and this night—it has been urged on me by others. Yes, *thou* tellest me to kill my father!'

'Yes,' she answered, kindling while she spoke. 'I tell you to kill your father, Percy. Your studies and exertions have shattered you, they have unmanned you. Do you not see that what I suggest is the only possible means by which you can escape from your difficulties? If he lives, you continue paying your enormous interests with the certainty of being obliged to refund your principal when perhaps you may have actually paid it and paid it again. This day your father met with an accident so severe as to render his life to appearance doubtful, though *we* know it is not so, for he is recovering. Caversham, Simpson, and the others, who at any other time would not wish you to pay up their principal but, rather, receive their twenty per-cent profit, just now want all the money they can command on some scheme or other, so I know they would aid me. In R. P. 'Sdeath, I foresaw a willing instrument.

'The accident, as I said, favoured the attempt, and therefore I boldly advised the deed. And, Alexander, have I to remind you now of the manner in which your father has treated you? Have I to relate your wrongs and injuries? Do you know of such a word as *revenge*? Yes! He has invidiously insulted me; he has opposed my marriage with you, determinedly thwarted it; and when he could not prevent it, he has striven to embitter it! He hates me as I hate him. He hates you from his soul. Believe me, the discovery of your Society originated with him!* He is a dark, a dangerous man! But' and she spoke with fierce emphasis, 'in thwarting me he has found his match! He has met a deadly, an inveterate foe. And you—your latter injuries have been owing to me! He knew how keenly I should feel your wounds, for I love you until your sorrows and your crimes are mine. And Holy Mary! What he has lent me, I will repay with his own usurious interest. I will return him percentage and principal. Jesus! Is my Alexander dying that he should thus regard this vengeance!'

'My Augusta, your voice only attempts to spur over the precipice a man who is determined to take the leap. I have made up my mind to kill him, because if I don't, I must make it up to kill myself. At College since August, I have been playing, hazarding desperate stakes in order to recover my tremendous fines and free myself from these human fiends, Caversham, Simpson, and Company. I was worried with exertion and anxiety, I was only twenty years old, and the result, of course, has terminated in the loss of *another hundred thousand pounds*! I was made Wrangler, the vacation came—my father forbidding my leaving the Isle then—but I did come over, simply in order to find *payment* for my victors. The attempt was desperate; from *him* I could get nothing, from Simpson and Company... Bah, my soul recoiled at a further entangling. I did think once of leaving Africa forever. It was a wild thought; and one thought of thee chased it, never to return. But how am I to pay? My debts are £300,000. When I enter on my father's property, I shall possess £500,000. I tell you, it is enough, my Love. It is finished, the Deed is done!'

'Then I am thine, and thou are mine, and hope of joy shall never fail us if I can trust in love from thee. But that heart is as wild as my own, and can evil trust evil?'

'I care not. I am what I was a year since. I know thee, and thou knowest how I love thee. We will not confess what needs no confession, but rather let me live an hour of heaven, love in the arms of one with whom I sacrifice all hope of it hereafter. Oh, Augusta, with you here I do feel as happy as I or you can feel. I know I am Alexander Percy who thinks that years with thee are bought cheaply from Eternity.* Where? I know not! You say, nowhere. How I have thought of you, Augusta, while I was away, and you are not one for many to think of. Others, did they love you, would take care to search your mind no more than skin deep. But I have thought of you till, trust me, I know you! Now, don't start, because you feel that you are what you wouldn't wish me to know. Remember, I do know you! And remember, I do love you!

'While absent,' he continued, 'could this form, this face, these dark Italian eyes be forgotten by such as I, and if unforgotten could they fail in their power? Oh, no, this life I foresee affords too little pleasure for me to throw what I possess away. The past also is fixing too firm a hold on me, and think what thou hast been through the past year—the first, the brightest, the most glorious Star that ever flashed on the eyes of—'

'My wild, wayward, wandering—yes, my divine Alexander Percy!'

'Divine! My God, is Hell divine?'

'*Thou* art divine, for what hath ever kindled my soul or brought tears into my eyes like *thee*? Thine own music is never so heavenly as thou, and what did I care for Hell or Heaven or death or misery? While I am here with thee, solitary evenings which in themselves had nothing except a dreary, desolate gloom and sounds of wind and rain have wrapt my thoughts like thine, not only far away but like doves— only themselves how un-dovelike!—they have all flown over sea and time to their mysterious home in thee.'

To burning words of which the foregoing are but a meagre shadow, the solemn, impassioned looks and melodious voice of the speaker gave a yet diviner feeling, and he to whom they were addressed from his own enthusiastic spirit called up in answer a language of the mind to which I cannot give a name. Ideas changing and uncertain, but which would gather from all time in a wandering flight a thousand associations of whatever contains the spirit of poetry, only in the end to fill that mind full of emotions connected with the noble being at his side.

He took her to a grand piano at the head of the saloon, and after a prelude of full solemn chords accompanied her voice to one of his own rich and melancholy compositions.*

> Son of heaven, in heavenly musing
>   Gaze beyond the clouds of time,
> Future glory rather choosing
>   Than the present world of crime.
>
> Thou whose heart that world caressing
>   Bows its bubbles to adore,
> On and hunt each fleeting blessing,
>   Still in sight but still before.
>
> Christian, worldling, hence and leave me!
>   Here with thee, my love alone,
> Things to come shall ne'er bereave me
>   While we two continue one!

'And are we not as one now?' said Augusta as they concluded, with her most winning smile. 'Yet, why, then, that sorrow and that wandering eye?'

'It's the thought of how I am repaying my Mother for her years of affection,' he replied. 'I thought I saw her! What would she think if she knew her son—! Oh, my Mother—my Mother!'*

Oct. 20th
1835
PBB

[Chapter II*]

Oct. 22
1835
PBB

With sorrow do I enter upon the detail of those events which marked the morning of January 17, 18—.* A wild and stormy morning it was, and well fitted for the work it was destined to perform.

Mr Percy lay on the bed, with Dr Duncan and Lady Helen seated beside him. But from time to time, through pauses of exhausted silence, he would articulate curses and imprecations upon the event which had brought him to his helpless condition, and doom to destruction everything which he fancied had joined to cause it. Though the symptoms were not dangerous, yet his fall had been very severe. One arm was broken, and he had received several violent concussions on the head. Copious bleeding had not allayed the fever of his restless mind, and no entreaty availed in imposing silence or softening his soured spirit.

'Helen,' he said, 'By God, if you disobey me in this matter when I cannot force obedience, depend on it that I will make you repent when I recover. I'll have the horse shot this instant—stumbling devil! And as to that insolent farmer who stopped me, on my soul he shall fall as low as I did. Thank Heaven he lives on my land, and I can make him smart for it. Steaton, Sirrah, there!'

'My dear Sir, you may rupture a blood vessel by calling in that manner. Shall I—?'

'Keep your cursed advice for your own lying quackeries. Ho, Steaton! By Heaven, doesn't the dog hear?'

Mr Steaton came hurrying in.

'Are you, too, determined to disobey me? But I'll have my revenge. Go and set to work with George Hawksworth this moment. Turn him out of his farm, out with him into the snow; and by God, I'm glad there is snow. Eject him, Sirrah, and set about it! Ho, stop, and go down to Montmorency. No, desire him to come up to me. He shall proceed legally against the slave for killing my game. But not till

I have shorn him of his money. First one blow, and then another. He shall see what stunning means! Begone!'

Mr Steaton gladly left the apartment, and Mr Percy then lay for some time still, but bending his black brows alternately at his wife and the doctor. After a while, with a groan he recommenced.

'I suppose now, when he hears of it, your damned son, Madam, will be ready to cut his throat with joy. But I'll cheat him yet, whichever way it turns with me. Neither he nor you shall juggle me out of my life and property! Call up 'Sdeath this moment!'

'Awm here, Master,' answered the fiendish old man, entering as he spoke, with Lady Helen and Dr Duncan both starting as if at the advent of an evil spirit.*

'Now, turn 'em out, 'Sdeath. Go out, Helen. Begone, Doctor. A word with ye, Robert.'

'Eees.* But me Leddy, Aw cam up to say there's Caversham and Vernon and some more's doan below and want to speak to ye uncommon partiklar.'

Lady Helen and the doctor rose to depart, but just as she was leaving the room, Mr Percy's eyes assumed a ghastly fixedness. But after a silent shudder, he only said, 'It's gone! God bless you, Helen!' Lady Percy afterwards remembered 'Sdeath's ghastly sneer as she closed the door in leaving the room.

In a drawing room below, she found Lord Caversham, Lord Vernon, Mr O'Connor, young Montmorency, and Colonel Wildwood waiting as if to make a call upon their friend, Mr Percy. After the usual salutation and enquiry after his health, the Earl said:

'My principal object in coming here this morning is not to see Edward, for I suppose he is not fit for conversation, but to acquaint your Ladyship with a piece of news more safely than I could do by letter. Mr Alexander arrived at the Segovia Palace last night from the Island, after having earned the honour of Senior Wrangler* there. Of course, he dare not let his father know of the fact, but he most earnestly desires to see you and entreated me to persuade you to come down this morning. And, my dear Lady, you need not be agitated at his appearance, for his studies have superinduced a nervous anxiety which a row or two with us will soon wear away.'

'Then you will excuse me, my Lord,' said Lady Percy, and without further remark, she drove off, with her usual promptitude, to town.

'Gad, she's gone,' said Montmorency when they saw her carriage drive down the avenue. 'Now, then, *he* must go, too. Where's Patrick?'

'Hush,' said Caversham. 'This is no business for talking. Let us call 'Sdeath in. But—stop. What was that?'

'Some clamjamfry with the servants, I suppose, ha, ha, ha!'

'Ha, ha, well. Conscience does make—you know the rest. But I had thought different of old veteran Caversham. He's had a touch of this sort before now, eh?'

'Hush, Vernon. Never with such inconsiderate confidants. It's time to commence. Where's 'Sdeath? Why tarry the wheels of his chariot?'

While they were sneering and talking thus, a noise was heard without. The door flew open, and 'Sdeath entered abruptly.

'What, here, old boy? Now, up and to your work!'

With a sardonic laugh, the old man standing before them answered, '*It's ower'd, Sirs!*' And directly left them, running through the house crying noisily for the doctor.

The party in the parlour stood petrified, gazing on each other as if doubting whether all was not a dream. *That deed done* ere they thought it entered upon!* Dr Duncan, alarmed by the cries for assistance, hurried upstairs with 'Sdeath clamouring before and the gentlemen from town after him. On entering the chamber, they found Mr Percy lying a corpse with discoloured face, clenched hands, and glass-like eyes.

'He wor threeping me ower Alexander, and swearing he suld'nt have a ha'penny o' his brass, so thinkin no wrong ower't, I just up and told him as haw he had comed into taan nobbut last neight, and the Measter at that starts bolt upright with an oath and a "What, Sir?" So Aw sez, "Alexander's comed hoam"; and then making a tear at me, his arm flang out o' joint agaan, and he fell backward wi a gasp and nivver spak more. Aw sead it wor apoplexy by 'bluid rushing intull's face, and soa Aw banged me daan stairs to fetch ye up to cure him. Lord safe us, he's like as he war dead!'

'Goodness,' cried Caversham. 'I fear it's something serious!'

'We must lose no time in seeing, my Lord,' answered Duncan, who has told me that it was all he could say, for he fancied himself among demons. Bleeding and every other means were promptly had recourse to, to restore animation, but all was in vain. The murderer's grasp had too effectually done its office, and those withered hands which had deprived their master of his life were now hypocritically busied in the office of attempted—but, as 'Sdeath well knew, useless—

endeavours to restore it. Lord Caversham, Vernon, Montmorency (that very man who is now the mouthpiece of reform), and Wildwood, with Mr Steaton, the steward, and one or two principal domestics stood round the apartment till Dr Duncan declared that Mr Percy was certainly dead.

Then, without a single tear being shed on the announcement, each man seemed eager to make what he could out of the event. The servants hurried about in full liberty. The steward drove down to pay his respects to the heir. All the visitors hurried away to acquaint their confederates with the event except the Earl, who remained behind to break it to Lady Helen on her return. This satanic nobleman, whose years only increased his crimes, walked alone through the drawing room, not in sorrow over the loss of his companion and fellow worker, but seeking every possible method of defrauding his son.

As he beheld Lady Percy's carriage coming up the lawn, he assumed a look of concern; and when she entered the room he said with his accustomed stately ease: 'I am sorry, Madam, to have to meet you with intelligence not so agreeable as my last. But you are agitated. Be seated, I pray you.'

'No, my Lord, no. How is Edward? Worse?'

'My dear Lady Percy—' and he hesitated as if unwilling to break the news so abruptly.

But she said suddenly, with a fixed look: 'He is dead, Sir!'

'There may be hope, Madam, but I fear—'

'My Lord,' she replied, repressing her feelings with her wonted firmness, 'my Lord, I shall judge for myself', and went up supported by Caversham to the room where Mr Percy lay. When she beheld the ghastly corpse, she trembled but recovered herself, looked long and earnestly upon it, and on a sudden turned to the Earl with a gaze which even his hardened conscience could hardly withstand.

'My Lord, you will excuse me. I desire to remain alone.'

'Certainly, it is most proper,' he answered; and as he departed, she closed the door within.

That day Lord Caversham spent chiefly at the Segovia Palace. But what passed there, I know not. In town, the report was soon spread that the well-known Mr Percy of Percy Hall had died suddenly from an apoplectic seizure while lying disabled by a fall received in hunting. A mystery hung over particulars, but in general people were glad at the removal of so dangerous and turbulent a man. I was myself in the country at the time; and when I returned home three days after, I was thunderstruck on opening a note from Mr Steaton of invitation to Mr Percy's funeral.

I had not heard a word of his illness and could hardly trust my eyes. I hurried out for information, but all save the mere fact was a varying mystery. Young Mr Percy, I found, was in the city but had not once been up to the Hall, and I knew he would not go up so long as his father lay there. But January the twenty-fifth arrived, the day for the funeral. Full of strange thoughts and old recollections, I proceeded toward the Hall; all round was the loneliness of desolation, for when the masters have departed, a domain will seem strangely drear.

Yet, within the noble old seat, though every room was hung with black and every inhabitant clothed in mourning, there sounded the joyless bustle of the preparations for the last dark journey. The Hall was filled with the various relatives of the deceased and many persons were there of the highest rank and title, not only the Earl of Caversham, Lord Vernon, and their group, but the Earl of Elrington, Lord Beresford, and Lady Hume (Lady Helen's cousin), with the youthful Earl of Jordan and many others whom it would be vain to name. At the appointed time, a long, solemn procession (among which, how few were mourners!) set forth from the park gates, the titled or wealthy leading the van, with the body servants behind, and in the rear a file of the hard-worked, oppressed tenantry of the deceased. When all had gathered round the opened tomb and while the solemn service was being read over the coffin, I looked up to view the aspect of those who were called Chief Mourners there. Lady Helen leant on the arm of her son, and though it would have shewn a folly very unlike herself to have then displayed* extreme affliction, she yet looked pale and sad and deeply thoughtful. Perhaps Mr Percy was not completely so bad as to depart forever and with such mystery without exciting some bitter pangs in the mind of his wife, the partner of twenty eventful years.

Faces well known to me and whom I knew could show no grief, his relatives and principal servants, pressed nearest to the grave, the first looking coldly and solemnly on, the last with flippant callousness. But Robert 'Sdeath struck me by his withering, fiendish sneer. I have long known its real meaning, but then I thought it caused by the religious service, for he had not put on the horrid cloak of hypocrisy which for the last few years has clothed his conversation. He was then blasphemously impious (and he is not less so, now). Miss

O'Connor, I saw, seemed very pale, and at this I wondered; but her conscience was not a scarred one, and the scene awakened its warnings. I neither saw Lady Augusta there nor expected to, but her husband I did see and on him my gaze was chiefly fixed.

I had not seen him since more than a year before, when he first set out for the Philosophers Isle. But I had thought and heard of him, and now I looked on him with the most intense interest. But I was, indeed, startled at the change time had made. How different was he from my former pupil! Much taller and nobler in figure, but thin, worn, and haggard, with wasted cheeks and restless, hollow eyes, his forehead furrowed with anxiety and his lips curled in hardened scorn. His arm supported his mother, and upon the recital of the words 'Our dear departed', he smiled derisively, but the words 'Earth to Earth, Ashes to Ashes, Dust to Dust' he seemed inwardly to repeat with bitter emphasis. And when the earth first rattled on the coffin lid, he looked upward with a desperate triumph that passed into anxious thought and, as his eye met Caversham's, a mysterious intelligence.

When the burial service was finished and as all prepared to leave the tomb, that nobleman came up to him, took his hand, and said, 'I congratulate you, my good fellow, on a return to the home of your father.* By Jove, a year's absence would wear out my patience!'

'Caversham,' was the answer, 'here is the home of my father; and by God, I wish he had entered it sooner! It would have saved me something second cousin to ruin. Curse him! Nor do I care who hears me. However, I do go up to the Hall, as the demon has left it. Come and hear *your* will read!'

'Ha, ha. Nay, not mine but thy will be done. You know, one must be devious on the occasion.'

'Gad, where's that jackal 'Sdeath?'*

'Awm here, Measter, and naw is the old Measter concerned* about going into the cold earth, for by gom, just as the coffin was covered, As see the arth hotch, and it whamled away daunt to th' fur spot, where just naw he's as het as ony coil in th' range.'

'Damn the old villain. I'll hear no more about him!' said Percy, and they walked away leaving the workmen alone about the vault. I turned back myself as I left the place and thought: Not a tear yet wetted that earth, or would it ever be gazed on with a sorrowful eye.

The Hall that night exhibited all the pomp and more irreligion than that of the great man's funeral. The will was read before all the titled and untitled relatives. Of course, as the property was entailed, all was left to Alexander Percy, with jointures to Lady Helen, and so forth, the whole amounting to little short of £500,000 and in condition to yield interest of £25,000 a year. The new master and Lady Percy were both present to receive their vast patrimony, which they knew would, vast as it was, dissolve like snow in winter.

And now I have concluded the detail of this bloody tragedy, this first step in a long career of crime and woe, where Alexander Percy showed himself the half-maddened accomplice* to the designs of a company of the most diabolically wicked men that Africa held in her bosom. His whole mind inflamed with hatred of his father's injustice and all his frettings, harassed by a dreadful weight of financial embarrassment, in order to free himself from the vast debts he had incurred and to revenge himself for injuries he would not forget, he became the desperate accomplice in the murder of his father. His wife—an Italian who comprised every bad and all the few good qualities of her nation—had first designed it, while his infernal creditors, *friends* of his father (save the mark!) and of himself but who nevertheless hated both (or what is as bad determined to get everything they could from both), being now in want of their principal for present speculations, directly urged it, and which plan Robert 'Sdeath, an old man whose name is synonymous with degraded villainy, who had brought up the victim and been his servant from almost his very birth, with a fiendish gladness executed.*

All now was over. The victim was gone, buried in the heyday of his crimes without a tear. His guilty son had entered upon his estate; and though many spoke of Mr Percy's mysterious death and a few suspected the cause of it, yet none felt interest in the deceased sufficient to probe it to discovery, Lady Helen Percy alone being excepted, none who dared to indulge the horrid idea of that parricide. And if the thought flashed on her mind, affection for her son, which nothing could abate, suppressed all desire of enquiry.

Such being the position of affairs on the termination of this horrible transaction, I find it my painful duty to enter upon the description of another deed scarcely less dreadful, but which almost total want of information prevents me from giving with anything like the fullness of the last. Time, which has discovered so much of the past, has not yet fully unravelled this event, but I have no doubt that what I relate is truth, so far as it goes. And I must remark, it is the first in a long series of expiations for blood, of awful punishment for crime where the wicked were brought to die by the snares they had used for others; and where in this great scene of sinners in such lofty stations, they one by one fell by each other's hands, or by the hand of the Arch-Sinner whom they had fostered for their own temporary purposes into such a lasting power.

I write this with sincerity when I look back and retrace the events which have chequered the last twenty years, for so long back fell the first blow of punishment; and then I look round me, gazing on some who yet survive and whose actions tell me that the last blow has not yet fallen but that as certainly it will sometime fall. What may be the fate of the principal actor in this mighty drama, I cannot foresee. He has done mighty and dreadful deeds; doubtless his end will answer with his life in importance, but will it be like it in sorrow and sin?

Ere I proceed with this life, I must remark that I have forgot to say anything of a person whose name I have often mentioned, Mr Simpson. Anything definite I cannot say, for he was and is a mystery. But I will say of him what I can. Mr Jeremiah Simpson, though moving in circles so aristocratic, was nothing more in rank than an extensive and fashionable dealer in linen, drapery, and the like in Wellington's Town, whose splendid shop attracted a mob of titled purchasers. Nothing more than this he would have been, had he not by his own qualities made himself a companion of peers and almost princes. Where he came from, no one knew. But on his settling at Wellington's Town, which he did shortly before Mr Percy arrived there, he set up a dashing business and appeared possessed of property. He was without family, and all thought him a person wrapt up in the aim of making money.

As Wellington's Town by degrees increased, it assumed that singular character of mingled abilities and profligacy which it has since maintained, and the multitude of dark and daring spirits who found settlement there congenial erelong raised it to an importance and elevation of society considerably beyond the other capitals of the Union. Of course, in its whirl of dissipation many fortunes were lost, while their once possessor* still wished to appear great. To this class of men, Jeremiah the Draper held forth the only hand of help. Money to any amount lent freely upon easy terms and for indefinite periods made his back parlour the resort of a host of desperate 'Westerns'.* When some titled head bowed at his threshold,* he took care to show all his shrewdness, sagacity, and mental power, to ingratiate himself by admirable advice on the means of escape from ruin, as well as capital schemes for accomplishing the ruin of others.

By these means, he soon became noted over the city as 'Gentle Jerry' and the Westerns spread his fame to their favourite Verdopolis. He extended his establishment to the mother metropolis, entered into wider connections, and soon was one who only wanted to be known to be appreciated. His mind was so masculine, his keenness so penetrating, his judgement so clear, and his conscience so callous, that his clients found him of infinite use in assisting them on their course to ruin. Men who themselves needed no advice, but whose years of crime rather qualified them to give it, and whose successful villainy had placed them beyond the usurer's gentle mercies, still found in Simpson a most able coadjutor in all difficult and treacherous undertakings. Sin, in the Lost, often assumed a sanguinary, as well as splendid aspect, and undoubtedly the hands of this shopkeeper have more than once participated in its stain. Foremost in their powerful class, Lord Caversham and Edward Percy, Esquire, discovered the merits of this worker of evil. Soon, he became their confidant, and along with them did his utmost to embroil the politics of, and do injury to, the parliamentary members of the West.

His keen eyes were continually bent on them. But yet, though he repressed and discomfited them, they went on, sowing too surely the seed which the subject of this memoir has since nourished into such bitter fruit. Simpson never entered Parliament, but his work lay under hand; and though a seat was offered to him by his noble friends, he declined acceptance, saying that his eyes could not bear the daylight. Nor his deeds, neither, he added, laughing with his accustomed suddenness. As he gained ground in the City, he increased his interests and erelong stood the most savage usurer among a most savage race of them. Indeed, I may say that he seemed destitute of every kindly sympathy or generous feeling. His cheerfulness itself was composed of taunts and sneers, his malice was like a dagger, and his wrath—why, he never showed it. Not on any occasion was Jeremiah Simpson seen in a passion; nothing could raise him beyond scornful jesting, and he despised any other state in the minds of others.

Robert 'Sdeath, the valet of Mr Percy, he took into greater confidence than perhaps any other man. Certainly these two knew more of each other than anyone else did and seemed on a better understanding. Often they would sit opposite, before the fire of the little

1. 'Bendigo "taking a Sight"'. Benjamin Caunt won the Boxing Championship of England in 1848 from Bendigo (William Thompson). The return match took place on 9 September 1845. The following day, Branwell included this drawing in a letter to Joseph Leyland, a clear instance of his enthusiasm for boxing. Bendigo regained his title in the match.

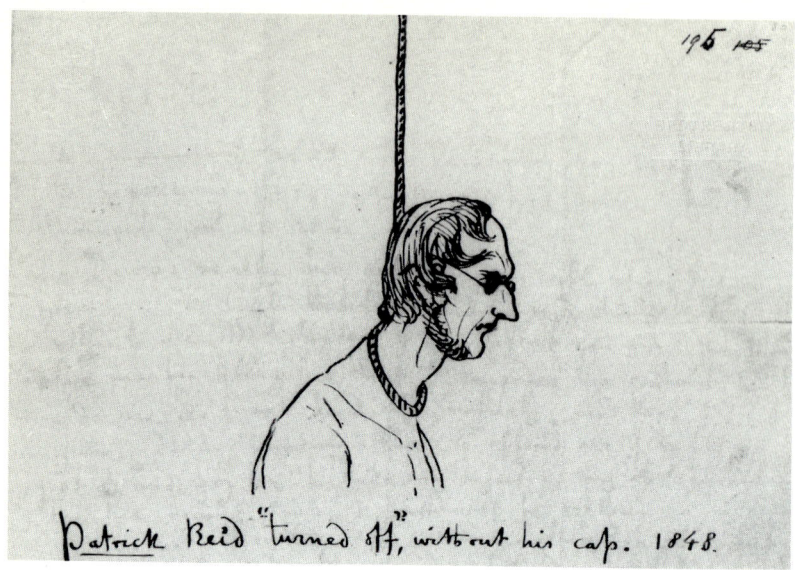

2a. Self-portrait, 1848. Francis Leyland, Joseph Leyland's brother, saw this drawing as expressing Branwell's sense of himself as martyred victim (probably in relation to the Lydia Robinson affair). It is, despite the later date, more probably a scene based on the Masonic initiation that he had undergone at the age of 18, which included a rope around the neck and a shirt opened to the waist.

2b. 'The Rescue of the Punch bowl, a scene in the Talbot.' The Talbot Inn at Halfix, of which the landlady was a Mrs Sugden to whom Branwell was at times in debt, was only one of several drinking spots that he shared with such friends as Joseph Leyland ('Phidias'), John Brown ('St John'), and Joe Drake ('Draco'), a carver and close friend of Joseph Leyland. 'Sugdeniensis' is probably the railway conductor, Dan Sugden. (Daphne du Maurier speculates that Branwell's double identification as 'St Patrick' and 'Lord Peter' may indicate that the group formed a hell-Fire Club from which Branwell's second title derived.)

3. 'Myself.' Self-portrait as Prometheus in chains.

4. top. Cartoon: 'Cooper's Anatomy'. Picturing Branwell (right) as 'Northangerland' and Joseph Leyland as 'Phidias'. January 1847.

middle. Self-portrait, on a catafalgue, c. January 1847.

bottom. *Hic Jacet*. 'Martini Liugi Implora Eterna Quiete!': 'Martini Luke implores for eternal rest!' (Italian Epitaph). c. January 1847.

counting house, enveloped in clouds of tobacco smoke, shut up till long past midnight and conversing with each other in low, nasal tones while a hollow laugh, rising suddenly and as abruptly silent, alone broke the monotonous murmuring to those without.

Simpson's bodily presence answered well to the spirit within. When I first saw him, I was struck by his looks; his demonic repulsiveness made one's blood run cold in one's heart. He was a great, bony man with a grisly black head and long, Herculean arms. His countenance was dark, heavy, and iron-like, with distorted eyes, and muscles moulded into a coarse habitual sneer. His attire was generally rusty black, and his harsh voice, on whatever subject he spoke, had always a tone of solemn scorn. Such a man as this, one would think, could never gain the confidence of a noble and beautiful lady, yet so it was; and Jeremiah Simpson was the Prime Minister to the Italian Queen, Augusta di Segovia.

'By Gom!' he would swear. 'If all the women on earth were like this one, my spots of work could yield me more profit than they do. Gad! My Old Chum* could never find room for them all. One might make a spot in the collieries for, 'Sblood, the price of coals would rise!'

And he swore, when Augusta and Alexander were married, 'May I be cursed if such a glorious event will happen again till the Old One has 'em all roasting together. Here's Sin and Death* with a vengeance upon us, and if such a conjunction doesn't forbode all that's heavenly to Africa, may I—'

But it is needless to give the concluding imprecation. All his conversation was blighted with the most blasphemous oaths and curses.

Well, such a man it was who had wound round the very vitals of Alexander Percy. To him he had lent £200,000 along with the cold-blooded Caversham and a few others like him; and now, to recover the sum, he had stood almost first in the murder of his friend, Edward Percy. But his keen sagacity foresaw that yet they had not received their principal, and his diabolical spirit suggested the means for ensuring it.

The night after Mr Percy's funeral, he called upon the Earl of Caversham and remained alone with him for several hours. Then Robert 'Sdeath joined them from the Hall.

That day, Lady Augusta with her usual impetuosity of character had passionately besought her husband to refuse payment of the

£200,000 loan. They dared not institute legal proceedings, she averred, for such would only implicate them in the business of the Society, whose members had received such punishment. They all, as heads of the party, would thus receive an irrecoverable shock in politics; it would ruin them. And as to their hatred, it could never be worse than their pretended friendship. 'Sdeath overheard this conversation and posted down to Mr Simpson's shop with an exact account of it.

Simpson knew that Percy was remarkable for improving on a hint like this, and that he possessed desperate resolution enough to brave its consequences. He consulted Caversham; 'Sdeath followed; and the deliberations of the trio in sin must have ended in a scheme for the destruction of her who had just before suggested the destruction of another—a plan for the death of Lady Augusta Percy.

It was a week after this dreadful meeting, late at night on the first of February, 18—, when Alexander set off on horseback for Percy Hall from a great party at Lord Ravenworth's, composed of the élite of the metropolitan aristocracy. As he rode on through the wind and darkness rendered yet more desolate from having so suddenly quitted the splendid saloons of Gambia Square, his ardent and ambitious mind engaging itself in some vast dream of future greatness, some shadow perhaps of those events whose coming yet lay in the future, his eye was arrested by a light which seemed approaching before him.

The wind and rain beating on his face rendered him uncertain of what it was, but it neared in the darkness, and he soon knew it to be the front light of some carriage driving townward. As he rode forward, that carriage approached, open, driven by four horses, and containing two persons on the seat. Notwithstanding the speed with which it came up, was it the storm which drowned the sound of its wheels? But he could not be uncertain whom it contained, for as it drove by him the single coach lantern cast its light back upon the figure of his own Lady Augusta, seated beside a dark form like Jeremiah Simpson's.*

'Augusta!' he would have called out as he rose on this stirrups, but a nervous emotion of the heart checked his utterance.

The carriage glided into the road leading up to Jordan Hall, and he turned desperately to follow it. But his horse with a start dashed forward on its road home, and he galloped on with a convulsive shudder of awe. His porter long remembered the ghastly oath which he swore when he was opening the park gates for his entrance.

'Has your Lady driven out in the carriage tonight?'
'She has not, Sir.'
'Then to Hell with both soul and body!' he replied and dashed furiously up the path. He sprung from the trembling beast and, as he met his mother in the Hall, asked, 'Where is Augusta?'

'In her dressing room, I believe, Alexander.'

He heard no further, but hastened up thither, opened the door and beheld Lady Percy reclined on a sopha near the fire. Springing joyfully forward, he exclaimed, 'Oh, my dear Augusta!' and clasped her in his arms.

Hers returned not the embrace; they fell cold and rigid. He started back—and—there she lay. Her black tresses dishevelled on her marble-like shoulders. Her face white and ghastly. Her eyes fixed upon him, not with their inspired emotion but in the black stare of *death*!

'Oh, my God!' he groaned, pressing his hand to his burning brow, and thus stood as he stared, almost stunned by that frightful shock. It was then that the hardened murderer entered, as if to speak to his master on his return; but at the first croak of his voice, Percy grasped a pistol and fired it straight in his face.* With a howl, the villain fled forth, his blood trickling as he ran, but his master dashed the door to and shut himself in the room of death. That act had not sprung from suspicion; it was the outbreak of a maddened mind.

All night Percy remained there alone with his Lady's corpse. I shall not give interjections, exclamations, and broken sentences, because I believe he uttered none. Nor can I analyse the feelings of a mind which was far too much stunned to feel. As when one shot by a musket bullet finds at first faintness only, and when he recovers his senses, pain, so exactly here that mind wounded just as suddenly as if by a bullet felt, as it were, stunned and bewildered till agony came upon it, such as its thrilling nerves were often doomed to feel. Perhaps through those dark and lonely hours the frightful truth which would press itself upon him was often repulsed with horror, till in the unreplying silence its voice pierced his ear too acutely to be withstood. And perhaps also as the daylight slowly revisited the room, its beams would bring a suspicion which became clearer to the inward sight as visible objects become so to the outer. But I cannot tell you whether from the chaos of that head could yet be created any thought so definite as this.

I only know that near the breakfast hour Mr Percy entered an apartment where Lady Helen was sitting and when he spoke the words 'Augusta is dead!' she started as if it was a voice heard in a dream. But almost before she could mark the agonized look of his face, he had turned and left the room.

'Where is 'Sdeath?' he said to the steward, who encountered him in an ante-room.

'Sir, he left the Hall last night, running downstairs bleeding and badly hurt after the explosion.'

'Enough, Sir,' interrupted his master, who directly departed on horseback toward the hills of Jordan Castle.

Lady Helen, hardly trusting her hearing, went up the Great Staircase, thinking of the beautiful lady whom she had left the evening before in all the enthusiasm of an unconquerable mind. But soon, indeed, the corpse on the sopha took the place of this picture with an impression which there can be none other to alter again. It lay there, splendidly attired in an evening dress with the dark satin and velvet mournfully contrasted to its cold and clayey whiteness, and the jewels still flashing amid the black curls over the pallid, lifeless brow. Twice, now, in the same house and so soon after each other, Lady Helen had beheld Death in its most sudden and unlooked-for form. Her husband and her daughter-in-law, both cut off in the pride of their life and spirit, with all their sins full blown and without a thought of repentance.

The strange and yet undiscovered mystery which hung over both these deaths could not but arrest the attention of one whose observation was more than usually clear; suspicions had already entered her mind regarding the first case. But in the last, who was there to attempt a life which all who dared attempt were in league with? If this event had not happened in the course of nature, surely the diabolical circle in the City would not murder their divine ally? The mean 'Sdeath unaided dare not effect what would be sure to ruin him? And Augusta's husband—no, it could not be her husband. Yet, horrible as the idea was, it pierced through the heart of his mother, because too well she knew what he had done and how unsettled was his mind. But in a little while an idea so remote from the truth cleared off, and the cloud of just suspicion gathered on the heads of the guilty alone.

During the day, while engaged in such appalling thoughts, Lady Helen in the utmost anxiety awaited the return of Alexander and an agitation amounting to pain seized her when, at night, she heard his footsteps in the Hall. She thought him at first approaching her apartment, but he strode hurriedly up to where Augusta lay; and Lady Helen, who had repressed her feelings when she thought him coming, sitting down again now burst into tears of sorrow for her unhappy son. To him, after his wild and lonely ride, re-entering that house where any day before he had rejoicingly hurried to his noble Lady, the rooms and the objects bursting on him where but a few hours before she would have been—and now hurrying up to meet her dead and stiffened corpse—was a trial whose anguish his soul could not possibly bear.

As he opened the door of the State Room where they had laid her out, the frightful change so flashed upon him that he stopped and fell, not fainting but in a dreadful consciousness to which fainting would have been a blessed relief. He spoke not, no tears could burst from his burning eyes; his heart beat with an intenseness of agony that *nothing* could relieve, for

> She was gone, his loved and lovely one,
> What was his being she had ceased to be!   (Byron)*

It was more than impressive, it was awful to see the voiceless, tearless silence of this, your Earl of Northangerland. The face he gazed on was not more corpse-like than his, its features not more fixed, but far did its still unconsciousness differ from the hopeless agony of his tortured mind. A wild and dream-like chaos of thoughts rose when he thought 'Oh, whither art thou gone!' But in what was to him the uncertainties of Revelation and vastness of eternity and horrors of atheistic annihilation, he only found a burning addition to Despair. Not an object around but added to it and not a thought within!

Knowing so well his strange spirit, no person dared to think of speaking to him, and therefore all the solemn pomp of the funeral was arranged by Lady Helen and those to whose lot its execution fell, the noble relatives of the Segovia House. Those of the Percy family, with those bloodstained beings whose names I have too often mentioned, though, of course, conferring upon the event with the mother of Mr Percy, did not think of seeing him or addressing him. In fact, he would not have listened to a word on any subject from any living soul. His own mother spoke not to him, though gladly indeed would she have striven to comfort him, but it was impossible.

Upon something being hinted about the mode, usual in all great families, of the deceased lying in state with relatives and others being admitted, Percy burst into terrific oaths; and he cried 'The first person who enters that room till the hour of burial shall go from it to Hell!' His agony and its cause this terrible spirit kept to himself, watching over the decaying form like a wild lion over his slaughtered mate.* And the hour at last approached when he should watch no more.

As the day of burial arrived, Lady Helen felt the utmost anxiety in going to mention it to Mr Percy. But he heard her calmly; and embracing the corpse, he looked that last long look which seemed as it would indelibly fix on his mind the features that he should never behold again.

'Let it be done as you wish, Mother. I have beheld now what through all eternity I shall behold no more. Oh, might there be another world! Oh, might we meet again!' And then there fell from his eye the first burning tear*—it was the only one—and when all the procession was marshalled, he joined it with a rigid and unnatural calm. Without speaking to anyone, he signed all to depart, and the gloomy hearse with its long train of noble mourners left the Hall for the Percy vault in Woodchurch, without the Park.

All gathered round the tomb with the music rolling from the organ above and the dark and narrow house yawning open below. I again beheld this man of sorrows,* but far more haggard and ghastly than when I saw him last before. His eminently beautiful features were deeply marked with suffering, and as the service drew to its close, his face grew paler, till he heard the words 'In sure and certain hope of a blessed resurrection to eternal life'. And then for a moment he lifted his eyes while his cheeks coloured, till the thought that these were but a man's words repeated according to custom darkened the momentary radiance. And when the first clod of earth struck the coffin lid, his lips whitened and his limbs trembled as if the 'burden were too heavy for him to bear'!

At last all was over, yet no one dared to speak to him. But it was with dimming eyes that many turned round to see the tall and noble mourner. So young, yet so smitten, and with a face whose paleness looked awful when contrasted with his deep, funereal black. All left him alone; but the last, who turned at the door, saw him burst suddenly into a flood of tears and, throwing himself on the covered grave, he knelt weeping bitterly.*

Lady Augusta Percy was now dead and buried, murdered by those whom she had instigated to murder, just having entered upon the enjoyment of the fruits of her crime and in the very flower of her age. She died aged twenty-six, six years older than her husband Alexander, and she had a far greater control over and influence with him than anyone has ever had since—that character of kindred passion, the Duke of Zamorna, alone being excepted. I certainly believe that, had she lived much longer, her influence would have passed off for she gained it because Alexander was very young, loving her ardently, and possessing a strange depth of feeling regarding such as she was that amounted sometimes to an indefinable awe. In the opening of his youth, she had crossed as a bright and leading star, and the overpowering effect of her majestic beauty and Italian passion when he was seventeen or eighteen was burning as strongly when he was nineteen and twenty.

But leaving out of the question this preoccupation of his soul, Percy's mind when matured and fixed in character was and is so tenacious and unyielding, his opinions so strong and peculiar, that, however he loves, nothing on earth or in heaven can guide him for a moment out of his own way. Often he seems led, and sometimes some worthless, artful creature like the M——s of W——y or Lady L——a V——n apparently for a time has ruled him. But this is superficial, and where they lead him he has resolved to go. I except one person, and I own that the extent or character of the influence that the wonderful monarch of Angria possesses over him is as much a secret to me as to others.

Augusta was dead, and those who had murdered her determined to press their advantage while Mr Percy's mind was yet utterly hopeless and desperate. They deputed Mr Simpson to press him for the money he owed them, and this Satanic personage chose his proper period for his cruel demand. He waited till Percy had paid off his £100,000 debt of honour due on his gambling transactions in the Philosophers Isle; and then his sagacious mind felt that Alexander, having commenced the headlong career of payment and seeing its certain termination, would take a mad, unconscious delight, as it were, in throwing his property from off him, and in his bitter grief would almost trample to the dust the faithless gold.

Then, and not till then, he made his demands, for so much caution was required to approach the chafed lion. To the first requests for payment, Mr Percy would neither listen nor answer. They became affrighted, but Simpson knew it was groundless fear. This was only an impulse of despair, for Percy had lost far too great a jewel to struggle for possession of the poor tinsel chasing.*

'Gom,' said the draper, 'I should be a poor tool* if I killed Lady Augusta and ran the hazard for nothing. Be Gor! Had she lived, he, high in hopes and spirits, heartened on by such a soul as hers would, I am certain, have refused us. But, Gad, it is different now. He is broken, desperate, cares for nothing, has begun to lose. The £100,000 has given him a shove down hill, and the £200,000 will increase the speed!'

So, for £200,000 he demanded, and with an oath of hatred it was given. Fearful of losing so admirable a leader, the faction had authorized Jeremiah to tell him that they would readvance him half the sum, upon reasonable mortgages. Percy, at first, did not seem to hear. It was pressed more intelligibly, and he answered, 'No. I will free myself from the net if I do leave skin behind me.'

'It were better', insinuated Simpson, 'to lose half than all.'

'Better', was the reply, 'to lose all and be free, than all and be a slave!' And then impatient of further conference with the man, he said with bitter emotion, 'Mr Simpson, a man struck as I have been will remember as well as feel the stroke. If he discovers the striker, he will return it. And by God, Sir, I know my enemies too well to mistake my blow!' With this unpleasant hint, Simpson departed; but he received the monies, and Mr Percy saw at once three-fifths of his estates torn away from him!

In this situation, oppressed with a tempest of miseries, without a single soul, save his mother, to look to for consolation or assistance, aware of the horrible truth that his friends and companions were the very persons who were ruining him, that it was his closest confidants who had murdered his Lady, that it was his own servant, the watcher over his childhood, who had done the deed, that the nation looked on him with distrust, and moreover that his own heart accused him of a terrible crime—it was in this state and by these events falling at once on so youthful a head that the foundation was laid of the cruelty, coldness, atheism, and utter melancholy of the man who would become Rougue, Elrington, and Northanger. Before this, he was full of passions and feelings as troublous as the roughest sea, but they had raved themselves to rest on shores of unutterable delight and joy. Now, that same wild ocean of passions raged louder than ever, but it beat on bleak and barren rocks.*

The spring of 1813 was to him a dreary winter. He wandered

about silent and solitary, his mind filled with these thoughts then but arising which have since deepened into such portentous gloominess. There actually was not one soul alive to whom he could look for assistance or sympathy. I have said so before, but I have to repeat it. There was not one to guide him, and I cannot wonder at the manner in which he has gone astray, for this was an important period of his life when whatever ideas he held would be likely to colour his future existence. All must know that the Earl of Northangerland is a perfect atheist, but he was not one during the life of Lady Augusta.* In his childhood, the Bible was his intense delight, and in boyhood the dim and glorious experience of that earlier childhood filled its days with associations of unutterable delight. Then, too, the awful glimpse it gave him into eternity, the sublime insight it gave him into far-off, long-ago times, the simplicity of its diction, all enchained him to religion.

I feel, Reader, that I am quite getting out of my depth when I speak of the *Essences of True Poetry* that filled his mind regarding Christmas Nights and Morns and divine summer Sundays passed away... Visions mingled with all the joys and sorrows of childhood and his mother's anxious affection and the freshness of an opening world and dim, indefinable theories of God and Heaven. Dreams of the Beginning of the World, the Patriarchs' days, the mighty Deluge, Abraham beneath his tent's shade, with the Angels slaying on their path of vengeance, Jacob the shepherd with his life of changes, Israel wandering through the Wilderness and amid so many vicissitudes guided to Jordan and the Promised Land. The mighty deeds of Canaan's conquerors, David's wars and sorrows and the voice of that harp so solemnly swept by the shepherd and Poet-King, Judith beneath her palm tree weeping over her Zion destroyed, the shepherds watching their flocks by night—but here he would think of the Christmas music and sacred winter morn; and thus each of these associations and a hundred, a thousand more all joined and revolving in a visionary chorus would fill his opening mind with thoughts of the spiritual world.

All this may sound foolish to the wooden-headed, but his head was not such a one, for then it rather beamed with the very light of heaven. It was *now*, after the terrible sorrows I have spoken of, that the clouds began to gather in that stainless blue. Now it was that Percy's mind, shut from all other consolation, began to look into religion with a keenness all its own; and as it was without any guidance, it ran into fatal and enduring error as he thought with all his intenseness and depth of the countless creeds of men all clashing one with another, their sickening follies and cant and hypocrisy, the many ways in which each read the Bible, the many ways it seemed capable of being read, its (superficially viewed) contradictions in itself, the mercy given and vengeance denounced, the Jewish history where a Chosen People slaying by command all the nations round them were allowed to retain all the light themselves and yet proved the vilest of sinners, though favoured so beyond a world which for a thousand years was purposely darkened and condemned, the grand failure of Creation itself.

A thousand arguments which I will not and ought not to mention, all entered into a spirit chafed to madness, a mind naturally now extraordinarily trustless, and moral feelings (bear witness, my unhappy country) miserably deadened in a very short period made Alexander Percy the firmest and most miserable of atheists. He believes that there is nothing except in this life, and he shudders at its hopeless woe.

'Oh,' he once said, 'if there were a God, a Heaven, an hereafter, I could feel some peace and have some room for divine imaginings. But there is not, there is not! And I am condemned to suffer here without the glorious thought that there is One above who knows what I suffer and who, if I serve him, will repay me in a life beyond my death. But none can tell what I suffer and whether I act well or ill. At death I must perish forever in the horrible annihilation of the grave.'

There are a few stanzas by him, the first found, which mark strongly the state of his mind in the year 1813.

> Life is a passing sleep,*
> Its deeds a troubled dream,
> And Death the dread awakening
> To Daylight's dawning beam.
>
> We sleep without a thought
> Of what is past and o'er,
> Without one glimpse of consciousness
> Of aught that lies before.
>
> We dream and on our sight
> A thousand visions rise:
> Some dark as Hell, some heavenly bright,
> But all are phantasies.

> We wake, and O! how fast
>   Our mortal visions fly,
> Forgot amid the wonders vast
>   Of Immortality;
>
>   In visionary joys
>   Of dreams of grief and gloom,
> We start to hear the thunder's voice
>   Arouse us from the tomb;
>
>   And o'erborne we arise
>   With 'wildered gaze to see
> The aspect of those morning skies;
>   Where shall that waking be?
>
>   How will that future seem?
>   What is Eternity?
> Is Death the Sleep? Is Heaven the Dream?
>   Is Life the Reality?

From a long and solitary wandering, as far as Elimbos and the borders of Sneachies Land, where he had travelled from place to place with a restlessness that showed not a mind flying from sorrow but torn and tortured with it, not even seeking an escape from it, for it had become a portion of his being and he knew that he could only lose it with his life—from this long, joyless journey, he returned in July. But Percy Hall and the Segovia Palace recalled every hour so many agonizing reflections that he found it impossible to remain in them any longer. Each moment there reminded him that a leaf had been turned over in his life, that the past was quite departed, and that all around him, even his own self, was the commencement of a new and iron road. He looked so utterly worn down and harassed that his acquaintances hardly knew him again; the man as well as the mind seemed new.

So, heart-sick of Africa and hating every person he saw, he made up his mind to leave his country behind him and embark on some long, endless voyage over the sea. But while his affairs were winding up and all things arranging for the departure, he plunged himself to kill time and memory into a heartless dissipation in the capital, flying from scene to scene, at every opened mansion the blighted and despairing visitor.

At this time

> When all around grew drear and dark
> And Reason half withheld her ray   (Byron)*

in the wilderness of Wellington dissipation first arose the Star of Hope, whose brightness for yet a few years longer dashed back the darkness that was fast closing him round. On a grand gala night at the fête made in the Ducal Palace on the presentation to the Westerns of the infant Prince of the West,* where Percy amid a whirl of pleasure and magnificence was asking his wretched spirit what business had it there, his eyes fell on the figure of Mary Henrietta Wharton, and a light first rose on his soul.

She was the only daughter of Lord George Wharton of Alnwick* in the Verdopolitan country and had grown up from infancy to youth half in the seclusion of an ancient country seat, half in the magnificence of metropolitan aristocracy. Her father, being a widower and an invalid, felt toward his daughter as to the sole stay and brightener of his life, and had taken care that hers should pass without many of the misfortunes that too often wait on our existence. She was brought up in indulgence, but like an exotic in an hothouse only rendered more beautiful by it. The two ladies of whom I have chiefly spoken hitherto, if they had many splendid qualities, had at least counterbalancing defects. Augusta with her majestic beauty of person and impassioned loftiness of soul was guilty of more crimes than I can mention. Harriet, with more cheerfulness and good nature, more mind and talents that I have often known united in one woman, had made herself completely miserable and from her extreme feebleness of principles was sure so long as she lived to continue so. But here I wish, Reader, that I had words to express the heavenly beauty both in person and mind of Mary Henrietta Wharton.

She was not one of those unnatural (for I will not call them supernatural) beings which disfigure the already worthless pages of sentimental novels with their amazing ignorance and inanity, beings who, if they had lived solely with their 'purities' and perfections, ought to be left withering like a sapless leaf in winter. She was a human being and a woman and had all the feelings of one as they ought to be, though she had not some as they are. Mary's mind shone in all her feelings and actions; it was as warm and as bright as a summer sunset and, like it, it had a shade of heavenly pensiveness which only made it the more lovely. When putting back the curls from her ivory forehead, she turned toward you with her musical laugh and the cheerful sunshine of her hazel eyes, you might see the heartfelt friendliness of her spirit brightening her lovely countenance.

Pride she possessed not, nor selfishness any further than must fall to the lot of every human being. But she had a silent, inward feeling; she had that feeling to which I can give no name but which, when alone and with nothing visible to touch the string, will yet sound in a chord which shall make a whole life seem but its echo, and feel in hours of struggle emotions that are never destined to fade from the mind.

I know that here I have ill explained myself, but this feeling is not to be explained. My fault lies not in my failure but in my attempt to succeed. It was that feeling to whose voice every nerve quivered in the man whose life I am writing. It was that which first spoke his name to Mary, and in it that she saw him and all his life. It was that which seemed to fill her dark eyes with tears, not only while wandering alone in the green groves and fertile fields of Alnwick, but while moving, one among a thousand, in the magnificent halls of the Palace of the West.

That night there was presented to the nobility in His Grace's Palace, the very man whose name now sounds through Africa, and whose life has been as wonderful, whose spirit has been as intense, as Northangerland's own. I was there, and the memory of that night has never left my mind. But what was that man like, then, twenty-three years ago? I think I see him yet, held forth to our loyal gaze in his nurse's arms, a little, helpless, speechless, beautiful child, the cross of baptism as yet glittering like dew, as it were, on his infantine forehead, and with large eyes whose gaze was attracted by nothing, on whose orbs nothing was yet impressed, the impetuous burning spirit then a blank, and that organ voice a faint, childish cry. His Majesty of Angria may smile, but these lines are a true picture of what was.

That man who in the wonderful future of time was to become the father-in-law and confederate to this Prince of Wellington's Land, then unknowing of what fate had written in its mysterious volume, cast scarcely a single look at the hero of the night and closed his heart to the bright and dazzling saloons, the gay and noble crowd, and the festive whirl of the gorgeous picture around him. At the repeated and anxious intreaty of many voices whose bidding he at another time would have obeyed most willingly but whose soft tones now fell hollow and unechoed in his mind, he had seated himself before a grand piano; and the noble and beautiful forms thronged around in eager expectation of the tones to be awaked by that master hand. His surpassing and unequalled skill in music, with the impassioned fervour of his genius and execution, was known to everyone; and at many a grand night in the capital, one half hour of Mr Percy's playing was a thing to be listened to and remembered as the most delicious *morceau* of the evening.

Oh, how I wish that I could transfer to paper the actual tones which those hands called forth as they ran along the keys or, all together, struck long chords of tumultuous harmony. He bowed to some one to take away the score books and saying, with a forced smile, 'My feelings are my own, and my music shall be my own', entered into a full, rich melody, whose solemn, sustained tones heard even in the distant saloons made the hearer unconsciously stop and listen. The worn and exhausted expression of his face gave way to an unearthly rapture, and while his melodious voice accompanied the music, he smiled one smile of bitter triumph that seemed to say, 'I have shaken off misery if but for a moment'.

It was but a moment, for when the memory of that scene similar to the one before him, the one which took place at that very piano before his marriage with Lady Augusta, flashed on his mind, the smile vanished, and his sudden change to anguish forced bitter tears from his eyes. This may seem strange to those who know only 'The Earl', but he bent his head and the curls fell over his shining brow. With his change in spirit, his music changed and became a mourning song.

> Thou art gone but I am here
>   Left behind and mourning on,
> Doomed in dreams to deem thee near
>   But to awake and find thee gone,
> Ever parted, broken hearted,
>   Weary, wandering all alone.
>
> Looks and smiles that once were thine
>   Rise before me night and day,
> Telling me that thou wert mine
>   But art dead and passed away;
> No returning—nought but mourning
>   O'er thy cold and coffined clay.
>
> Beauty banished, feelings vanished,
>   From thy dark and dull decay.

It was but a fragment, both in poetry and music. Yet, that music filled the hearts of all round and their eyes, too. He sang the last word and the chords rang, changing upon another key.

> Frozen fast is my heart at last
>   And unmoved by thy beams divine,
> Wild o'er the waste the wintery blast
>   Has withered and weakened thy shine.
>
> The pulse that once beat to each look and each word
>   Is congealed by the frosts of care,
> Thine eyes are ungazed on, thy voice is unheard,
>   For love ever flies from despair.
>
> Farewell then, farewell then, for parted forever
>   The blooming and blighted should be,
> Soon shall the ocean eternally sever
>   My heart from my country and thee.*

And ending in that wild melody, he turned to his auditors with a look that showed it was themselves he addressed, and that it was their beauty which sorrow had darkened in his mind. The music had not ceased. He was gazing on them with a wandering look; they, on him, with eyes almost in tears. But the full tones of the instrument sounded on in successions of thrilling melody, stealing insensibly on the hearts of the listeners.

As it was struck from the trembling hands of the musician, he again seemed wrapt in his inspiration and gave measure after measure of some grand ancient requiem whose swelling strains seemed to be bearing his thoughts from the world. They rose and deepened, and he relapsed into his feelings so that it was not until he had struck the last long chord that he looked around and seemed aware of the effect of his performance.

But when he did seem to notice the countenances of his auditors, the emotion he had kindled in their eyes, the looks of earnestness they were bending on him, their entranced and unbroken silence, he felt a flush of excitement which belied the words of his song and showed him to be Alexander Percy still. Many were the beautiful faces that regarded him with admiration, but one young lady who stood beside the piano he looked at with a flash of lightning keenness. The tears sparkled on her cheek, and the glistening of her large eyes was unshadowed even by the curls that fell above them. With clasped hands she had listened till her soul was carried away with the music. Her lovely face beamed with a sympathy which she did not think to hide; and there she stood knowing that in the man before her she beheld the founder of a society whose principles she regarded with horror and whose punishment she knew to be just, a man of whose profligacy few were ignorant, and on whose head tonight rested the dark shadow of a suspected parricide.

She knew this, and she was thinking of it. But the unconcealed agony of his tormented spirit roused all her sympathy, and the magnificent stature and aspect, the beautiful though ghastly face, the power, the splendour of that wonderful mind had infused all their influence into a heart which felt too exquisitely to soon lose the impression. Mary knew not herself that power (which others have often owned since) until in after solitariness, when there would be nothing around to sustain her.

But Percy knew the impression and saw in her face the spirit that had received it; and as he looked at the beautiful girl with her tearful hazel eyes and bright curling hair and gentle sylph-like form, a light did burst on him that showed not the dark waters of the Atlantic but the once-more shining woods of Wellington's Land. The Star had risen, whose rays for yet a few years were to delay the terrible night of misery. That Star whose setting brought a darkness which has never passed away.*

P. B. Brontë*
November 17th
1835

REAL LIFE IN VERDOPOLIS.
A TALE
By Captain John Flower. MP. FRS &c
IN III VOL'S
VOL, I.
CHAPTER I.

DURING the latter end of April, in the midst of those Forewarning which seemed to forebode to our general country another dreadful and protracted struggle, like those from which she has lately escaped, soon and raised to by the same means, A Trial came on in the Great Public hall of the Glasstown, which from the strange secrets it was expected to disclose and the manner in wich it was expected to involve several of the principal Mob Leaders and thus perhaps quashing the incipient rebellion, created the greatest interest ever at such a political period. Five fellows distinguished by the cognomens of Dick Naseby, Tom Cobham, Frank Twitchem, and Jack Ned Stinguishem, had been convicted of Robbing in the most daring manner a Government Courier on the road to Wellingtons land laden with large sums of money and several important dispatches, the intent of these fellows with regard to the "Blunty" as well as their reason to the wit the might make of it was very apparent and readily explained. But when it was understood that their first exclamation on shooting the Courier was "have at the papers" and the "Flimsys" and moreover when pursued they dropped the a of gold, yet retained the to the bit the higher prized dispatches, men began on to suspect that something more than met the eye, was concealed in this business. For why, in the name of every thing, that's reasonable should four such vagamuffins as these were feel any desire for slight escape. Gold of "plunder" unless directed from high quaters and actuated by hopes of reward. Feeling the weight of this argument and desiring as perhaps in the present crisis of criminating the Mob Leaders is possible since so doing would contribute to quell the approaching Commotion, the Government Judge the and the Government advocate in the case determined to pump the prisoners to at the approaching Trial to get from them by every means of crying the supposed important secret.

This Trial whose result was so much was expect and whose advent was so an xiously waited for came on at length on the 27.th of April, on that day, the Public Hall was filled, crammed, choaked with spectators of all classes and every opinion, the Mayor Col Grenville presided to keep out JOHN GIFFORD, to rethis seat as Judge and Sergeant Bud, acted as advocate for the Government. The counsel for the prisoners was called, a known thoroughs bred Lawyers well known in own city by the title of Lawyer Tweazy, of great repute for ability though honesty had never once been mentioned in a conjunction with his name, Proceedings opened by the Crown Advocate stating the nature of the case to be tried, its criminality, and the punishment which would first one its subject. He next hinted, to something of the suspicions affoat respecting the affair, and then proceeded to question the prisoners who stood at the dock perfectly unmoved by all that could be thought said or done respecting them. His First question was, what were your motives for the action you have committed." Stinguishem, answered, "Now if we're to be treated in jith a fashion as this Ise-Ise- I-.oh. you end of the jail a Bull hyed you, Cod Fish. you hide of a sheep. what do you mean by Motive and Action on-you Jew, say? Bud come now my man remember where you are." Stinguish, "I rayment ber well enough we was next door to a Rearing Pothouse and we cont get in to it we've just Sovereont, a haggerly swipe stakes and we coult. get our Knives into him." BUD. well well that not what I mean, now my Sure men. you'll have a chance of getting into the pot house and me to if you like. "If youll just bolt out why you d played this plisky what you thought. of the papers and who told you to take them eh".
TWITCHEM. Now my men day. if you set a squeazing us in this gate why well Just bolt thats all.

BUD come come my boys. this isn't— All the prisoners at this moment cried. "hope boys does the Cheplock call us boys if thing is coming on in this fashion we'se see why we do do of my vate spe. if we are to be called hogs they here ill. burst out in crying for it is well we know. those vaga lads cannot bear to be called by a name of which they are unknow to had Bud call ed them a spee "end of the Tail of a louse" or names yet more grotesque but to which they had been insistened they would have bust it over but a it was that end unfortunate wood. had ruined the proceedings of the whole evening Bud saw that this suit Turning to the Judge he said "My lord we can make nothing more of these with this night they had better be remanded. "Here Lawyer Tweezey rose up and said "My lord at a proper time and place I shall enter my protest against this mode of proce eding. I am well aware of the suspicions which have set afloat respecting this business but never were suspicions more wretchedly. Sounded, these men have a informed me that their reasons for approving so so aager about the papers arise from in an idea they entertained that they were Bank notes, And as the natural ly supposed that some dozens of the notes would be contained more value than a box of Sovereigns they so naturally upon being warmly pursued, flung the latter away rather than the former, this my lord explains the whole of this formidable mystery."

REAL LIFE IN VERDOPOLIS
A TALE

By Captain John Flower. MP. FRS &c

In II Vol's

VOL, I

CHAPTER I*

[Chapter I]

During the latter end of April, in the midst of those forewarnings which seemed to forebode to our general country another dreadful and protracted struggle like those from which she has lately escaped—and raised too by the same means—a trial came on in the Great Public Hall of the Glasstown. From the strange secrets it was expected to disclose and the manner in which it was expected to involve several of the principal mob leaders and thus perhaps quash the incipient rebellion, it created the greatest interest ever at such a political period. Four fellows,* distinguished by the cognomens of Dick Nose'em, Tom Catchem, Frank Twitchem, and Ned Stinguishem, had been convicted of robbing in the most daring manner on the road to Wellington's Land a Government Courier laden with large sums of money and several important dispatches. The intent of these fellows with regard to the 'Blunty'* as well as the use they might make of it was very apparent and readily explained.

But when it was understood that their first exclamations on flooring the courier were 'Have at the papers', and 'Mind the flimsies', and moreover when pursued that they dropped the gold, yet retained to the last the higher-prized dispatches, men began to suspect that something more than met the eye was concealed in this business. For why, in the name of everything that's reasonable, should four such ragamuffins as these feel any desire for aught except gold or plunder, unless directed from higher quarters and actuated by hopes of reward? Feeling the weight of this argument and desirous perhaps in the present crisis of incriminating the mob leaders if possible, since so doing would contribute to quell the approaching commotion, the judge, the jury, and the Government Advocate in the case determined to pump the prisoners and at the approaching trial to get from them by every means of coaxing the supposed important secret.

This trial from whose result so much was expected and whose advent was so anxiously awaited came on at length on the 27th of

April; on that day, the Public Hall was filled, crammed, choked with spectators of all classes and every opinion. John Gifford* took his seat as Judge and Sergeant Bud acted as Advocate for the Government. The counsel for the prisoners was a keen, thoroughbred lawyer, well known in our city, by the title of Lawyer Tweezy, of great repute for ability, though honesty had never once been mentioned in conjunction with his name. Proceedings were opened by the Crown Advocate stating the nature of the case to be tried, its criminality, and the punishment which would rest on its authors. He next hinted something of the suspicions afloat respecting the affair and then proceeded to question the prisoners, who stood at the dock perfectly unmoved by all that could be thought, said, or done respecting them.

The first question was, 'What were your motives for the action you have committed?'

Stinguishem answered, 'Now, if we're to be treated in sich a fashion as this, I'se—I'se—I'se. Oh, you end of the tail of a bull! You cod fish, you hide of a frog! What do you mean by motive and haction—you rare dog, you!'

BUD: 'Come now, my man, remember where you are.'

STINGUISHEM: 'I remember well enough where we are; we're next door to a roaring pothouse and we can't get our heads in to it. We're just forenent, a beggarly swipe-stakes, and we can't get our knives into him.'

BUD: 'Well, well, that is not what I mean. Now, my rare men, you'll have a chance of getting into the pothouse, and me too, if you like, if you'll just bolt out why you played this plisky, what you thought of the papers, and who told you to lift them, eh?'

TWITCHEM: 'Now, my rare dog, if you set asqueezing us in this gate, why, we'll just bolt. That's all.'

BUD: 'Come, come, my hogs.* This isn't . . .'

All the prisoners at this moment cried, 'Hogs, hogs! Does the cat's flesh call us hogs? If things is coming on in this fashion, we'se see what we can do! Oh, my rare ape! If we're to be called hogs!'

They here all burst out in a fit of crying, for it is well known these rare lads cannot bear to be called by a name which they are unused to. Had Bud called them apes, 'end of the tail of a louse', or names yet more grotesque but to which they had been accustomed, they would have past it over; but, as it was, that unfortunate word had ruined the proceedings of the whole evening. Bud saw this and turning to the Judge he said, 'My lord, we can make nothing more of these men this night. They had better be remanded.'

Here Lawyer Tweezy rose up and said, 'My Lord, at a proper time and place I shall enter my protest against this mode of proceeding. I am well aware of the suspicions which are afloat respecting this business, but never were suspicions more wretchedly founded. These men have informed me that their reasons for appearing so eager about the papers arose from the idea they entertained that they were banknotes, and as they naturally supposed that some dozens of the notes would contain more value than one box of sovereigns, they naturally upon being warmly pursued flung the latter away rather than the former. This, my lord, explains the whole of this formidable mystery.'

'A very plausible explanation,' said Gifford, 'but, however, let these men be remanded for the present, till something more is brought to light. Officers, take the prisoners back into custody.' This order was promptly obeyed; and the prisoners having departed, the Hall soon began to pour forth its vast multitudes and in a short time remained empty, gloomy in the decaying evening.

One figure alone, that of Tweezy,* remained pacing its shadowy pavement. He constantly kept looking at his watch, and when the hand pointed to the hour of ten, he hurried out of the building and with hasty footsteps bent his course toward the Great Jail. After threading a multitude of dark alleys and darker passages, he arrived in front of the outer portal of this mighty building. He paused not to survey its vast proportions nor the sublime appearance of its shadowy walls rising black and indistinct against the starry sky, but to knock loudly at the gate.

The porter opened. An aged man of the old days, he held in his hand a lighted lamp, the beams of which fell concentrated on his shiny locks and stern, time-worn visage and on the more insidious lurking countenance of the lawyer. Tweezy desired to be admitted to the four prisoners in the tower.

The porter shook his head and said, 'The time is past, my man; for sich as you, my orders are against it.'

Tweezy drew him toward a corner and began to converse with him in an earnest tone of voice for some time. At the conclusion of the dialogue, the porter, casting a hasty look round, silently unlocked a small postern in the wall, and they both entered. With noiseless footsteps they glided through many dark passages and up a steep staircase till stopped by a small iron door. This the porter opened and Tweezy having entered, he left the lamp. He descended and disappeared. The room in which the lawyer stood was the cell of the prisoners. It was low, damp, and dark, but from all appearance the hardy fellows it contained cared little about all its inconveniences. They lay on the floor in different postures, but all sound asleep. Tweezy, advancing, awakened them one after another; and when, after many yawns, execrations, and grumblings, they became conscious who was speaking to them, he said, 'Now, my rare apes, stick fast. Your trial comes on again tomorrow. Say what you like, but don't reveal your secret.'

'Ay,' replied Stinguishem, 'we will say what we like, my rare man; we've all made up our minds upon that matter. But as to not revealing our secret, that's a different case. Listen, my rare ape. We're determined, whatsomever comes of it, if you don't help us out of this dog hole this very night, why, we'll balk, we'll let out ivry thing. Our mind's made up, so no more speaking. Will you or won't you release us?'

From the determined look of these fellows, the lawyer's searching eyes saw that there was no reply except one. For a moment he stood thunderstruck, but at once, as if he recollected something, he replied 'Courage, my rare men. I'll let you out this very night. One o'clock. One o'clock, be ready.' Then, stepping out, he closed the door after him and descended the steps. At the landing place he was met by the porter, who silently conducted him back to the great gate. There Tweezy, turning round, said hastily, 'Tom, is your time out by one o'clock?'

The porter answered, 'Ay, my rare lad; if that's what you trust to, you're lost. I'm just going now to deliver the keys to the next watch.'

Tweezy again seemed petrified. He hastily cried, 'Would you think your next watch might be—?'

'Oh no,' said the porter, cutting him short. 'Oh my rare man, he's Ned Standfast, an's been a servant to the Duke of Wellington.'

'Oh, then,' replied Tweezy, 'that's over, now. Well, we'll try some other way. Good night, Jack.'* The lawyer stepped out; the porter shut the gate, and each departed on his way.

[Chapter II*]

May 20, 1833

That night, as Lady Zenobia Elrington* was resting alone in her splendid saloon, deeply engaged in the discussion of Seneca's *Epistles* in the original, the door opened, and her husband entered the room. He advanced to her sofa* and lying his hand on the back of it stood a little while musing in silence. He first broke it by saying, 'Madam, you must neither go to nor receive any parties or persons here this evening.'

'What, my lord?' she answered. 'What do you command? You may give way to your humours as you like, but do not expect me to do the same. Let me see. I shall receive three parties and go to five in the whole, my lord.'

'Do you dare to disobey me?' replied Rougue in that calm, deep voice which with him is the sign of utter determination.

Zenobia started at the tone and started still more when, on looking at him, she observed the paleness of his countenance and the deadly and even awful gleam of his eyes. She knew this was neither time for contradiction nor reply and remained silent.

'You have me?' he continued in the same calm, unaltered voice.

'Yes, my lord,' she replied rather faintly, for his expression and manner convinced her who so well knew him that there was 'Something dreadful in the gale'. He nodded and withdrew.

That night the splendid square of Elrington Place seemed deserted. The ceaseless roaring of carriages, the cracking of whips, and the dismounting of countless multitudes was silent, and the heavy golden knockers rung not with the incessant annunciations of visitors. It seemed that the lord of the mansion was lying dead in its apartments. But this was not the case. Rougue, Viscount Elrington, was seated alone in his study, silently reading a volume of Lucian's *Dialogues*. The cold, atheistic sentiments, the continual sneering at humanity and human life agreed well with his disposition and served for a while to fix his attention, but cares and thoughts too mighty to be driven long away soon seemed again to press on his mind.

He laid the book down and, rising, began to pace round the apartment. Several times he turned to the window and looked out upon the vast city spread below him. Its mighty edifices, its various streets, its crowds of houses and mills and palaces, all sweeping away in the darkness like black clouds on a midnight sky, while the million lights twinkling and glancing, appearing and disappearing below him, seemed like the stars in a reflected heaven. But if there were stars below, there were none above, for the sky was covered with moist, rainy clouds. Like his own soul, all looked dark and comfortless.

But meditation and contemplation were not the attributes for which Rougue was famous. He soon turned from this scene to a rosewood cupboard in the corner of the apartment, and taking therefrom a bottle and glass sat down in his accustomed seat. Here he remained drinking silently but constantly, glass after glass of pure, undiluted brandy. But just as the clock struck eleven,* he heard a gentle tap at his door. He cried 'Come in', it opened, and there entered, with slow, insidious footstep, Lawyer Tweezy.

Rougue, starting, exclaimed,* 'Ha! Dog, you here! Well! What news? Quick!'

Tweezy, first taking a chair and giving an affectionate hug to the bottle, replied by stating what had happened in court with regard to the four prisoners, his pilgrimage to the jail, and his interview with them.

In concluding, he said, 'The Porter or Watch, Sir, is now changed. The men at present watching are not to be tampered with, and for my part I am at a loss entirely how to act. To have the secret divulged would be dreadful, to attempt to liberate them would be no less so.'

'For your part? Fool, what should you know? Look at that straw on the carpet. To you, I suppose, to let it remain there would be dreadful, to take it up, not less so?'

Rougue with his usual penetration and energy had, while Tweezy was speaking, contrived and determined upon a scheme, which however required more resolution to act upon than skill to invent. He shoved away bottles and glasses from him and opening a desk began to write. He soon indited four or five letters which, after sealing and directing, he gave into the hands of Tweezy.

'Now,' he said, 'go instantly and take these letters each to the man for whom they are intended. For your better expedition, you may take a horse from my stables. In default of speed, your life shall be the forfeit, Tweezy, I swear it.'

The Lawyer too well knew his patron's temper and spirit to disobey his injunction. He gave a last kiss to the bottle, jumped up, and taking with him the letters left the room. Rougue listened till he heard his horse's feet leaving the square. All weight of care then seemed dismissed from his mind. Instead of the cold, sneering misanthropy which had hitherto seemed to pervade his countenance, his eyes now flashed fire, and his aspect seemed filled with the ardour which he always displays on the eve of some great crisis. He rung the bell for his valet who, appearing, soon attired him in a strong travelling suit. He then seized his hat and sword and, first ordering his fleetest horse, hastened to the apartment of Lady Zenobia. She had thrown by her reading and was now engaged in writing. Rougue as he entered smiled.

'Active, active. Well, I like that. It's better than to be like some Ladies whom I know who, when without company, die through ennui and with it die through fatigue.' The more than usually cordial tone of this speech did not, as it would from any common person, please Lady Zenobia but alarmed her. She knew well enough that her Lord seldom used words so kind but when on the eve of some great enterprise, some awful plunge. His fiery eye and his travelling dress increased her fears.

She said hastily, 'Rougue, where are you going, what will you do?'

'Never mind, Zenobia, I hope I'm not going home,' replied Rougue, pointing downwards. He continued, 'But listen, I have to go a journey now. You say as little of it as you can. Keep all things as they are till I come back. Good night. Good bye.'

He turned round and left the room. Descending the stairs, he hastened to the yard where his horse stood ready saddled. He mounted, cast one look at his vast mansion rising gloomily in the midnight sky, and then putting spurs to his steed disappeared in the darkness.*

That night between the hours of eleven and twelve o'clock, the dark, desolate alleys lying on the north side of and shadowed by the lofty towers of the General Prison exhibited a scene of bustle and animation unusual to them. In general their high, crumbling buildings and narrow, forsaken pavements at this hour only echoed to the solitary footsteps of some drunken rare lad or Frenchy going to or reeling from the rotten doors of the low pothouse whose red light, glinting through a thousand chinks and crannies in wall and window, was the only one that broke the doleful gloom. Perhaps, too, at such times it might be the lot of him who chooses to explore these dangerous recesses to stumble over something soft and yielding which, perchance, upon his coming into contact with it he might perceive to be a human being gashed over with wounds and rotting in the air. But whatever might in general be the appearance of these places, it was widely different now. The light from a hundred torches glared upon each huge, decaying wall or fell in wild confusion upon the ferocious and upturned faces of the multitudes crowding the space below. All present seemed to come together by one consent but not one seemed to know for what he came.

They were agreed upon two points, to be here present, and all to have arms. Everywhere muskets, rifles, knives, and bludgeons flourished in profusion, all waiting for general employment.

In the meantime, to pass away the period till the grand plot should open, many a little episode was acted through the multitudes. To an Englishman, to a stranger, it would have seemed as if two rival and savage armies were combatting together for life or death. But in reality the case was otherwise. Though the report of guns was incessant, though knives were everywhere brandished, though numbers fell dead or wounded, the 'rare fellows' were 'nobbutt spreeing a bit till Rougue should appear'.

A general shout through every lane and alley in the neighbourhood soon hailed the advent of this distinguished personage. He appeared advancing on horseback, pistol in one hand, and his sword in the other.

Tightening the reins of his steed, he halted and, pointing with his sword to the immense walls of the jails which rose above them in the darkness like a band of formless Genii, said in his usual loud, clear voice, 'Friends, I believe that you all see yon towers before us, and I believe that you all know what they are.' (A general yell.) 'Very well. It is, you must know, very essential to our general liberty that several men there confined should this night be liberated.' (Another yell louder than the first.) 'The reasons I have given to your leaders, Naughty, Lawless, Carey, and the rest. That is sufficient. They may deliberate, you must act! Have you got all your arms in order?' (Loud howls of assent.) 'Very well. Form into three lines.' (This was accomplished amid direful howling, thrusting, fighting, and eclipsing of the torches.) 'Well, again. Now, you torch bearers come in front. Naughty, you head one rank. Carey, you another. Lawless, take the third, and I'll head you all.'

'Hurra, Rougue forever! The Jail and Victory!' A horrid and tyger-like yell followed this speech.

Rougue, spurring his horse, galloped on in a direction opposite to the Prison for the purpose of disentangling himself from the narrow lanes and attacking it in front. The armed multitude of many thousands of men followed him in due order, scouring the streets from side to side, threatening, shouting, and constantly firing their muskets. As they rolled on, their numbers increased, so that when arrived at the Grand Market Place the crowd became truly alarming. The whole area was filled with the blaze of torches and ringing with their confused uproar.

By this time a report had spread through that quarter of the city that some great popular commotion was on the eve of breaking out, and hundred-tongued fame magnified it into an attempt at a revolution. The Government, anxious not to give the mob one instance of 'showing fright',* hastily assembled as large a body of troops and military as could be got together at such an unfavourable hour. But where to place them was the question. For an hour, all was uncertainty on this point, but from the continued cries of the advancing mob, 'The Jail! The Jail! Down with the prison', this doubt was soon put to rest. Three regiments of cavalry and a large body of police were instantly dispatched under the command of John Sneaky to guard that important building and to block up every avenue leading to it. This they did and, having surrounded the place, waited with fixed arms the approach of the mob.

At this moment the scene was solemn and even sublime. It was night. Over the huge building the black clouds rolled thick and gloomily, opening now and then to show the cold, silent moon, which for a moment made visible the mighty city, the summit of the Tower of Nations, and the vast buttress of the threatened walls. Its pale light gleamed fitfully on the long lines of armour which surrounded the gates, and then all rolled back in their former gloom.

In a short while above the general hum of the city distinctly rose the distant yet advancing cries of the mob. They rose hoarse and discordant as the wind swept past and wakened the soldiers to double ardour. In a while vast shoals of boys, nondescripts, and all the usual shoals of idlers attending a popular commotion began to pour forward into the square; and suddenly through the darkness, at the opening of a distant street, one vast blaze of torchlight flashed forward upon all.

Now the word of command past quickly from rank to rank. With short, shrill screams, the boys hailed the approaching contest.

The mob was coming!*

All down the street in long and tumultuous array poured the resistless torrent; the lights, though in such vast numbers, though they glared on all round with a crimson blaze, yet could not dissipate anywhere the utter darkness, and the wild, ferocious features of the rioters crowding on in black masses toward their gloomy goal. First in the front on his noble horse, which had borne him safe through a hundred conflicts, advanced the leader Rougue, his gigantic spirit raised now to the highest pitch of which it was capable. This was his sport, his pastime. The scenes around him were the only ones which could light a glow of pleasure on his noble countenance. In the gambling house, in the Senate, in private, however elated he might be, his features always preserved their iron sternness and cold sarcastic smile. But in the heat of a midnight conflict, all reserve was thrown by and he gave his fiery spirit full liberty to revel in the darkness and dangers of battle.

But enough of this, to our narrative. Before the officers could utter the word 'Fire', before the men could prepare their muskets, the whole body of rioters had precipitated themselves pellmell among them.

Among the Glasstowners in such cases it is scarcely customary to read the Riot Act or to fire blank cartridges. For such a proceeding our tempers are neither sufficiently patient nor phlegmatic. Here with bayonet and sword, with musket and bludgeon, did both parties at once 'join issue'. Now so long as the numbers on each side continued pretty equal, the more regular and better-trained body of military had greatly the advantage. As fast as their antagonists rushed in, they heaped them dying before them. Once, indeed, they had rolled the whole torrent backward and obtained space to pour upon their black and congregated masses a well-directed and destructive fire of musketry; but as the smoke rolled off and the echoes of the guns rattled upon the vast walls before them and thundered among the wilderness of buildings darkening behind them, it seemed the knell of these brave soldiers.

To a Glasstowner, the sound and smell of gunpowder is, indeed, dear as the nut to which his soul conforms.* And therefore, the moment that this volley ceased, the mob, impetuous, again rushed forward. Rougue seemed guarded by supernatural aid for, though always in the very front of the firing, he remained untouched, unwounded.* But now new masses of men joined the mob; their numbers swelled as if the earth were restoring its dead around them.

Rougue but cried, 'Now for the Jail and Victory!' and, with one tyger shout, over soldiers, walls, and bulwarks was hurled onward one blazing mass of men.

Where are the Military now? No trace of them is to be seen. Oh yes, under the mob there is a dreadful heaving, and soon the middle of the crowd breaks open and armed men are seen fighting for life with desperate energy. But all is lost. Here new shoals of men rushing from every street precipitate themselves over their fellows and rushing forward hide every remnant of the gallant regiment. Now the great postern of the Gateway is surrounded by the foremost rioters. Rougue and Naughty like furies rage before its huge iron-bound frame:

> 'There Rougue' among the foremost deals his blows,
> And with his axe repeated strokes bestows
> On the strong doors, then all their shoulders ply
> Till from the posts the brazen hinges fly.
>
> Dryden*

Doubled and trebled were the blows from pickaxe and crowbar and bludgeon. Incessant were the heavings from gigantic and brawny shoulders, and at length it gave a crash, burst inwards, and fell back in the gloom. Now the great yard was in a moment filled, choked with armed men and the hissing firebrands threw their strong, lurid light high up on the buttresses of the assaulted prison. Here it stood before them in all its gloomy majesty, but how were they to enter? Here every door, and there were many, was framed of solid iron. But they were not long in deliberation.

'Bring fire!' cried Rougue in his loudest and clearest voice. 'I could ken it among a thousand.'

The words were scarcely spoken when a thousand torches were bent forward toward him. Beams, barrels, everything combustible rose rapidly in an immense pile before the principal doorway. Black smoke rose hissing from the heap. In a few minutes a clear red sheet of flame rose high in the darkness. A loud and long-continued yell announced this grateful event, a yell which was from time to time renewed as one bright flake upon another burst against the fast blackening walls. The shining sparks and splinters like stars whirled and shot overhead, and the dense clouds of smoke blocking up the air produced feelings much akin to suffocation. At length over the astounding tumult, three loud cracks in the fire announced the vast door had given way; and in an instant, over every obstacle like an army of locusts extinguishing the fire, in poured the resistless mob.

An hour ago and nothing could be more dark, more silent, than the interior of this mighty building. Nothing could be heard but the keys creaking in the doors as the jailors, before retiring, went round to ascertain that all was safe. But now, in a moment, every endless passage, every winding avenue, flamed and thundered to the footsteps and torches of the entering rioters. Hundreds were heard, rather than seen, racing along those passages, the lights glancing like falling meteors. Every cell door was torn open, and the lately chained inmates joined the mob, swelling it like the rivulets to a mighty stream. Up the strong wooden stairs rushed the resistless multitude, and with loud yells and shouting performed the same kind office to those above. Stinguishem, Twitchem, Catchem, and Nosem were seen now, free among the thickest of the uproar. The walls seemed to split with the clamour and high overhead the roofs echoed like peals of thunder.

Now the awful voice of their leader cried, 'Fire the prison!'

This was in unison with the most heartfelt wishes of the rare lads. Every heart bent itself to the 'sport', every torch was put in requisition. All being cleared from the upper stories, the lower rooms were filled with vast beams, rafters, piles of wood, wool, any thing that would flame. Torches were scattered among them, then all living rushed from the building, and at a respectful distance with groans, yells, and shouting waited the breaking-forth of the conflagration.

For some time an incessant hissing in the building was the only thing that told what was going on. Then the thick smoke began to curl out from the gaping door. Quickly it came out, blacker, thicker, and intermingled with sparks. Then tongues of red flame darted forth from the front windows, and all knew that the fire had arisen and was devouring all within. The flames now came out thick and fast. All were gazing on them when, with a mighty and astounding crack, the roof gave way above. Many slates and blazing beams burst into the area, while the main mass, hissing and blazing, crashing into the interior tore through ceilings and floor. From the lowest 'bed of flame' now, as from a mighty furnace, the smoke rolled red and wavering. From the gaping building the fires streamed upward to the sky, cast their light through the whole frightened city. The front towers and walls stood black and shattered against the glowing light, but every moment portions of them would burst into the blaze and be seen no more. But, however, another scene now presented itself which turned the thoughts of the rioters away from this sublime but terrific spectacle.

The streets seemed to shake and tremble behind them; and ere they were aware, a vast body of cavalry, bloody with spurring, fiery hot with haste, headed by the Marquis of Douro dashed boldly in among them. The Government had become aware of their movement and had sent 6,000 men to disperse them. Now, among the surprised rioters nothing was to be seen but utter consternation. The horsemen had dashed in among them and were hacking them down by hundreds. With a frantic fury they threw themselves over the walls among burning ruins, poured in a thousand columns down every lane and alley, burst impetuously in thousands all down the grand streets, and in an hour had all evaporated in the general mass of this mighty capital.

When the first crimson light of morning began to stretch through the darkness over the sea, no trace remained of the insurrection but the vast heaps of dead bodies covering the field of fight, the thousand pieces of armour scattered through the city, the houses standing with torn walls and glassless windows round the bloody area. And high over all in the dusky twilight, the vast, blackened, shattered pile of towers and wall: 'The Jail', torn, riven, smoking, and flaming like a bursting volcano.

[*Chapter III**]

May 23, 1833

Reader, let us escape from these bloody scenes. Stand here with me. We are in the open country; the white mists of morning are softly and coolly rolling back into the stainless blue, and are beginning to fleck the sky with light, fluffy clouds. As these vapours ascend upward, they unveil the landscape before us. And what is this landscape? It is the Glasstown Valley. Yes, backward and backward sweeps a wide, a magnificent sea of verdure, golden cornfields and hedges of glowing green intermixed with a hundred stately parks and a thousand stately mansions standing white in the morning sun. Each side of this plain, undulating at first, softly then bends up into a ridge of majestic and luxuriant hills. Long and high, yet gentle and cultivated, they sweep away through the sunshine toward the purpled and golden horizon. Through this mighty and fertile valley winds stately on what at first looks like an arm of the sea, but its pure glassy surface and the lofty palms and oaks intermingled feathering down to its margin at once destroy that likeness. It is a vast river, it is the Niger, rolling to the Glasstown the collected waters of Africa.

Through this noble valley and 'at the sweet hour of dawn', the morning after the events recorded in our last chapter, there proceeded from the great metropolis, up the Grand Northern Road, a man mounted on horseback. The reins were thrown loosely over the arched neck of his steed, whose appearance together with the costly equipment and above all the lofty and graceful bearing of his rider betokened both, each in his way, to be of 'salt of the land'. The mind of that rider seemed taken up entirely with something of great interest and importance. He neither looked around nor seemed to know whether it was night or morn, fine or foul. His aristocratic features bore impressed on them the marks of stern care and also, I must add, of deep dissipation. No other expression hovered over them except what might be contained in one cold, sarcastic smile which he gave as, at one point of the road, he turned his horse and stopped to survey the city he had left.

That city, the Glasstown, lay about 13 miles behind him, wrapped in a thick cloud of smoke and vapour which stretched along, brown and murky over the whole southern horizon. Through its hazy curtain only three or four objects showed themselves, such as the glorious Tower of Nations and far, far inward, the huge dome of St Michael's Cathedral.* But what most attracted the attention of our cavalier was the now-fading, now-blackening piles of smoke which, wreathing heavily through the haze, denoted the spot where stood the yet-smouldering Jail.* He looked steadily upon this for a moment and then with that bitter smile turned round his steed and went on his way. After proceeding several miles further through this magnificent valley, he stopped at the splendid gateway of an extensive park which for a great distance lined the Grand Northern Road. This gate was opened with wonderful alacrity by the bowing porters, and he galloped swiftly up the sunny lawns and shady avenues till he reached the front of a splendid modern mansion.

Here springing from his horse he desired of the servants to be shown into the presence of their master. He was accordingly conducted through a gorgeous suite of apartments to the door of an extensive library. He entered. At the upper end was seated at a table surrounded by, immersed in, piles of books, papers, and writing materials, the owner of all he saw. He was a man of about 40 years old, gigantic in size, firmly-built and evincing vast muscular power. His hair, of which he had a considerable quantity, was even-grey with study and hung wildly down over an immense and knotted forehead. His eye was keen and restless, showing the true fire of ambition; his whole countenance was cast in the sternest mould, energetic, harsh, and repulsive, shattered like his visitor by marks of deep dissipation. The moment his guest entered, he started up and looked at him with great astonishment.

'What, Rougue,' he said, 'You here, too?'

'Aye,' replied Rougue, for he it was whom we have followed on his journey. 'Aye, Montmorency,* I am here but what mean you by saying "too"?' Saying this, he threw himself languidly on the rich Indian sofa.

Mr Montmorency replied, 'Oh, why only Ned Sydney.'

'Ned who?' asked Rougue, starting up.

'Ned Sydney, the new member for Freetown.'

A frown of blackest and most tremendous appearance darkened the whole visage of Rougue as he replied. 'Hang that viper, and has he, too, started up to cross me?'

'Oh,' said Montmorency, 'don't take on so. The more difficulties encountered, the more glorious our victory, while (with a strange smile) I could crush that one with a word or two.'

'Not so,' said Rougue, the frown however passing off like magic and giving place to his usual heartless sneer. 'You haven't seen the toad's maiden speech, made two nights ago. You don't know his keenness. He's not like you, Montmorency, in body, but he's something like you in soul.'

His host returned, 'Now there is nothing, Elrington, which I detest more than cant, and just now you seem about to fall into it, eh?'

Rougue answered, 'Stop. You saw smoke on the horizon this morning? Well, the Jail is on fire. How? The four prisoners threatened "they'd peach an' we didn't lause 'um". You'll guess what followed.'

Montmorency at this hint started, and his face assumed a yet darker expression. 'Well, Rougue, if it does get to light, it's all up with me.'

Rougue replied, 'Now, Mont, to prevent undue disclosures, would it not be best to make off with these fellows? Tweezy and the four. I, you know, am going to our firm in the Mountains. Therefore, I'll just leave you to superintend all that business. You're going to the City to light your lamp, so you can also attend at the same time to our bit of an affair, likewise, eh?'

'I will, my man, but let us see whether I've got anything in my cellar,' answered Montmorency, and rung for the waiter.

His domestic, appearing, was ordered to bring forward a large measure of wine and brandy. In the interval, these two heroes continued talking together in a strain so obscure and technical that it would be useless to repeat their conversation. The 'Spiritual Waters' having made their appearance in the form of two vast jars of brandy, with several dozens of the 'the weaker brethren', Rougue and Montmorency by mutual consent set in to profound drinking. For a long time they continued to pour down amazing quantities of the 'lush' in perfect silence; but in a while their faces became flushed, their eyes flashed, and Montmorency first broke silence by uttering in a *sotto voce* tone the words 'Dog, dog'.

This expression Rougue understood as applied to himself, and he therefore, first turning down* a glass of brandy, cried in a rather louder voice, 'You hound, you villain!'

Montmorency, in return, swallowed his drink with the words, 'Beast! Wretch! Scavenger!'

His guest answered him with a loud execration and then both together, amid repeated draughts of brandy, continued roars of imprecation, and incessant shouts of cursing, beheld the table, floor, and at length the whole room whirling around them like a top. Dropping innumerable bottles and glasses and catching hold of everything around them, they, grappling with each other in a dying frenzy, descended on to the floor amid the crash and tumult of tables and chairs hurled above them in promiscuous confusion. The domestics, who well knew what was likely to happen, in a while entered the apartment and conveyed each of these 'Nobles of Nature' away to their quiet beds.

Here we shall leave them till the following morning. At which time, just as the sun was rising over the glorious valley, we behold Rougue mounting his horse at the hall doors with a firmness of step and brightness of eye which showed that such scenes as the one we have been describing were quite trivial with him. By him Montmorency stood, to whom Rougue on taking his leave said, 'Now, Mont, my dove, you know my mind in this matter. The upshot of our course concerns yourself as much as me. Therefore you'll just do as I told you respecting our gentlemen yonder. Now you know where I'm going and what I intend to do. And I say, should I, when I return, find that you've played the oaf and slackened your ways, I'll—why, you shan't have one farthing of our proceeds.'

'Won't I?' returned Montmorency. 'You shall see wither I won't. But howsoever that be, I'll do the thing to a toucher. If I light my own lamp, be sure I'll quench theirs. Adieu, my sweet one!'

'Farewell, my darling,' answered Rougue as he turned his horse's head and cantered merrily down the avenue.

He still continued his course toward the North and up the Glasstown Valley, but he passed the splendid scenes which continually met his eye without even once looking upon them; or if he did, it was with the vacant gaze which shows a mind concentrated upon some overwhelming theme within. In the evening he arrived at Freetown, from which early next morning he started to proceed on his journey. This day, the scenery began to show symptoms of a speedy change.

First he left the great vale for the wide, sunny, fertile plain, covered with fields of gold and trees of gold and fruits of gold. Then that plain began to raise itself into long, low, wavy undulations, like the billows of a rolling sea, and just as the sun rested its flaming disk on the north-west horizon, taking one look ere it left this fairy scene and flinging its level rays all round the sky, Rougue's piercing sight perceived the summit of a long and distant range of mountains beneath the very centre of the flaming light. His stern features at the sight lit up with a friendly smile, for with no refined feelings he yet adored and reverenced the hills and mountains. All other scenes but those of moors and wastes and rocks he with all his usual heat and decisiveness contemned and despised.* But now so eager was he to reach his beloved hills that all that night did he ride on without stop or rest. And had not he and his horse both possessed a more than common share of strength, they would neither have found themselves as they did, when morning dawned on a wild, rocky, heathy flat, elevated far above the smiling plains of Ashantee,* which like a sea stretched back in the haze behind them, while before, for many miles huge, dull swells of heath rose one after the other in monotonous succession. Yet this species of scenery Rougue admired above every other. He had long left the Grand North Road, and striking on to a mountain path pursued his way along its unfrequented track, at every turn plunging farther and farther into the mazes of the wilderness. But all these moors and turns were perfectly well know to him, and even to his horse who, with the reins suspended on its neck while its master indulged in his reveries, continued to trot on in the safest and indeed the only path. This, the fourth evening from his setting out from the Glasstown, beheld him gain the summit of one of the long, swelling hummocks, and the sight he saw from it was one which none could grudge fatigue to view.*

Far down before him swept the side of that hill, black with heath and mottled with rock, no path, not even a solitary sheepwalk, stretching over its face. Its base was* washed by the waters of a large and rapid brook which, after running with a hundred turns through the rushy and marshy plain beyond, disappeared among deep gorges and confused heaps of heathy hillocks. Over this chaos stretched moor after moor, lying in mighty terraces, one over the other, and all sloping on each side to the plain, forming a wide and dark valley for the bed of some great stream whose broad surface could be observed shining at intervals amid the waste. Thus far the scene possessed sublimity more from its vast extent, its utter desolation, than from any other quality.

But look forward and see what it is that casts such a shade over this highland landscape! The clouds are all rolling off into the sky, and gradually unveil first the skirts, then the sides, of a ridge of terrific, enormous mountains, which sweep forward first and then far, far backward over the whole extent of view. Their height alone is terrible but much more so are their terrific chasms, their white and hoary rocks, their precipices towering a thousand feet into the sky, and their vast heads capped with great clouds and shining snow. These Alpine mountains are the 'Robbers' Towers' and that great stream is 'the Red River'.

All these scenes Rougue was well acquainted with. Many of the acts of his past life had been laid among them, and every foot-track could he trace amid their recesses, were all as dark as the 'Last Night of Coomassiee'*—but it is high time to return to our story.

Rougue stopped a short time to view the vast piles before him and then descended the steep. It gave him small uneasiness to view the depth of the torrent before him. He dashed fearlessly in and after some hard struggles gained the opposite bank and continued his way through the marsh amid sloughs and pools where, had he not been accurately acquainted with the place, both he and his horse might have found sure stabling and a lasting home. Soon he neared the wild, raging waters of that king of hill streams, the Red River, and here he stopped. For these were not waves to be passed by a child, no, nor man either, for with that red colour from which the stream is named they rushed onward, one over another, foaming and chafing the rocks and steeps beside them. One would think that this opposed an effectual barrier to our traveller's journey but it was not so. He directed his steed a little way down the bank to the mouth of what seemed a gigantic badger hole or otter's den. Here he alighted and holding his horse by the bridle entered the gloomy cavity and disappeared downward. Not many minutes had elapsed when he again emerged, on the other side, and continued his journey. This hole ran along under the whole bed of the stream and ended like a tunnel in an entrance or exit on the opposite bank, but few knew of so great a convenience.

When Rougue had arrived among the aforementioned chaos of rocks and heath and hillocks lying at the bases of the Robbers' Towers, he halted his wearied steed and gave a loud, shrill whistle. But who was there to answer the call? All looked to be the extreme of desolation. A human foot seemed never to have trod or a human voice to have sounded amid this gloomy wild. Oh, never mind for this. Rougue had scarcely ceased his whistle when it was answered by another from among the rocks and rubbish. Shortly, two men, armed at all points, rushed toward Rougue from their hiding place. When they saw him distinctly, nothing could exceed the astonishment which seemed to overcome them; but he forbade speech and commanded them to take his horse to the stables. They did this with the utmost obsequience.

Rougue himself passed forward among the chaos till he came before the entrance of a huge cavern, black as death but scarcely so silent, for from its inmost recesses came forth distant shouts, screams, and peals of laughter. Rougue walked, still forward, with the air of one well acquainted with every secret of this wild den. In a while, after threading many intricate passages, flashes of red light burst through the gloom, and he speedily had his hand on the lock of a great iron door which he opened quietly, and silently entering the apartment to which it led stood unobserved, a witness of the proceedings therein. That apartment was a huge inner cavern of great length and height, the sides damp rock and the floor black clay. At the farthest end of this apartment roared up a sort of chimney a huge, bright-red fire of peat which cast a crimsoned and unsteady light through the whole room. Stretching nearly from the fire to the door was a long oak table covered with and groaning beneath immense dishes of roast and boiled beef, mutton, deer, hares, birds, piles of bread, and mighty jugs and casks and bottles of brandy, rum, whisky, arrack, and beer.

Round this noble fare flashed a hundred knives and daggers, assaulting with eager fury its noblest bulwarks and brandished by the brawny arms of as many stern, iron-looking men of the 'rare lad' species, with here and there a northern highlander interspersed. These fellows beseiged the lower end and sides of this table, but the head was governed by men of different appearance. In the midst sat a wretched, withered, fiendish-looking old man. Little in stature, dirty, and clothed in a shabby, tattered blanket, this old wretch seemed lord of this ample feast. At his right and left hands, there sat about a dozen tall, gentlemenly, and officerlike men, dashingly dressed but of sinister and reckless aspect, evidently given up to the vilest dissipation and perhaps the most lawless courses, for huge pistols were seen sticking in every belt. The knives that all used were short poinards; and muskets, bayonets, swords, and heaps of packages, boxes, carpets, with innumerable other things lay in wild confusion round the floors.

While Rouge stood concealed behind the door, a hundred conversations from high and low produced the wildest disorder, till the scarecrow at the head of the table, by repeated knocks on the table and vast exertion of his screech-owl voice, produced a slight cessation of this din. Addressing one of those gentlemen on his right hand, he said 'Now, Carey, where do you intend to stump tomorrow?'

'Nowhere,' replied he, 'while I can see an ounce of meat or a stoup of wine in this doghole of ours.'

'I fancied', said his superior grinning, 'that Rouge set you such a spot of work to do while he was off that, if you left it undone, my . . . but he vowed he'd blow your brains out!'

'Let him. Hang it if I care, provided he'll just fill the brain pan with a pint of whiskey! Howsoever, I'll not stir from hence for you, 'Sdeath, or that sour dog, either.'

'Listen, gents,' said a second gentleman on the left, one of a most deadly and ferocious aspect. 'I say, supposing next time the whole rascal shows his face among us, we all rise up at once and each man aims his pistol at him till he blows up into the roof like a football. You, 'Sdeath, would then be chief and I—'

'I say,' answered Carey, 'supposing to practice in this pretty sport, we now shall all rise and aim our pistols at yourself, O'Connor,* till you smack into the earth like a leaden coffin.'

'Oh, Carey,' answered 'Sdeath. 'You should say *in* a leaden coffin.'

'Nay,' answered another, 'but we always put our leaden coffins into the man and not the man into them.'

A roar of laughter followed this exquisite joke, but O'Connor was not to be pacified by a jest. He, first swallowing a draught of brandy, started up and clenching his sword cried, 'Carey, I say. What in the name of Murder did you tell them to practice on me for? Why, you thorough bloodhound, I'd have you to know that for any such insolent jests I'll sliver you in pieces like a turnip. Draw, you villain.'

Carey needed not that command; but ere anyone could hold him, he grasped his sword and dashed over the table at his antagonist. Both were slashing and hacking at each other, while the crowds stood round, laughing, fighting, cursing, and enjoying the fun, when Rouge stepped from his concealment and advancing toward the antagonists cried suddenly, 'Stop, there!'

That awful and well-known tone rung through the cavern, recoiling on the hearts of all present, and the huge confusion in an instant ceased. Every man was amazed and frightened. Old 'Sdeath ran cowering into a corner and the two duellists, each opposite to the other, stood with flashing eyes and bloody faces but not daring to continue their conflict.

Rougue stepped up to the chair vacated by 'Sdeath and, after taking a long pull at a bottle of claret, called out, 'You, O'Connor! For mutiny attempted against your leader, and you, Carey, for creating disturbance in our community: I here condemn and order to each of you straight away, 500 strokes with a cart whip. Such dirty conduct deserves a degraded punishment. Lawless, and Scroven, do your office.'

These two gigantic executors of the Demagogue's will came forward and bore their two sullen and determined culprits from the room to the place of punishment.

Rougue, meanwhile, casting round him an eye of fire, cried, "Sdeath, I say, where's 'Sdeath? The dog, the rascal! Come here this moment.'

'Sdeath appeared, crouching and fawning upon his incensed superior. 'Now,' said Rougue, 'Why in the name of robbery have you in this manner disobeyed my orders? I told you, I believe, to send these villains each upon his errand and yourself to go immediately to the great seat of filth, the Glasstown. You'll be wanted there, sir, I assure you.'

'Sdeath replied, 'What, eh? How? What secret divulged? Oh. I'll go, I'm off. Good day. You'll serve my turn no more, an that be the case.'

Rougue replied by a dreadful kick, which sent the old vermin yelling to his accustomed corner.*

But now, 'The night drave on wi sangs and clatter'.* Rougue, umpire of the feast, poured down his throat torrents of the most fiery liquors. His satellites followed faithfully his example; their inferiors lacked not in keeping up with them. Barrels upon barrels were rolled into the hall, and there being staved were at once emptied of their contents. An incessant storm of conversation rung through the room, intermixed with blows, curses, threats, and execrations, the whole seasonably varied by a dozen or two of pistol shots, stabs, and other violence by which several men were killed or wounded. The morning had begun to dawn over the huge Robbers' Towers, ere silence and sleep could obtain the ascendancy over those wild and ferocious men.

[*Chapter IV*]

July 10, 1833

The sun was already blazing high over the hills of Sneakysland* ere Lord Elrington awoke from his deep, dead sleep. The fatigues and harassing which he had undergone since the night of the attack on the jail would have unhinged the frame of an ordinary man, but on him they only produced an impression obliterated by a single sound sleep. He arose this day stern, strong, and calm as ever, his mind filled with new projects and fresh schemes of iniquity.

After conferring a while in private with 'Sdeath, Carey, O'Connor,* Dorn, and Co., he took his gun and walked out to stroll in search of game among the banks and braes of the Robbers' Towers. While wandering on the sides of these desolate hills, observing at the distance of a musket shot from him a 'rare ape', with 'summat up his back', from his tallness and the agility with which he moved Rougue conjectured that it was Ned Laury.* He called to him. Ned bounded forward and stood before him to receive his commands.

'What in the name of Robbery have you got on your back?' inquired Rougue.

Ere Ned could speak, his burden (but a light one) lifted up a round, roguish face and a head of curly hair and cried out. 'Oh, Rougue! I'm the Rev. Peter Poundtext, flying from the face of John Balfour of Burley,* who is enshrined in the carcase of Arthur, Marquis of Douro.'

'Hem, you little fool. When did you leave the city?' asked Rougue with some earnestness.

'A few days ago. The evening after the jail was tuk,' replied Lord Charles Albert Florian Wellesly.*

'Oh,' replied Rougue, 'you must come with me to our counting house. Ned, you may locate yourself by a brandy cask.'

Ned bowed most obsequiously, and the three wended their path to the cave. On their road Charlie pulled from Ned's pocket an octavo volume and handed it to Rougue, telling him to 'peruse it carefully' for it was of his doing and he would see why he was flying from 'the sour puritanical milksop', his brother.

Rougue opened the volume. It was the celebrated 'Something about Arthur',* then just published. With great satisfaction, for Rougue hated the Marquis of Douro, did he read the mischievous exposé therein contained of several of that young nobleman's earlier scrapes and frolics so caustically told by his impish brother. On arriving at the cavern, he sent Ned to the promised brandy cask, and beckoned Charlie into an apartment where, shutting the door and offering him fruit, he commanded him to relate the news of the City. Charlie, though rather awed by finding himself before so stern, dark, and dangerous a nobleman as Lord Elrington, began in his usual light, mischievous air.

'Eh, Rougue, what a scrape you'll get yourself into. Why, my book came out the morning after the Jail was burnt, so that being engaged with my publisher in important business which you, Rougue, will not understand, I had little time to inquire into the passing politics of an hour. However, after breakfasting upon an onion and 3 grey peas, I strolled to Ned Sydney's. I found him immersed in papers and newspapers. Says I to him, says I, "Sydney, my nose isn't blue this morning. I am not cold today. What a fire there is up by yonder. A kiln's in a blow, I am given to understand, eh?"'

'Sydney cocked his eye and said some unutterable nonsense about fiendish rebellion, execrable treason, bloodshed, and so forth, also cheeping of government secrets, quash the demagogue, have a hold on his nose, pull him where we like—and much more to that effect which has leaked through my memory. Thereupon I arose and rode upon a wheel-less chariot* to Elrington Hall, intending to converse literarily with her ladyship. But her I found too much bound to affairs of the nether world to listen unto my celestial language. Her words ran upon the actions of a certain person who shall be nameless. I remarked suavely that I cogitated he was hot enough himself not to set ablaze the whole "urbs", or city, in the vernacular. I affirmed that he scarcely possessed a "mens et animus" or as the vulgate renders it, that he was a red mad Bedlamite. I remarked, again suavely, that he ran much danger from his wild courses; and she being inclined to weep and lament, so beautifully pictured I the effigies of impeachment, gallows, bloody bodies, bodiless heads, et cetera that I kindly hinted that one who was not a hundred miles from her possessed influence even in the highest quarters, and that that influence we would use for the alleviation of punishments, and so forth.

'Thence I departed, to parade the city for the purpose of seeing how my book worked, and "Thus passed the day till evening fell".*

At which time I again honoured the paperworm Sydney with my presence. I beheld him now giving adieux to Lawyer Bud and another gentleman whom by his shovel hat, lean figure, keen visage, and musty smell I calculated to be of the same profession. They all, upon one casual glance by me* vouchsafed to them, appeared to be conversing on political subjects. The strange lawyer more than once, aye or twice, either, mentioned your name, Sir; and on the whole much of the confab seemed to turn upon your reputable procedures.

'But now at the witching hour of night, when taking a turn through the street, hearing the opinion of my opus or, in the received edition, my book, mine orbs beheld Arthur a-tramping at a stone's cast distance. Now his visual organs seemed so contracted and obverted and twisted with fiendish fury that, though he beheld not me, I for fear of consequences called out to Ned Laury who I knew was departing for the far-off mountains of Sneakysland to lend me a hoist on his back bone for two or three hundred miles or so, and thou, O Wretch, knowest the end.'

Rougue could not resist laughing at the conclusion of this doughty speech, but ceasing suddenly, he asked with perfect calmness: what like was that Lawyer whom he saw with Sydney?

'Oh, a middle-sized, middle-aged man, hooked nose, brown face, douce* pate, and lean carcase.'

'Very well,' replied Rougue. 'Now go to the rare apes in the Hall yonder. Amuse them with your chatter. You may stay here till the storm has blown over.'

So saying, he led him to the Hall, and as he himself turned back again he called out, ''Sdeath, Carey, O'Connor, Dorn, here this instant.'

Those celebrated personages followed him back to the little cavern, half drunk and reeling from wall to wall. All being entered, he shut the door.

'Hey,' said 'Sdeath. 'What now? Oh, I see. Black as blood. Blown up. Divulged. I'm off.'

'Silence!' cried Rougue. ''Sdeath, how are your shoes?'

'Why, pretty well, I think, considering they're without bottoms.'

'Oh, they'll do for that matter. But you know the road to the Glasstown.'

'Aye.'

'And you have a bottle with you?'

'Aye.'

'And a sharp knife?'

'Aye, aye.'

'Well, you old wretch. I fancy Tweezy has been or is about to let out.'

'Now. You've a heavy plan of preventing that pass?'

'This night tramp for the Glasstown and—'

A fiendish light gleamed from the old wretch's eyes. As he touched the haft of a huge knife which stuck in his belt, he replied with a hateful chuckle. 'Oh, my knife wants scouring. It's been too long in the sheath. I'll give it some rust ointment, heh! But, howsomdever, the wind's up, and 'Sdeath's a-cold.* I'll take a draft or so just afore I tramp.'

Thus speaking, he began to smell about the room with his twisted nose and soon scented a large barrel of spirits in a corner. He crept to it and with a strength far above his appearance rolled it into the middle of the floor. O'Connor, Carey, and Dorn, whom thirst had kept silent, now rushed in to share the spoil; and when whisky had given them tongues, began to volley forth oaths and execrations, sometimes upon the liquour, sometimes each other, and often on their friends in the far-off city. Rougue standing above them poured down huge draughts in silence, looking with his usual sarcastic smile upon his lieutenant and minions round him. The darkness had come on and the clock was chiming ten when Rougue lent 'Sdeath a tremendous kick which hurtled him to the farthest corner of the room and drove the good liquor out of his head.

''Sdeath, thou villain, it's time. Off! Tramp! Use your shuffle,* and that, too, with good effect.'

'Sdeath got up, took his hat, and without seeming to give a thought to the length and fatigue of his journey went maundering and groping to the door of the cavern, then climbed his way up the hill side and was lost in the darkness. He being gone, Rougue and his satellites adjourned to the Great Cavern or Hall where around an ample mountain feast were ranged, as I have before related, the hundred inmates of this suspicious dwelling.

After eating and drinking till a late, or rather an early hour, Rougue started up and cried out, 'Now, my lads. Let's have a little sword-play. Let fifty go to this side, and fifty to that, and then we'll begin.'

But I must here leave our hero and his gang in the enjoyment of the fiery and dangerous sport.*

[*Chapter V*]

PBB. August 5th

The early dawn of another morning beheld the dewellers in this mysterious cavern assembled on the tongue of land formed by a bend in the river and attentively listening to the commands of their leader, who standing on the summit of an emptied beer barrel thus addressed them.*

'Gentlemen, we have been too long idle and must pay for that sloth with interest. O'Connor, take ten men. You know where Carnac* lies. Return in two days. Dorn, with ten of you, will march into the south, and back, in the same time. Carey, with your ten take this letter of instruction. Open it on the second day from hence. March you along the confines of this country, down from the Nevada to Parry's Glasstown. You'll see what must be done there. And now, let twenty men, the quickest-sighted among you, take post upon the heights just yonder, in different spots. Keep hid, observe attentively, communicate your observations faithfully. For the rest, this is our receiving day, and we expect news from various quarters. Therefore, we must remain in the halls. Now, away to your posts.'

Thus speaking, Rougue dismounted from his eminence and entered his room, while his minions each prepared their troops and, well-armed but with little provision, set out upon their different 'mercantile' expeditions. In an hour or two, a messenger arrived on horseback from the south. He was ushered into Rougue's apartment, where he continued some time. This man was followed by parties and posts from a hundred different quarters but all from seemingly a great distance. In fact, the whole of this day Rougue neither had nor allowed himself to have a minute's rest from his huge heaps of papers, boxes, and dispatches and the Glasstown publications.

The latter class of parcels he did not open until, having declared that he would not sup in the hall, he had sat down a little freed from his press of business before his writing desk and a flask of powerful brandy. With his usual supercilious sneer, he drew toward him those bales marked 'From the Great Glasstown' and opened them one after another, displaying their literary treasures before him. He first eagerly seized upon *The Glasstown or Monthly Intelligencer*, dated just after he had escaped from the city and burnt the Jail. With a sneer thrice refined, he looked over its account of that catastrophe and perused its puzzled expressions of doubt and uncertainty as to the reasons of the Arch-demagogue for this atrocious act. From this portion of the news his eyes glanced to a letter signed 'J—T—y' and which ran as follows:

'Sir: I would advise the public to look closely to that seat of vice and villainy, Elrington Hall. Circumstances will shortly, perhaps, transpire that may make clear the reasons for this my advice.

Yrs. J—T—y.'

This letter was short and indefinite, but Rougue read it over a second and third time. Then, slowly taking from his pocket a little black book with steel clasps, he marked in it with a pencil 'John Tweezy—death' and proceeded calmly to look over the other paragraphs in the paper till his eye rested on the notice of *Lord Ronan*, the new poems from the pen of Marquis Douro. He hastily opened the packet marked 'books' and flinging out heaps of pamphlets, tracts, and volumes, all published during the few days of his absence from the Glasstown, he at length lit upon the work he sought. Holding it by the boards* at arm's length, he surveyed with a bitter sneer its gilt leaves, embossed cover, and the name on the back. He then opened it and rapidly looked over its glorious pages, now and then stopping at particular passages which he read twice or thrice over. Upon laying down the book, he exclaimed 'Very well! This won't do', and rung the bell violently.

A minion entered, to whom he said, 'Get my horse ready by midnight, and begone, you hog!'

The man departed. Rougue for a while paced up and down the room in deep thought, and then by an effort sat himself at his desk to close up, as he termed it, 'our arrears', and to answer the thousand letters received that day and now lying beside him. The answers were most remarkable for their astonishingly laconic expression. For instance, to a letter requesting to be informed when the writer should 'lead his clerks' to the firm at W.G.T. and when to the Sierra Nevada, Rougue merely answered:

'Grand firm
For S.L.
M——33:

Sir
W G T—May 21.
S—N—June 3.

Rougue. C.'

To another letter from 'Off Fidens' wishing to know when Rougue would visit that 'Office', he merely answered by a scolloped line, intimating that it would be doubtful when he should come, for such were the symbols used by this mysterious and suspicious trading company. In fact, to cut all short, the directions of these letters were always longer than the letter itself.

Yet, with all this speed and brevity, it was long past midnight ere Rougue had concluded his voluminous correspondence. He arose then and ordered his minions to see that the letters were dispatched immediately and anticipating mishap ... he swallowed some food,* together with a pint bottle of brandy. He without further preparation mounted his horse, and by the light of the early dawn ascended the hills and galloped out of sight.

[Chapter VI]

August 6, 1 [8—]

The stranger who on a summer's day passes through one of the principal streets of the Great Glasstown, upon observing the mighty crowds and shoals of carriages, horses, foot-passengers, and persons of every clime and character, all mingling and blending together, flying and running and wending first this way, then that, crossing and recrossing, jostling, sidling, retreating, and advancing in a thousand different places and a thousand separate ways, each among the inumerable countenances lighted up by a different passion, and all at once speaking and shouting and cursing in Babylonic chaos—that person, I say, coming unawares upon this astonishing spectacle would, did he not himself become too confused to think, fancy that one mighty spell from the assembled Genii had brought all the inhabitants of the world together, struck at once by fatal and frantic madness.

I myself have often stood wondering, admiring, and speculating upon the enormous groups thus daily exhibited. Yet always, after a little thought and observation, I have found each person whom I saw pursuing his own distinct and definite aim. Come here today and observe with me.*

Look, for instance, at that magnificent young nobleman who so truly bears out his fame, dashing in his gorgeous chariot through the crowd of plebians and scattering them like mud on every side. His object is, first, to exhibit himself to the eyes of a wondering people; secondly, to make all haste to his publisher's shop; and, thirdly, to keep within the hour his appointment at 'M. Eat-him-up-sloop-and-roop's' New Elysium* for gentlemen who love to moult the superfluous. Next, view that shoal of fragments from this principal block, a hundred chariots guided by a hundred sprigs of nobility, each directing his eye to their great Original and copying from him their every move and motion. Leaving out the affair of the publisher, these young nobles have the same decisive end in view as him.

Next, see that stout, corpulent gentleman on horseback. Lo, how he hastens on his way, how he turns up his nose into the air as if he smelled his quarry from afar. This one is going to a grand dinner, to feed upon fat and flattery. Then, see that knot of men on foot, pacing with knitted brows and compressed mouths along the pathway, each copying the motions of that youth before them upon whose visage care and study has placed every wrinkle. Often so are statesmen, politicians, men who hold the affairs of Africa at their tongue and finger's end. Their road lies toward a cabinet council or to the House of Parliament.

Following the same road, look at those three men walking, arm in arm, tall and military: the middlemost firm, strong, and of searching aspect; the right-hand one taller but more stooped, marked by age and of a cautious and a sarcastic appearance; the left-hand one much like this, save more upright and of a franker aspect. These three are kings,* and it scarce behoves us to speak of their motions. Then, interspersed among all these whom I have sketched, you see soldiers and officers in full uniform, racing and galloping about, helter-skelter, yet each with an aim. Some too late on parade, some too early from parade, others going to Elysium, other again going to a place different from Elysium;* this one riding to a meeting, and the two hasting as seconds to the same meeting. Then view the plebians, the crowds of poachers and 'Rare Apes' with movements eccentric as those of so many comets but each attracted or repelled by his peculiar Sun. One part with stern and ferocious aspect about to assault a mill. Others looking gaily toward the country and cocking their guns for the far-off moors, thinking while in the streets of Regina of the heathcock now crowing in the pride of power on the wild steeps of Aornos* or the heaths of the Robbers' Towers (but then doomed to lay an anointed head as low as death before the unerring shot of a Scroven or a Naughty).

But, Reader, he with whom we have most to do at present is yon young man walking by himself along the path. He is well, aye, dashingly dressed and seemingly aged not much above twenty; his unbronzed cheeks, accomodating manners, and the want of that fiery eagerness in the eye which characterizes our young nobility proclaim him perhaps but lately returned from the Philosophers Isle. But the manner in which he stops to reconnoitre through his eyeglass every 'Stand up', 'pausing toss', or 'dashing chariot race' pending in the streets shew that he is game and will, ere long, be a passable Glasstown youngster.*

But to return to our narrative. This promising young fire-worshipper passing through several streets and turning down a dark lane at length stopped before the corner door of a range of old mean-looking houses, dark, damp and dirty. That door was worn and rotten; yet, strange to relate, during the few minutes during which he had stood by it no less than nine or ten persons had entered, all of whom from the outward man seemed to belong to the very élite of the city. In a little while, an old man, little, mean, and of shabby attire, stepped up and motioning to our hero opened the door and entered the house. He followed this guide through a multitude of dark, musty passages and cold, windowless rooms, until they reached not a poor, unfurnished apartment but a very large and lofty hall paved with marble and decorated with furniture of old and shining oak. Round this room were placed rows of hat-stands whose fruit, for its abundance, amazed our uninitiated hero. But he had only time to notice that a single wax taper illuminated this spacious hall, and that its doors and walls were so thickly coated with matting that sound from another room, however loud, could never penetrate here, when he was led by his elfish guide to a door at one end, to which the old dog applied a key from his pocket. It instantly flew open and such a blaze of glory burst upon their eyes as for a moment caused the young nobleman to start back in astonishment. But his companion, more accustomed to the sight, urged him forward and himself entering closed the portal.

They were on the threshold of a vast and gorgeous room, without windows but lighted by a long range of splendid chandeliers whose branches and drops sparkled like diamond and gold. The floor was covered by the richest carpets, the wall hung with crimson and purple. Velvet sofas, rosewood and ebony tables, luxurious and yielding ottomans were placed round the room, and down the middle, from top to bottom, were ranged two long tables, with on each side a corresponding sideboard. On these sideboards were heaped bottles, goblets, glasses, fruit, confectionary, gold, silver, crystal in magnificent confusion. Round the tables were seated or standing crowds of men, in appearance and carriage worthy the name. Many in their numbers, of the highest rank judging from their appearance, none of them past the middle age, they were head over ears engaged in deep play.

Flushed already by the splendour and excitement of the scene, our hero turned to his companion and asked whether this was a public or private dwelling?

'It's no dwelling at all, you young foal,' answered the old wretch in gruff, snarling tone, as if envying the gaiety, life, and manliness he saw around him. But his voice was heard at the tables and in an instant a hundred heads were turned to the door.

''Sdeath, you here? What have you got there?' asked a hundred voices.

''Sdeath, in the name of murder,' cried a stern, deep voice, and Montmorency rushed from the table toward him. They spoke together for a few minutes in an undertone, and then Montmorency, laying his iron hand on the arm of the young nobleman and drawing toward the tables, said 'Gents! Ho, waiter! A glass of something. Gentlemen, a young sprig here lately sprouted wants to be planted in the gardens of Paradise. Another glass, I say! I'm murdered with thirst. You'll admit him into Elysium, I've no doubt. Grand pluck. Twenty thousand per annum. Hem, hem! Volo! If you laugh, Lofty, I'll smash your brain pan.'

'His name?' asked a tall young man of an eagle aspect who was seated at the head of one of the tables.*

'Out with it, you blockhead!' cried Montmorency. 'Fork it, you scurvy, lumbering degenerate, loathsome, dirty—'

Here his volley of imprecations was stopped by a stunning blow on the mouth from the fist of our young hero who, though flustered and shy at first, began to show evident tokens of 'pluck' upon being called in this manner. A roar of laughter from the lofty bystanders made him, however, relapse again into his former bashfulness.

'Well done, capital!' 'You've got it, Monty!' 'A dog, this!' 'something decent here!' was ejaculated by the gentlemen round; and the tables were deserted in order to view the 'young dove give play'.*

'Gentlemen,' said our hero, gazing upon the crowds of stern, supercilious countenances gazing at him. 'I am here unknown and unacquainted with your proceedings or society, but I must say that the manner in which I have been treated would be disgraceful if used to the lowest and most degraded inhabitant of our city. I declare to you that if any one among you intend to amuse yourself at my expense, he must do it armed, and out of range of my pistols' shot'.

As he said this, drawing out at the same time a brace of firearms, the laughter redoubled, and that officer-like gentleman who had asked his name, pushing back the crowd, laid hold of his arm and said, 'Young man, we see that you possess pluck. Follow me and we'll initiate you.'

So saying and at the same time, in spite of his resistance, wresting from him his pistols with an ease which showed his muscular strength, this nobleman hurried our hero through the room to a door on the opposite end, which was opened, and they entered a small apartment fitted up like a chapel with the most costly decorations. The galleries, pews, and so forth were rosewood, and the altar was ornamented with the most gorgeous gold and velvet. To this altar they led him, and the lofty nobleman before mentioned, ascending the steps, said, 'Young man, what is your name?'

'My name is Viscount Castlereagh.'*

'Your age.'

'Twenty-one.'

'You, I have no doubt, can guess some of the purposes of this society, but others you cannot. However they will appear in time, therefore I need scarce detail them here. This Society is called the "Elysium or Paradise of Souls", and here are our rooms of assembly. No one can enter unless he prove himself above the age of eighteen. Are you so?'

'I am.'

'Perfect in limbs and without deformity; are you so?'

'I am.'

'One who has once in his life slain a man. Have you?'

'I have.'

'Worth at least 5,000 a year, are you so?'

'I am.'

'Very well, then,' he said to the young man.* 'You will never under any pretence whatsoever violate the rules of this Society, abscond from it, or disclose the least matter connected with it.'

'I swear.'

'Rise, then, Frederic Viscount Castlereagh, a member of the Elysium or Paradise of Souls. You, Montmorency, write down the entry in our book, and now, Sir, before we go into the hall I will tell you the Officers of our body.

President.	Alexander Rougue, Viscount Elrington.
Vice President.	Myself, who am Arthur Wellesly, Marquis of Douro.
Treasurer.	Edward Lofty, Viscount Lofty.
Secretary.	Hector Mathias Mirabeau Montmorency, Esqr.
Under Secretary.	George Charles Gordon, Esqr.

Officer of the Household.   John Flower, Esqr.*
Usher.   Robert Patrick' Sdeath.

           *Champions**
     Richard Naughty.   First
     Edward Laury.   Second
     Jean Pigtail.   Third
     Thomas Scroven.   Fourth

Council for AD 1833
James, Marquis of
  Abercorn.
Robert Henry, Viscount
  Molineux.
Richard Carey, Esqr.
Arthur O'Connor, Esqr.
Edward Geoffrey Stanley
  Sydney, Esqr.

The assembled multitude now rushed from the chapel into the hall where they saluted each other with cries of 'What's to be done tonight?'

'Stake!' replied the Marquis of Douro, who presided in the absence of Rougue.

Crowds instantly collected round the table, while others sauntered about the splendid room conversing, turning over their portfolios, or through the glasses quizzing* the company. Several of the political cast were diligently perusing newspapers or quaffing large draughts from the sideboard. The Marquis was playing Hazard with Castlereagh for 1 or 2 guinea points, but the hawk-like glance with which he now and then looked at him boded ill to the luckless pigeon.

Montmorency had drawn 'Sdeath to a corner of the sideboard. Here they were deeply engaged in stirring two stiff rummers of punch. "'Sdeath,' said Montmorency, 'I thought, my dear, that you were off at the firm.'

'No, you fool, I have been but d'ye think I'll keep there all—'

"Silence your grumbling, I say. 'Sdeath, we're endangered. Does Rougue know of it? Oh, there are two fellows at your board, the eagle and the wren, whom I could crush, crush! Hah, and I'll crush them yet. But what do you think? Our Law—'

'Hush, you hound,' muttered the old wretch, 'Sdeath. 'Look ye here', and so saying, with the usual gleam of his old grey eyes, he touched with his withered finger a dagger protruding from his waistcoat pocket. 'That's the mission Rougue sent me on.' With a fiendish laugh, he drunk off his tumbler and retired from the room.

Montmorency was not puzzled at 'Sdeath's broken sentences. He grinned, took a pinch of snuff, and walked to the back of a nobleman's chair, from whence he could view at leisure the hundred striking countenances ranged round the table.

There were no women's faces, no vapid, fashionable, lounging visages. True, there were handsome ones in plenty, but all presented stern, corrugated brows, keen eyes, and mouths with endlessly varied expressions. Montmorency turned his eye to where stood the magnificent form of the Marquis of Douro, who risen from his chair was attentively watching the progress of a stake with Arthur O'Connor.* Often he passed his hand across his lofty forehead and over his aching eyes, for not only tonight was he involved in the whirl of passion, but for nights before he had been engaged in the House of Parliament, combatting almost unaided the assaults of a bitter and formidable faction. 'Or involved in a wide whirlpool of politics, fashion, and dissipation', Montmorency thought as he bent upon him his stern searching eyes.

'Ha, that youngster must slacken. It won't do to run on. At this pace, the sword will wear out its scabbard. I wish it would, I do.'

By the Marquis was seated O'Connor, whose forehead and countenance presented the wreck of a mind and person originally of the highest order, but now worn and harassed by the warring of passions, degraded by the use of everything mean and low. From him Montmorency glanced to a figure at the other end of the table, slight, girlish, and seemingly of small account in life, but Montmorency knew the mind, the talents, the vast ambition, the determined spirit which dwelt in his antagonist, Edward Sydney. Then he passed his eye over the handsome and fashionable figure of Lord Lofty, the wild, dissipated forms of Abercorn and Molineaux, and the dark gloomy countenance of Secretary Gordon. Last he took a long, keen look at young Castlereagh; and as he surveyed him over and over, he muttered, 'Hah! I'll have that youngster yet; he too shall not fall to the share of that cursed omnipotent.'

At this moment, two men started from the table and tottered to a sideboard. One of them took vast draughts of brandy; but the other, with trembling hand, snatched a pistol and blew his brains out. At the report, all present turned their heads round, but most of them with a scornful laugh turned again to their absorbing employment. The Marquis of Douro cried 'Off with him', and two gentlemen took up this lamentable victim to gambling, and hauling him on their shoulders disappeared through a dark passage.

Castlereagh laid down his cards and shuddered. He looked at the hundreds round him, but not in one could he see an emotion answering to his own. All were absorbed in the hopes, fears, or desperation of their tremendous occupation. He saw the Marquis of Douro scrape together, with a smile of joy, a huge heap of gold, the produce of a night's winnings from O'Connor, who said with the utmost nonchalance as he rose from his chair: 'Here's my last farthing, the last ounce of £70 or £80,000. But I'll off for a day or so, and then come back.' Saying so, he turned and strode out of the room.*

At this moment the door opened, and there entered a man of lofty stature who strode into the apartment, dashed his hat on to the floor, and emptied at a draught a whole bottle of brandy. Montmorency started back, the whole company rose aghast.

It was Alexander Rougue. He seemed raised to an appalling passion; his hand shook, his eyes flashed, and his hair was wild and disordered as if he had returned from some long and harassing journey. The moment he saw the Marquis of Douro, who stood gazing at him with a Wellingtonian smile, he advanced toward him, elevated his iron fist, and dashed it into the face of the Marquis, who fell back with violence, his countenance covered with blood.

The whole apartment rose in an uproar, but Arthur rising pushed back the crowd and threw his coat to Sydney, charging him to stand by as second. Rougue cast off his coat and threw it to the first bystander, who happened to be Castlereagh. To him Rougue said, 'Now, young man, you're my second. Mont, my love, hold the bottle.' Montmorency obeyed, the bystanders cried out, laughing and joking. 'A ring, a ring!' It was formed, and every one gathered round in the highest expectation to see their President and his vice 'Stick it into one another like men of the real stamp'.

In the whole City there were not known two men who for blood, mettle, and science could in the slightest compete with these two renowned noblemen. They scarcely needed the preparations* for the fight; but the moment that their arms were free and shirt-sleeves tucked up, they put themselves in attitude and set to. The Marquis had the advantage of the Lord in youth and vigour, and his well-compacted and supple frame promised well, contrasted with the shattered and decayed nerves of his antagonist. But Elrington was the taller, the more seasoned of the two. Their arms were epitomes of themselves: the Marquis of Douro's, well-made, fleshy, a fine display of round muscles, and light as a bird in action; Lord Elrington made bare two long, bony arms, devoid of muscle or flesh, but sinewy and nervous to an amazing degree, hard as oak and garnished with fists that scarce needed the aid of gauntlets. Dead silence was observed.

You might have heard a pin drop when Rougue, with a quick glance of caution, darted at the Marquis a tremendous facer which, however, Arthur beautifully parried and, like lightning, popped Rougue a dig at the ribs which made them sing like a bell. Rougue staggered but threw his shot right and left, ending with a blow upon Arthur's collar that dashed him on to the ground with the victor over him. Arthur scorned this and began round second by a cautious guard of his person and a toucher on Rougue's smeller which brought out a beautiful stream of claret. First blood was cried for the Marquis, and the odds for him were 3 to 2. Rougue with much malice aimed always at Arthur's face, which malice was returned by his antagonist with interest. Soon their eyes became black as the midnight, their lips red as coral, their cheeks like those of a milkmaid. Rougue's face made less show than that of his enemy, for the extreme dryness and scantiness of flesh could not bring much blood or bruise, but after the first hour and the thirtieth round, he began to shew evident signs of exhaustion while the vigour and youth of the Marquis bore the fight in an exquisite manner.

The battle displayed perfect science and vast powers of endurance, yet after the second hour fatigue and dissipation began to tell visibly upon the shattered powers of Lord Elrington. His falls were more frequent, he was generally undermost, and the heat and passion with which he had entered the ring did him damage contrasted with the Wellingtonian coolness of the Marquis. But now neither could stand, unless in active fight. They seemed unconscious of what they were doing and only to continue the combat from the instinct of surpassing courage. In the third hour of the combat and the 91st round, Arthur, opening his eyes or at least one eye, gave Elrington a hit on the 'cellardoor' that dashed him back on to the ground, with the Marquis senseless above him. Both were taken up by their seconds, quite lifeless, and laid on two sofas.

'My eyes!' said Montmorency. 'They must have been mad to

choose such seconds. Look how Castlereagh trembles and as to that hound, volo—'* He rushed up to him and inflicted upon the young member Sydney such a kick as hurled him across the room.

'Ho,' cried Lofty, 'sits the wind in this quarter!' and he snatched a pistol from the sideboard with the intent to set Mont asleep.

In an instant a scene of confusion followed which it would be in vain to describe. Our young hero Castlereagh, albeit he enjoyed such work, amazingly felt the weakness of unpractised nerves and was tossed about with the combat, stunned and bewildered, until the bell of St Michael's tolled four in the morning. This being the hour for departing, by the rules of the society, an universal rush commenced out of the room through the long, long passages and into the street. Castlereagh was borne foremost, and ere he knew anything of the matter, he found himself propelled into a mighty square, in the raw, fresh dawn of returning daylight.

Capt. Flower

End of The
First Volume*

P. B. Brontë
Angust 17, 1833.

REAL LIFE IN VERDOPOLIS
A TALE

By Captain John Flower, MP &c.

In Two Vols.

VOL II

CHAPTER I

P. B. Bronte
Aug. 17th
AD 1833.

Before we proceed farther with our tale, we must endeavour to recapitulate sundry political events of the day and to retie the thread of our narrative. It was evident that in the fact of Rougue being a declared robber, there was more than met the eye. He either carried on his operations in a different way or upon a different scale than men generally supposed, and our readers must have seen that he scarce wished his actions to be scrutinized, or known. How it was for fear of undue disclosures that he liberated the four prisoners and burnt the Jail. But this maneuver being contrary to law, he was forced to fly to the 'Office' in Sneakiesland of 'The firm of Rougue, Montmorency, 'Sdeath and Co', or in plain terms the den for receiving the goods stolen by the worthies above-mentioned. Here he remained till sundry hints in the papers convinced him that his emissaries in the City were scarcely playing him fair and till he read the poem 'Lord Ronan', by the Marquis of Douro, a piece directed against him. These things put Rougue into a flame. He left his mountain cavern, rode post-haste to the Glasstown, and entered the moment he alighted the rooms of that society of which he was President. Here he saw the Marquis of Douro whom, unable to contain his fury, he violently assaulted. A battle was the consequence, and our readers know the result.

Now, with relation to the political posture of present affairs, we must observe that the Great Glasstown countries are and were divided into two grand parties, the ARISTOCRATS, consisting of all men of rank, wealth, and standing headed by the Twelves, and the DEMOCRATS, consisting of the lower orders, poachers, rare apes, and so forth, with various dissipated, broken, or ambitious men, soured by merited mishaps, and burning against all those whose luck was fairer than their own. This party was headed by Alexander Rougue, Viscount Elrington; and in spite of its worthless materials comprised much energy, talent, and firmness in the persons of its leader, Montmorency, Gordon, O'Connor, Carey, and several others. To counterbalance which, the other party brought in the Marquis of Douro, Mr Sydney, Lord Lofty, Captain Flower, Captain Goat, and many other men of powerful and active talent. At the period of which I write, these two parties were in active array against each other and the height to which political feeling had risen boded mighty and lasting evils to the state and country. But after making these necessary explanations, we must return to our tale.

Castlereagh, upon finding himself thrown from the mouth of this volcano into the midst of the open city, paused to take breath and recover his stunned senses. When he looked round, he found himself in the middle of a mighty square. In heaven the night was just retiring from the day; and while overhead the stars peeped out and the clouds looked black, cold, and night-like, in the horizon the red and yellow lines stretching and fading round the sky betokened that morning was now near at hand. In the City no smoke yet curling above the houses announced the busy hour of dawn, but the countless buildings of Verdopolis all stood, cold and raw, with their dark outlines standing out from the crimsoned sky. The mighty palaces round him frowned aloft in sombre shadow, and the rising wind swept round their walls and howled down the long, deserted streets.

Castlereagh knew that his hotel was yet locked up, and that there he could scarce gain admittance. He therefore paced down the street, starting at the distinct echo of his footsteps, and stopped on the parapet of the great Bridge to survey the gradual unfolding of another day.*

As the clocks of the city chimed four and then five, mortals began to rouse from their beds. First there appeared the rare apes going forth with their guns on their shoulders to their early sports and employments. Then the Naval men, with all connected with shipping, moving toward the quays and harbours. Then the windows of the houses gradually opened; the shops unfolded like flowers. A horse or two pattered along the streets, a troop or two of cavalry, a file of infantry going to a parade. In a while the hum became louder, the smoke curled across the city, and Castlereagh, when he reflected upon the late darkness and silence, could not help feeling astonished to view the rapidity with which the sun blazed out in heaven, the shadows disappeared, and the whole city glistened and thundered and shook with life, light, and the bustle of its millions of inhabitants. An hour ago, and not a living being had passed across the darkened bridge. Now, as the sun glinted over its parapets, what thousands of carts and horses, carriages and chariots, foot-passengers and merchandise of every clime and country teemed incessantly over its expanding arches! It now seemed as if sooner might the vast waters below him cease to flow forward than the tide of mortals above disappear and be still. Castlereagh, yawning frequently, for the night had to him been a rough and sleepless one, returned to his hotel and passed his time dozing on the sofa until breakfast was announced.

During that day he remained principally indoors until toward evening a note arrived, addressed to him and dated 'Sydenham Hotel, Georges street, GGT',* from the pen of Mr H. M. M. Montmorency.* In its purport, it requested him, nay, commanded him, dine at his house that evening. Castlereagh ordered his carriage and drove off from the hotel.

Upon his announcing himself, he was shown by a footman into a library furnished in the highest style of elegance, which was the study of its far-famed owner. No one was in the room, but the open desk, loaded table, and instruments of writing showed that it had been but just vacated. Castlereagh, curious to see the line of reading pursued by Montmorency, approached his table and examined the books thereon.

The first he took up was a Greek copy of *Lucian's Dialogues*, finely bound and bearing on the fly-leaf the words written 'Alex. Elrington to Hector Montmorency. Read this book. Mark, learn and inwardly digest. Ap. 1, 1830.' Under this lay odd volumes of Voltaire, Rousseau, the two volumes of Hume's *History* containing the English Revolution of 1630 to 1660, Mignet's and Thierry's *French Revolution*, Dent's *Wars with the Genii*, several volumes relating to the Roman

Commonwealth, from Gracchus to Marius and Sulla, well-fingered and open, and one or two other books. But what gave our visitor the most striking notion of the vast cares, anxieties, weight, delights, and labour attendant to Montmorency's present high station in politics were the enormous piles of new political pamphlets, newspapers, parliamentary papers, circulars, and all the tremendous etceteras obliged to be read by a parliamentary leader. Lastly, to complete this literary survey, there glittered on the desk a half-full decanter of brandy and a tumbler drained to the bottom.

Further research was here interrupted by the entrance of the stern, Herculean figure of Montmorency himself, who casting a searching look at the young nobleman said, 'Well, my lord, short acquaintance is oft surest. You acted as second to Elrington last night, and it's decent that your services should be repaid by an acknowledgment. I have invited you to spend this evening with us here. Of course you'll be easy; there are only few at dinner, but be quick or they'll pass off. I'll usher you into the dining hall, once I get this into me.'

He stepped to the decanter, poured all the contents down his throat, and followed by Castlereagh* left the room. They entered the dining room, an apartment presenting the most aristocratic attention to grace and ornament. At the dinner table were seated three persons; the first, a stately old lady, advanced in years, tall in person, and of a most majestic and almost regal deportment. She was introduced to our hero as the Dowager Countess Elrington, mother of Rougue, himself. (By the way, she was the only person to whom that Arch-Demagogue showed the least glimmer of respect and affection, the only one who could control his smallest action.) The other two were given as Harriet and Julia Montmorency, the daughters of the stern statesman, two exceedingly graceful and elegant young ladies of seventeen or eighteen, from their appearance but lately arrived at the Glasstown and possessing all the elegance without any of the frivolity of the highest circles of fashion. Harriet, the eldest, was taller than her sister and of a rather Italian appearance; and it was strange to see the resemblance she, and even both, bore to their tremendous father, albeit their features were so finely and fairly chiselled and his, so fierce, shattered, and so exaggerated by energetic and conflicting passions. However, Castlereagh, being a young nobleman of elegant manners and prepossessing address, a complete hero, in short, with, to use the cant language, much light hair, fair complexion, blue eyes, vivacity and spirit in conversation, and a decent desire to show off in the presence of ladies, he and they soon entered into conversation; Lady Percy, the stately old Countess, bearing her part with a shew of mind and dignity befitting the mother of Elrington.

Dinner being over and the evening being as cool and mild as ever closed a summer day, the Countess proposed a walk in the ground, which was acceded to, and Castlereagh taking her arm, they proceeded down the ample walks of this noble mansion. Deep shadow had settled on all around, and the full moon was rising over the towers and domes of St Michael's Cathedral. The vast palaces and Hotels, as the rented houses of the nobility are termed, were ranged along the river in lines of dazzling light. But there was one which flung forth such superior radiance, whose windows blazed out with such uncommon lustre, that Castlereagh remarking the circumstance begged to know to whom it belonged.

Lady Julia replied that it was the Hotel of Lord Thornton Witkin Sneaky, lately arrived at the City, who had sworn in the most public square of the City that he would make such a rattle in Verdopolis as only himself should be spoken of for months to come. Lady Julia (by the bye, her title had descended from her mother) spoke of his character and of the character of many others in the City in such a manner as shewed the most acute perception and the most lively fund of imagination. The unsophisticated manners both of her and her sister threw such a charm of naïveté over their conversation that Castlereagh felt far from pleased when the stern voice of Montmorency from the window desired him to attend him to the study.

Castlereagh reluctantly left his fair companions and followed Montmorency to the room. As he entered, a blazing fire threw its light over the apartment. Candles were placed on the table. On a sofa reclined the figure of a tall man, his head bound up and his face swollen and bloodless. It was Lord Elrington.

'Ha! Mont,' he said to their host as he entered with our hero. 'You villain, look at the bottles.'

Montmorency removed a large quantity of emptied decanters and from a secret recess procured an astounding number of bottles of wines and spirits.

'Why, volo,' he said. 'You'll drink off a man's income. But you villain, here's Castlereagh, your second.'

'I see him,' answered Rougue, not deigning to take another glance at the visitor. 'I say, Mont. The moment it strikes ten, I must go. Is the carriage ready?'

'Yes. But in the name of Murder, can you possibly sustain this work? Just think, you were thrashed and battered senseless last night. The moment you recovered your reason—hem, he-em, I mean, your want of reason—you ordered yourself to be borne to a pothouse, where you drank yourself into a state of bestial intoxication. Here I found you. I ordered the carrion to my own house. I again supplied you, and myself, too', taking a vast draught of wine, 'with most fiery spirits until you again drank yourself senseless. You then slept an hour, and now that you have awakened you mean to intoxicate yourself a third time, then to go to the House of Parliament, to rise up in your present state of frightful weakness to speak, perhaps against a first-rate orator, certainly against astounding opposition, for hours on end. Your subject-matter unthought of, unprepared, and attacked on all sides. Truly, you horseleech, an' you bear that, you'll bear everything!'

'I'll bear that and ten times more. Mont, pass the bottle to that young man. Sir, you'll accompany us to the house?'

Castlereagh was about to decline, but Rougue laid his hand on his pistols in a manner which showed that refusal might not be safe. Besides, in fact, Castlereagh had the most intense curiosity to see how Rougue could bear this fiery trial. Montmorency, in the meantime, stood at the table and filled himself glass after glass of the most ardent spirits until his eyes began to flash with intoxication. Rougue and he looked at each other with such incomprehensible sneers of hatred, contempt, and seeming astonishment of their respective powers of mind and body that the impression they produced on Castlereagh was deep and singular.

'What mean you to do?' said Rougue to his fellow labourer.

'I told you,' Mont answered in a deep determined tone.

'Ha. Right—good—kill them, weary them out, worry them to death.

'Oh,' he continued, starting to his feet with a strength produced by his extreme fire and emotion. 'Oh, what a glorious Ministry they will soon be. How they will stalk into the house, night after night, pale, haggard, worn to spectres. And how Elrington and Montmorency and O'Connor and Gordon and Carey and Dorn—' here he stopped a moment for want of strength. 'Oh, how those glories will rise up the moment they enter and blaze out with such unwearied sarcasm, such life-destroying taunts and abuse and invective as shall make them shrink, shrink, wither within themselves. How, by my glorious goad, that toad, that villain, that hateful leopard, the Marquis of Douro, shall exasperated to agony start up and defend himself, his kings, his country, the Ministry until Nature, tired, exhausted, spent, shall refuse him strength for utterance!

'Oh, how glorious to see his place vacant, himself raging with fever and the whole weight of the lower house fallen on the shoulders of Lofty, or—or—that—that hateful spider Sydney. To see him, him, the wretch, spitting out his burning venom, retaliating the a-thousand-times-urged attacks of thee, Montmorency, confuting thee, harassing thee, yet still himself confuted, harassed, overpressed by the mighty forces of O'Connor, or Gordon, or Carey, or Dorn.

'Then,' he stopped again, 'then the report will go out. Douro is dead, Sydney has cut his throat. Flower has absconded. The Ministry is—is broken, is dissolved. The House of Lords wearied with opposing, the kings—Oh, then comes on with full forces the Mob, the Rare Lads, storming, attacking, rising *en masse*! Oh, Rougue—Rougue. Revolution and Vict—'

Here Elrington sank down in a swoon, overpowered by weakness contending with energy. Montmorency, who during this description had lighted up like fire, laughed with delight of anticipation.

'Tonight we'll begin,' he muttered and proceeded to lift Rougue from the floor, who slowly opening his eyes snatched a pint bottle of brandy and drunk it off at a draught.

For a moment he sunk back as if shot; and then, starting from his seat while the blood rushed to his face, he said, 'The clock has struck. Now we'll go.'

Montmorency seized his hat, poured off a tumbler, and they left the room, followed by Lord Castlereagh who, stunned and appalled by the scenes, the sentiments, he had heard and seen, scarce felt conscious of what he was doing. They all three mounted the chariot and it drove off to the House of Parliament.

On their way they were joined by the carriages of Gordon, O'Connor, and many other of the most influential demagogues, so that on arriving at their destination Rougue marched up the stairs into the House followed by a troop of ninety or one hundred of the most resolute and daring members, all warmly attached to his interest. He took his seat on the Opposition benches with his minions gathered round him.

And here let me describe 'A Night In Parliament'.

The vast hall was not yet lighted up, for comparatively few of the Members had yet arrived. Thus the crowds of Members trooping in and moving across the hall like shadows in the darkness, passing from one to another, conversing, assuming their seats, the macers hustling about to keep order, and a hundred other etceteras connected with the scene, was striking enough. Shortly after Rougue entered, the chandeliers one by one lit up, cast their light through the room, and the increasing influx of members pronounced the hour of business near. The Ministers' seats were yet vacant, and to them Rougue and Montmorency directed an anxious eye. And into what a sneer of hatred did they distort their features when there entered a pale, care-worn young statesman, who moved quickly to the table and arrayed thereon sundry heaps of papers necessary to the business of the day and then, as hastily retiring, settled on to his bench with an anxious look around the crowding house.

'Sydney's in rare trim for worrying tonight, I guess,' cried Gordon to Montmorency.

In a short while, the Paymaster-General entered, Captain Flower,* whose firm, manly frame, and unwrinkled forehead betrayed no signs of vigils and watching. Behind him came the Secretary of State, Marquis Douro, pale, shattered, and scarce to be known by those who had viewed him as he usually appears. The benches of the Ministry were filled up by Goat of the War Office, John Sneaky of the Foreign Department, Lofty, and the other ministers of the lower House.

'What sort of a night, think you?' asked Sydney of the Marquis.

'Rough, I believe,' was the answer. 'They muster black under those windows, but I only fear for myself physically, for our numbers are beyond the risk of defeat.'*

'Is not Lord Thornton Witkin', asked Lofty of Sneaky, 'to be presented as a new member tonight?'

'I believe he is, but little indeed do I trouble myself with his motions.'

At this moment, the well-known voice of Rougue was heard loudly addressing the House.

'Viscount Thornton Witkin Sneaky, in consequence of an illness brought on by a too violent exertion of the corporeal functions (*loud laughter*), begs to be excused from tonight presenting himself before you as Member for Sneaky's Glasstown in room of *Colonel Arthur, dead—'

'Ha,' said John,* 'that young blade—'

'Stop,' cried Douro. 'Remark the singular circumstance of a son of the Twelves entrusting his excuse to such a man as Rougue, to his party indeed! John, I scarce knew this turn in the politics of our friend.'

'Indeed, Douro,' replied the prince. 'Nor I, either, but I expected something odd from him. However, if my father hears of this, good day to Witkin Sneaky!'

But at this moment, Colonel Grenville, the Speaker, entered and, upon his taking the chair, the regular business began. I can scarce call it regular, however, for some hours it consisted of ceaseless and vexatious attacks made by Montmorency, Gordon, and the Democrats in general upon minute affairs relating to expenditure, foreign missions, et cetera, all directed against the Ministers. Rougue always persisted in bringing the motion to a division though the result nearly always came to the same thing: One hundred against the Ministers; six or seven hundred for them. Then Sydney rose and protested against this vexatious mode of proceeding.

'What!' said Montmorency in reply. 'Will you, Sir? Dare you, Sir? (*order, order*) Silence, fools! Will you attempt to draw a veil over your actions? Over actions in the remotest degree connected with you? Why, the very sound of Mr Sydney speaking in favour of this motion would cast a doubt over any motion or bill! Let me tell you that in the whole of these four kingdoms united there is not a man so much mistrusted as yourself! The time is come and I must speak out. If the present Minister of Finance remain another month in office, it will shake the Ministry in their seats. (*Cheers and hisses*.) What right, I ask, had the Government at a moment's warning to place in full control over the persons of millions of their Majesties' subjects a young man—eh, *man*? (*Laughter and loud disapprobation*.) A young man totally unknown, untried, untrusted; nay, whom I should say was known but known only for peculation (*dreadful uproar which continued for some minutes but over which the Herculean tones of the orator rose like thunder*), known only for weakness, known only for baseness, known only for bribery, for corruption in his election, for slavery, for grovelling, after his election now playing the king and tyrant over the people, again playing the slave and flatterer to a king. Truly such a man neither ought to have a voice in the representation of his country, much less a voice in its government. What party, what class of men I ask does this man represent in parliament? Not the Aristocracy, surely? As surely not the Rare Lads, the democracy, neither the merchants, not the military profession, nor the literary professions, and what, then?'

'The mental profession, sir, the Intellect of the country,' replied the Marquis of Douro (*loud and long cheering*).

'What profession does he say? The *rental* profession? By him who never drew a rent in his life? The mental profession, then? Ho, ho. Mind must seek a higher, a worthier representative here! Yourself, my lord Marquis? My noble colleague beside me? Aye, myself even, for any one rather than him! The gentleman represents in this House of Parliament the slavery, the trickery, the poltroonery, the united grovelling habits of our mighty nations, and I ask can we not dispense with such representatives here?'

Montmorency here sat down amid thunders of applause from his own party and the most deafening marks of disapprobation from the majority of the house.

Sydney, hastily getting up, responded. 'Gentlemen, however mean and base is the attack just made upon me, however worthless the character of the attacker, yet seeing from so considerable a portion of your house his speech so warmly applauded, I cannot refrain from rising to confute his aspersions. I know, Gentlemen, that I am unknown, young, little-tried. I know that I may be eager to be involved in that unfortunate pursuit, politics, but is this a fit reason why an individual should presume to attack me before you?'

'Now, far be it from me to attempt replying to his aspersions in detail. You all know of what I am the representative. I am the representative of the populous borough of Freetown in this country, where I was elected by an overwhelming majority of electors. My noble friend, the Secretary of State, has arrogated for me too high an honour in seating me as the representative of your mind and intellect. Mr Montmorency has been pleased to taunt me with respect to my personal appearance; but let me tell him, if I am like a woman he is like a demon, and of the two which is the worst? (*Loud cheers.*) Sir, too much time has already been taken up with my affair. I shall now, then, scorning alike the person and the character of my attacker, sit down and let our business go forward.'*

Much talking and recrimination now commenced between the different parties, and some trifling motion respecting custom duties was brought forward by Mr Sydney and Flower, for the Marquis seemed too much shattered by his late victory to speak much. This motion was carried, of course, by a large majority.

At the conclusion, Rougue started up and began an address. His utter weakness, however radically covered by the fumes of brandy, shewed itself at first. He leant against the bench for support and spoke in a hoarse, low, hollow tone. But as he proceeded, his face lightened up, his voice became more distinct, and snatching his arm from its support he advanced forward a few steps with all his usual overpowering tone and attitude.

'Again and again,' he said, 'has the country or part of it asked: What right have you to attack the ministry, to oppose them, to endeavour to unseat them? What right have we, say you? What right has the torn stag to turn on its pursuers, what right has the persecuted outlaw to turn on his country, what right has the armed soldier to fight and slaughter for that country? They have the right, Sir, of self-preservation, the right of the first and greatest impulse planted in our nature. The present Ministry, by virtue of their Office, rule over and govern this vast country; they have a mighty share in the administration of justice throughout this country, and this gift, this power, placed in their hands they do all in their power to twist and distort. They were placed there for the good of the many, they act for the benefit of the few! They were placed to have a single eye toward justice, and they judge and punish without the slightest reflecting or, if reflecting, only to the end "Will it benefit or injure *us*!" They were placed there to hold an equitable jurisdiction over the laws, lives, liberties of the subject, to obey those laws, to protect those lives, and to insure* those liberties, to repeal taxes, not to lay them on, to pardon, not to slay, to soften, not to make hard. But alas, all these precepts, these commands, have they most wretchedly and wilfully violated and trampled down. Upon the present occasion it is not my object to lay fully open their thousand crimes and flagrancies. This, my friends, I will do when, tomorrow night, with your permission I bring forward a bill for the ejection from office of all the present Ministers and for the better securing of the laws and liberties of their Majesties' subjects in the appointing of all future Ministers.'

Here while his own party was vociferously cheering and the opposite one still more loudly deprecating this eloquent invective, Rougue, who had slipt behind several of his friends, fell back fainting from his seat. A ring gathered round him, and he was borne off to his carriage by Montmorency, Gordon, and several others. But now, the morning having begun to appear and the night's business being got through, the House after a few broken words from the Marquis of Douro, whose exhaustion had rendered him incapable of taking an active part in the night's debates, adjourned and separated.

[Chapter II]

Aug 20.
AD 1833

Lady Zenobia that night sat alone in her splendid saloon in Elrington Hall. For more than a fortnight, ever since, indeed, the beginning of our work, she had never heard the slightest intelligence of her lord. He had departed in an ominous manner and at an ominous period, nor could any conjectures avail respecting his return. She now sat at her table, her head leaning on her hand, when she was startled by a thundering knock at the great door, even as a carriage was heard drawing up before it. Much bustle was heard in the hall below; and ere long, her room door opened and several footmen entered, bearing Lord Elrington. They laid him on the sofa and left the room.

All this, transacted as it was in a few moments, seemed to Lady Zenobia like a thunderstroke, and it was some time ere she could advance toward the sofa where he lay extended without motion, speech, almost without breathing. She bent over him, striving to recall her sensations scattered by so strange a circumstance. She saw the proud figure of Alexander Elrington stretched there, rigid and motionless, his lofty forehead wrinkled with care and his face sunken, ghastly and deadly pale. She shuddered as she saw the demoniac expression of hatred moulded on his features, but she saw no clue as to the reason for the situation he was in. True, his head was bound up, and a lock of bloody hair strayed from under the bandage. His hands, too, were swelled and scarred, but these wounds had evidently been made a day or two before. Utterly unknown to her then remained the reason for this atrophy. Seeing no sign of breathing, she believed him dying or dead; and stern and unsocial as was this man, fearful and cruel as was his character, he yet possessed too many noble qualities, and those qualities were too much in unison with her own, to make her careless of his death. She might have once feared, even detested him; but at such an hour, in such a time, old feelings, old associations return, and now leaning over him she wept bitterly.

But Rougue was not dead. His constitution yet triumphed over his frightful exertions. She saw him move his hand, then drawing it from hers, raise it to his forehead. His eyes opened, and he attempted to sit up but immediately fell back.

'Through miserable exhaustion,' he muttered. 'Oh, Monty dove, all's up with us. We're defeated. Don't back out, Mont. I say, sweet, I shall kick up, toss off, and I'll leave thee a legacy. Zenobia? Fire, I say! Zenobia, dog (for Rougue had a dim consciousness of her being in the room), give me that knife! Now, Mont, kneel down and I'll create thee a baronet! Kneel, hound—and, and—die!'

Rougue, in his eagerness for the death of his friend, started up, which motion seemed to revive him considerably. He leant against the back of the sofa and looked slowly around the room.

Seeing Lady Zenobia standing by him, he exclaimed, 'Hey, where am I? You here, Zenobia? What are you doing? It's a long time since I've seen you. Do you know what I've been doing, eh? Tell me—out, this moment! Tell me at once you've—' casting at her a bewildered look. 'You've pois—poisoned me, you wretch, you murderer! No! 'Sdeath, there! Old wizard, fiend, take this woman and—and—'

He stopped here, and then continued but in an altered tone. 'Eh, no. This won't pass. Zenobia, what have I been doing? It's sadly up with me, however. Was I fighting with Arthur just now, eh? That fiend! No (feeling his head), that won't pass. It's some time, I think. How did I come to be here?'

'You were carried here from your chariot, my Lord, by your servants and—'

'What, Zenobia! By who, by my—my servants? They dared to—? Bring them here, this moment! Ring that bell!'

Lady Zenobia was going very reluctantly to obey, for she knew that some other ridiculous or horrid scene would take place were they to enter, when the door opened and Mr Montmorency was announced.

'In with him!' said Rougue, and this second Mirabeau entered the room.

Not immediately seeing Rougue, he asked Lady Elrington joyfully, 'Is he dead, oh?'

'No, sir,' replied she indignantly, for she liked not such a tone in such a question.

Montmorency's face fell immediately, but advancing to the sofa, he said, 'Well, you scavenger, I'd thought you were as gone as a herring.'

'Where did my husband faint?' demanded Lady Zenobia.

'In the Parliament House, Madam.'

Zenobia sighed, for she guessed the scenes that had taken place, the exertions of him before her. She shortly left the room, leaving these two statesmen to themselves.

Montmorency, knowing how to treat the illness of his friend, poured down his throat a bottle of mixed gin and brandy, which draught mightily revived the nobleman. He sat upright and took another tumbler and a third of wine that effectually strengthened him—for the time, we mean, for our readers may think of the exhaustion which must follow such a cure.

'Now,' he said. 'Now Mont, dove, I want to speak of that young man visiting at your house.' Rougue grinned as he said this, a demoniacal smile.

Montmorency put his finger to his mouth. 'He's there still. I've got it out of him that he's worth twenty thousand a year.'

'That's well, but we also must have him for a tool, Sir. He's a Lord, Mont, and a Lord does not sound ill in our ranks, eh? Does he take?'

'Grandly, Rougue. He'll come to like murder. Only give him pleasure, and he'll give you in return body and soul. I know that if I told him so now, it would shock him like death, but volo, degrees, by degrees!'

'Don't teach me, Mont.'

'Teach thee! Thou'rt past teaching!'

At this moment several carriages drew up, and visitors were announced. They came storming and swearing up the stairs and into the apartment, proving to be Gordon, O'Connor, Carey and Old 'Sdeath. Vast quantities of wine and spirits were brought forth; but as the aristocratical splendour of the apartment did not suit their plebeian stomachs, they all agreed to adjourn to the nearest pothouse. Rougue, he who so lately had been brought in to the house dead to all appearance, cold and still, now—but an hour after—was seen reeling out, cursing, swearing, with his glorious lieutenant, Montmorency, and a whole band of followers, shouting, fighting, and disturbing the neighbourhood as they went along. Soon turning down a lane, they all disappeared in its shadow, to some frightful den of their dissipated orgies. There, amid crowds of rare lads, of degraded French men and women no less degraded, sat the Greatest Orator of Africa, mounted upon a taptub and giving laws to his devoted subjects.

Meantime Lord Castlereagh had emerged from the House of Parliament, his soul inspired by the exciting and stormy scenes he had witnessed, longing to be one distinguished in the same station and ready to catch at any means of becoming so. Montmorency saw this, pressed him to a longer stay at his house, and asked him what he thought of a statesman's life. Castlereagh said something warmly admiring of it.

Montmorency whispered, 'There's a borough in our interest just vacant.' He had then set him down at Montmorency Hall and drove off himself to Elrington Palace.

With Castlereagh, meanwhile, the hours passed pleasantly on. The soft but sprightly manners of his fair entertainers afforded a striking contrast to the [...]* highly wound and ferocious characters of his late associates. And Ladies Harriet and Julia Montmorency, being but lately arrived at the City and encountering only the society, if it might be termed by that name, of their father and his dark associates, felt a most pleasing contrast in the elegant manners of the young nobleman.

At dinner Montmorency himself appeared, just returned from his orgies, where he told Castlereagh he had left Elrington 'in the thick of it'. He bore an invitation to them all to attend a grand entertainment to be given that evening by Lord Elrington to the principal nobility and Fashionables in the Glasstown. At the hour for setting off, the carriages were ordered, and Montmorency with the Dowager Countess Elrington taking one, and Castlereagh with the two younger Ladies taking the other, they drove off to the stately buildings possessed by the Arch-Demagogue.

On reaching the square of which it forms one side, they found it almost blocked up by the countless multitude of splendid equipages driving up to the doors of the kingly mansion, disembarking their crowds of dashing Fashionables and then wheeled round the open space by their respective coachmen, each eager to show off the beauty of respective horses. Montmorency pointed out to his daughters, quite new to the scene, the dashing carriage and magnificent horses of the Marquis of Douro, which shone like gems amid the crowd of quadrupeds, the comfortable wealthy-looking equipages of Colonel Grenville and Mr Bellingham, the neat business-like barouche* of Sergeant Tree and young Bud,* and the other hundreds of splendid vehicles of rank and fashion, among which his own two carriages shone pre-eminent for their costly appearance. While looking on this gay and stirring scene, all eyes were directed to a gorgeous chariot which recklessly dashed thundering through the crowd, and drew proudly up before the door, its sides and top of shining, glossy green, its cast light wheels of polished brass, its six blood horses, red and glossy, tossing their heads, snorting and pawing the ground as if conscious of the magnificent carriage they drew.

'Who is that?' 'What goes there?' 'Who does that belong to?' burst from the crowd of gazers.

Various guesses were made, but none satisfied, till a single person dismounted and entered the hall.

The gazers cried, 'It's Lord Thornton!' Lord who? Lord Thornton Witkin Sneaky;* the riddle was explained.

Montmorency's carriages, which had been hitherto detained by the press of visitors, now took their places before the door amid an admiring throng, and the inmates dismounting were ushered through a vast, vaulted marble passage of classic plainness into the great Hall. The huge rosewood folding doors were wide open to admit the constant stream of visitors. In the opening stood the servants to announce the names, and beyond stretched the mighty apartment, its vast, airy roof raised high overhead, its grand velvet curtains flowing from thence to the ground, its light and lofty windows opening on to the wide river and distant harbour, now darkening in the shades of evening. The blaze of a hundred dazzling chandeliers, the furnitures of such wondrous cost and value, and above all the crowds of nobility, rank, and beauty thronging its ample extent, absolutely blazing with costly ornament, presented to the eye a picture of overwhelming brilliancy.

Near the entrance stood to welcome the visitors the stately forms of the Lord and Lady of the mansion. Both of commanding height, of noble figure, and of extreme loftiness of manner well beseemed their splendid mansion. Lady Zenobia was attired in a robe of velvet, her usual plume of ostrich feathers surmounting the curls of her raven hair and her Italian physiognomy lighted up with smiles of courteous welcome.

As to Lord Elrington, those who could have seen him that morning intoxicated, harassed, swearing, and quarrelling amid the most despicable society, those who did see him last night, battered, bound-up, hollow, storming in Parliament, pushing forward his democratic faction, levelling his atrocious falsehoods at a dignified Ministry—or, worn with his exertion, laid down on the floor of the house livid and lifeless—would be and were indeed astounded to behold him now, erect and stately, free from all signs of the fight. Pale, indeed, but of composed and lofty manner, looking around him with an aristocratic expression as if he would have scorned to mention such society as that in which he was that morning engaged. Such as saw him now might believe him a dark and wicked man, for such was always the expression of his curled lip and treacherous eye, but still would they believe him an honourable, aristocratic nobleman. He and his lady, of course, made no ceremony in receiving his mother, Montmorency, and the two young ladies. Castlereagh, he warmly and condescendingly shook by the hand.

The company still kept pouring in, in vast numbers. Name after name was announced and person behind person was introduced, till late in the evening when the arrivals ceased and Elrington with his lady led their guests into the Grand Ballrooms. There, dancing was commenced by Elrington himself, leading out Lady Julia Montmorency, a high honour which he conferred to oblige her father. Her beauty, elegant manners, and above all the fact of her being a new arrival instantly attracted the attention of all; and the elderly Ladies above all indulged themselves in eternal guessing respecting her.

But upon her returning from the dance, a young nobleman presented himself before her, soliciting the promise of her hand at some future period of the evening. She answered she was engaged to another.

'Well, well, but you are not for the whole evening surely, Madam?'

'It is scarcely proper for a young person, I think, to appear thrice in the same evening.'

'Volo, put off your engagement to oblige me.'

'To oblige you, Sir!' she answered and turned haughtily away.

Castlereagh noticed this young man and felt a hatred to him at first sight, more than he could distinctly account for. He was apparently rather under than above the middle size, was firmly and strongly built, possessed red hair, light, quick eyes, and a whole countenance naturally of a frank, open, determined character,* buoyant and cheerful under any circumstances. But somehow this pleasant character seemed changed, the frankness and determination to effrontery, the cheerfulness to recklessness, and the whole openness of countenance expressed a determination to do only as he wished, a consciousness that his wishes were wrong but a carelessness as to that wrong. He walked through the room with a free and dashing air, not coxcombical or dandyish, but still scarcely like a true gentleman or nobleman. Castlereagh pursued him with eyes expressing hatred and contempt strongly mixed, aye, probably wholly caused by a latent jealousy.*

He stepped up to a tall, stately person far past the middle age who stood aloof from the company, eyeing them with a frozen smile and eyed by them with much mingled awe and dislike. To this elevated old gentleman Castlereagh asked, 'May I ask, Sir, who is that young man who has just passed?'

'What, Sir?' was the scornful answer.

'Sir, I shall not submit to be treated with contempt. Who is that sinister-looking young fellow, I ask?'

'Do you know who I am?'

'No, Sir, save that you're an impu—'

'In the name of murder! What are you at?' asked Rougue coming up, and then turning to the stately old aristocrat, he said, 'Your Majesty* must pardon this young person. He does not know you.'

'Of course,' said the Twelve, for such it seemed he was, and elevating his stern voice he called for his carriage to be drawn up immediately. Half-a-dozen servants ran to execute his bidding and he, walking down the room, with an exclusively frigid air turned to the company all of whom had obsequiously made way for him, and with a 'Good evening, Ladies and Gentlemen', bowing coldly left the room. The host and his lady attended him to his carriage.

'Oh, Oh,' said the young man so much hated by Castlereagh. 'Dad is as snap as gingerbread tonight. I'm up with him, however.'

'How stiff and cold', remarked the Marchioness of Douro to Lady Julia M, 'Sneaky is.'

'Is he always so?'

'Yes, nearly. But I observed him speaking scornfully to that young nobleman who handed you from the carriage. Perhaps it may have contributed to, to—'

'To starch him, eh?' interrupted the arrogant young noble so often mentioned. 'My lady Marchioness, the favour of your hand tonight? Eh?'

'Engaged, Sir.'

''Pon my soul, tart as lemon! Put off.'

'No, sir, I cannot.'

'Volo, won't you?' he replied and turned abruptly away.

Castlereagh now begged the favour of Lady Julia.

She accepted, and he led her out directly. The elegance and grace of both dancers attracted the attention of the company; and while all were gazing on them in admiration, the arrogant young nobleman cried out, taking a cigar from his mouth. 'Eh, what? Perjured, forsworn, eh?' and pointed to Lady Julia.

'Thornton, how can you?' exclaimed twenty voices round him.

'Why she's broke her promise.'

'Who's broke her promise?' asked Castlereagh, breaking from his partner and stepping furiously up. 'Sir, who are you?'

'One at a time. Your partner's broke her promise with me, and I'm Lord Thornton Witkin Sneaky.'

'Then let me tell you your name disgraces you, Sir. We must meet another time.'

'Nay, nay now, not so warmly, lad.'

'Mr Montmorency,' called out Castlereagh. 'Here, sir. Transact business with this person. He is unworthy another word.'

'Hey, what?' cried Montmorency reeling from the sideboard. 'Where's Elrington? A duel! Order! Order!'

'Elrington's off,' exclaimed O'Connor from the table, giving a significant touch to his nose.

'Oh, I guess,' replied Montmorency.

Lord Thornton cried, 'Well, well, I'll accept. But O'Connor, you'll do the needful for me tomorrow? 2:00 P.M., Scavenger's Pothouse. Pistols. All's settled and now—' raising his voice, 'Now, Ladies and Gentlemen. Hear me. I invite all this company to a grand fête to be given at Thornton Place tomorrow evening. I ask all, all friends and foes and if I should chance not to appear through the evening owing to unavoidable accidents (bowing to Castlereagh) why, volo, you must share out my goods, chattels, and furniture, among you while you are there. You must—'

Further conversation was here broken by an outrageous din heard in the square below, as if a hundred cats were fighting as many duels. All ran to the windows to reconnoitre,* and by the blaze of light flung from the windows of the illuminated mansion all perceived a huddle of mortals in the middle of the square, thrown about as if in mortal combat, cursing, swearing and venting showers of execrations. One voice was distinctly heard over the rest. Many started, and Lady

Elrington cried, 'What voice is that, Mont?' But Montmorency with many of his friends had sallied out into the square for they smelt the master directly.

There was Lord Elrington, the owner of this kingly mansion, the giver of this splendid feast, him lately so proud, so noble, so aristocratic, now in the last stage of intoxication reeling through the square, his hat dashed from his head, kicking along with his whole force Old 'Sdeath, his lieutenant, who sprawled at every hit, gasping and yelling for mercy. Rougue himself often fell flat on his face; but then rising, with his countenance blackened by dirt and blood, he vented forth a torrent of oaths and execrations, laying round him his kicks with frantic vehemence and striking to the ground all who ventured to oppose him. All this paroxysm arose perhaps upon some most trivial occasion, for he had drunk himself to a pitch of absolute frenzy, so that when Montmorency and his friends rushed down to lay hold on him, laughing however at the joke as they termed it, he felled the foremost with a loud oath and rushed up the steps to the Hall. He stumbled against them there, and fell rolling to the bottom of the flight, wounding his head further till it streamed with blood.

This only raised him above all bounds. He bolted into the house and made his way toward the grand hall in which the company were assembled. As his demoniacal figure rushed through the folding doors, the ladies screamed, the gentlemen drew their swords. But he, not heeding them, rushed through the room and taking a desperate leap flung himself headlong into the blazing fire.

A cry of horror ran through the assembly. He was drawn out by Montmorency and his friends, who throughout shewed far less surprise than any others, owing to the not uncommon ocurrence of these freaks among them. When extricated, he was quite senseless, and his face was streaming with blood.

The company, thoroughly startled, only waited till surgeons had arrived, when he was conveyed to his room, and then they departed. Lady Zenobia took leave of them firmly and without seeming emotion, but she looked pale and extremely faint. She was too lofty to shew her feelings openly, but for all that they were not less acute.

[Chapter III]

PBB

'Well,' said Montmorency to Castlereagh as soon as they had alighted at the Montmorency Hotel. 'Our friend Elrington has drunk himself up to it tonight, I think. The fool. When such important matters were to have been brought out, he might had had the decency not to knock himself on the head in this manner. I'll cut him. I'll—volo!' So saying, the Senator, seizing by the ears a large bottle of brandy, retired to his study.

Castlereagh remained behind. He felt hot and feverish; therefore, seeing the morning cool and fresh, he stepped out from the sash-window and paced to and fro through the grounds. The lights, as the dawn increased, were fast fading in the splendid mansions ranged along the river. But one still remained blazing out as if to insult the returning day.

'Arrogant wretch,' muttered Castlereagh to himself. 'But either I tame him this day or—' New thoughts and feelings, Castlereagh was aware, had risen in his heart since last morning. Or at any rate, old feelings were concentrated upon one new object, for the young Viscount was not raw in anything. But now, however, the fact was plain; he was in love, and for that love was in a few hours about to fight a duel.

A very romantic situation and one, of course, in which the 'ars poetica' must descend upon one, were he as dull as Morpheus. He stepped into the room and taking from thence a lute he sat himself down beneath the window of Lady Julia's apartment, performing with a practised hand and a mellow voice the following serenade.*

A SERENADE*

The guardian is old and the castle is dreary;
  Fair was the Maiden and fond is the swain,
But the tempest is high and the night is uncheery
  And ne'er may she see her true lover again.

The morn on her marriage must gloomily lighten
  Mid tempests and torrent and glittering rain;
    And her guardian has told her
    A Noble must hold her,
Who owns, round his castle, hill, valley, and plain.

> Oh, to that Maiden fair,
> Ocean and earth and air,
> All seem resolved her destruction to claim,
> But love will ne'er cower
> To tempest or shower,
> And nature's worst madness its bright beams can tame.
>
> The Niger is broad and its waters unruffled;
> Far through broad Afric its waves wind along,
> A thousand wide kingdoms its billows have watered
> In history renowned and immortal in song.
>
> Rage, then, O Ocean! and hurl thy white billows
> High o'er the rocks of this desolate shore;
> Drive shower on shower o'er temple and tower
> And down each dark valley thy sleety storm pour!
>
> Plains may be flooded and roads may be broken
> And torrents may burst o'er the traveller's way
> But Never, o Never, can Niger's vast river
> Fall like a roadbank or rise like a sea.
>
> There, then, fair Maiden, thy boat lies at anchor;
> There the rough sailors recline on the oar;
> There thy true lover beneath thy proud castle
> But waits thy forthcoming to sail from the shore.

The last notes had scarcely died from the lute, and Castlereagh had arisen to depart when he heard from the trees near at hand another voice and another instrument begin a tune in reply to his own. He started, but the voice was that of a man, deep but mellow. It sang as follows.

> Why dost thou pine, fair Maiden,
> Within thy castle tower?
> Why does the tempest chain thee there,
> O'er Ocean's driving shower?
>
> What recks it if the night be dark,
> Or roughly roars the seas?
> What needs it that a feeble bark
> Shall bear thee far away?
>
> There are gates enow within this wall
> And posterns, safe and sure.
> Then rise, awake, command thy page.
> To unbar the hostile door.

> Why need we fly o'er Niger's stream
> Or wander through the storm?
> When I may enter quickly here
> And clasp thee in my arm!

The free ideas and the bold, ready voice of the singer could not be mistaken. Castlereagh snatched his pistol and dashed among the trees. He gazed round with eyes of fire, but the singer and the lute were gone and had left no sign. Castlereagh 'moved heaven and earth but he would obtain revenge!'* He returned to the house, threw himself on a sofa, and tossed there until the sun had risen over the city.

Lady Julia met him at the breakfast table with a silent greeting. I must here remark to my readers that duels were too common among the Glasstowners for the ladies to show any very great distress upon the approach of one; for did they weep on such occasion, I could scarce insure them a dry eye through the year. Therefore, though Lady Julia guessed the one pending that day, she was scarce less cheerful or lively than usual. After breakfast, Montmorency appeared, his hat in his hand and two horses saddled at the door. After cursing everything round him, he exclaimed, 'Castlereagh, come to your dinner', and putting his finger to his nose, 'Castlereagh, do you like black pudding?'*

Castlereagh arose and with him left the room. They rode through the street until they reached a dirty, dark lane, down which they turned, and then stopped at the door of a wretched old damp pile of a building, the very appearance of which would dampen a man's soul. Their horses were there taken by that old fiend, 'Sdeath, and they both entered the building.

It was a pothouse of the very lowest order, a real tavern, dark, low, rotten, corrupt within and without, the roof rotten, the walls rotting, the floor covered with rotting substances. All presented the smell and aspect of a charnel house though, unlike it, it was furnished with a rousing fire, two or three rotting forms, and several tubs and vessels of spirits and ale. No one appeared in the room, but a powerful steam of whisky from an inner area announced the occupants to be engaged at a still somewhere about. Castlereagh who, be it remembered, was only a novice in Glasstown life, shuddered as he surveyed this wretched scene, and questioned his companion, who was emptying out from a can a measure of 'life'.

'And whom are we to see in this miserable hotel?'

'Pho! It's what I call a grand place. Why, O'Connor and Thornton and Rougue.'

'Rougue! Why, Sir, remember where we left him! How we left him!'

'Aye, and see where he is now,' exclaimed a voice from behind the heaps of cans and barrels.

They ran to look, and Castlereagh started back. Montmorency laughed loudly. It was actually Elrington himself. Yes, there lay that lofty nobleman, grovelling in a black, musty hole, behind a heap of casks, drunk, miserably drunk, his head wounded in last night's revel now bound up, his face pale and ghastly, and himself so weak as to be unable to lift himself or sit upright.

'Well done, Elrington!' cried Montmorency. 'My darling has done it! However, why, man, how will you get on at this rate?'

'Oh dear, I don't know. I am weak. Heave me up, Mont, on to that cask by the fire.'

Montmorency did as he desired. The nobleman leant his head against the fireplace, but did not speak. He presented an appalling spectacle as he sat there, his forehead absolutely white as ivory, save where spotted with blood, and shining with cold perspiration, his hair appearing in bloody curls beneath its bandages, his sunk but yet lightning eyes flashing fire, his pale, hollow cheeks and his lips and hands trembling with nervousness. In fact, the mere exertion of sitting up was too much for his shattered frame. He gazed languidly round the apartment, smiled with a ghastly expression, and would have fallen back senseless, had not Montmorency caught him in his arms and, laughing all the while, poured down his throat a draught of hot brandy. It revived him slightly.

Castlereagh, startled at the spectacle, said, 'What on earth, Sir, has his Lordship been doing?'

'Oh, naught extra. You know what work he had the night before last. All yesterday he was writing, reading, forming, and executing his scheme for tomorrow's vengeance.'

Here Montmorency grinned horribly, a ghastly smile. 'In the evening he presided at the feast, the night he presided at—humph, you may yet see where. All this morning, he's been laid up. This day he has worked so hard in politics, besides other little matters, that just now he is clean done up. But, howsoever, Thornton will be here presently, and I'll just sit a bit till he comes.

'Come Castlereagh! Sit on the other side of this barrel. Noble cards, you dogs—ho! What, Sirrah? Cards, I say! Not come? Volo, dog, beast, hound, calf's tail fiend!'

Here the Senator strode from the apartment into the still, returning soon, a flask of spirit under one arm and a wretched, ghastly Frenchman under the other.

'Produce your cards or, my teeth!'

The startled monsieur with a trembling hand pointed to a pack in the corner. Mont seized them and hurled the Frenchie out of the room. He made Castlereagh sit at one end of the barrel, placed himself at the other, and they began a light game to pass away the time. But before many minutes, Rougue motioned them to come nearer him and give him a hand. The barrel was drawn before him, and after steadying himself with a draught of brandy, he entered into a rubber of whist for a few guineas.

But they had not proceeded far in their game before a series of thundering kicks at the door announced the entrance of Thornton and his second, O'Connor. They entered the filthy hole, singing and swearing in great glee.

'Come,' said Thornton, 'let's make it up, Casty, and gang wi me to my doghole out by Thornton.'

'Make it up, Sir!' cried Castlereagh, and took out his pistol.

'Humph, he's brave,' exclaimed Thornton admiringly, and took his place at one end of the room. 'You're in the dark there, lad.'

'Well, rouse the fire.'

A barrel was instantly flung on to the coals and a blaze soon shot up which made them hot to suffocation. Preliminaries were settled. The word was given, 'Fire!'

Instantly flashes succeeded, and all were enveloped in dense smoke. When it had cleared away, the two combatants were found standing, Witkin with his arm shot through, and Castlereagh *sans* a portion of the ear. All here except Castlereagh burst out a-laughing.

'Fair hits, but clumsily missed, somehow.'

'No, Castlereagh. Beg pardon, Sir; never do so no more,' cried Witkin.

Castlereagh stared at such ungentlemanly conduct, while the rest laughed.

'Well done, Sneak, a prime one!'

Lord Thornton then inviting them all to his house that night, retired with his second. As he passed by to the door, Castlereagh staring at his disgraceful conduct just lifted his foot and fairly kicked him out of the tavern. Lord Thornton, as soon as he had gained firm ground, arose but still laughing heartily ran off as fast as he well could.

'A disgraceful scoundrel,' exclaimed Castlereagh.

'A capital young fellow,' replied Mont. 'Isn't he, Rougue?'

'I care neither for him nor you, you vile scoundrel. Get out of my sight this instant! Piece of impudent folly and presumption, you great, gross, leather-headed Jacobin!'

'I'll report, Rougue, an' you go on in this way. Volo, I will, you fiend, you—'

'Mont, help me to the carriage.'

'Aye, Rougue.'

Thus saying, all three left the pothouse.

'Oh,' asked Montmorency on their way home, 'Castlereagh, our game's not out. Let's finish it here before we go home.' He pointed to the door of the Elysium.

The nobleman hesitated, for he was not far enough drawn into the maze of dissipation to treat this matter so lightly, but Elrington and Montmorency, winking at each other, prevailed on him to assent. They dismounted, stepped in; and that night, between O'Connor and the Marquis of Douro, Castlereagh lost a thousand pounds.

'Dear play,' remarked Montmorency as they drove home, 'but I'll teach you tomorrow how to handle it better.'*

[*Chapter IV**]

Sept. 18, PBB
AD 1833

Two or three weeks I must now pass over with short notice, only briefly remarking the events transacted during this space of time. That mysterious but urgent business relating to the 'great firms' which at the end of our first volume had called Rougue so hastily to the Glasstown seemed now to be entirely hushed up, if we might guess from the perfect silence maintained upon the subject. Parliament, too, had been prorogued, and the members were for a little time released from their overpowering cares and labour. This proved of the highest consequence to Lord Elrington who, as we have seen, could not have borne long with his own policy but was fast breaking up and reducing himself to the doors of death.

Now, however, he relaxed a little and his iron constitution began slowly to recover its wonted spring. Do not, however, imagine him to be idle. No, all this time of general holiday he was actively, energetically preparing to meet another campaign, forming his coadjutors and associates into a hundred revolutionary clubs, bribing and persuading to his party every straying spirit with whom he could meet, supporting and causing to be written a hundred newspapers, pamphlets, and the like calculated to poison the foundations of society. And, finally, he was exerting himself to the utmost to raise also his own private affairs, to shine out amongst the nobility, to seek funds for supplying his boundless expenses.

The style in which he was living far exceeded the bounds of even the most ample fortune and would swallow up hundreds of thousands. Half-a-dozen splendid dwellings in town and country, a palace almost equal to those of our noble kings, feasts, balls, and entertainments day after day, servants, equipages, horses without number to support. And, worst of all, a constant stream of perfect bloodsuckers, associates, tools, engines, bribers to pacify and supply. Add to this that his passion for gaming was insatiable, that he strove with all his energies to be the leader in the race course, the ring, the

Paradise; nay, also in the Halls of Philosophy, as patron of music, of the fine arts. In short, he hungered to be pre-eminent in everything, little or great, good or evil, in which pre-eminence could be attainable.

Now, this mention of such a boundless ocean of expense leads one to ask how in the world he could find funds for the slightest indulgence in them. I don't know.* Some things, however, will come out. This curious mercantile concern several times mentioned seemed a good reservoir, but what was it? We don't know; but, however, the question leads us to bring forward again My Lord Viscount Castlereagh, who was one means to defray a few expenses.

Now, our Readers must see that, somehow, Rougue and Mr Montmorency professed a wondrous friendship for this young person. The truth was, he was possessed of £30,000 a year.* These two, Satan* and Belial, instantly fixed their eyes on him as one admirably calculated to serve two ends. They determined to draw him over to their party and to fleece him of all his property, then to cast him off and, if he proved refractory, to, as Rougue said emphatically, 'get rid of him'.

Now, Castlereagh was like most of our young noblemen; wild and thoughtless, he liked pleasure and excitement and heeded little how he obtained it. The commanding spirit of Hector Montmorency first seized on him, and made him believe in him as his friend. He invited him to his house, instructed him in the ways of life, initiated him into the mysteries of the Elysium and finally presented him a powerful object of attraction in his daughter, Lady Julia Montmorency. Then, lest this should fail, in effect this victim was brought under the talons of the great Elrington himself, whose vast ability, enchanting powers of conversation, splendid entertainments, and presiding genius so enchained him that, though he—having naturally enough sense—distinctly saw the dangerous nature of the men among whom he was placed, yet it was vain for him to attempt to free himself from their shackles.

To all Rougue's entertainments he was ever invited. He constantly appeared with him, Montmorency, and others so that, as every one instantly began to regard him as a confirmed anarchist, he himself slipped gradually into the error; and ere he knew, he found himself among the meshes of a ferocious faction. Of course, his name became enrolled among their club. Rougue offered him a seat that he held in his interest, and he became, too, a mark in the Elysium's races and other activities for the most noble Arthur, Marquis of Douro, and his followers to practise upon and destroy.

Now, at the beginning of the three weeks we have passed over so lightly, Castlereagh felt many twinges of conscience, had many sleepless nights, and little liked the race he was just about to run. At the end, though his sleepless nights were not abated yet, his spirit had become metal, and—why, his metal had also become spirit, for he felt himself minus £80 or £90,000. This seems a tremendous amount, but it was not destined to satisfy the treacherous and inexorable Elrington and Montmorency. They, it must be remarked, never won from him. No, they advised him to leave off play; they lent him large sums to free himself from immediate embarrassment. It was O'Connor, it was Witkin, it was Douro* that fleeced him and bled him so.

The last named gentleman, of course, they had no control over; he worked on his own ground, not in their interest, and here they from their souls wished Castlereagh to win. But, sad to say, of his money Douro had pocketed some odd £9,000 or £10,000; Lofty and others, four or five. Then for the remainder £75,000—Witkin had £30,000, O'Connor £25,000, and Carey £15,000, of which they by special agreement made with Elrington and Montmorency were to refund four-fifths to those two grand springs of this conspiracy.* But as yet, much was to be done. Castlereagh's property yet exceeded £400,000.

Now, leaving this miserable mass of treachery and fiendishness, we must mention the state of Lord Castlereagh with regard to Lady Julia. His sensations here had ripened into silent but ardent love for her, and loud and burning hatred for his rival. Lord Thornton Witkin Sneaky with persevering effrontery continued his addresses to the person of Lady Julia and the purse of Castlereagh. However, the lady, disgusted with his arrogance and presumption (for strange to say, though so high in rank and title, Lord Thornton contrived to seem presuming even to those far in those respects below him), would have little to say to him.

The fine, animated countenance, genteel appearance, elegant manners, and still good reputation of Lord Castlereagh far, far more inclined her to that quarter. In fact, she could not deny that her interest in him had not decreased on acquaintance to the usual attentions in fashionable society. Castlereagh possessed a high skill in music; here she could participate with him. A fine taste in literature, large acquaintance with books and nature; here, they too agreed. Here he also could and did instruct her.

But now to go on. We are about to describe an account of the manner in which Castlereagh spent his day. Concluding the third week of our 'passover', it will serve as a specimen.

[*Chapter V*]

AD 1833
PBB*
Sept. 18

About 12 o'clock Castlereagh, who still resided at Montmorency House, awoke from sleep, not over-refreshed nor of an over-serene mind. After an hour occupied in dressing, he descended into the breakfast room where he found Lady Julia alone. She was standing before the window and her handkerchief was in her hand. Her eyes glistened. It was plain she had been weeping; and Castlereagh knew that it was plain, too, she had heard from some hint or other given by her father how last night at a great meeting on the 'North Ground', where a trial took place between Douro's black horse 'Eagle' and Abercorn's bay colt 'Blow It', Castlereagh had sustained serious and heavy losses. In fact, he had disbursed to the tune of £13 or £14,000.

After the usual salutation, on his part made with embarrassment, she asked him:

'My lord, what do you see before you?'

'An angel,' he answered.

'No, my lord, I mean in life.'

'Ah,' he replied, rather starting. 'But it matters not to reproach, Julia. I know well enough what will befall, but you should see a way to get out of it and see whether I won't accept it.'

'You know the man who made such a show on the course last night?'

'Yes, the Marquis.'

'Very well. From what my father mentioned of your proceedings there, I should scarce have supposed that nobleman possessed of many evil or good qualities. I should have thought him worthless and broken, but so it is not. He is secure in fortune, in the estimation of the world. What is it owing to, now?'

'Ah, good fortune, I fear.'

'No, I do not think so. He has firmness, he knows when to stop. Look at him, copy him, and—'

'Yes. Yes, Julia. But you are scarcely ignorant of those two men with whom I am so much entangled. Elrington and—'

'My father, you could say. I know—' She seemed afraid to say what was on her tongue.

Castlereagh began to think, for yesterday had staggered him, and he was near, at once, for a month to come forswearing the course and Elysium. Then, the stern, harsh voice of Montmorency was heard in the passage.

He entered, shook Castlereagh warmly by the hand, and reforming the frightful expression of ferocious cunning impressed on his countenance into a peaceful but serpent-like sneer, he said, 'Hey! Well, what now, Castle? What, volo! In the suds, down-cast? Murder, this won't do! What, man, grieve for a trifling matter of £10,000? It shan't pass. Look you, Elrington came up to me this morning, half smashed, he was; and he said, that is, a matter of a few ciphers could startle you? Why he would just forkit at once for you. John, bring the desk. Now, I'm commissioned to give you over—my! Volo, let's see. 1, 2, 3, 4—5—6—what a long purse Elrington keeps—7, 8, 9, 10, £11,000 in good bank bills, endorsed Bellingham (Co.).* Now, what say you to that, eh? And listen, we don't require bonds; we will do with your word, my hound! But the grandest piece of news is to come, yet. This afternoon at Astley's course we shall have a real turn-up between "Swasher" and "Clinker"! And then, volo, in Astley's Rooms, it is rumoured there will be, aye, more than rumoured, a real turn-up between the Marquis and Lord T. W. Sneaky. Quite a treat but private, strictly private; none but the first grade will be present, and of them, all.

'Now, if you don't go, why—volo, you must pass a step lower. That's all, but I'm cursedly dry. Ho, hang your tea, Julia. I shall take a glass or so in my study, hear me? There's a general card of invitation* to the fête at Waterloo Palace this night. But come, Castlereagh, into the study. We must settle the bond* and then, off.'

Montmorency led the way out of the room. Castlereagh followed, looking back on Lady Julia with a shake of the head and a melancholy smile.

After Montmorency had remained sitting in the study opposite to Castlereagh, fortifying his inner works with a drink or two of B.R. and Y. or O.D.V.* for half an hour, a servant entered and visitors were announced. They came, in the half-frank, half-arrogant figure of Lord Thornton, the sinister Belial, O'Connor, the mean, filthy wretch Old 'Sdeath, and a whole host of dark spirits, men to be known only by deeds of villainy.

As they entered, they cried out, 'Come, Montmorency and Castlereagh, all's ready. Rare, rare sport, my Masters, today! Rougue's waiting for us at Elrington Hall to meet him.'

Montmorency looked black. 'Could not he have come with you?'

'Oh, no! He's over-high for that!'

With a few curses and execrations, Montmorency led the way out of the room. They mounted their horses and made off, Castlereagh, however, looking much cast down, which they all observed and so set upon him with their bitterest ridicule. On dismounting before the proud porch of Elrington Hall, he strove with all his might to shake off this inconvenient shame and this troublesome knave, Conscience. The party moved forward with songs and curses, into the study of Rougue. On the door opening, there they saw him fronting them, standing behind a table, his hands upon an open book and his high forehead showing forth an aspect of the deepest solemnity.

'Hey,' muttered Montmorency. 'What moonstroke now?'

'Shame,' cried Rougue with an affected twang through his nose. 'Shame, that upon the dawn of so glorious an outpouring, men should be found so little carried forward by a spirit of reviving grace! Open your tongues, fools, for some other purpose than to vent your ungodly execrations, and join with me in a little savoury rising of the Spirit, a psalm of pleasant thanksgiving for the awakening flowers about to appear among the dunghills of a carnal, self-seeking world.

> Raise your triumphant songs
> To an immortal tune;
> Let the wide earth resound the deeds
> A Saving grace has done.
>
> Now, Sinners, dry your tears,
> Let hopeless sorrow cease;
> Bow to the Signs of Saving grace
> And take ——'*

Here a roar of laughter, for some time suppressed, burst from the edifying assembly.

'My heart, Rougue does go it!'

'Is he mad?'

'Aye, mad as the wind.'

'I'll stick my knife into you, an' another were!'* Such were the expressions of his auditors.

For himself, Rougue closed the book, and standing with his hands clenched, uttered forth such a volley of the hugest oaths, curses, and execrations, as must have startled even some of his hardened hearers. Then calling for his horse, he led the way to the square. As they all mounted he said calmly, 'Now, what number expect you shall we amass?'

'Thirty-seven men.'

'Oh. Well, just by way of sport, I intend that if we meet any of the Aristocrats, we'll just have a row on the course.'

A laugh of approbation burst from the assembled, and they rode on through the streets* to the place of meeting, one well known to many of my readers. There they found assembled all the élite of the spirit and fashion of the city. They trooped into the rooms till the race should begin. It was broad noonday, but here in the halls of misery, thick stone walls shut out every ray of daylight, and its absence was supplied by the red, lurid glow of the hundred lamps within. Here, as entered Rougue's party, his antagonist, Douro, withdrew to the other side until the desire of betting impelled them to join the others; and soon the cries of '2 to 1 on Swasher', '5 to 1 on Clinker', 'Taken!'

'6 to 1', '7 to 1', 'All taken!'

'Ho, Clinker's the favourite!'

The Marquis of Douro's firm voice, '8 to 1 on Swasher.'

Castlereagh, who had inquired and inspected minutely the points of the horses: 'Taken!'

'Is it?' replied the voice of the Marquis. 'Come with me, Sir.' Castlereagh retired with him to a sideboard.

'Again?' asked Lofty, speaking of the Marquis's 'pigeon'.

'Why, a cropper.'* Then, 'But, Sir. What are your stakes on the subject?'

'Nay, your lordship shall lay them.'

The Marquis scanned him over with his keen eye, saying in a low voice, '£20,000.'

Castlereagh started, but instantly cried, 'Done.'

The Marquis turned to seek more game, he met Rougue.

'Humph, a stiff one,' winked Lord Lofty.

'Douro,' said Elrington, 'I am willing to risk heavy for Clinker.'

'A broken-winded trump,' said Lofty contemptuously.

Rougue fixed his fiery eye on him. 'Well, Sir. Since he is so, you'll not refuse a layer.'

Lofty was caught. Elrington pressed him hard. Lofty took bait to the amount of several thousands. Montmorency, eyeing poor Sydney in the crowd, instantly bribed a man to go up and praise the qualities of Clinker to him with all his heart. The man did so and prevailed entirely on the simple statesman to bet anything in favour of Clinker. Montmorency then stepped up, and giving Swasher a doubtful preference he offered £10,000 upon him. This Sydney accepted, though terribly startled.

The officers soon came to say that the horses were ready. All rushed on to the Grandstand, and the room was cleared in an instant. But in this room will we remain till the race is over. We have seen too much of such work to find the detail of it particularly novel. An hour has elapsed, and you may hear by the noise that the race is over. The betters return headlong into the rooms. There is the Marquis, his countenance illuminated by a satisfied smile. Rougue, cool but dissatisfied. Castlereagh, pale as death. Sydney, perfectly bewildered. Montmorency, venting his laughter, sneers, jokes on all round him, crying to Sydney 'Cash up, Cash up' till a great blow from an unseen hand hinted him to be quiet. He scratched his head and looked dismayed. It was miserable to view Castlereagh, giving out £20,000 to the hands of the Marquis, who stood over him with a most provoking, good-humoured smile.

As Arthur glanced round the room, he perceived Sydney doling out with hands as blue as steel his £10,000 to the iron Montmorency. His eyes instantly flashed, he flung the parcel of bills on to the table, and with a great exclamation rushed up to Sydney. What in the world was the ass doing?

'Did I not tell you not to lay one guinea without my advice?'

'Oh, he's thought better on it,' exclaimed Montmorency. Douro, glancing at him with a look of blackness, retired with his inconsiderate* friend.

But the hour was now drawing on to the promised fight, and the two champions, Douro and Thornton, retired to the drawing rooms to prepare. The favoured ones who were to view the fight trooped into the Sanctum Sanctorum, the inner betting rooms. In a while, they prepared to commence; the two sons of kings (humph, if their fathers knew of it!) were placed opposite to one another. Elrington was Thornton's second; Lofty, the Marquis's. Bets were immediately given and taken to immense amounts. Our hero, Castlereagh, who hated Thornton Witkin though he was of his own faction, determined not to back him but bet on the Marquis of Douro.

The champions were true-blood first-raters, and in the highest condition for breadth and bone. Thornton had for height,* and for experience the Marquis. They began. The battle was long, and tough to the last. Sixty rounds were fought with equal success, till at the end Witkin began to fail, and some exquisite hits on the part of the Marquis brought him to the ground senseless.

They were both carried off by their seconds in a weak condition. Blood was let and the surgeons required, but the Marquis was declared winner of the fight. Various were the fortunes of the betters, but for Castlereagh, he won £6,000, which in some degree alleviated his terrible losses before. The crowds now began to separate and depart. Elrington, Montmorency, Castlereagh, and others rode together to Bravey's Inn on the command of the former, who swore that they should not go home, as they ought to be at Waterloo Palace in the evening. He, however, ordered servants to be sent round to their respective residences to fetch their carriages to the hotel. Here in the Refectory, they sat down to dinner among several hundred persons.

Elrington with the utmost ease walked to the head of the vast common table, took a chair, and after emptying glasses of strong waters cried, 'Now, dogs, look up to me for direction. I believe I am your superior.'

Under the direction of such a president, the bottle was not wanting in circulation. The company soon became outrageous. Several English gentlemen were present, and Rougue, with his usual inclination to mischief, pointed them out as objects for sport. The diners, like true Glasstowners, set upon them and committed the most atrocious injury to their persons and effects. Elrington then incited all round to drink; and when the waiters entered with their bills, our unlucky young nobleman, Castlereagh, felt such a buzzing in his brain that it was with difficulty he paid his reckoning.

Evening now drew on, and by the time that he, with Rougue, Montmorency, and the others mounted their chariots for the feast at Waterloo Palace, his dizziness had in some degree abated. It was night when they reached the front of the noble mansion of the Duke of Wellington, crowded with equipages, blazing with splendour.

Elrington's possession did not here forsake him. He boldly walked up the steps to the Hall, his followers behind him, and was received with becoming courtesy by their host, the Duke, who was, by the bye, a very respectable gentleman in black, with a pleasant smile, keen eye and eagle nose. The vast crowd entering here broke one person from another and mingled all in one mass. Castlereagh, with whom we have most to do, thus separated from his seeming friends, walked up to the upper end of this magnificent saloon and looked on the scene before him.

Its stir, glory, and gorgeousness I need not describe, but this was a usual entertainment given by a mighty monarch. No Duchess of Wellington was here, but she who officiated as Lady of the Feast, though simple as a May Day maiden, yet well beseemed her high rank and station. She was the Marchioness of Douro.* Castlereagh saw her surrounded by a bright and glowing circle of beauty and fashion, among whom he easily discerned the proud, lofty Lady Elrington, the gay, sparkling Lady Sydney, and the fair form of Lady Julia Montmorency.

But what distinguished this fête above others in the city yet more than its magnificence was the five or six men whom he saw standing together alone at the upper fireplace, conversing together as too high to notice much around them. These were some of the Twelves,* the first founders of our mighty kingdom, who could only in the feast of the nobility be found, singly, or dropping in occasionally for a moment to shed a lustre over a whole gathering. Yet in appearance were they far from sunlike. On the contrary, there stood a little, broad, stout, elderly man, stiff and upright as his own cane, smelling suspiciously of the times of old. His Majesty Stumps, of Stumps Land. A still broader, stouter but younger one with red cheeks and frank aspect: His Majesty of Ross's Land. A great, corpulent, bluff, carbuncled, rosy-nosed, drunken ox, Bravey. The big, burly, brawny, brutish, Herculean-armed Bady. The tall straight, Scottish, unamiable Monarch of Parrydise. The still taller, far more unamiable, bald-headed, elderly, sinister, cold-blooded, polite old Gentleman of the North. These formed that nucleus of planets round which crowded all the boldest and brightest of the Glasstown, and to these, Castlereagh could not help directing much of his gaze.

But we must pass over much of this feast for our space permits us not to enlarge. Let it be enough to state that it contained more than the usual portion of stir, variety, and splendour. When the company had adjourned to the great saloons, there commenced the usual flow of brilliant and varied conversation such as one might listen to for hours with highest enjoyment. And here the garrulity and egotism of professed talkers and authors was finely awed and counterbalanced by the military gentlemen among whom they stood. Gifford, Bud, Tree, young Soult, Goat, and others were counterbalanced by Elrington, Douro, Montmorency, Lofty, Cavendish, Abercorn, Sneaky, and a host of spirits of the same stamp.

But amid this feast of reason and flow of soul, up rose Elrington and, taking a little volume from his pocket, he mounted a table and then with his loudest voice commanded silence. A hundred swords were half unsheathed to repress his audacity, but curiosity returned them back. As for Rougue, rolling his eyes round the assembly and pressing his hand to his forehead, he began.

'Oh vain, oh foolish Generation, wise I know in your own Council. Aye, wise as the dust, the stones you tread upon. Do not, now, I intreat you, continue your path through this so-long travelled, so-weary wilderness. The darkness of this night just passed may well excuse you from thus far stumbling into it and wandering over it. But no further, children, no further. Look up, now, O Sons of Men. Look, behold. What is it you see in the heavens? I see a light rising in the morning, a light not of a natural sun, but the great overwhelming all-changing light, which is destined now to rise, hereafter to shine eternally, friends. You have never seen the plains of Parry's land from Mt Elimbo, you have never seen the natural resemblance of a spiritual world. Yet the frightful wastes of that haughty hill are above those far-off golden plains. In nature the hideous chaos of a carnal world lies deep, deep below the heaven of a coming grace.

'But oh, how vainly do I speak, and then am I tinged with a touch of earthly, carnal thoughts, vain, un-godly images. Pass off now, all of you, and visit me no more! Oh, that I could emulate the men of old and arise in spiritual strength, declaring unto you the things which are to come! Oh, might the mantle of those mighty Worthies descend here on me in this, the most waste, most unprofitable Vineyard man ever laboured in. It needs, indeed, a noble faith to believe morning at hand when we are walking in darkness, cannot see even the pitchy sky, but hope against hope, have faith in the wildest danger. Yes, and I have, and having it I keep raised above this earth, above you all.

>Faith is the brightest evidence[*]
>Of things beyond our sight,

> Breaks through the clouds of flesh and sense
>   And dwells in heavenly light.
> That sets times past in present view,
>   Brings distant prospects home
> Of things a thousand years ago
>   And thousand years to come.

'Hah, children, by faith I believe that morning comes, by faith I believe Myself its Messenger, by faith I believe this world was formed, by faith I believe it now reforming.* Oh, Men of this World! Ho, carnal, selfseeking, ungodly souls! Howl, gnash now, for your time is at an end. Look backward, children of light, upon this night of darkness. Look back upon your original fall; look, see your natures dashed and broken, fallen in the fall of your fathers—rising with your rising sons. Sons, no more shall we have sons, no more daughters, no more fathers or mothers. I tell you All, All, are alike now; no one is over another. None oppresseth another. Hah! Long have I laboured to remove oppression, but it too is smote away by another hand than mine, and faith and grace and the spirits and a continual Godly savour of the incense of thanksgiving shall rise instead and rule. Howl, I say, ye men of dust and ashes! Howl, aye, ungodly lukewarm feeders of children! Howl, Man of Belial; howl, thou of false Gravity! Aye, howl thou Old Man, thou full of days! Behold, thy days are done, and thy age is as nothing before me.'

Here the preacher became sensible that he had gone too far by a simultaneous movement among his hearers and a pistol shot or two fired at him.

'Vanity of Vanities,' he shouted, 'All, all is vanity! Down upon your knees, ye men of pomp, pride, power; down to the earth, ye unholy pomps and gaudities! Down to that dust from whence ye sprung, from which ye shall not, cannot rise! Ha, what is this I see riding on clouds? This the heavenly sun of regeneration, this sweet harbinger of reviving grace! Lift up your head. Oh, all ye ages, bend down, mountains, bend down that grace and godliness may enter in. Now, now, let me close my eyes, let me die since I here behold the crown of all my hopes, the sum of all my joys. Now, we all can read out titles clear, now we all can see our heavenly Mansions; and now in like manner let us bid farewell to all fears and shortcomings and doubts and relapsings! Enter, enter, my children, into the Morning of Light and Life, of saving grace and eternal joy!

'Heh, O'Connor, there, or you, Thornton, fetch me that bottle of claret and help me off this table. It's like Adam's desk, your Grace; it has my footmarks on it.* Oh, my Lord Marquis, I say, I would entreat a few moments—but stop a while—really now I am so thrashed that this claret seems worth fuishionless.* Nay, Old Elrington, Old Scoundrel, are you at the cordial waters, eh? Give me a toss!* Now (pulling out his watch), I would just hint to all gentlemen concerned here, it is near time to go there. Ye ken where. I'm pressed, ye ken. Oh, what? Dancing, eh? No, my dear Lady, Marchioness Douro, I beg, I intreat of you the honour of your hand. Then shall be accomplished the saying which was written: the lion shall lie down with the kid—I mean the wolf and the lamb—never mind! Don't refuse me, Lady, or I shall break my heart.'

The Marchioness, one of the most astounded during the whole of this extraordinary speech, for to her these exhibitions were uncommon, was startled to find so near a request made to her by the great actor in this late extraordinary scene. However, he stood by, half-entreating with a menacing eye. She could not refuse. Elrington led her out with much satisfaction. The company had seldom seen such a contrast as was here presented to them. Her slender, fairylike figure, her face of such elegance, sweetness, and innocence, his overbearing stature, the haughty glance of his triumphing eye, the mixed and extravagant passions displayed in his face formed an odd and curious sight. The Marquis of Douro looked on gloomily during the dance and, when finished, instantly beckoned his Lady beside him.*

All this while Castlereagh had been looking on with vast interest, admiring the preaching of Elrington, the figures of the fair dancers; but on a pause being made when these last had retired, his soul relapsed into itself and became the seat of bitter and gloomy reflections on his future life. The men among whom he had cast his lot, his losses that day, his probable losses that night: how could he meet Lady Julia?

Here he was roused by hearing that baleful, arrogant voice, well known as the voice of his rival. He looked up. There was Lord Thornton standing before Lady Julia Montmorency.

'Volo, your hand, Ma'am?'

'It is engaged, my lord.'

'Now fire, murder! I'll be cut off no longer! I demand—'

Castlereagh had stole beside him unobserved. He seized Thornton by the collar and, catching a cane from Old Lofty, he dragged

Thornton into the middle of the room and gave it him over the shoulders in the most handsome style.

'Now, here I declare before all men that this is the only reproof of avail on this degraded, shameless, arrogant scoundrel!' So saying, he flung both the cane and the culprit from him with the utmost contempt.

The company stood amazed at this spectacle, many laughed outright, all tittered. A smile was even seen to steal over the frigid, aristocratic features of Old Sneaky. As for his worthy son Thornton, he upon recovering his breath clapped both hands to his sides and burst into an uncontrollable fit of laughter.

'Flat as a fluke, broad as a pancake! He has herculeanized my shoulders. They were broad afore, they are twice it, now. Oh, I ache, I ache, pathetically. Didn't I, ladies, show unco grace?* Stop, waiter, hand me that glass of spirits! I assure you, I am thirsty! Ladies and Gents, your health. Yours, too, Castle. Oh, sir, I want to speak to you,' he called to a tall, elderly, frigid, proud-looking nobleman,* who stepped up to him. They retired to a corner and continued whispering to each other, all the time looking frequently to Castlereagh. In the midst of this, Elrington took out a peculiar little ivory whistle from his pocket, blew one shrill call, and nodding a graceful adieu to His Grace and the visitors, withdrew. In about a quarter of an hour, not only his own followers but the Marquis, Lofty, Abercorn, Cavendish, and dozens of young noblemen also withdrew from the rooms.

[Chapter VI]

PBB-te*
Sept. 21. 33

We shall rejoin the gentlemen, whom we left departing from the Palace, at the rooms of the Great Elysium, or Pandemonium,* the same night at 12:00 pm. There are, as usual, congregated amid a blaze of lurid light and midnight splendour the brightest and darkest spirits of Verdopolis. Elrington is seated at the head of that long, long, rosewood table. There are hundreds of noble countenances, all darkened with doubt, pale with despair, flushed with hope or in joy, standing with native coolness. Our hero Castlereagh is standing opposite the elderly, crafty nobleman mentioned before as conversing so eagerly with Thornton. Douro holds the stakes, Rougue looks on with a strange wink at the nobleman who was, it may be time to state, the celebrated Lord Caversham, enshrined in equine and monumental memory. The game was brought to a conclusion.

'Lost,' said Castlereagh. 'Here, my Lord. Count them.'

'Aye. Five, ten, £15,000. Very well for a night', he said and stalked away from the table to the sideboard. Castlereagh's hands trembled violently. He too walked to the sideboard and poured down his throat large draughts of claret and brandy.

But a thought strikes me. It were better, reader, for us to step out of the street door of this awful dwelling and there wait till four o'clock. Then that door flew open, and there rushed out a wild multitude of men, actuated by the strongest, most different passions and feelings.

Among them came Castlereagh. He, in spite of the various calls of his friends (*eh, friends?*), rushed from the crowd, ran through the dark, silent streets, and only stopped on the Great Bridge which spans the noble Niger. He stopped here and gazed wildly round. It was, as usual, a raw, solemn morning, dark and dreary.

'Here,' he said after a long silence, 'here I stood before first meeting the accursed Montmorency. Oh, what changes have visited me since then! Then I was worth £400,000; now, I am indebted

£40,000. All through him! But, save once, I will never darken his doors again.' He turned down a street hastily and disappeared.

Montmorency that day at noon was seated in his handsome study at one side of an ample fire, Elrington on the other, as croose and canny as twa auld friends.* Bottles and glasses were before them and the floor and table piled with papers, letters, and books.

'Humph. Well, Mont, he's proved true pluck, anyhow. Let's see how stand the accounts.

O'Connor has gained from him	£13,000
Carey from him	16,000
'Sdeath from him	1,600
Caversham from him	26,000
Gordon from him	31,500
To Elrington's share:	£88,100*
Dorn gained from him	£11,000
Thornton	41,000
Eagleton	3,800
To Montmorency's share:	£55,800*

Total of both: £143,900. To Douro, Lofty, and others he has lost, it seems, £60 or £70,000 which, lackaday, is also lost to us. But, however, we've made a bright job of it, Mont. Volo! Well, let it pass, I say, Mont. Now we've blown him, next we'll cut him, cut him out. And hear me: I'll hire some desperate fellows to shoot him, aye, some night in the street. Mont, dead man's blood never cries.'

'Why Rougue, if it did, your ears would seldom be of stretch.'*

'Right, Mont, right, hand me the bottle. Whisht! Who's here?'

A servant entered with a bundle of newspapers, proclamations, and other papers, laid them on the table, and departed. Montmorency took up the first. It was a proclamation for the calling together Parliament that evening for the more fit discussion of several important questions on hand. He looked at it and without speaking handed it to Elrington, who soon laid it on the table. The two worthies gazed a while on each other in mute astonishment, and then each burst out into a fit of laughter. This paroxysm ended.

'By my soul,' said Elrington in his darkest tone. 'Out with your speeches. Convene the clubs. Set the machinery going! Have at them! Woe to the slackest! Don't talk, I'll off this moment. They have found all out. Hang the cursed, the thrice despicable scoundrels.'

Here a servant again entered, announcing Viscount Castlereagh.

'In with him,' cried Montmorency. The young nobleman entered. Without bowing, he walked up to Montmorency. He was pale, dressed in black and habited for a journey.

'Sir,' he said, 'We must part, without regret on your part, of course; without either regret or pleasure on mine. Sir, I will not reproach you. May I be permitted to speak an hour with Lady Julia?'

'With Julia? My teeth, she is gone, gone to be married. Why, Thornton asked her of me this morning.'

'In reward for merited services', interrupted Rougue.

'Aye, Rougue, and as knowing that between cup and lip—you guess the proverb—why, we ordered the carriage. Volo, a king's son is something, though she scarce thought so! However—hah-hah-hah!'

'Where is she gone, Sir?' asked Castlereagh calmly.

'Oh, that is neither here nor there,' replied Montmorency. 'I tell *you*, Sir? Look here, by my soul, you shall have it! Begone! Out of my house, and never darken these doors again!'

Castlereagh lurched round. He could not respond;* his brain was on fire. He dashed down stairs while, as he went, the loud bursts of fiendish laughter from his two betrayers above seemed to scald his ears.

He threw himself on his horse and with whirling brain galloped through the streets, stopping as by instinct at the residence of Lord Thornton Witkin Sneaky. As he gazed on the front of that splendid Hotel, a pang of anguish stole over him when he reflected on the sum which he had only squandered on its hateful owner. He fiercely demanded of a servant, 'Is your Master within?'

'No, my lord. Gone off in the carriage this morning.'

'Which road?'

'That to Sneaky's Glasstown.'

Castlereagh turned his horse and rode furiously off.

That evening at sunset on the Great North Road there was seen galloping forward a young cavalier mounted and spurring in hot haste, his hat struck over his eyes and urging his lively steed to its utmost force as he gained sight of a carriage rolling along with outriders at a distance. A little behind this carriage there was a single horseman. Toward him this cavalier, who was Lord Castlereagh, furiously rode, and as he came up to him he cried, 'Draw, villain or die!'

The horseman looked hastily round and then cried out 'Ho, John,

'Sdeath, push forward, for life! Don't wait. For life, I say!' He turned to Castlereagh, saying, 'What—what now, Sir?'

'Lord Thornton, draw!' was the only answer, as Castlereagh rushed on him, bore him to the ground, and plunged a sword into his body.

It scarce hit fairly. Thornton drew, grappled with his adversary, and by his superior strength had got him under and prepared to run him through when Castlereagh, drawing out a pistol, fired it at him. Thornton fell. Castlereagh jumped up, spurned him with his foot, and ran into a cottage on the road side. There he called out. 'Ho, is Scroven here?'

'Aye lad. I am, I seed you play that pliskie* just now. What in the—?'

'Scroven, no questions! Help me to drag him into your cottage.' They both ran to the road, lifted up the bleeding Thornton, and conveyed him into the hut.

When he was set down, Castlereagh said, 'Scroven, you have companions here. I'll trust you with the carrion. I must ride back to the Glasstown for assistance to rescue her contained in that carriage which some time ago passed by. Keep him till I return.' He mounted his horse and dashed back to the City.

Here he arrived after several hours. The morning was dawning; he had ridden through the night.* As he passed through the streets, he beheld vast confusion reigning through them, prodigious considering this early hour. Even his anxiety and fever of mind could not allow him to pass on till he had inquired the nature of this disturbance.

'Parliament is broke up for the night,' was the answer. 'The moment they met last evening, up got the Marquis of Douro. He declared that all the robberies and plundering committed through the whole country for some time past were without a single exception the result of one grand, united, concerted system of wholescale plunder. It was headed and directed by a few individuals who had in secret established firms* and depots throughout the whole country for the reception of the spoil and the organization of plots and schemes of robbery, and for paying the subordinate agents their allowance of profit.

'The heads of this frightful body were Alexander Rougue, Lord Elrington, and Lord Thornton W. Sneaky, Mr H. M. M. Montmorency, R. P. 'Sdeath, L. Gordon, A. O'Connor, M. Dorn, Carey, and others. And the burning of the Jail a month ago was owing to the fact that in it were confined four under-agents of this conspiracy who were taken up simply for, it was thought, a common robbery, and who had threatened to their employers to divulge the whole secret of the combination if they did not liberate them. And so Elrington had had recourse to that desperate measure of storming the Jail for this purpose. Further: Douro said that this combination was first discovered to the Government by the Lawyer Tweezy, and that since then they had been employed in ascertaining the truth of it, that now they moved that Lord Elrington, Montmorency, Witkin, and the others should be impeached for their share in this frightful transaction, and that warrants should be issued for the detention of all the other agents of the conspiracy.

'The moment the Marquis had spoken, up rose Elrington, Montmorency and others and after a torrent of execration and abuse they with their followers rushed forward and made a desperate struggle to attain the doors. But they were strongly guarded, the government foreseeing the likelihood of an attempt of this sort. Most of them were caught and secured, but Elrington, Montmorency, O'Connor, and one or two more by dint of desperate valour made their way through and disappeared in the darkness. The bill was instantly passed and they are now hunting after Elrington, Montmorency, and Thornton; for the detention and presenting of any of whom, dead or alive, the government offers a reward of £50,000.'

'Do they?' replied Castlereagh. 'I can answer for the last one, anyhow', and he rode forward to the Office of the Home Department. Here he found Sneaky, Douro, and Sydney. He explained to them that with proper officers, he could engage to secure Lord T. W. Sneaky, but whether dead or alive uncertain.

Sneaky, the culprit's father, instantly ordered horses and a carriage be got ready, and officers to be procured. They followed Castlereagh, who urged them out of the City with breathless haste along the North Road for many miles to Scroven's cottage. There entering with handcuffs, the officers found Thornton stretched on a settle, wounded indeed, but wondrously recovered, for that shot had not proved at all fatal.

He cried out when they had explained why they were conveying him off.

'Oh, Castle, I say! I'll give up my Lady Julia if you'll engage to free me. Eh, boy?'

'Villain, where have they conveyed her?'

'Off to Freetown, 20 miles forward.'

'If I find her and bring her home unharmed, thou mayst hope for thy wretched life. If not, woe to thee!'

So soon as Castlereagh had seen Thornton lifted into the chaise and conveyed back toward the City, he prevailed on a party of the officers to accompany him to Freetown in search of the fair prisoner. They drew up at the Northern Hotel. The officers rushed into the yard and secured Old 'Sdeath and his escort. Castlereagh flew into the parlour. There, welcome sight, he saw Lady Julia Montmorency, in tears, indeed, and dejected in the extreme.

I cannot and need not describe their welcome and cordial meeting, the joy and rapture on both sides. They mounted the chariot and it rolled back to the Glasstown.

When arrived there, Castlereagh acquainted the Government with the success of his journey, and informed them that Thornton, at least, was secured. The Marquis of Douro informed him that he, for his part, through the whole of his short and adverse aquaintance with him had seen and marked his spirit, his mind, and accomplishments, and had mourned the evil men among whom he was fallen. Of course, he could not restore him the money he had gained from him,* but he was happy to state that the government had, on his representation, declared for his services the highly advantageous post of Secretary of the Foreign Office at his disposal, and entreated him to accept it.

Of course, Castlereagh did not refuse. He was sick of his late faction, convinced of his errors. This post, with the prize £50,000, restored him to his former station, and repaid his losses. And after sojourning two weeks at the Marquis of Douro's, his marriage with Lady Julia Montmorency was solemnized before his new and illustrious friends of the Wellesly, Sneaky, and Lofty families. The bride was given away by his Grace of Wellington.

Of Thornton Witkin we can only say that his part in the robbery scheme was found very slight, as rather, indeed, suggested by the general indifference of his character. He was released as a Twelve's son and dashed about as usual.* The other rascals accused are about to undergo trial. The ringleaders Elrington and Montmorency still remain hidden. I fear they will first work in secret and then come forth again, to inspire dread and create confusion.

Lord Viscount Castlereagh and his bride have gone with the

Marquis and Marchioness of Douro to spend their honeymoon in the Country.

End of the 2nd volume
P. B. Brontë.
September 21st
AD 1833*

Books published this Season

By Seargent Tree. G. G. T. No. 587. G. S.*

Lord Ronan, a poem by the Marquis of Douro.
    I vol. Oct.   12s.
Something about Arthur, by Ld C^s Wellesly.
    II vols. Oct.   20s.
The Fate of Coomassie, a poem by Young Soult.
    £   s   d
    I vol. Quarto   2. 0. 0.
The Foundling, a tale by Captain Tree.*
    £   s   d
    I vol. Oct.   1. 0. 0.
The Green Dwarf, a tale by Ld C^s Wellesly.
    I vol. Quarto   12s.
Real Life in Verdopolis, a tale by Capt. Flower.
    II vols. Oct.   30s.

———————
———————

N. B.* The tales entitled Something about Arthur and The Green Dwarf may also be had of Sergt. Badenough, neatly stitched, in from 12 to 24 Nos. Price, one penny each.

Sergt. Badenough
Pothouse Alley
G. G. Town*

P. B. Bronte, Sept. 22 AD 1833.

EXPLANATORY NOTES

The Life of Northangerland

3 *the man who has it... unlock the casket*: Branwell's narrator, John Bud (whose title advances from Sergeant to Captain in the course of his career) is developed carefully as a contrast to Alexander Percy, voicing a respectable conservatism that frequently verges on pomposity. In some accounts, Sergeant Bud and Captain Bud are separately identified as father and son; see Barbara and Gareth Lloyd Evans, *Everyman's Companion to the Brontës* (London, Dent, 1982).

4 *Transpire*: used here in the old sense of 'to become known, leak out or emerge from secrecy'. Branwell used such archaic diction, it would appear, far more often than did his sisters, and generally with complete accuracy, suggesting a highly developed vocabulary at a quite early age.

5 *half-lord, half-robber*: interestingly, this description of the Percys as robber-kings fits the career of the famed seventeenth-century Malabar pirate Angria, whose name was extended to his private kingdom, and whose 'sons and immediate descendants' held their power for the better part of a century until crushed by an English force led by Clive in 1756.

... to the union of rival crowns: that is, from the end of the War of the Roses to the succession of the Stuart line.

Raystrick Hall: Branwell gradually modernizes the name: Raystracke–Raistrick–Raystrick. The name is found in the Haworth churchyard, and the family is still represented locally. (Coincidentally, one member of the family is a long-time employee of the Brontë Society and works in the administrative offices of the Brontë Parsonage Museum as of the present day.)

the Pretender's invasion: James Francis Edward Stuart (1688–1766), the 'Old Pretender'.

6 *back to Northumberland*: Branwell's frequent references to rack-renting may well have been tied to accounts of his father's early life in Ireland, where Patrick's own father, Hugh Brunty (or Prunty) was an illiterate labourer and sometime tenant, with a large family to feed. In any event Edward Percy's career at this point is a summary account of the typical absentee landlord made famous in Maria Edgeworth's *Castle Rackrent* (1800). John Wilkes (1727–97) was a radical political reformer in

Parliament, known for his recklessness and still frequently mentioned in *Blackwood's* and other periodicals during Branwell's youth.

6 *Gerald, Earl of Mornington*: was an actual figure, the name and title of the Duke of Wellington's father, the title later inherited by his older brother, Richard, first Governor-General of India (where Arthur Wellesley, at that time a colonel with his own regiment while still in his early twenties, gained his initial distinction as a soldier under his brother's reign).

7 *Robert Patrick King*: known more familiarly as 'Sdeath, is an extremely important figure here as an avatar of violence and corruption—He is, too, an anticipation of the old Yorkshire hypocrite, Joseph, who quotes scripture in a litany of hatred towards others in *Wuthering Heights*, though the latter is both more subtle and more realistic.

8 *one of these heroes*: the figure in question is the post-Waterloo Duke of Wellington, but later fused with his son Arthur Wellesley, who in turn comes back to Africa as the youthful hero Duoro (one of Wellington's actual titles), also known as the Duke of Zamorna. The original Wellington at this point in the chronicles has become a shadowy imperial figure as ruler of the entire Verdopolitan Union, while his son, having saved civilization (an obvious reference to Waterloo), demands and receives the new kingdom, Angria, as reward for his achievement.
the new seat of her capacious reign: this view of the Empire as a new world in which England would duplicate itself around the globe is echoed in the Brontë Juvenilia. What is striking about these writings is the completeness with which the ostensibly African setting is transposed to a new England in both culture and landscape by Branwell and his sisters.

9 *1500 AD*: although Branwell continues to refer to the land generally as Africa, at this point an English manor-house built over 300 years earlier seems to be an obvious anachronism, with the settling of Glasstown/Verdopolis only a generation earlier.

the Great Rebellion against the GENII: almost the last reference to those master-builders, the Genii. While spoken of as demonic, they represent a fairytale element that is forthwith abandoned by Branwell. 'The Great Rebellion' here does suggest a parallel with Lucifer's rebellion against heaven, however.

10 *the King*: the reference here is to the old Duke of Wellington who, as a member of the English aristocracy in Ireland, is said to be related to Lady Helen Beresford, Edward Percy's spouse.

12 *Northangerland*: the name has associations for writer and reader other than the obvious one of Jane Austen's comic *Northanger Abbey*. The

northern heritage of the Percys, in part at least, reflects the Yorkshire sense of separation from a more populous, more cosmopolitan, and more effete southern England, expressed not only in *Wuthering Heights* but in Mrs Gaskell's *North and South* and countless other nineteenth-century novels. The name 'Percy' for a rebellious northern family is, of course, derived directly from history and Shakespeare, and the defiant young Harry Percy (Hotspur), an alter-ego of Prince Hal in the *Henry IV* plays, is probably a partial model for Alexander Percy. As contrasted with traditional heroes, his ego and disdain for others results in an almost constant *anger* against the world. Thus, Percy's own precariously held domains, both tangible and psychological, are appropriately North-Anger-Land.

14 *from 1796 to 1800*: that is, the earlier part of the Napoleonic Wars.

Bide the brunt: another instance of Branwell's use of archaisms, which convey a certain learned quality to the thought of his narrator.

15 *Leaf's History, with Commentaries*: '*Leaf's* History', along with Sergeant *Bud* and Captain *Tree*, are playful arboreal names surviving from Branwell's childhood writings; there is nothing of the fantastic left in them at this point.

16 *I obeyed the assignment*: in this long rationalization, Bud is revealed as both prig and opportunist, however inoffensively so. Throughout, he is an obvious contrast to the ruthless Percys.

upon my being . . . a: in the MS the top line of fo. 2 (verso) is largely illegible; the reconstruction is based on the surviving visible letters and the context.

17 *. . . never absent*: In this passage, the MS reads 'where Queenship and aristocracy were never absent'. The change is probably the most radical of our emendations made on rare occasions because of questionable syntax or diction.

his most frequent disposition: here used to refer to the boy's characteristic tendency of mind, or humour.

18 *'I shall arrange this'*: Branwell was a genuine lover of music, who became skilful on piano, organ, and flute; his transcriptions for the latter instrument still survive in 'Branwell's Flute Book' in the Haworth Parsonage Library. In his teens he became the organist in his father's church in Haworth.

the seal: probably a device or impression, but it could be a closed mouth on the small cannon.

19 *Sullivan O'Connor*: an earlier reference to O'Connor gave him the Christian name of John. A later reference to Arthur O'Connor refers to a son who is a peer of Alexander Percy's.

20 *blowing behind the instrument*: pumping the bellows of the organ.

21 *wanderings*: here referring to the vagaries of his imagination rather than actual straying.

23 *... likes of yaw*: 'Sdeath's dialect throughout is not consistent. This seems to be less a matter of Branwell's failure than of a character trait of the old villain who is duplicitous in every way. Frequently he abandons dialect altogether; at other times he clearly uses it for a particular purpose.

24 *strode*: an indecipherable adverb follows this word in the manuscript. Its omission seems not to affect the narrative in any way.

25 *of this world?*: in the MS this question is (inconsistently) addressed to 'Mamma'.

spoken: the MS page ends in mid-sentence here, but the bottom of the page shows a doodle of trees and hills, a not-uncommon practice of Branwell, who at times will even write his text on a sheet earlier used for such a casual bit of sketching.

... his favourite hymns: the central portion of this sentence is partly illegible in the MS. The hymn-titles following are by Isaac Watts, a copy of whose work was in the Brontë family library.

26 *always darkened*: some words at this point are not fully legible but are consistent in their visible parts with the passage as reconstructed. While an unusual phrasing, it is clear enough in meaning.

27 *spurning at*: 'kicking at'.

28 *Percy Hall ... the Capital*: this long sentence has been slightly altered from the MS to avoid incoherence in the original phrasing.

beside: in the archaic definition of 'nearby'.

30 *Rougue*: a name used during Alexander Percy's more riotous years or earlier adulthood (in 'Real Life in Verdopolis', for example); it becomes displaced by 'Northangerland' in both this manuscript and Branwell's own subsequent references to himself.

Branwell's reference to Percy's mathematical genius coincides with a probable source for one of Percy's titles, that of Viscount Elrington. Thomas Elrington (1760–1835) was a distinguished Irish mathematician who became professor of mathematics at Dublin University in 1795, provost of Trinity College in 1811, Bishop of Limerick in 1820, and was translated to the see of Leighlin and Ferns in 1822. His well-known edition of Euclid was still being used as a textbook at Dublin University some forty years after his death; he also published an edition of Juvenal.

31 *Augusta Romana di Segovia*: in her nature, Augusta is a close parallel to

EXPLANATORY NOTES 217

Augusta Geraldine Almaida (AGA) of Emily Brontë's Gondal narratives, as deduced from the surviving poems (see Fanny Ratchford's *Gondal's Queen*, 1940), and very probably was Emily's source for her Gondal figure. The name 'Augusta' is undoubtedly borrowed from Byron's half-sister Augusta, with whom the poet was deeply involved and for whom he named his own child Augusta Ada.

35 *a middling night*: the MS appears to read 'midding night', but since their ride is completed without inteference from the weather, 'midding' is probably a mistake in spelling. (Conceivably it could be a vulgarism, using an adjective derived from 'midden'.)

Montmorency: in the various chronicles of Branwell, Hector Montmorency is alternately Alexander Percy's closest confidant or his bitter enemy, in either case represented as equally dissolute. However, this relationship never attains the psychological complexity of the relationship between Percy and Zamorna, which is described at length in several other Angrian chronicles, though not brought out in those presented here. See Bud's reference to both Montmorency and Zamorna as possible biographers at the beginning of this narrative.

36 *rich*: this word is not clear in the MS and could conceivably be 'Jew'.

37 ... *traffic on*: depending on how the note is interpreted, in the four years until Alexander's twenty-first birthday the borrowed sum of £25,000 will grow into a debt of from £57,203 to nearly double that amount.

38 ... *repulsed it*: this specific analysis of character is remarkable for the way in which, at the age of eighteen, Branwell anticipates his own adult life as reported many years later in Charlotte's letters and Mrs Gaskell's biography.

39 *eighteen years*: born on 'the first December, 1793', Alexander can have no more than barely reached his seventeenth birthday on this 'wild autumnal evening in 1810'.

... *know its own feyther*: the Devil as the true father of the great sinner is here stated explicitly. This introduces a circular element, since the central character is simultaneously a creation of the Devil, and responsible through his own actions for the diabolical figure's successful activity. The note signed with Caversham seems an interesting parallel to the pact with the devil, since 'Sdeath (who had been a witness signatory), now cheerfully declares himself to be a devil incarnate.

40 *£30,000*: the discrepancy in the amount is as given in the text.

42 ... *interest centred*: in the MS the words between 'soon' and 'on him' are not legible. However, the bridge portion used here obviously fits the narrative sense.

EXPLANATORY NOTES

44 *...fate and circumstance*: the phrasing here seems to anticipate that of *Wuthering Heights*, with the 'pale-faced beings' suggesting the Lintons. There is an obvious parallel with the fated lovers Heathcliff and Catherine, both pairs showing in similar ways the intensity of a shared world from which others are excluded and which is throughout coloured by a sense of doom.

45 *Sun of Angria*: a cognomen of the Duke of Zamorna, just as 'Star of the West' is of Northangerland, the two names reinforcing the Miltonic Christ–Lucifer opposition.

48 *Daniel Montmorency*: apparently a brother of the Henry Montmorency described earlier, and uncle to Hector Montmorency, Alexander's friend, who is also a lawyer.

50 *untiring Ambition*: echoing here the Luciferian figure even more than the standard Byronic figure so often seen as the source of the Brontëan hero, Branwell quite explicitly defines the characteristics of the romantic archetype embodied in the figure of Lucifer in Byron's *Cain*, a work over which Charlotte enthused in an early letter to Ellen Nussey; see Gaskell, p. 134.

Like a bright exhalation...more: Shakespeare's Henry VIII, III. ii. 226–7. In the original, the pronoun is 'me' rather than 'him'.

51 *the wreck of his fortune in 18—*: probably the 1832 Rebellion referred to at other points in the Angrian writings.

jilting: again, an archaic usage: 'jilting' as 'casting off'.

53 *...ere he is cured of*: this passage is again reminiscent of dialogue used by Hindley and Heathcliff a dozen years later in *Wuthering Heights*.

54 *Ellen*: one of several references in the Juvenilia to a nurse figure called Ellen/Nellie, who would later come fully alive as the chief narrator of *Wuthering Heights*. (Another name source is Ellen Nussey, Charlotte's close friend and ceaseless correspondent, with whom both Branwell and Emily were well acquainted.)

55 *as the weapons of my arm*: this passage accounts to some extent for the league of young rakehells with whom Percy surrounds himself; they parallel the demon lieutenants of Lucifer in Milton's epic. Note Percy's reference to his own ego as 'that Deity within'.

squire: illegible in the MS, but the sense of the statement suggests the word 'squire'.

accustomed: here used literally to mean 'characterized by custom or tradition'.

...or feeling can: this passage is a disquisition on ambition that is virtually synonymous with Pride, in the epic sense. It recreates the

EXPLANATORY NOTES   219

image of the hero, reaffirms the primacy of passion over morality, and makes sensitivity and powerful feeling the sole measure of value.

56 *a Sicilian and a miner*: the final clause in this sentence is indistinct as it appears in the MS. If accurately transcribed it would seem to reject the kind of idealism that was manifest in Byron's experiences in Greece and the Mediterranean or Shelley's lifelong republican statements. (The two poets had died, respectively, only eleven and thirteen years before, in Branwell's early childhood, and their work was well known to the Brontës.) A more specific identification may be possible, but the context with its three-part division—*imitative* youth, heroic *ardour*, and sordid passion—all disavowed, seems to make use of the Sicilian and miner purely as metaphors.

57 *... Satan, I am he!*: the idea of an incarnated Lucifer as a dark parallel to the positive incarnation of Christ persists in the villain/hero as a great sufferer. The lines that follow this passage may profitably be compared with Branwell's poem 'Lucifer' (see Winnifrith, *Poems*, 219).

58 *Aveola ... after this*: major battles of the Napoleonic Wars, though only a few years past, are part of historical myth for Alexander Percy, reinforcing the demands of destiny in his own life.

what am I ... at the end of that time?: this speculativeness was common to the Brontës in both the Angrian writings and the published novels, as well as their personal writings (cf. the four-year diaries of Emily and Anne, where the same questions are asked). Branwell's subsequent speculation about 'our nation' is as relevant to England as to Angria (although he remembers to refer to Africa later in the passage).

the Western Aristocracy: a reference to the inhabitants of the Angrian provinces as distinct from Verdopolis.

mighty shackles of religion: Branwell's atheism was a grievous concern for Charlotte right up to the deathbed scene that she reports when, allegedly, her brother while unconscious murmured prayers after his father. That Branwell was already anti-religious while still in his teens seems evident from this passage.

59 *Earth to earth*: in the MS this phrase is repeated here, an obvious lapse by the author.

Augusta, though I am far away: this poem was later copied out in Branwell's 1837 Notebook, with several word-changes from the original version found here. See Winnifrith, *Poems*, 190, which follows the Notebook version.

62 *presently*: that is, 'immediately'.

63 *a period of three months*: the MS phrasing here is 'a period of five or six weeks'. However, later in the same paragraph Branwell refers to

63 *demeaned himself*: that is, 'conducted himself'.

64 *...from various colleges*: the list of Alexander's accomplices at the university seems to include some about whom he had queried Augusta in his earlier letter. Theoretically, they could have subsequently joined him as students. (Hector Montmorency, already in a profession and some years older than Alexander, is conspicuously absent.) The 'old man' referred to in the preceding part of the paragraph is, obviously, the ubiquitous 'Sdeath, Alexander's diabolical familiar.

65 *so help me, my mind*: an interesting, if awkward, variant of the oath 'so help me, God', the latter obviously being inappropriate, given the anti-religious aim of the society. A probable model incident for Branwell's 'Society' was the expulsion of the poet Shelley from Oxford University at the age of 18 because of his circulating a pamphlet, *The Necessity for Atheism*.

66 *St Michael's Church*: readers familiar with the life of Branwell will recognize the name as that of the Haworth parish church where Patrick Brontë was the perpetual curate and, ironically, in the vaults of which Branwell himself would be buried in 1948.

67 *assigned punishment*: an example of Branwell's haste: the MS here reads 'their assigned consequence was so high as to involve severe consequences...' It will be noted that, in the following paragraph, 'Sdeath apparently knows the punishment before it is announced, given the prior date of the meeting of Alexander's financial backers.

68 *...on the death of his father*: the £30,000 originally borrowed from Caversham has ostensibly been supplemented by a loan of £20,000 from Simpson, the occasion of which has not been dramatized in the narrative.

71 *Major General*: while the reference to Bud as 'Major General' in the MS is here retained, it seems probable that it was an unwitting repetition of the title given above to Percy. Although a soldier, Bud has been spoken of primarily as a writer, and it is scarcely probable that he would have reached the very highest of military ranks, one that Northangerland himself holds.

...1835: in the MS, 'Chapter II' is written above 'Vol. II': it would appear that Branwell was undecided on his division references or simply neglected to strike out the chapter reference on the draft. Similarly, he wrote the date as 'June 3, 1825', obviously meaning 1835, in accord with the preceding portion of the manuscript.

EXPLANATORY NOTES 221

72 *foppish*: that is, 'foolish', a now-obsolete usage. In the following paragraph an interesting, even if playful, series of allusions to Branwell's sisters occurs. The 'foppish person' is quite clearly his younger sister Emily, characterized as a soul-searcher and visionary. The succeeding 'person of the weaker sex' is 15 year-old Anne, with her 'pretty tales' or 'gambols of fairies in a flowery vale'. The third, 'of the shorter sex' (a familiar gibe against her), is manifestly Charlotte, whom Branwell here excoriates at length for her romantic and traditional interests and her unwillingness to write of 'real life and real feelings'. In light of this fairly extended critique by Branwell, it is interesting to note Charlotte's reaction to *Wuthering Heights*, particularly in her Preface to the posthumous Second Edition (1850), with its reservations about Emily's plot.

73 *a Barmecide feast*: an illusory meal (taken from a story in *The Arabian Nights*, another favourite Brontë family book).

the mightiest poetry: Branwell here and in the following paragraph affirms that 'the mightiest poetry' is that in which the force of personality is the subject. Although he speaks as Bud, the sentiment is less suited to that narrator than to the author himself.

the fallen spirits in the West: again, a correlation of Percy's cronies with the fallen angels in *Paradise Lost*. In some ways, Branwell is more logical than his predecessor, for the 'fallen spirits' surrounding his Lucifer are both accomplices and betrayers. There is no loyalty to speak of in his underworld.

75 *dived downward*: an old term for going underground.

76 *I daily strove to maintain there*: six words of this sentence are illegible in the manuscript, but the reconstruction seems to be the only logical phrasing for the context in which it occurs.

... what I feel?: Bud's bitterness at the daily humiliation of serving as a tutor anticipates the reaction of Anne Brontë to the role of governess, expressed a dozen years later in her *Agnes Grey* and by Charlotte in numerous letters and other writings.

another pen than mine: the other pen is that of Charlotte. Marian Hume was the first wife of Zamorna; the family gave its name to the Angrian region of Humeshire.

77 *Harriet O'Connor*: later becomes a devoted mistress to Alexander Percy. She resembles in some ways Charlotte's later creation, Mina Laury, in the story of that name.

miserably ended: Arthur O'Connor is identified elsewhere in the Juvenilia as a revolutionary leader; beginning as one of the Council members of the Society for the Creation of the World, he ends as one of the casualties of Northangerland's bloody rebellion.

77 *'Mr Harry'*: as a pet name for Harriet very probably was inspired by Charlotte's frequent use of the signature 'Charles Thunder' (Charlotte as the female form of Charles, while Brontë is a Greek word for 'thunder'). A further parallel, later, occurs with the masculine pen-names 'Ellis, Acton, and Currer Bell', under which the poetry collection and the first novels appeared. (Bell, of course, was the name of the curate whom Charlotte married, while all the first names were family names of the Haworth region.)

80 *... who used it*: in the MS the structure of this sentence is badly jumbled ('and for this reason, it came upon my ears, while writing in the very time of those who used it as the well-remembered name bestowed on her by when she was seen associating with such freinds and meddling with such matters as she did ...')

81 *Hal, Percy*: Shakespeare's Hotspur Percy and Prince Hal of the *Henry IV* plays are again echoed here.

... succession of visitors: this passage, reflecting Bud's isolation from others in the company, indicates that he is still a menial, further raising question about his military title as given at the beginning of Volume II in the manuscript.

Mr Charles Steaton: probably is a lapse and should be Thomas Steaton, the Steward for the Percy estate, referred to earlier. (The name may well be derived from the village of Steeton, six or seven miles from Haworth.)

83 *'tilted off 't fur spot'*: that is, damned to Hell—the 'far spot'.

84 *... plaused at o' me life ower ye*: 'Sdeath's ejaculation 'Od!' apparently indicates pique at being called 'old'. He sees himself as straddling the life-span of each of the generations involved in the story: 'I'm placed at all my life over you.'

85 *... to DEATH*: the fatal irony of this exchange between 'Sdeath and Augusta is obviously meant to be realized retrospectively, after her death.

... kneel before her: the grotesque court that 'Sdeath arranges here for the murderous 'Queen of Heaven' is a clear mockery, with the arch-demon assuming the role of stage director as he places the totally unprincipled nobleman, Caversham, and the arch-usurer, Simpson, as attendants around the beautiful but absolutely egoistic and pitiless Augusta. He himself, with pointed irony, is placed as a "mere tool," a servant paying homage to her noble attributes. In her role Augusta di Segovia again evokes comparison with Emily's unprincipled Gondal

heroine, Augusta Geraldine Almaida whose second lover is Lord Alexander of Elbe.

87 *What thou doest, do quickly*: *Macbeth* is clearly running through Branwell's mind during the episode of the killing. This first direct reference is obviously from Shakespeare's 'If it were done when 'tis done, then 'twere well | It were done quickly' (I. vii. 1–2). A few pages on there is an explicit reference to 'my Lord and Lady Macbeth', while on p. 90 Augusta's reproach, 'they have unmanned you', is reminiscent of Lady Macbeth's gibe at Macbeth: 'What, quite unmanned in folly?' (III. iv. 74). On p. 94, 'A wild and stormy morning' recalls the stormy night of Duncan's slaying and, of course, the name 'Dr Duncan' for the attending physician further confirms the association of ideas. In this later scene there are other incidental parallels, like the word 'juggle' in 'Neither he nor you shall juggle me out of my life and property' (p. 95): compare Shakespeare's 'And be these juggling fiends no more believed' (V. viii. 19); or 'that deed done' (p. 96) echoing running allusions to the assassination as 'the deed' in *Macbeth*. Branwell's familiarity with Shakespeare at this point is obvious, too, in casual references such as 'conscience does make—' (p. 96), the tail end of Hamlet's 'To be or not to be...', or, 'with all their sins full blown' (p. 106), paraphrasing Hamlet's 'With all his crimes broad blown, as flush as May' (III. iii. 81) from the 'Now might I do it pat' soliloquy.

Careful readers will assuredly find many other echoes in the impressionable young Branwell's narratives at this time, particularly from Shakespeare. It is, after all, no accident that he borrowed the name of the arch-rebel, Percy, from the Shakespeare histories, even if he subsequently ignored the characteristics of the idealistic Hotspur and strove to make his Percy a representation of Milton's nihilistic dark rebel.

89 *... at least*: the speaker is not identified, but seems to be Alexander Percy.

Vi et armis: 'by force of arms'.

90 *... originated with him!*: Augusta's attributing 'the discovery [exposure] of the Society' to the elder Percy reinforces the image of his agent in that episode, 'Sdeath, as the eternal *betrayer*, since 'Sdeath now is about to betray his old master, after having already betrayed the younger, and as he will subsequently betray Augusta herself.

91 *from Eternity*: while the MS reads 'by Eternity', the context logically calls for 'from'.

92 *melancholy compositions*: the poem 'Son of heaven' was subsequently copied by Branwell in his 1837 Notebook, with minor changes. The

fourth line, in which he changed the definite article 'the' to the indefinite 'a' is illustrative of the effect of such a minor variation, however; the earlier phrasing given here provides a darker view, more appropriate to the narrative situation in the Northangerland biography. (See Winnifrith, *Poems*, 209.)

93 *my Mother!*: of biographical interest: earlier on the MS page here transcribed, there occurs, written sideways in the margin, the phrase 'My Mother!' Maria Branwell, his actual mother, died when Branwell was in his fourth year.

94 *Chapter II*: Volume II shows only two chapter headings compared with four for Volume I. The divisions are obviously arbitrary ones.

January 17, 18—: since the manuscript has previously alluded to Philosophers Isle growing quiet again 'in the winter of 1812', we may assume this to be the year 1813.

95 *evil spirit*: characteristically, 'Sdeath appears as if supernaturally when summoned up by the thoughts of a vengeful person; that is, someone 'needing the devil to do his work'.

Eees: 'yes'.

Senior Wrangler: the reference is to the Cambridge 'first' in the mathematical tripos.

96 *... entered upon!*: at this point there is a completely illegible half-line in the MS. Its omission seems not to raise any problem.

98 *displayed*: the MS reads 'felt extreme affliction'; the scene more logically calls for 'displayed', given her devotion to her husband.

99 *home of your father*: while the MS here reads 'fathers', we have been told that Edward Percy is an immigrant who has bought the Hall; thus, the singular form is clearly the right one. Alexander in his response, speaks of the grave as 'the home of my father'.

... that jackal, 'Sdeath: this sentence is not separated in the MS from the two preceding ones, but it is clear that Caversham speaks the first two while 'Sdeath responds to the third as coming from Alexander Percy ('Awm here, Measter....').

the old Measter concerned: the preceding phrase, illegible in part, is reconstructed from the logic of the remaining part of the sentence.

100 *accomplice*: the word in the MS is obscured and could be either 'consenter' or 'conspirator'. 'Accomplice' fits the context more accurately.

... gladness executed: while this protracted summary of the preceding events remains somewhat rambling, it has been broken into two

sentences from the one in the manuscript and slightly restructured for the sake of coherence.

101 *Their once possessor*: that is 'former possessor'.

'Westerns': as with 'Western aristocracy' earlier, the people of Wellington's Land and theoretically other countries west of Great Glasstown.

at his threshold: the MS here reads 'While some titled head bowed *beneath* his threshold'. An awkward image.

103 *My Old Chum*: another reference to Lucifer as the intimate of Branwell's villains.

Sin and Death: see Milton's *Paradise Lost*, Book II. where Sin is born out of Satan's head as thought; he then couples incestuously with her, conceiving Death, thus incarnating a twin blight upon the world.

104 *... Jeremiah Simpson's*: the apparition of the murdered Augusta in the ghost carriage with Simpson not only confirms his demonic nature, it establishes Augusta as a damned soul collected by the creature from Hell on her death. Precedents for such an apparition of the murdered figure were everywhere available to Branwell in the Gothic novel; see, for example, Hogg's *The Private Memoirs and Confessions of a Justified Sinner* and Lewis's *The Monk*.

105 *... in his face*: 'Sdeath can be wounded but, apparently, he can never be killed since he has a form of demonic immortality. An old man when first introduced, he remains physically active and still murderous a half-century later.

107 *(Byron)*: The identification is on the MS; however, it was probably added by someone other than Branwell since the hand is very different from his. The quote is from *Childe Harold*, II. 891–2.

108 *... slaughtered mate.*: at this point in the MS the sentence continues but is illegible except for disjointed words: 'once was heard to say ...' 'I will ... without her.' Since what follows is not dependent on it, I have omitted this brief missing passage without attempting reconstruction.

first burning tear: Branwell here inserted in the margin the words. 'I saw it' with a hand drawn below them. This insertion was evidently intended to mark eventual revision and to be attributed to the narrator, Bud, who has said that he was present at the funeral.

this man of sorrows: the image of the suffering Percy as a Christ figure is developed in the passage that follows. Interestingly, *A Man of Sorrows* is the title of the modern biography of the Revd Patrick Brontë, Branwell's father, by J. Lock and W. T. Dixon (London, 1965). It is an ironic parallel at that, for the title refers to the multiple family deaths endured by the elder Patrick Brontë, not the least of which was that of his cherished only son and namesake, Patrick Branwell.

108 *weeping bitterly*: at this point the number '15' is written in pencil on the manuscript page; successive numbering is written in the same fashion on other pages and probably was added by a later reader.

110 *chasing*: either referring to metal filigree or, in the old form, a 'casing' for a jewel.

poor tool: while 'poor fool' might be expected, the MS clearly reads 'poor tool'.

bleak and barren rocks.: here follow two-and-a-half lines which are completely illegible except for the words 'a fair isle arose once on the waters', and ending with what appear to be the words 'one, a shovel.'

111 *... life of Lady Augusta:* earlier references to Alexander's atheistic beliefs, particularly with respect to his Society for the Creation of the World, seem to be contradicted here. This lapse could be ascribed to Bud's obtuseness.

112 *'Life is a passing sleep'*: under the title 'The Doubter's Hymn', this poem has been collected in *The Poems of Patrick Branwell Brontë*, as taken from the 1837 Notebook, where it reveals several significant changes, including the omission of stanza 5. See Winnifrith, *Poems*, 210.

113 *(Byron)*: See note to p. 107 above.

114 *Prince of the West*: the new-born son of the Duke of Wellington, the future Duke of Zamorna and the King of Angria.

Alnwick: a town in Northumberland; another pointer towards the common use of an English setting in the Angrian chronicles. Ironically, it was also, in life, the home of Charles Thorp, the allegedly hostile brother-in-law of Lydia Robinson. For thwarted love of her, by Branwell's own testimony, he lost all will to live, resulting in his physical degeneration.

117 *'Thou art gone... my country and thee'*: see Winnifrith, *Poems*, 211–12, for the 1837 Notebook versions of these two songs, there somewhat rearranged and re-punctuated.

118 *That Star... passed away*: there are two readings relating to 'Star' here. On her first appearance Mary is referred to as 'the Star of Hope'. However, Percy now is fully risen as Star of the West, matured both through the tragedy of the past and the sustaining force of Mary's love, which is newly achieved. (None the less, the Star of the night sky retains an association with the newly fallen archangel of Milton.) As such, the narrative does reach at least a certain level of completion as a biography, that is, of the childhood and youth of Northangerland.

EXPLANATORY NOTES 227

118 *P. B. Brontë*: on the MS signature, Branwell seems to use a horizontal accent (macron) over the 'e' in Bronte, rather than the diaeresis ultimately adopted by Charlotte, which became subsequently the standard accent on the family name. (Patrick, Senior, used no accent, apparently, after changing his name to that of the honorific bestowed on his hero, Lord Nelson (Duke of Bronte)). In 'Real life in Verdopolis', written two years before 'Northangerland', Branwell uses a macron as an accent in two places where his full name is given.

Real Life in Verdopolis

121 [*title-page*]: on the first MS page there are, under Branwell's text, some pencilled characters scattered across the sheet. Probably written earlier, they are for the most part illegible. However, some are recognizable as random numbers (50, 17, and so on), and may have had some association with the erratic page-numbers found on the companion MS 'The Life of Northangerland'. Just under 'Chapter I', in longhand that does not seem to be that of Branwell, are written two words, the second not clearly decipherable: 'Lord['s] Mi[dst].' In a lighter ink on the bottom right-hand corner of the page, in Branwell's hand, is written '5th September September', the repetition a clear indication of Branwell's characteristic haste and lack of revision.

123 *Four fellows*: the MS here reads 'Five fellows', an apparent lapse, since four are subsequently identified, here and following. The number five does occur again, however, on pp. 128 and 138 where it has again been changed to 'four' for consistency.

'Blunty': a variant of the slang term 'blunt', meaning 'ready money'? It could, alternatively, be a coined word intended to combine 'booty' and 'plunder'.

124 *John Gifford*: as identified in other Angrian writings, Sir John Gifford is the Chief Justice of Glasstown.

hogs: the epithet here is first written as 'dogs', with 'h' written over the 'd'.

125 *Tweezy*: in the MS 'TWEEZY' is written in block caps, with the 'Z' reversed. In the preceding lines, the word 'time' had been omitted, along with the '-ed' from 'remained', another indication that Branwell did not reread much of the prose that flowed from his pen.

126 *Jack*: the porter was referred to as 'Tom' seven lines earlier. The contradiction is preserved, on the slight possibility that it might indicate Tweezy's casual use of a common name for a person he did not know earlier.

127 *Chapter II*: written as 'CHAPTER IId. May 20, 1833', with an elabo-

ration of the roman numeral 'II' that is characteristic of Branwell's MSS from the first childhood imitations of *Blackwood's*.

127 *Zenobia Elrington*: Rougue's wife, through whose family he derives his title of Lord Elrington, is herself a formidable personage of intense passion and high intellect. A woman who is elsewhere in the Juvenilia, particularly in Charlotte's writings, identified as deeply enamoured of Arthur Wellesley, she is wooed and wed by Rougue in 'The Pirate'. As Christine Alexander has pointed out, she is very probably drawn from the historical Zenobia, Queen of Palmyra and the East, who is described admiringly in Gibbons's *Decline and Fall of the Roman Empire* (see *The Early Writings of Charlotte Brontë*, 23–4). As with Alexander Percy's first wife, Augusta, the marriage is based on tension between strong-minded individuals that at times approaches a love-hate stand-off, as seen in several other of the Angrian writings of both Branwell and Charlotte.

sofa: as the Chronicles proceeded (as in 'The Life of . . . Northangerland', for example) Branwell came consistently to prefer the old spelling 'sopha', to the modern form 'sofa' used here. The 'ph' spelling may very well have seemed to him to be more evocative of luxury as he became more conscious of language.

128 *eleven*: written in numerals as '12', crossed out, and with numeral '11' superimposed.

starting, exclaimed: at this point, and extending for a dozen lines, there appears a faint background drawing of a seated figure. The text is written over it; such use of an already partly used sheet is a customary economy measure.

129 *in the darkness*: between this line and the next there occurs in pencil the number 18. Among the numbers scattered on the first page of this manuscript is a character similar in appearance, 17. Since the manuscript pages of both 'The Life of . . . Northangerland' and 'Real Life' sometimes bear what appears to be part of the same succession of numbers, and in view of the fact that they were written at different times, it seems probable that these numbers were added by a later hand.

131 '*showing fright*': the MS reads 'showing fight', but that is contradicted by the context, which seems quite clearly to call for the government's not giving 'the mob one instance of showing *fright*', by hastily assembling 'as large a body of troops' as possible. While Branwell not infrequently drops a letter in his breakneck pace, it does not normally result in a totally different and contradictory reading.

132 *The mob was coming!*: in another instance of Branwell's hasty composition, the MS reads 'The mob were coming'.

nut to which his soul conforms: 'nut' is apparently the slang term for one's

EXPLANATORY NOTES 229

head (here used in mocking reference to Glasstowners as having little soul, but much concern for their heads).

133 *...unwounded*: again, marks in pencil appear on the MS, including the number 19, which is consistent with the 17 and 18 on the two preceding pages. However, since other, more random numbers appear, there may have been further identifications merged with the successive sequence.

133 *Dryden*: see his translation of the *Aeneid*, Bk. II. Branwell has, of course, interpolated Rogue's name

136 *Chapter III*: the manuscript here reads, with capricious punctuation (that may be accounted for by Branwell's tapping pen): 'CHAPTER. TH.E, IIId.' Some doodling appears on the right side of the manuscript page at this point. Part of it resembles the estuary of a river, with what might be the smoke-hole (fumarole) of a volcano.

137 *That city ... St Michael's Cathedral*: Glasstown is here some sixty years old and apparently extensive enough to have the heavy, choking smog of an English city in the 1830s, such as Leeds, Manchester, or London itself. The following reference to 'the huge dome of St Michael's Cathedral' obviously pulls together the name of the Revd Brontë's village church and the physical reality of St Paul's.

the yet-smouldering Jail: Branwell nods, here: the manuscript reads that heavy piles of smoke 'denoted the spot where stood the *yet-consuming JAIL*.' (Italics added.) Obviously he was thinking of the *fire* as still consuming the jail.

Aye, Montmorency: the MS here first identifies Rogue's host as Sydenham, which name is crossed out and replaced with that of Montmorency. Sydenham's role in the murder of Percy's first wife, Lady Augusta di Segovia, is recounted in 'The Life of ... Northangerland'.

138 *turning down*: 'swallowing'.

140 *All other scenes ... despised*: there is a clear anticipation of the Earnshaw/Heathcliff love of wild landscape here.

140 *Ashantee*: the Ashanti (or Ashantee) Wars were much in the news in Branwell's childhood. The actual location of that African kingdom was north of the ostensible Angrian territories and was probably responsible for Angria's being placed in Africa in the first place, rather than in India (the site of the actual pirate kingdom of Angria) or elsewhere.

fatigue to view: in the bottom right-hand corner of this MS page occur several words that are not part of the text (and probably were written earlier): 'Oh thou ... who/whose' and a little above them what appears to be the word 'solo'.

Its base was: the MS shows another small doodle that resembles tributaries feeding into a river. There is a similar one some thirty-four lines down the sheet.

141 *'Last Night of Coomassiee'*: Kumasi, the Ashanti capital. The manuscript in question was not necessarily ever written; see the 'book-list' at the end of 'Real Life'.

143 *O'Connor*: Arthur O'Connor, son of one of the companions of Edward Percy, Alexander's father, in the flight from Ireland some decades earlier (in 'The Life of... Northangerland'), is first shown as a companion of Rougue in Branwell's earlier 'Letters of an Englishman', as well as being a character in some of Charlotte's stories such as 'A Day Abroad'. (In her 'Four Years Ago' of 1837, she would describe him as a '"dead maniac" buried in the yard of the lunatic asylum in Adrianopolis'.) Branwell retains him as a companion in dissipation with Northangerland, along with Montmorency, Quashia, and Carey, down to his final work 'And the Weary are at Rest'.

144 *accustomed corner*: another doodle starts here. It is not clear but could be either a paintbrush or, as shaped, a vaguely phallic figure.

wi sangs and clatter: see Robert Burns, 'Tam o' Shanter', 45.

145 *Sneakysland*: another variant spelling, Sneakysland is commonly spelled 'Sneachiesland' in the later writtings, a change which somewhat obscures the more childish nomenclature of the original Twelves.

Carey, O'Connor: the 'cart whip' punishment earlier alluded to seems to have been forgotten. The OED identifies a cart whip as 'a long, heavy horsewhip', and cites an 1811 *Edinburgh Review* article: 'after a cart-whipping, he was carried to a sick-house.' Clearly, then, the reference is not understood as a light whip such as might be used in a dog- or pony-cart. None the less, both Carey and O'Connor are obviously in normal operating condition the morning after their punishment.

Ned Laury: here a fairy-tale prodigy of strength, as he was in Branwell's 'Letters of an Englishman' some years earlier. Later, he becomes the forester of Wellington's estates, and the father of Mina Laury, the title heroine of Charlotte's more-or-less realistic romance of 1838, written when she was 22 under the psendonym of Charles Townshend, an alias taken by Charles Albert Florian Wellesley.

Peter Poundtext... Balfour of Burley: allusions to Sir Walter Scott's *Old Mortality*, in which the historical figure of the Presbyterian fanatic, John Balfour of Burley, is the most striking of the central characters. In Branwell's fragmentary novel 'And the Weary are at Rest' he has Alexander Percy (Rougue) playing the satiric role of a fundamentalist preacher of the 'Poundtext' school.

Charles Albert Florian Wellesly: a comic figure here in Branwell's hands; Charlotte frequently used him as a persona in her early fiction ('The as Branwell used Bud and Captain Tree as authorial characters. (Conversely, Charlotte mocked Branwell's style of writing by making use of Captain Bud; she characterises Sergeant Bud as 'a clever lawyer and great liar'. See her sketches of Glasstowners in 'Characters of the Eminent Men of the Time' (1829).) Branwell throughout 'Real Life' spells the name 'Wellesly', rather than the actual spelling 'Wellesley' which Charlotte invariably used.

146 *'Something about Arthur'*: an Angrian manuscript written by Charlotte Brontë under the pen-name of Charles Wellesley. The manuscript is described in detail by Christine Alexander.

a wheel-less chariot: that is, he walked to Elrington Hall.

'Thus passed the day . . .: given as a quote, this line is unidentified and is sufficiently characterless to remain so, which may be Branwell's point in assigning it to Charles Wellesley.

147 *glance by me*: at this point in the MS there is another indeterminate illustration drawn under the text.

douce: in Scots dialect most commonly means 'pleasant' or 'amiable' in temperament, but probably here is intended in a secondary meaning as 'sedate' or 'sober'.

148 *'Sdeath's a-cold*: an obvious echo of the lament of Edgar as 'Poor Tom' in *King Lear*. The literary reference serves as a mocking clue to his own spurious nature, since 'Sdeath can, on any occasion, be either vulgar or quite sophisticated in his speech.

Use your shuffle: 'shuffle' here can be understood in an obsolete secondary meaning, that is, as 'trick', 'evasion', or 'equivocation', to put, trust, or bring about trickily; or simply, if somewhat doubtfully, as 'use your awkward walk' (the latter not quite suitable since 'Sdeath reveals himself to be both a durable and swift pedestrian).

. . . dangerous sport: this MS page is an interesting example of Branwell's economical habit of writing on sheets on which he had previously made rough drawings. The entire page is covered with various small sketches, including rivers, a castle on a hill, and a further country scene of hills, fields, and a foreground gateway. At the bottom-left side of the page is, incongruously, a projecting leg.

149 *. . . thus addressed them*: Rougues' men are both revolutionaries in the anarchistic sence and freebooters, as the frequent reference to their stronghold—Robbers' Towers—has indicated. While no specific details are given, Rougue's instructions here are clearly intended to be the dispatching of robber gangs on forays of violence. (The northern border country of England has a long tradition of moss-stroopers, or freebooters, infesting the land that dated back through the seventeenth century and, in the lawless independence of unprincipled

border chieftains, long before. See the early history of the Percy family, recounted by Branwell two years later, in 'The Life of... Northangerland'.)

149 *Carnac*: although the name itself is not important in its present context, its occurrence is interesting with respect to the Angrian nomenclature. While it is conceivable that the MS could read 'Carnae' or even 'Caruse' in Branwell's hasty hand, it seems quite clearly to be 'Carnac'. A region of south-east India carries the name 'Carnatic' or 'Karnatik'. (Alternatively, the 'Carnic Alps', between Austria and Italy, might have been a source, although the 'Carnac' of this manuscript seems to be a place-name *out* of the mountains.)

150 *by the boards*: the MS reads 'by the leaves', but the immediate subsequent use of the word 'leaves' in a different action indicates inadvertance on Branwell's part.

151 *he swallowed some food*: this initial line on MS page 6 verso is fused to the matting and some words are not clearly legible; however, the reading given seems to be accurate.

152 *... observe with me*: the scene here following is, paradoxically, anticipatory of Thackeray, the later idol of Charlotte Brontë. Thackeray had not yet become known in 1833, when he was himself but 22 years of age.

M. Eat-him-up-sloop-and-roop's New Elysium: apparently a slang expression incorporated into a gambling entrepreneur's nickname. While 'stoop-and-roof' would make some sense, it does not seem to be an accurate reading of Branwell's written hand. However, the alternative—'stoop and roop'—according to the *OED* is north-country slang meaning 'completely'.

153 *These three are kings*: this 'meeting of kings' is a reference to the original Adventurers, or 'Twelves', four of whom became founders of separate kingdoms which, in imperial fashion, were united as the Verdopolitan confederacy under the supreme leadership of the Duke of Wellington. As described, although otherwise inappropriate, there may also be an echo of the meeting of the exiled kings in Voltaire's *Candide*, a familiar work to Branwell.

...from Elysium: while the MS is difficult to decipher here, the sense of the statement seems to be accurately rendered. 'Elysium' is the private gaming-club which is to be the scene of action later this night. It would seem to be a different establishment from the 'New Elysium' described a page or two earlier, where an entrepreneur fleeces the gambling gentry-at-large. Probably Branwell has simply used the name 'Elysium' ironically, as a metaphor for the doubtful nature of the 'bliss' found in such places.

EXPLANATORY NOTES

153 *Aornos*: the Angrian Olympus, the mountain where dwell the Genii, the powerful spirits who, in an act of magical creation, built the original city and remain the guardians of the Twelves. Elsewhere, the chief Genii are identified as Talli (Charlotte), Brani (Branwell), Emmi (Emily), and Anni (Anne).

... *Glasstown youngster*: here, at the beginning of MS page 7, are eight lines crossed out which are almost identical with the first eight lines of MS page 3. The word 'youngster', completing the sentence begun on the preceding sheet, follows the cancelled passage. Apparently this sheet was a previously discarded one, probably from a false start, of which Branwell decided to use the clean portion.

155 *a tall young man... tables*: the first appearance in this manuscript of Arthur Wellesley, the central figure of Charlotte's early fiction, antagonist as well as son-in-law to Northangerland.

young dove give play: probably a gambling term, indicating a pigeon being given the opportunity to wager; alternatively, providing amusement to them.

156 *Viscount Castlereagh*: Robert Stewart, second Viscount Castlereagh (1769–1822), was an Anglo-Irish aristocrat born in Dublin, whose career was closely associated with that of his countryman, Arther Wellesley. Although damned by some for his suppression of the Irish in 1798, when he was the Tory chief secretary for Ireland, he played a considerable role in the politics of the time, including reorganizing the army, planning the Peninsular War, putting Wellesley in command, and organizing the successful European Coalition against Napoleon. Branwell's youthful character is, apparently, much more sympathetic than the actual Castlereagh.

Very well... man: this first line on MS page 7 verso is obscured by the fused mouning but appears under backlight to read as given.

157 *George Charles Gordon... John Flower, Esqr*: George Gordon was the Christian name of Lord Byron; John Flower is the ostensible author of the present narrative.

Champions: the four Champions named here are 'rare boys', in Branwell's earlier fiction identified as gigantic and lawless figures.

quizzing: that is, 'peering at'.

158 *O'Connor*: described as being here at the Elysium Club when 'Sdeath arrives from 'the Firm', although in the preceding scene at the Robbers' Towers, many miles away, Rougue had sent O'Connor along with the others on a mission elsewhere the morning after 'Sdeath's departure for the capital. Apparently this is a time-lapse not accounted for by the events described.

159 *Saying so ... room*: this sentence is partly illegible and has been, in part, extrapolated from the letters that can be read.

preparations: starting at this point there is a faint background drawing of a muscular arm and torso, which illustrates the story content at this point, that is, the physical characteristics of the two men preparing to fight. Branwell loved prize-fighting and made frequent reference, as in his letters to John Leyland, to the pugilistic champions of the day. Mary Butterfield in *Brother in the Shadow* (1988) has described Branwell's association with the sport in considerable detail, including a cartoon by him based on the Jack Painter–Jack Shaw battle of 1815, as well as the Bendigo (William Thompson)–Ben Caunt historic rematch of ninety-three rounds on 9 September 1845, of which the Branwell drawing reproduced as plate 1 between pages 92–93 was made the very next day. Obviously, Branwell knew the full modern history of prize-fighting. According to Francis Leyland in *The Brontë Family*, when Branwell visited London in 1835 he visited the Castle Tavern in Holborn, an establishment frequented by sporting characters of the day and kept by the retired prize-fighter Tom Spring. Allegedly, the habitués were so impressed by the young Yorkshire visitor that they accepted his decisions on certain details of well-known prize-fights of the past. For a characteristic picture of sporting life, and particularly pugilism, in the first half of the century, see Pierce Egan's Tom and Jerry sketches in his *Life in London* (1820–1) and the weekly paper *Pierce Egan's Life in London and Sporting Guide* which developed from it in 1824 and subsequently turned into *Bell's Life in London*, which Branwell allegedly read in whatever pub he happened to be in. Egan's *Boxiana: Or Sketches of Ancient and Modern Pugilism* appeared in parts in 1812–13, and as a five-volume supplementary edition between 1815 and 1829. Not surprisingly, it is not a title in the Brontë family library, but Branwell almost certainly knew it.

161 *Volo*: an epithet used often in the masculine social world of drinking and violence described by Branwell. A slang term, it is probably the Latin *volo*, 'I am willing', or a related contraction of a Latin expression meaning 'the bird is on the wing' or, essentially, 'Let's go!', 'Let's do it!'

End of ... Volume: the end of the page is embellished by a drawing of an uncoiling decorative ribbon.

163 *the gradual unfolding of another day*: in the passage that follows Branwell reveals one of his real strengths as a writer, his ability to describe the physical reality of nature or a cityscape. It is a quality that was already developed in his writing as early as 'Letters of an Englishman', a major project undertaken when he was only 12 years old.

EXPLANATORY NOTES 235

164 *GGT*: the abbreviation for 'Great Glass Town'.

Montmorency: in the MS the name is spelled here with an Italian ending: 'Montmorenci'. Since nothing is made of it in the narrative, the usual spelling is here restored.

165 *Castlereagh*: the MS reads 'Montmorency' where the context obviously calls for 'Castlereagh'.

169 *Captain Flower*: Branwell seems to have forgotten at this point that Captain Flower is the ostensible author of this narrative.

'They muster ... defeat': though the text follows the MS, where there is no new paragraph marked for this sentence, there is some ground for believing that the sentiment should be attributed to Sydney rather than the Marquis Douro, since the latter is always shown elsewhere to be obsessively courageous.

170 *in room of*: that is, in place of Colonel Arthur.

John: the speaker here is John Sneaky. There are two by that name, the first the son of Alexander Sneaky, the ruler of Sneachiesland. This John Sneaky is the first Duke of Fidena. His son, John Augustus, is the second Duke of Fidena (see note to p. 180 below).

171 *... go forward*: the last two lines at this point in the MS are obscured but on careful study seem to read as here given.

172 *insure*: in the MS could conceivably be 'inure', 'to come (or bring) into use'. It is worth noting that while Branwell, like all his family, pays lip-service to the conservative aristocracy as opposed to the anarchic demagogue, he gives Rougue and his party all the good lines, as well as the dramatic action. A comparison with Charlotte's *Shirley* is instructive on that point.

177 *contrast to the [...]*: the dots indicate an illegible word or two (possibly an adjective beginning with 'sl-' or 'st-'). Even without them, the syntax remains coherent, so no extrapolation has been necessary.

barouche: Branwell's not infrequent misspelling, combined with the only partially legible manuscript at this point, produces a question since the carriage is identified, as it appears, to be a 'burou...'. It could be 'brougham' but could equally be 'barouche'; the latter choice is more probable since the brougham coach was not in very common general use as early as 1833 when the manuscript was written.

Grenville ... Bellingham ... Tree ... Bud: Colonel Grenville, identified a few pages earlier as the Speaker of the House, is a wealthy mill-owner; in the Great Rebellion fomented by Alexander Percy, he is shot by the striking workmen (cf. Charlotte Brontë's *Shirley*). Bellingham, narrator of Branwell's earlier 'Letters of an Englishman' and 'The Pirate', is a London banker involved in the financial development of the Confederacy. 'Sergeant' refers to a law title, since Tree is a jurist. 'Young Bud' could be either Captain Bud or Sergeant Bud, the son. He is sometimes the voice of Branwell, as in the later 'Life of... Northangerland'. Sergeant Bud, elsewhere described as Captain Bud's son, and as a clever lawyer and liar, would seem to fit the reference to a young man in company with Sergeant Tree.

178 *Thornton Witkin Sneaky*: some transcriptions of other Angrian writings identify the middle name of Lord Thornton Sneaky as 'Wilkin'. In this MS it seems quite clearly to be 'Witkin', which seems suggestive of his character, and I have left it so, accordingly.

179 *... open, determined character*: interestingly, the physical description of Lord Thornton Witkin Sneaky very closely corresponds to Branwell's own appearance. This might be seen as surprising, since the author clearly presents him negatively and is far more sympathetic to the opposite figure, Castlereagh. In fact, the character analysis of Lord Thornton that follows seems even more of a reflection of the author and the ingrained weaknesses that were to trouble his life later. Branwell, of course, admired rogues from his earliest days.

180 *latent jealousy*: at this point in the MS there follows a passage that has been crossed out: 'Stepping up to Lord Lofty'. | [a] Stately old man who stood by himself | he asked. 'who is that young man[?]' 'What young man[?]'. 'The one with red hair.' 'What he's not so very young its Rougue.' 'No my Lord you. know t who I mean.' 'Yes I do kiddy. but let me tell you. that I'm not. the person. of whom to ask idle questions. its Lord...'[*sic*]. Branwell immediately rewrites the scene, changing Lord Lofty to Thornton Witkin Sneaky's royal father.

Your Majesty: originally a sailor and one of the adventurer Twelves who settle the country, Alexander Sneaky becomes King of Sneachiesland, one of the four countries in Africa of which Branwell writes.

181 *to reconnoitre*: at the bottom-left corner of this MS page appear the apparently random words: 'open open and hateful', probably a note of earlier or later date. The end of this MS page and the first three-and-a-half lines of the next have been crossed out. The deleted section is an earlier phrasing of the scene in the square: 'it was dark outside but. | plainly could the[y] hear. the sounds of swearing cursing and execrati | ons. they were not long in doubt. for as the square nosie attract[t] | ed. crowds from the. adjacent streets. lamps were brought s[...] | and. the. light from'.

183 *serenade*: there follows in the MS the following twenty-one lines of verse, which are crossed out there but which are indicative of

Branwell's penchant for romantic nature poetry of a Gothic quality. The last line is obscured but the reconstruction is believed to be accurate. (Punctuation has been added as needed but otherwise the poem is as written):

> The eve is dark'ning down on heaven;
> Black stormy clouds o'er the skys have driven,
>   And ~~dark~~/dull/the shades creep down;
> With piercing sleet, with drenching rain,
> With cold blasts howling from the main,
> Now rolling back, now poured again,
>   O'er hill and tower and town.
>
> Each streanlet [sic] ~~by~~ to a torrent's force
>   Is swelled by ceaseless rain,
> And, bursting through its downward course
>   roars raging round the plain.
>
> The banks ~~are broke by~~ have slided down the stream;
> The uncertain paths in evening's beams
> Lead to some darke deep precipice,
>   or wind above some vast abyss,
>   Or stretched along the Moor
> lead to some quaking black~~xxx~~ morass,
>   or ~~through~~ o'er some mighty summit pass,
>   Where ~~it~~ shrinking from the shore
> Howls the loud blast with furious tone,
>   Both on the clouds of mist and rain . . .

183 A SERENADE: this dull bit of Keatsian romance is scarcely an improvement on the discarded poem that precedes it in the MS. However, as a characterization device it presents Castlereagh effectively—even if more unfortunately—as the pining lover as seen by the 16 year-old author. A redeeming scepticism, or at least humour, is perhaps seen in the bold invitation that makes up Witkin's answering song.

185 *'moved heaven . . . revenge!'*: while in quotes, the passage has not been identified and, again, seems too general to benefit from identification.

black pudding: a dish made from congealed blood. The reference here seems to be a vulgarism referring to a casual beating.

188 *handle it better*: marking the end of the chapter is an ornamental design of flourished scrollwork. Also, at the right bottom of the page is a doodle, perhaps a river and tributaries once again.

189 *Chapter IV*: in the MS given in block capitals, 'CHAPTER. IVth.', somewhat embellished.

190 *I don't know*: the narrator's ignorance seems to overlook the robbing and looting activities already described at the Robbers' Towers earlier. However, Branwell seems to be hinting at even more nefarious enterprises still to be brought out.

£30,000 a year: earlier referred to by Montmorency as £20,000 a year. That might be regarded as a speculative figure, however.

Satan: in 'The Life of...Northangerland', written two years later, Branwell repeatedly refers to Alexander Percy (Elrington, or Rougue) as a Lucifer or Satan figure. Here, the label seems only casual, indicating the greater depth of the later work.

191 *Douro*: the character of Arthur Wellesley (otherwise Baron Douro and the Duke of Zamorna), more idealized by Charlotte, seems little better than Alexander Percy in Branwell's chronicles. In fact, it seems to confirm that Branwell himself admired the dissolute life that he ostensibly condemns in Percy.

...of this conspiracy: a hasty count; Branwell's figures amount to only £70,000 rather than the £75,000 total he referred to earlier.

193 *PBB*: after Branwell's familiar initials in the MS there appears the markings '= 1' with, possibly, an additional character obscured at the edge. There is no obvious meaning to the marks, and they may well have been a non-pictorial doodle.

194 *Bellingham (Co.)*: as noted earlier, Bellingham is the London-based banker who handles the overall funding of Glasstown (the finance minister in some of the tales). The last syllable, given in this transcription as 'Co.' is partially illegible. It could be 'coy'. On the top quarter, centred, of the next MS page (fo. 14 verso) is a deleted poem of some nineteen lines, apparently an abandoned effort written earlier, with the Rougue narrative written around and following it on the page. The poem, transcribed here (punctuation corrected to facilitate reading), is reminiscent of Castlereagh's 'Serenade' to Julia, given earlier in the text and may have been a first attempt at that piece. It is also somewhat reminiscent of Byron's verse narratives, which Branwell knew thoroughly by this time.

> Rattles the Hail like ~~shower~~ storms of stone
> Then pass down bellying o'er the plain
> ~~Thou mayst not~~/Fair Maiden/in such/drear/hour ~~as this~~
> Thou mayst not from thy castle tower
>   Flee o'er the waste with me.
>
> But, Oh the sullen rolling main
> What heeds it storms of sleet and rain?
> Behold thou its dark silent plain

> That huge Atlantic sea.
>
> Our boat is ready on the Shore
> Our sailors rest beside the oar;
> Not such light wind as wailing now!
> Covers with sleet the Kumrii's brow,
> Can raise the ~~sullen wave~~/billow dull/.
> Not such vain storms, though cold they blow,
> Though earth they hide in clouds of snow
> Can hurl the billows round our prow
> Or rock our sturdy hull.
> Then ~~come with me~~/daring free/upon the sea,
> Oh Maiden, fly from thy fate with me.

194 *There's a ... invitation*: crossed out in the MS, this line originally read 'There's a note/card from Marchioness Douro requesting. inviting us.'

settle the bond: Montmorency calls Castlereagh to the study to 'settle the bond' on the entangling loan, having said that 'we don't require bonds' a few lines earlier. This seems, however, to be less an author's lapse than a demonstration of the duplicity of Elrington and Montmorency.

B.R. and Y. or O.D.V.: Branwell is amusing himself here with phonetic abbreviations for strong spirits; at 16, he is clearly no stranger to brandy and eau-de-vie.

195 *and take ——*: the blank word at the end of this verse may well be understood as a vulgarism, given the response of his listeners. In Branwell's last prose manuscript, the fragmentary novel 'And the Weary are at Rest', generally dated from internal evidence as 1845, a dozen years after the composition of this chronicle, a major scene consists of Alexander Percy and his followers (including some of the same ones) engaged in mock sermonizing in a Methodist chapel.

196 *an' another were*: dialect ellision. That is, in response to the question 'Is he mad?' the speaker answers 'I'll stick my knife into you *if any other person* ("an' another") were' [as mad as he is].

through the streets: crossed out at this point: 'galloping, tossing their hats and fighting with each other in a manner most disgraceful'.

Why, a cropper: though not clear in the MS, Douro apparently answers Lofty's implicit reprimand defiantly and turns back to his 'pigeon', Castlereagh. (One other definition of 'a cropper' is 'a plant that yields crops'.)

197 *inconsiderate*: here used in the sense of 'ill-advised', or not carefully judging a situation.

198 *had for height*: that is, had the advantage of being taller, though earlier

Thornton is described as somewhat *below* the middle height, while Douro is always described as tall. The background on the MS page from about this point to the bottom of the sheet shows a sketch of what appear to be birds in flight, probably swifts.

199 *the Marchioness of Douro*: of Douro's wives, this would be the first, Marian Hume, mother of Wellesley's first son, Julius, Marquis of Almeida.

some of the Twelves: six of these are mentioned: *His Majesty Stumps*, in some of the other Angrian writings, has successive identities, the later one as King Frederick Guelph, the Duke of York, who is said to have died in battle on the same day as the real Duke of York; *His Majesty of Ross's Land*: derived from Sir John Ross, the Arctic explorer, for whom Anne's soldier was named in the childhood game with Branwell's toy soldiers; *Bravey*: otherwise known as Sir William Bravey, a co-founder of Glasstown. Bravey's Inn was a gathering place for the Wellesley circle to meet for discussions. The personal description given here, that of a Falstaffian figure, accords with his profession of innkeeper; *Herculean-armed Baby*: also known as Dr Hume (an actual figure, Dr Thomas Hume, 1769–1850), the Duke of Bady or Badry, he was physician to the Duke of Wellington. His title is originally a childhood derivation of 'bad' with the familiar 'y' ending (cf. 'Sneaky'); *Monarch of Parrydise*: 'Parrydise' is, of course, a pun. The figure of Parry is drawn from another Arctic explorer, Sir William Edward Parry. As with Ross, Parry was the name of a living hero given to one of Branwell's toy soldiers years earlier—in this case, by Emily; *polite old Gentleman of the North*: this is, again, Alexander Sneaky, King of Sneachiesland and father of Thornton Witkin Sneaky, an eminence already encountered by Castlereagh.

200 *Faith is the brightest evidence*: this poem, along with other lines of verse incorporated into this manuscript, was not included in Winnifrith's published collection. Given the context, a question is raised regarding the excision of such poems for separate publication: should such a poem be offered as the tribute to faith it pretends to be, or should it be set aside as the doggerel mockery that Branwell intended? As the text continues, Northangerland mocks his own role as a revolutionary demagogue as well as the idealized social egalitarianism that formed part of contemporary republican ideas.

201 *now reforming*: there is a large background sketch behind the written text on this MS sheet, another instance of paper conservation by Branwell. The figure seems to be a seated nude with the upper portion incomplete, although the written text obscures it. At the bottom of the page is drawn a flourish of scrolls, indicating a chapter ending.

EXPLANATORY NOTES 241

202 *Adam's desk... footmarks on it*: the word 'desk' is chosen here, although the MS letters are partly illegible, as the apparently right one. It raises, obviously, some question of meaning in context. The 'footmarks' left on it suggest the presence of the devil, a role seized often enough by Rougue, and that may be the thought implicit here.

worth fuishionless: an apparent nonsense phrase indicating worthlessness.

Give me a toss!: while the MS does not clearly indicate the speaker or speakers, and the last few sentences may have been spoken by Douro or Montmorency, as the text continues the speaker is certainly Elrington, and it probably is the same person throughout despite the reference to himself in the third person ('Old Elrington, Old Scoundrel'). Background doodling obscures Branwell's always doubtful punctuation.

beckoned his Lady beside him: ironically, the second wife of Douro will be Lady Mary Henrietta, the daughter of Alexander Percy, who is more or less abandoned by Douro out of hatred for her father, even though Douro loves her. See 'History of Angria', and Charlotte Brontë's poem 'Zamorna's Exile', dealing with the same story.

203 *Didn't I, ladies, show unco grace?*: the MS wording could be 'Didn't I, ladies, look unto grace' (though not clearly punctuated). Alternatively, it might have been corrected to read 'look unco grace*ful*'.

proud-looking nobleman: identified in the next chapter as the villainous Lord Caversham.

204 *PBB-te*: the letters 'te' following Branwell's initials here remain obscure in meaning.

Pandemonium: again, the reference from Milton's *Paradise Lost* suggests Elrington's cronies as parallels to Satan's minions.

205 *as croose and canny as twa auld friends*: a convergence of Yorkshire and Scottish dialect. 'Croose' (or 'crouse') is a word which can mean both 'irascible' and 'cosy' or 'jolly'. Clearly the latter sense is used here.

£88,100: Branwell's calculation in the MS is £78,100, off by £10,000. The total comes to £88,100; Branwell was always careless with money, it would seem.

£55,800: again the subtotal in the MS is inaccurate; rather than the £53,800 given, it should be £55,800. Even the two subtotals are added in hasty fashion. They would total £131,900 if we used Branwell's mistaken figures, rather than the total of £127,900 which he determines. The actual total of the winnings said to have been taken off Castlereagh most recently is £143,900. Obviously, had Branwell been

possessed of Castlereagh's fortune in real life, he would have been in even more desperate circumstances than the fictional youth. On the right side of the MS sheet at the point of Rougue's calculations is further doodling, resembling the face of a mountain cliff.

205 *Seldom be of stretch*: slang term meaning 'relieved of fatigue'.

206 *not respond*: the MS reads 'He could not resent', but what follows indicates that he was incapable of responding, whether with resentment or anything else.

207 *pliskie*: or *pliskey* (see p. 124), Scottish dialect, meaning 'a trick'. Tom Scroven is a poacher. In 'Letters of an Englishman' he is a giant figure, an intimate of Ned Laury.

The morning... through the night: the MS line here reads 'It was dawn of morning; he had ridden during the night', which seems to require the altered phrasing given.

firms: the word sometimes seems to read 'firms' as here, and sometimes 'farms' in Branwell's quirky hand. It is probably the former, though a case might be made for the latter in the context in which it is used.

209 *the money... gained from him*: money is always sacred in Branwell's chronicles. Douro's 'inability' to return what he had won from Castlereagh, even though won by obvious deception, indicates the unified figure of hero and villain in Branwell's narratives. The very wealthy Douro is not a highwayman as is the dissolute aristocrat Alexander Percy/Elrington, but he is equally respected as a predatory gamester.

dashed about as usual: in other Angrian writings, Lord Thornton Sneaky, dignified under the title of 'General', is shown as married to another Julia (Wellesley), while Julia Montmorency does not appear.

210 *1833*: the MS concludes with the date '1835'. However, the text throughout has read '1833', including the beginning of this short final chapter, a few pages earlier.

211 *No. 587 G.S.*: this is a hangover from Branwell's pseudo-publishing formality—a 'Glasstown Stationers' volume-registration number. The initials following Sergeant Tree—'G.G.T.'—refer to 'Great Glass Town'.

Of the advertised volumes on the end-pages, '*Something About Arthur*' is one of Charlotte's narratives about the early youth of Douro, under the pen-name of Lord Charles Wellesley. '*The Fate of Coomassie*, a poem by Young Soult' is one of Branwell's titles, Young Soult being a pen-name used in the composition of his early poetry. The name itself is taken from Napoleon's distinguished general, Marshal Soult (again reminding us that Branwell, from the time of the

EXPLANATORY NOTES 243

toy soldiers incident, identified himself with Napoleon in opposition to Charlotte's championing of the Duke of Wellington). Coomassie was an Ashanti capitol destroyed by the Twelves in their fictional conquest of Africa; the Brontës borrowed the name from the actual Ashanti centre, Kumasi, on the Gold Coast of Africa.

211 *Captain Tree*: while, as on this list, he is distinguished from the publisher Sergeant Tree by title, Captain Tree is probably the same person at times.

N. B.: written vertically across the following last two titles is a large scrawl that appears to say 'Mark Off off Sor', This is, I believe, in Charlotte's hand. Both books referred to are hers, and the scrawled message may be a demand that Branwell not include them in his fictional book-list (although both are actual compositions). On the other side of the sheet, written in the same hand but more obscured are what appear to be the words 'Not I [illegible word] the one I know—'

G. G. Town: to the right of this address line are two or three words, inverted, in a printed hand that is not that of Branwell. The first word has been subsequently written over by the address 'G. G. town'. The second word may be 'shafts', the third word is clearly 'plains'. Again, this suggests an earlier note or phrase on a mostly blank sheet later used by Branwell as an economy measure.